He clasped his  **the last bite of chocolate hanging between them.**

"Take it," she urged.

Her voice was too sexy to ignore. He grabbed her hand and drew it to his mouth. Cade enveloped the chocolate with his mouth and swallowed it down. The motion was both carnivorous and sexual.

Abby's brown eyes widened in surprise.

"What did you expect?" he asked.

"I don't know," she said. "Something more…"

"Polite?" he asked.

Her eyes darkened. "Maybe. If so, I'm glad I was wrong."

His gut tightened. "You need to be careful. You're asking for trouble."

"Just from you," she said.

His heart hammered against his rib cage. "This is a bad idea."

"There are worse ideas," she countered.

He felt himself begin to sweat. How could Laila's little sister affect him this way? It wasn't possible.

A MAVERICK
FOR CHRISTMAS

BY
LEANNE BANKS

First published in Great Britain 2013
by Mills & Boon, an imprint of Harlequin (UK) Limited,
Eton House, 18-24 Paradise Road, Richmond, Surrey TW9 1SR

© Harlequin Books S.A. 2011

Special thanks and acknowledgement to Leanne Banks for her contribution to the Montana Mavericks: The Texans are Coming! continuity.

ISBN: 978 0 263 90149 8
ebook ISBN: 978 1 472 00539 7

23-1013

Harlequin (UK) policy is to use papers that are natural, renewable and recyclable products and made from wood grown in sustainable forests. The logging and manufacturing processes conform to the legal environmental regulations of the country of origin.

Printed and bound in Spain
by Blackprint CPI, Barcelona

Leanne Banks is a *New York Times* and *USA TODAY* bestselling author who is surprised every time she realizes how many books she has written. Leanne loves chocolate, the beach and new adventures. To name a few, Leanne has ridden on an elephant, stood on an ostrich egg (no, it didn't break), gone parasailing and indoor skydiving. Leanne loves writing romance because she believes in the power and magic of love. She lives in Virginia with her family and four-and-a-half-pound Pomeranian named Bijou. Visit her website, www.leanne banks.com

This book is dedicated to Susan Litman.
You know why.

Prologue

Abby Cates remembered the moment she fell for Cade Pritchett. She had been nine years old at the time, and he'd been giving swimming lessons at Silver Stallion Lake. At seventeen, Cade had been tall, strong and blond. He was nice to all the kids, but demanded they learn their strokes. Abby was pretty sure he didn't remember scooping her out of some too-deep water when she'd choked and panicked. In her little-girl mind, Cade was a god.

Despite her best efforts, Abby had never found any man who could top Cade in her mind, not even now that she was twenty-two. And that was a terrible shame, especially since he'd never noticed her and, on top of that, wedding fever was running through Thunder Canyon like a bad flu.

Now that her older sister Laila was engaged to Jackson Traub, the discussions of weddings were nonstop. Her mother was usually so eager for Christmas that she began decorating plans in early November, but this year she was clearly distracted. If her mother didn't take a little break from wedding talk, then Abby was going to explode through the roof of her family's home. She tried not to listen to her mother's phone conversation as she finished cleaning up the kitchen after dinner.

"A double wedding for Marlon and Matt," her mother cooed. "Love is definitely in the air. And soon enough, there will be babies," she continued, her tone giddy with delight.

Abby glowered. *Love is in the air.* Yeah, for everyone except her. Her mother began to dig for more details on the double wedding of her cousins, and Abby turned the water on high as she washed the last pot. She wished she could wash out her brain as easily as she could clean the dishes.

Why in the world had she fallen for a man who couldn't seem to even notice her? Talk about unrequited love. Then it had gone from bad to worse when he'd dated her beautiful oldest sister, Laila, the town beauty queen. Then it went from worse to tragic when he'd proposed to Laila. At least her sister had turned him down, but she'd hated the idea that Cade would suffer from Laila's rejection.

The past couple of years it had been so hard to see Cade with Laila. Abby had felt as if she'd walked around with a permanent knot in her stomach. In love with her sister's on-again, off-again boyfriend? It was like a bad soap opera. Although she loved Laila, Abby had been torn between guilt and resentment. She'd successfully kept it hidden, but she didn't know how much longer she could manage it, especially since it felt as if everyone around her was finding love and getting married. And as far as Cade Pritchett was concerned, she might as well be invisible.

Irritated with her bad mood, she muttered to herself, "Suck it up. Wedding fever won't last forever, and Christmas is right around the corner."

One second later, the door opened and her sister Laila waltzed in wearing a smile and flashing a cover of a bridal magazine. "I guess I need to start planning for the big day."

Abby felt something inside her rip. The beginning, she feared, of turning into a rocket and shooting through the roof. If she didn't get out of here. "Gotta go," she said, tossing the towel she held on the counter. "I'll be back later."

Laila shot her a bemused look. "Where are you going?"

"I need to do some research for a paper," Abby manufactured, although it was partly true.

"Can't you do it online?" Laila asked.

"Nope. Tell Mom when she gets off the phone," Abby said and grabbed her coat. She jammed her hands through the sleeves and raced outside. Full of so many different emotions, she walked blindly away from the house. She skipped getting into her orange Volkswagen Beetle, hoping the cold air would freeze her feelings.

She was torn between swearing a blue streak and crying. She hated to cry, so she began to swear under her breath. Walking toward town, Abby whispered every bad word she could call to mind. At a younger age, she would have gotten her mouth washed out with soap, but there was no one to tattle on her unless she counted the bare November trees and whistling wind. Unfortunately she used up her repertoire very quickly, and despite her best efforts, her eyes filled with tears.

Chapter One

It had been a long day and it was colder than a well-digger's backside. Cade had been working like a dog and wanted a little reward. He wouldn't be getting it from a woman tonight, so Cade Pritchett looked inside the café, trying to decide whether or not to indulge in a slice of cherry pie.

Cade looked away. Since that insane moment he'd proposed to Thunder Canyon's beauty queen, the woman he'd dated casually the past few years, he'd become all too aware of his burning need for a family of his own. It didn't make sense because Cade wasn't interested in falling in love. He'd done that once and lost the woman to an accident. He wasn't interested in risking his heart, but he wanted more than what he had now. A partnership in his father's business, his own spread just outside of town and his hobby rebuilding motorcycles. Oh, and his hound dog, Stella. He should have listed her first.

From his side, he heard a sniffling sound. Curious, he glanced over and saw Abby Cates wiping her nose as she leaned against the café window. His stomach clenched. Abby, little sister of the woman he'd asked to marry him during the Frontier Days celebration. That had been a monumental mistake.

He heard Abby sniff again and Cade felt a surge of concern. He should check on the girl. The poor thing looked upset. He moved toward her.

"Hey, what's up? Or down?"

Abby glanced up in shock, her wide eyes blinking in surprise. "Hi," she said and gave another sniff and surreptitious wipe of her nose with her tissue. "What are you doing here?"

"Thinking about getting a piece of pie," he said. "Long day."

She nodded and blinked away her tears. "This is the beginning of one of your busy seasons, isn't it?"

"Yeah, how'd you remember?" he asked.

"Osmosis," she said. "I guess I eventually noticed during the last few years when you didn't hang around the house as much."

"Yeah," he said. "So, what's with the sniffles? I don't think it's allergies or a cold."

She shrugged and lowered her gaze, her eyelids hiding her emotions from him. "I don't know. Lots of changes going on at my house. I guess I'm going to miss

Laila now that she's getting married," she said, then froze and met his gaze. "I'm so sorry. I didn't mean to say—"

He waved his hand in dismissal. "No problem. My pride was hurt more than anything else. Laila and I were never crazy in love. I shouldn't have been such a darned fool by proposing to her," he said.

"You weren't the fool. Laila was. She should have never let you get away," she said.

Cade laughed and shook his head. It felt nicer than he'd like to admit for Abby to rush to his defense, but he knew more than most that romance and emotion could be fickle and elusive. He shoved his hands into the pockets of his sheepskin jacket. "You shouldn't be out here in the cold," he said. "Let me buy you a cup of hot chocolate."

She met his gaze for a long moment, and he saw a flurry of emotions he couldn't quite name except one. Defiance.

She licked her lips. "I'd like something a little stronger than hot chocolate."

Surprise punched through him. "Something stronger," he said. "You're a little young for that, aren't you?"

She gave a husky chuckle. "Are you suffering from a little dementia due to your advanced years? I'm twenty-two."

"Whoa," he said. "When did I miss that?"

"I guess you weren't looking," she said wryly. Her chocolate-brown eyes flashed with humor, and his gaze slid over her silky, long brown hair.

"I guess not," he said. "So you want to go to the Hitching Post?"

"Sure," she said with a shrug, and they walked down the street to the town's most popular bar and hangout. It was crowded when they walked inside, so he hooked his hand under her elbow and guided her to the far end of the bar.

"Hey, Abby," a young man said from halfway across the room.

She glanced up and shot the guy a smile.

"Hi, Abby," a young woman called.

"Hey, Corinne," she said.

"You seem pretty popular here," Cade said, finding a space next to the bar. "How often do you come?"

She shook her head and rolled her eyes. "I know those people from my classes at college. I'm usually too busy to spend much time here. They're probably surprised to see me here."

He nodded. "What do you want to drink?"

"A beer's okay," she said with a shrug.

He noticed her lack of enthusiasm. "What kind?"

"Whatever you're having is fine," she said.

He felt a twinge of amusement. "You really don't like beer."

"I'm working on it," she said. "At least once a year."

He laughed out loud. "I'll get you one of those pink girly drinks. Cosmo," he said to the bartender. "And a beer for me. Whatever you have on draft."

Moments later, she sipped her pink martini and he drank his beer. "It's loud in here," he said.

She stirred her drink with the tiny straw. "Yeah, I guess that might bother you older folks," she said with a naughty smile.

He shook his head. Her teasing gave him a kick. "Yeah, I'm thirty. Don't rub it in. What have you been doing lately?"

"School. College," she corrected. "I'm also working at the youth center. And as you know, my family can get a little demanding. I have a part-time job teaching skiing lessons at the resort when I can fit it in. What about you? How's that new motorcycle coming?"

He was surprised she'd remembered. "Close to perfection, but I'm still tinkering with it."

"You wouldn't know perfection if it slapped you in the face," she teased.

Cade liked the way her long eyelashes dipped over her eyes flirtatiously. Someday, Abby could be trouble, he thought. "What do you mean by that?"

"I mean you have that perfection complex. Nothing you do is ever good enough. Not with your woodworking. Not with your motorcycle."

She nailed him in one fell swoop, taking him off guard. "How'd you know that?"

"I've known you for years." She took the last sip of her cosmo martini. "How could I not know that?"

For one sliver of a second, she looked at him as if he was a dork then shrugged. "You want another one?" he asked.

She shook her head and smiled. "No. I'm a lightweight. Already feel this one. I'll take some water."

Cade ordered water for her and continued talking with Laila's little sister with whom he'd played board games and computer games when he'd been waiting for Laila. He was distracted by her mouth. Especially when she licked her lips after taking a sip of her water. Her lips were plump, shiny and sexy. He shouldn't notice, but he sure did.

"So you're busy at work," she said and took another long sip of water. "Bet your father's driving you crazy."

"Yeah," he admitted. "No need to repeat that."

She laughed. "I won't. That could be tricky working with your dad. I mean, I love my own dad, but I can't control him."

"That's for sure," he said, thinking of his own father.

She clicked her half-empty water glass against his beer and dipped her head. "We agree. Cheers."

"So, what are you majoring in?" he asked.

"Psychology. I finish next spring, but I may need to get an advanced degree. I like working with the teens."

"I can see where you would be good at that," he said, thinking that although Abby appeared very young, she was pretty mature for her age.

"I don't know what I'll do after I graduate. I haven't decided if I'll leave Thunder Canyon or not," she said.

Her statement gave him a start. "You would leave town?"

"I may have to if I want to get an advanced degree. Plus, with everything going on with my family, it may be time for me to strike out on my own by then."

He nodded. "If you wanted to stay, you could get an

advanced degree online. And just because you move out of your parents' house doesn't mean you have to move out of town."

She smiled. "You almost sound like you'd like me stay. That can't be true. You barely notice me."

"You're a quality girl—" He broke off. "Woman," he corrected himself. "I hate to see Thunder Canyon lose a good woman like you."

"Ah, so it's your civic duty to encourage me to stay here," she said.

He felt a twist of discomfort. "Lots of people would miss you."

"Well, I haven't made any decisions yet. I need to finish my classes first. I'm just glad the end is in sight. What do you think about the rivalry between LipSmackin' Ribs and DJ's Rib Shack?"

Cade would have had to have been deaf and blind not to know about the controversy between Thunder Canyon's longtime favorite barbecue restaurant DJ's Rib Shack and the the new rib place, which featured waitresses dressed in tight T-shirts. "I'm a DJ's man all the way. I don't like it that the Hitching Post started featuring LipSmackin' Ribs on the menu and I refuse to order them. I'll buy drinks here, but no ribs."

"So you've never even visited LipSmackin' Ribs?"

"I went a few times just to see what the fuss was about," he said.

"You mean the skimpy uniforms the waitresses wear," she said.

He shook his head and rubbed his jaw. "I pity your

future boyfriend. He won't be able to pull anything over on you."

"Future? How do you know I don't have a boyfriend right now?" she asked. "I don't, but I certainly could. There are even some men who think I'm attractive, some who ask me to go out with them."

"I didn't mean it that way. And you be careful about those guys. You make sure they have the right intentions."

She shot him a playfully sly look so seductive he almost dropped his beer. "What would you say are the right intentions?" she asked.

His tongue stuck in the back of his throat for a few seconds. "I mean just that—you need to make sure they have the right intentions. You shouldn't let anyone take advantage of you."

"Unless that's what I want him to do, right?"

He choked on his beer. Where had this vixen come from? Although she'd been a spirited competitor whenever she'd played games and been far more knowledgeable about sports than most females he knew, Cade had always seen her as Laila's sweet little sister. "I think it's time for you to go home. I'm starting to hear things come out of your mouth that aren't possible." He waved for the bartender to bring the bill.

"Oh, don't tell me I scared big, strong Cade Pritchett," she teased as he finished his beer and tossed some bills on the counter.

"There's more than one way to scare a man. Let's go," he said and ushered her through the bar to the door.

* * *

Abby felt higher than a kite. She'd been waiting forever for the time when it was just her and Cade. She'd had a secret crush on Cade since even before her sister had dated him, and watching Laila's wishy-washy attitude toward Cade had nearly put her over the edge on more than one occasion during the past few years.

But now, she thought, her heart beating so fast she could hardly breathe, she had Cade all to herself, if only for a few more moments. "So is most of your work right now for people who want to get special Christmas gifts?"

"A good bit of it," he said. "But there's a potential for a big order. We'll find out soon." He stopped abruptly. "Is that old man Henson trying to change a tire on his truck?" he asked, pointing down the street.

Abby tore her gaze from Cade's and felt a twist of sympathy mixed with alarm. "I think it is. Isn't he almost eighty-five? He shouldn't be changing a tire during daylight let alone at this time of night," she said.

"Exactly," he said and quickened his pace. "Mr. Henson," he called. "Let me give you a hand with that."

Abby joined Cade as they reached the elderly man, who'd already jacked up the truck. "I'm fine," he said, glancing up at them, his craggy face wrinkled in a wince of pain. "It's these dang rusted bolts."

"Let me take a shot at them. Abby, maybe Mr. Henson might like a cup of that hot chocolate I was talking about earlier."

"I don't need any hot chocolate," Henson said. "I'm fine."

"I'm not," Abby said. "Would you keep me company while I drink some to warm me up?"

Henson opened his mouth to protest then sighed as he adjusted his hat. "Well, okay. But make it quick. I gotta deliver some wood in the morning."

Abby shot a quick look at Cade and shook her head. Mr. Henson was legendary for his work ethic. She admired him for it, but she also knew he'd gotten into a few situations where he'd had to be rescued. Flashing Henson a smile, she hooked her arm through his and walked to the café.

She made chitchat with the man while they sat in a booth and waited for their hot chocolate. She noticed Mr. Henson kept glancing out the window. "Your truck will be fine. It's in good hands with Cade."

"Oh, I know that," Mr. Henson said. "Cade's a fine young man. You'll do well with him."

She dropped her jaw at his suggestion then gave a wry laugh. "I think so, too, but I don't believe he sees me that way, if you know what I mean," she said and took a sip of the hot drink.

He wrinkled his already deeply furrowed forehead and wiggled his shaggy gray eyebrows. "What do you mean? You're a pretty girl. I'm sure you turn quite a few heads."

"Thank you very much," she said. "That means a lot coming from you."

"It's true. I've never been known for a silver tongue.

My Geraldine, rest her soul, would tell you the same. Although she *was* the prettiest woman to ever walk the streets of Thunder Canyon. I still miss her."

Abby slid her hand over Mr. Henson's. "I'm so sorry. How long were you married?"

"Fifty-three years," he said. "That's why I keep working. If I sit at home, I'll just pine. Better to be moving around, doing something."

"But you could afford to take a break every now and then. We don't want anything happening to you," she said and made a mental note to stop in and visit Mr. Henson. His loneliness tugged at her heart.

He shrugged. "I'll go when the good Lord says I'm ready, and not a minute before." He glanced outside the window. "Looks like Cade's finished changing my tire. We should go now. Let me pay the bill. And don't you argue with me," he said when she'd barely let out a sound. "I don't get to share some hot chocolate with a girl as pretty as you very often these days."

"And you said you didn't have a silver tongue," she said. "Thank you."

The two left the café and caught up with Cade, who appeared to be looking for a place to wipe some of the grease off his hands. Abby offered the paper napkin she'd wrapped around her cup of hot chocolate.

He made do with it. "Thanks," he said then glanced at the truck again. "It's no wonder you had trouble with those bolts. I had to bang on them to get them loose. You'll get that tire repaired soon, won't you?" he asked.

"I'll get to it. I'll get to it," Henson said in a testy

voice as he inspected the job Cade had done changing his tire. "Thank you," he said with a nod. "What do I owe you?"

Cade shook his head. "Nothing," he said.

"Aw, come on. I gotta give you something for your trouble," Henson said.

"Okay, I'll tell you what you can give me," Cade said. "You can stay out of trouble."

Henson glared at Cade for a moment then laughed. "I'll see what I can do. Thank you again. And, uh—" He glanced at Abby. "Take care of that pretty girl. You shouldn't let a good one like her get away."

Abby shot a quick look at Cade's disconcerted expression. Her face flamed with heat and she quickly focused her attention on her hot chocolate—blowing on it, sipping. "Thanks for the hot chocolate, Mr. Henson. Good night, now," she said.

She stood beside Cade as the old man got into the car and drove away.

"I'll give you a ride home. My car's just down the street. That Henson is a character, isn't he?" Cade muttered, leading her to his vehicle.

"I have to agree. So are you," she said, wishing the evening wouldn't end.

He opened the car door and glanced at her. "Me?"

"Yes, you," she said. "You're always trying to stay in the background, but here you go again saving the day."

"What do you mean?" he asked as he started the car.

"I mean you're always rescuing somebody. It's just what you do. White Knight syndrome?"

He looked at her for a long moment with an expression on his face that made her breath stop in her chest. He looked at her as if he were seeing her as more than Laila's little sister. "I didn't think anyone noticed," he finally said.

"Of course I notice," she managed in a voice that sounded breathless to her own ears.

He glanced away and put the car in gear, driving toward her home. Abby was torn between relief and disappointment. She had wanted that sliver of a moment to continue, yet she could breathe a little better now.

"Is that an official diagnosis? White Knight syndrome?" he asked, his mouth lifting in a half grin of amusement.

"No. I don't think you're clinically maladjusted. You're just a good man," she said, although *good* was putting it lightly. Cade was much more than a good man.

He glanced at her and chuckled. "Thank you. I feel better."

"That will be five dollars," she said and laughed at his sideways glance at her. "Just kidding. I'm not licensed to practice."

They approached her street and her stomach knotted. She tried to think of a way to continue this special time. She didn't want it to end. "I always thought that was strange. A doctor practices medicine. An attorney practices law. What if they have a lousy day practicing?"

Cade pulled the car to a slow stop and shifted into Park. "Good point. I try to avoid both if possible."

Abby drank in the sight of him, meeting his watchful blue gaze and noting the vapor of his breath from his mouth. His strong chin matched his character and determination and his broad shoulders had always made her think he could carry anything life threw at him. He'd suffered some deep losses. She knew that beneath that sheepskin jacket, his muscles were well developed from the times he'd played touch football with her extended family in the backyard.

She knew a lot about him, but she wanted to know so much more. She wanted to slide underneath that jacket and feel him against her. Maybe it was time to take a chance. A crazy chance. Her heart raced so fast she felt lightheaded.

"I've always liked your eyes," she said in a low voice.

His gaze widened in surprise. "What?"

"I've always liked your eyes," she repeated. "They say so much about you. You have this combination of strength and compassion and the first place you see it is in your eyes." She bit her lip then leaned closer to him. "Of course, the rest of you isn't bad, either."

"It's not?" he echoed. She saw a lot of curiosity and flickers of sensuality in his gaze.

"Not bad at all," she said, sliding her hand up the front of his jacket. Taking her courage in her hand, she tugged at his jacket to bring his head closer to hers. Then she pressed her mouth against his, relishing the sensation of his closeness and his lips meshed with hers. He rubbed his mouth against hers and she suddenly felt his hand at her back, drawing her breasts against his chest.

His response sent a flash of electricity throughout her and she opened her lips to deepen the kiss. He took advantage, sliding his tongue inside her. Craving more, she gave what she knew he was asking. Despite the cold temperature, she felt herself grow warmer with every passing second of his caress. Warm enough to strip off her coat and…

Cade suddenly pulled his mouth from hers and stared at her in shock. "What the—" He shook his head and swore, taking a giant step away from her. "I'm sorry." He swore again. "I shouldn't have done that."

"But you didn't start it," she said, her heart sinking at his response.

He held up his hands. "No, really. I shouldn't—" He cleared his throat. "You go on home, now. I'll watch from here."

"But, Cade—"

"Go inside, Abby," he said in a voice that brooked no argument.

Still tempted to argue, Abby had pushed her courage as far as it would go tonight. She swung away from him, hopped out of the car and slammed the door behind her. Striding home, she was caught between euphoria and despair. He had kissed her back and he sure seemed to like it. For those few seconds, he had treated her like a woman he desired. This time she hadn't imagined the way he tasted, the way his lips felt against hers, his hand at her back, urging her closer. This time, it had been real.

But then the man had apologized for kissing her. The knowledge made her want to scream in frustration. Was she back where she'd started? Was she back to being Laila's little sister?

Chapter Two

Cade would have mainlined his third cup of coffee after lunch if it had been possible. He hadn't slept well last night and had felt off all day. He stripped another screw for the designer desk he was making for an entertainment hotshot in L.A., and swore under his breath.

His father and partner, Hank, was talking, but Cade was trying to focus on the desk instead of the way Laila's sister had kissed him last night. And worse yet, he thought, closing his eyes in deep regret, the way he'd kissed her back.

Cade tried to shake off the thoughts and images that had been tormenting him since he'd apologized and burned rubber back to his house. Thoughts about her had haunted him. Her wide brown eyes, her silky, long brown hair and her ruby lips swollen from the friction of his mouth against hers. His own lips burned with the memory, and he rubbed the back of his hand against them, trying to rub away the visual and the guilt. What the hell had he been thinking?

Impatience rushed through him and he grabbed a file. His mind torn in different directions, he stabbed his other hand. Pain seared through him, blood gushed from his hand. Cade swore loudly and stood.

"What are you doing, son?" his father demanded, striding toward him to take a look at Cade's hand.

"It's fine," Cade said. "I'll bandage it and it will be fine."

"You better be up-to-date with your tetanus shot," Hank said.

"I am," Cade said. "I'm not that stupid."

"Based on your performance this morning…" his father began.

"Lay off, Dad," Cade said, looking down at the man who had taught him so much about carpentry and life, the man who'd never recovered from the death of his wife several years ago. None of them had really recovered from the death of Cade's mother. She'd balanced her husband's stern taskmaster nature with softness and smiles.

"Son, I don't want to have to say this, but you need to snap out of your funk. Laila is getting married to someone else, and you're just going to have to get used to it," Hank said bluntly.

Shock slapped through Cade as he stared at his father. He opened his mouth to say he hadn't been thinking about Laila then closed it. He sure as hell didn't want to tell his father he'd been thinking about Laila's little sister Abby.

"You bandage up that hand and go check in on the community center. They've requested a few things for their Thanksgiving program."

Cade shook his head. "We don't have time for me to go to the community center now. We have too much work."

Hank shook his head. "Get some air, do something different. You'll come back better than ever."

"You know that since we're equal partners, you can't be giving orders," Cade said.

Hank sighed and rolled his eyes. "Okay, consider it a request from your elderly father."

Cade felt a twitch of amusement. His father was still a hard driver, especially in the shop. "Elderly my—"

"Get on out of here," Hank said.

Cade pulled on his jacket and walked out the door, feeling his father's gaze on him as he left. He didn't want his father worrying about him. With a few exceptions during his teen years, Cade had made a point of not causing his parents much grief. Once his mother had gotten sick, his younger brothers had acted up, and Cade knew his father had needed to be able to rely on him. Work had gotten them through the rough times, and for Cade, the loss hadn't stopped with his mother. There's been Dominique and he'd felt the promise of happiness with her before she'd been taken from him.

Stepping outside the shop, he walked toward the

community center a few blocks away. He shook his head, willing the cold air to clear it. He shouldn't be thinking about Abby. It was wrong in so many ways. Putting his mind on the community center's Thanksgiving needs should point him in a different direction. He welcomed the change.

Cade walked inside the glass door of the community center and headed toward the gym at the back of the building. He pushed open the door and his breath hitched at the sight before him. The object of his distraction handed a baby to the community center's children's director, Mrs. Wrenn, and began to climb a ladder holding a humongous horn of plenty.

"What the hell?" he muttered, walking toward the front of the room.

Abby continued to climb the ladder while she lugged the horn of plenty upward. Cade couldn't permit her to continue. "Stop," he said, his voice vibrating against the walls.

Abby toppled at the sound of his voice and whipped her head in his direction. "Cade?"

"Stay right there," he said, closing the space between him and the ladder. He grabbed each side of the metal ladder. "Okay, you can come down now."

Abby's hair swinging over her shoulders, she frowned at him. "Why? I've just got a little farther to go."

"Not while I'm here," he said, his voice sounding rough to his own ears.

Abby shook her head. "But it won't take another minute for me to finish—"

"Come down," he said. "It's not safe. I'll handle it."

She paused long enough to make him uncomfortable. "Abby," he said.

"Okay, okay, but I was doing fine before you got here," she said, descending the ladder.

"That's a matter of opinion," he muttered under his breath as he watched her bottom sway as she wobbled.

She missed the last step and fell against him. He caught her tight and absently grabbed the horn of plenty, his heart pounding.

"Oops," she said after the fact.

Some part of him took note of the sensation of her breasts against his chest, her pelvis meshed against his as she slid downward. His brain scrambled, but he fought it.

"I really would have been fine," she insisted.

"Yeah," he said, unable to keep the disbelief from his voice. "I'll handle the rest of this."

"You're not being sexist, are you?" she demanded. "Because I really *can* do this."

Cade felt his heart rate rise again. "Not sexist," he said. "Just practical. I'm more athletic than you are."

"I don't know," she said. "I played soccer and—"

"I have more upper-body strength," he said, deciding to end the argument once and for all.

He felt Abby's admiring gaze over his broad shoulders. "I can't argue with that," she said.

He felt an odd thrill that he quickly dismissed. "I'll

go ahead and hang this horn of plenty," he said. "Do you mind holding the ladder?"

"Not at all," Abby said cheerfully.

Cade climbed the ladder and hung the horn of plenty. He descended to the floor. "My father told me you need a few things for your Thanksgiving show."

Mrs. Wrenn jiggled the toddler and Abby extended her arms to the small boy. "Come here, Quentin."

The toddler fell toward her and Abby laughed, catching him in her arms. "Hiya, sweetie," she said.

The mocha-colored child beamed and giggled as Abby cradled him, clearly feeling safe with her. Cade saw a flash of Abby, laughing, burgeoning with pregnancy and another baby on her hip. Her brown eyes were sexy with humor and womanly awareness.

Cade shook his head, snapping him out of his crazy visual. "How can I help you, Mrs. Wrenn?"

The elderly woman beamed at him. "Thank you so much for coming. We need a ship hull and a table for the pilgrim and Native American dinner. It doesn't have to be too special."

"We can take care of that," Cade said. "We'll get a donated table and dress it up."

"That would be wonderful," Mrs. Wrenn said.

"And I'll work out something with a ship's hull during the next week. How many people do you want on it?"

Mrs. Wrenn winced. "Twenty."

"Whoa," he said. "Good to know. We can take care of that."

Mrs. Wrenn gave a big sigh and clasped her hands together. "Thank you. I knew we could count on you, Cade. We want to give all of the children a chance to feel like stars."

Cade nodded, catching Abby's eye and feeling a flash of kinship with her. He was surrounded by people who either were or felt as if they needed to be stars, but he couldn't be less interested. If he read Abby's wry gaze correctly, then she felt the same way.

"I can do that," he said.

"I knew you could," Mrs. Wrenn said.

He glanced at Abby and the sexy look in her gaze took him off guard. He fastened his gaze on the graying Mrs. Wrenn. "Any particular colors you have in mind?"

The director shrugged. "Harvest colors."

He nodded. "I'll take that back to the shop. Anything else you need?"

"Nothing else I can think of," Mrs. Wrenn said and glanced at Abby. "Is there anything else that comes to mind? Abby has been nice enough to fill in since my volunteer helper Mrs. Jones had to have bunion surgery."

Abby glanced at the director, then looked at Cade. "Not a thing, but if you get lost, you can contact Mrs. Wrenn or me."

"I don't get lost," Cade said.

"That's a shame," Abby said under her breath, then lifted her shoulders. "Then if you need suggestions."

He shot her a sideways look. "Who does Quentin belong to?" he asked, unable to squelch his curiosity.

Abby's gaze turned serious. "His mother, Lisa, has passed her G.E.D. and has completed her L.P.N. She wants to get her R.N. She's just nineteen and one of my ROOTS girls. I told her I would step in as often as possible during her education. She's halfway through her R.N."

He felt a shot of admiration. "You're a good friend."

"She's a good mom. It's the least I can do."

Cade's respect for Abby grew. Big brown eyes, long brown hair, she was just Laila's little sister, but now she seemed like so much more. He glanced at the toddler and couldn't hold back a smile. "How are you babysitting with your courses?"

"Just call me Superwoman," she deadpanned. "Kinda like you're Superman."

He felt a crazy hitch in his chest and inhaled quickly. "I'm no Superman."

"Nobody else knows that," she said and shifted the baby on her hip.

His mind flashed. Body. Baby. Come-hither smile. Heaven help him.

Cade cleared his throat. "I'll get back to the shop."

"Thank you for coming, Cade," Mrs. Wrenn said in her squeaky voice.

"Let us know when you need a break," Abby offered, her eyes lowered to a sexy half-mast.

Cade felt a rush of arousal race through him. He

swore to himself and turned away. "See you ladies later," he said.

"Anytime," Abby said, and the sexy invitation sent his blood rushing to his groin. Cade swore again, but he suspected the fresh air might not cure his distraction.

Abby was surviving at home, but barely. Although she was happy her sister Laila had found true love and wanted to marry, it was hard to deal with the constant wedding plans. Plus, her cousins were headed down the aisle, too.

Enough was enough and it felt like pulling teeth to get Cade to look at her as if she was more than a fourth grader. Reality beckoned, however, and Abby was forced to join her family for a dinner with Jackson Traub and his sister, Rose. Jackson had managed what many other men had tried by winning over her sister Laila.

"To Laila and Jackson," her father toasted, lifting his glass. "May your love be bigger than your wills."

"Here, here," Abby's mother said.

"Yeah," Abby muttered under her breath and took a big gulp of sparkling wine.

Laila beamed and looked at Jackson. The love between them sizzled. Laila lifted her glass to Jackson and her eyelids lowered in an intimate gaze. "Who would have ever known?"

"Who?" Jackson echoed and clicked her glass against his.

Abby felt a sliver of envy that traveled deeper than her soul. What she wouldn't give to have Cade look at her that way. *Not in this lifetime,* she thought.

Thank goodness the Cateses understood their priorities. Food was near the top of the list. Soon enough, a platter of roasted chicken was passed her way, followed by mashed potatoes. After that, green beans and biscuits.

Abby took a small spoonful of each dish as it passed. Her mind was preoccupied with Cade. Her appetite was nearly nonexistent. The good news was that everyone's attention was focused on Laila and Jackson, so no one would notice the fact that she wasn't the least bit hungry.

Abby nodded and smiled and pushed her food around her plate then murmured an excuse to get her away from the table. She sought peace in her backyard. It was freezing, but that was no surprise. Abby enjoyed the freezing air that entered her lungs. Despite the fact that it was too cold for words, she was thrilled with the solemn quiet her father's ranch offered at moments like these.

She meandered past the porch and shoved her hands into her pockets.

Seconds later, she heard voices from the back porch.

"I know it's crazy, but Laila is my dream come true," Jackson Traub said. "I never expected it, and she took me by surprise."

"I'm so glad," Rose Traub said. "I was surprised, but

happy when it happened. I love that you never thought it would happen to you."

"Thanks," Jackson said, unable to conceal his amusement.

"Humility is the beginning of wisdom," Rose said.

Jackson swore. "You're tough."

"You taught me. I'm just not sure I'll ever find my true love. Maybe he doesn't exist. I feel like I've dated every man in Thunder Canyon."

Abby swallowed a sound of frustration that threatened to bubble from her throat. Rose had been out with a *lot* of Thunder Canyon men. She'd even gone out with Cade, and that hadn't set well with Abby, at all.

"You haven't dated every man. There's still old man Henson and his friends," Jackson joked.

Abby resisted the urge to laugh, but Rose didn't. Her warm chuckle drifted through the cold air. "Thanks for the encouragement. Mr. Henson is eighty-five if he's a day."

"Just kidding," Jackson said. "But the truth is you can find your true love. I did. Don't give up."

"I'm not sure I can count on that," she said.

"Give it a little longer," Jackson said. "You might be surprised."

Seconds later, silence fell over Abby as she stood outside the deck in the dark. She wasn't quite sure what she should take away from the cold night and the conversation she'd overheard.

Abby stared into the horizon, feeling the stars from the sky watching over her. She should leave, she thought, but she felt the stars tracking her. She wanted—no, needed—to feel the stars guiding her to her future. More than anything, she wished a lucky star was shining down on her. A star of love. If not love, then an antidote for love.

Fixing her gaze on the brightest star, she felt a ripple of realization shimmy down her spine. She's wanted Cade as long as she could remember. She'd pushed herself to flirt with him the other night. Abby felt as if her passion for Cade would never be returned. But she would never be sure if she didn't put herself out there.

Abby had never been much of a flirt, and she had no idea how to be a seductress, but maybe she needed to give it her best shot now. Maybe she needed to do everything she could to make Cade see her as a woman, a desirable woman who wanted him. At that moment, she made a promise to herself. No more shy little sister, hiding behind Laila. Abby needed to find her inner sexpot.

Abby cringed at the thought. Okay, maybe not *sexpot,* but *seductress* had an empowering ring to it…when it didn't make her snicker.

Two days later, Cade took a break from work at the shop and headed for the new bakery in town, the Mountain Bluebell Bakery. He was feeling deprived lately and figured giving in to his sweet tooth was the least of possible evils. Cherry pie or something better sounded great.

He exhaled and his breath sent out a foggy spritz.

Noticing a crowd ahead, he slowed as he approached. A news team was interviewing several different citizens of Thunder Canyon.

"So, do you think a down-home ribs meal is good enough to keep customers happy?" the newscaster asked. "Or do you think tight T-shirts and short shorts are necessary in today's market?"

"Nothing wrong with short shorts and tight T-shirts," a man from the crowd yelled.

"But is it necessary?" the newscaster asked.

"Well," the man said, "I guess not. But it sure doesn't hurt."

The crowd laughed.

Suddenly a microphone was put in Cade's face. "What about you? Do you think a tight T-shirt and short shorts are more important than a home-cooked meal?"

"No," he said without hesitation. "The food and service are great at DJ's. No need for tight T-shirts."

The reporter moved past him and Cade automatically searched the crowd. His gaze landed on Abby on the opposite side of the street. He wondered what she thought of all this. She'd seemed a bit skeptical of the skimpy outfits of LipSmackin' Ribs.

Her gaze met his, and he lifted his hand and gave her the hi sign. She nodded and moved toward him.

Cade noticed the way her long brown hair swung over her shoulders. Her cheeks were pink from the cold and her plump lips shiny and distracting. She had the kind of lips any man would want to kiss.

"Hi," she said as she approached him. "Can you believe this?"

He nodded at the crazy press. "Not really. Who would have thought a debate over ribs would bring national news to Thunder Canyon?"

"I'm with you," she said, glancing over her shoulder at the crowd behind her. "What are you doing out and about?"

"I'm taking a break and checking out the new bakery down the street. I hear they've got some good stuff," he said.

"Mind if join you?" she asked.

Something told him he should refuse, but he didn't give in to it. "What about school?"

"I don't have a class until tonight."

He frowned. "You take night classes? Why don't you stick to day?" he asked.

Her lips twitched. "Because not all of my classes are available during the day."

"Hmm."

"Are you going to buy me a chocolate tart or not?" she asked.

He blinked. "Yeah, I'll buy you a tart. Let's go."

He led the way to the bakery and they ordered their pastries and coffee.

Moments later, the two of them sat at a table with coffee, a chocolate tart and a slice of cherry pie à la mode. Like many of the shops around town, the bakery featured both Thanksgiving and Christmas decorations. The shop owners in Thunder Canyon weren't dummies. They would maximize the holiday season to get the most out of it. Cade, however, wasn't big on Christmas since his mother and Dominique had died years ago.

Abby took a spoonful of chocolate tart into her mouth and closed her eyes in satisfaction. "Now, that is good."

"Yeah," Cade said, fighting a surge of arousal as he took a bite of his cherry pie.

"No, really," she said, lifting a spoon toward Cade. "You should try this."

Cade glanced into her brown eyes then felt his gaze dip deeper to her cleavage. When had Abby Cates gotten cleavage?

Cade cleared his throat. "I'm game," he said and opened his mouth.

He felt her slide the spoon and decadent chocolate past his lips onto his tongue. His temperature rose. He swallowed.

"Good," he managed.

"Of course it is," she murmured.

Cade met her gaze and felt a wicked stirring throughout him. Something about Abby made him…hard.

She took a sip of coffee and looked at Cade from the rim of her coffee mug. "Coffee's not really my favorite," she said. "When it comes to hot drinks, I'd rather have hot chocolate or apple cider."

"I'll take coffee," Cade said.

"But what if you had a choice?" Abby asked. "What would you choose?"

"Coffee with cream and hazelnut," he said.

"Smells delicious," Abby said, closing her eyes and smiling.

"But do you want to drink it?" he asked.

"Not so much," she said. "But I would love to smell it."

He chuckled and she opened her eyes. "What's wrong with smelling?" she asked.

"Nothing," he said. "Nothing at all."

She got to the end of her tart and there was one bite left. "Bet you want it," she said, waving the spoon in front of his mouth.

The motion was incredibly seductive, and he found himself craving what she offered. Or maybe he was craving what he wanted. He couldn't quite tell what Abby was offering, but it was a big no-no. Or was it?

He clasped his hand over hers, the last bite of chocolate hanging between them.

"Take it," she urged.

Her voice was too sexy to ignore. He grabbed her hand and drew it to his mouth. Cade enveloped the chocolate with his mouth and swallowed it down. The motion was both carnivorous and sexual.

Abby's brown eyes widened in surprise.

"What did you expect?" he asked.

"I don't know," she said. "Something more…"

"Polite?" he asked.

Her eyes darkened. "Maybe. If so, I'm glad I was wrong."

His gut tightened. "You need to be careful. You're asking for trouble."

"Just from you," she said.

His heart hammered against his rib cage. "This is a bad idea."

"There are worse ideas," she countered.

He felt himself begin to sweat. How could Laila's little sister affect him this way? It wasn't possible.

"Go away, little girl," he said and pulled back.

"I'm not a little girl," she said.

"You're too young for me," he said.

"Says who?" she challenged.

Her defiance caught him by surprise. "Says anyone with any sanity."

Abby leaned toward him, her eyes full of everything he shouldn't be thinking. "Haven't you heard? Sanity's overrated."

"I don't know what game you're playing, Abby. But I'm not playing," he told her with finality.

Chapter Three

Abby's ego bruised *again,* she buried herself in her schoolwork and decided to follow up on her intention to visit Mr. Henson. She hadn't seen his old truck in town during the past few days and decided he might enjoy some leftover chicken and dumplings Abby and her mother had made last night. She also brought along a wreath to add a little holiday cheer to his home, hoping it might lift his spirits. She drove her orange VW toward his place and slowed as she turned onto his dirt driveway. The ground was too frozen to allow the dust to kick up the way it would in the summer, she thought as she pulled in front of the old white farmhouse.

Although Mr. Henson did far more than most folks thought he should, Abby knew he'd finally given up on ranching several years ago and leased his acreage to a local rancher. The old blue truck with peeling paint was parked next to the house, which meant he should be home.

Abby picked up the container of food and got out of her car. She noticed the steps to his porch were still crusty with ice and wondered if he had any salt she could throw on them for him. Knocking on the door, she paused and listened, but there was no response. She knocked again and heard a faint reply.

"Mr. Henson, it's Abby Cates. Are you okay?"

She heard the sound of slow footsteps and moments later, the door finally opened. Abby was surprised at the sight of him. His face was grizzly with white stubble, his hair hadn't been combed and his clothes were rumpled.

"What are you doing here?" he demanded in a cranky voice.

"I came to see you and I brought some chicken and dumplings," she said.

His eyes lit with faint approval. "Oh, well, that's nice of you. Come on in," he said and hobbled inside. "Where's that Pritchett young man? Aren't you two married?"

"No," she said. "Cade Pritchett barely knows I'm alive."

Mr. Henson glanced over his shoulder. "That's his mistake, I'd say."

She noticed his grimace as he took a step and her alarm buttons started to go off. "Mr. Henson, you're limping. What's wrong?"

He waved his hand. "Oh, it's nothing. Couple logs fell on my leg when I was delivering wood. You mind if I heat up those dumplings? I bet they're tasty."

"They are, but I think you might need to get your ankle checked by a doctor," she said.

"Doctors usually can't do anything. Medicine is just one more racket, I say."

"But—"

"You gonna make me beg for those dumplings?" he asked.

She sighed. "No. Sit down and I'll heat them up for you," she said and walked toward the kitchen, then turned as something occurred to her. "If you'll let me take you into town to see the doctor as soon as you finish eating."

He scowled at her. "I'm telling you, it's a waste of time and money."

"It will make me feel better," she told him. "I'm worried about you. You're not yourself."

His gaze softened. "Well, you're being silly," he said gruffly. "I'll go," he said, sinking onto the sofa. "But not until I eat those dumplings."

Thirty minutes later, he'd finished the food and she hung the wreath on his front door.

"What's that for?" he asked as he shuffled toward her car.

Abby adjusted the red bow. "To give you some Christmas spirit."

He muttered and got into her car. Abby drove toward

town with Mr. Henson fussing the entire way about her car.

"What can you carry with this thing, anyway? Bet my lawn-mower engine is bigger than this. What keeps it running?" he asked. "Sounds like squirrels."

"The only thing I have to carry is me," she said. "I don't haul wood, and this car is surprisingly good in the snow."

"Can't believe that," he said. "You'd get stuck in six inches."

"It's light, so it doesn't sink, plus the gas mileage is terrific. What kind of gas mileage does your truck get?"

He made a mumbling sound that she couldn't understand. "Excuse me? What did you say?"

"Fifteen miles to the gallon," he said. "But I could haul most of the houses around here if I wanted."

She bit her tongue, refusing to point out the obvious, that there was no need to haul houses. Turning off the main drive, she pulled next to the clinic door.

"This is a no-parking zone," he told her.

"I know," she said. "I just wanted to get you as close to the door as possible."

"Hmmph," he said and opened the car door.

"Just a minute," she said, cutting the engine and rushing to the passenger side of the car.

"Gotta be a darned pretzel to ride in that car," he grumbled, but leaned against her as she helped him inside the clinic. Two hours later, she helped Mr. Henson back to the car as he hobbled on crutches.

"Just a sprain," he said. "I told you it wasn't anything

and I'm not taking that pain medication. It makes me loopy."

"It's not a narcotic," she said as she carefully arranged the crutches in her backseat. "Do you have plastic bags?"

"Yeah, why?" he asked.

"For the ice. The doctor said you need to put ice on your ankle."

Mr. Henson shrugged.

"Well, if you don't want to get better and you want to keep feeling rotten, you don't need to follow his instructions."

She felt the old man whip his head toward her. "I didn't say that," he said.

"The doctor said between the bad bruise and sprain it's a wonder you didn't break it. So you need to take care of it. RICE is what he said."

"Yeah, yeah," he said. "Rest, ice, compression and elevation."

"You can sit back and watch some TV," she suggested.

"Hate that reality stuff. Give me a book or a ball game instead."

"That could be arranged," she said. "I think my mother said something about fixing some beef stew. Maybe I could bring some over for you if you behave yourself."

The old man licked his lips. "That sounds good."

She smiled. "You'll get better faster if you do what the doctor says."

"Maybe," Mr. Henson said and paused. "You know, you would make a good wife. You nag like a good wife would."

Abby didn't know whether to feel complimented or insulted.

"Cade Pritchett will be chasing you sooner than you think," he said.

"Not in this lifetime," she said.

Mr. Henson lifted a wiry gray eyebrow. "You disrespecting your elder?"

"No," Abby said reluctantly. "I just can't fight reality."

"Girlie," he said, "I'm eighty-five and I lost Geraldine, my reason for living, eight years ago. I fight reality every day."

She couldn't argue with that.

After that, Abby focused on her schoolwork and her work at ROOTS, a community group founded for at-risk teens. Abby led her girls' teen group on Tuesday nights where they talked about everything from bullies and sex to cosmetics and higher education.

The truth was most of the girls in Abby's group were pretty cool. They were older than their years and saw Abby as the person they wanted to become. She was humbled by their admiration.

"So, we've told you about our guys. When are you gonna tell us about yours?" Keisha, a wise-to-the-world fifteen-year-old, asked.

"I don't really have a guy," Abby said.

Silence settled over the group and Abby felt an unexpected spurt of discomfort. "Well, I *could* have a guy. It's just that the guy I want doesn't see me."

Shannon, a sixteen-year-old with purple hair, frowned. "Is he blind?"

Abby chuckled. "Not in the physical sense. He used to date my sister, so he sees me as the little sister."

"Oooh," Katrina, who wore faux black leather from head to toe, said. "Drama. I love it. Does your sis know you like the guy?"

Abby shook her head.

"Does *she* like this guy?" Keisha asked.

"Oh, no. She's engaged to someone else."

"Well, then, you should definitely move in on him," Katrina said.

Abby laughed uncomfortably. "He sees me as the little sister."

"You should change that," Shannon said. "Maybe you could dye your hair pink."

"I'm not sure that's me," Abby said.

"Well, you have to do something different," Shannon said, her gaze falling over Abby in a combination of pity and disapproval. "You're, like, everything but sexy."

"She's not ugly," Keisha said.

"I didn't say that," Shannon said. "She's just not sexy."

"I don't know," Katrina said. "She's got that fresh, natural, girl-next-door look."

"But *not* sexy," Shannon repeated.

Silence followed.

"We could help you," Shannon said.

Alarm slammed through her. "Help?" she echoed in a voice that sounded high-pitched to her own ears.

"Yeah," Keisha said, clearly warming to the idea. "We can sex you up. Your guy won't be able to ignore you then."

"I'm not sure…" Abby said.

"Hey, it's like you always tells us," Shannon said. "If you always do what you've always done, you'll always get what you've always gotten."

Abby blinked at the sound of her words played back to her. True, but how much of a change was she willing to make?

"If you won't do pink or blond hair, then we can do big hair," Shannon said, pursing her profoundly pink lips.

"And cat eyes," Keisha added.

"And a short, black leather skirt," Katrina added.

Abby winced inwardly. *Black leather skirt?*

Shannon nodded. "Kim Kardashian hair. He won't know what hit him."

Abby managed to redirect the conversation, but she knew her girls were determined to perform a drastic makeover. She ran into her fellow ROOTS volunteer, Austin Anderson, after the meeting. Austin was twenty-four years old and the two of them were good friends, thanks to their time spent working together.

"How's it going?" Austin asked and stepped beside

her as she walked toward her car in the small parking lot.

"Okay," she said and knew her voice didn't hold the commitment it should have.

Austin laughed. "Let's try this again," he said. "How's it going?"

"I think I may have just gotten myself into a situation," she said as she drew close to her car.

"What kind of situation?" he asked, putting his hand against her car door before she could open it.

Abby sighed and turned to lean against the car. She reluctantly met his gaze. "I did a bad thing," she said.

"You sold drugs or killed a baby," he said.

She couldn't withhold a chuckle. "Neither. I did, however, get drawn into a discussion about my personal life with my ROOTS girls group. Now they want to perform a sexy makeover."

He laughed. "Hooker time."

She shot him a sideways glance. "Kinda. But they make an important point. They repeated my words of wisdom back to me. If you always do what you've always done, you'll always get what you've always gotten."

He nodded. "Okay."

"Well, if I go through with this makeover, I may need a cohort."

Austin stared at her for a long moment. "I'm not sure this is a good idea."

"It probably isn't, but I need to shake things up."

Austin gave a heavy sigh. "What do you have in mind?"

"I dress up in makeover mode. You and I hit the town in places where people will talk. My unrequited love wakes up and sees that I am the answer to his heart's desire."

Austin winced. "Abby, I'm really not sure this is a great idea."

"I'm sure it isn't," she said. "But I have to do something to shake up Cade's impression of me."

"Cade?" Austin echoed. "Cade Pritchett." He gave a low whistle and shook his head. "Isn't he the one who proposed to your—"

"Yes," she said in a flat tone.

Austin took a deep breath. "Okay, I'm in. Let me know when you want to do this."

"Apparently Saturday night," she said in a wry tone. "It's the most visible night."

Austin nodded and raked his hand through his hair. "All right. Text me with the time." Austin brushed his finger over her nose sympathetically. "You're a great girl. If he doesn't realize it, he's an idiot."

"So far, he's an idiot," she whispered, her heart hurting.

The following Saturday, the ROOTS teens performed their magic on Abby. As she stared into the mirror, she wasn't sure if it was magic or something more gruesome.

"Are you sure…" she began as she looked at her dark eye makeup.

"It's perfect," Keisha said.

"You are so hot," Katrina said. "You're going to knock every guy off his feet."

Abby was not at all sure. She squinted her eyes at her teased hair, trying to see a remnant of her usual self.

"Ready to go?" Austin asked from the back of the room.

Abby took a deep breath and turned to look at him.

"Oh. Wow," he said.

Abby felt a sudden spurt of panic. "What does *'Oh. Wow'* mean?"

Austin strolled toward her. "You look hot. You'll turn heads. Look out, Thunder Canyon."

Abby rose and walked toward him. "You're lying like a dog, aren't you?"

"Not at all," he said. "You're going to turn heads like nobody's business tonight. Are you ready?"

She met his gaze and quieted her crazy heartbeat. "Not really," she said. "But that first jump in cold water is the hardest. It may as well be now."

Abby and Austin visited the hottest bars and made sure she was seen by the maximum number of people. Their last stop was an old bar on Main Street. Surprisingly enough, Cade was at this bar watching a ball game. He didn't even notice her as she sashayed inside with Austin.

Austin, however, noticed Cade. He ordered Abby

another soda water, her fifth of the evening. She countered with a martini.

Austin raised his eyes. "Lemon drop?" he asked. "I'd say you've earned it."

Abby propped on a bar stool and tried to look flirty as she sipped her lemon-drop martini.

It was a little bitter, so she switched off to ice water. She jiggled her leg from the bar stool and wondered if Cade would ever tear his gaze from the screen.

Suddenly, Austin gave a loud laugh that startled her and vibrated throughout the bar. He leaned toward her and nuzzled her.

Abby blinked in shock. *Holy buckets.*

"Play along," he said in a low voice.

Oh, yeah, she thought and nuzzled him back and giggled. That was what she was supposed to do. Right?

Out of the corner of her eye, she saw Cade looking at Austin and her. He didn't look happy. She forced a light laugh.

"He's looking, isn't he?" Austin said as he lifted his fingers to her cheek.

"Yes," she said in a low voice.

"It's what you wanted, isn't it?" he asked.

Abby felt torn. "I guess."

Austin shook his head. "Better make up your mind. He's right behind you," he muttered. "Cade," he said. "Old man, how ya doing? I see a friend on the other side of the room. I'll be back in a minute—darlin'," he added to Abby.

Abby turned to look at Cade. His face looked like a thundercloud. "Hi," she said. "How's the game?"

He shrugged. "It's California against Clemson."

She smiled. "Not close enough to care."

"I guess. What the hell have you done to your hair?"

Abby frowned. "Dressed it up. Dressed me up," she said.

"You don't need to dress up," he said. "You're asking for trouble dressed like that."

Abby frowned at him, feeling a double spurt of frustration and anger. "Some people might say I looked pretty."

"Some people would say anything to get you into bed," Cade said.

Offended, Abby narrowed her eyes at him. "You just need to butt out of my date. I'm having a good time. There's nothing wrong with that."

Austin appeared from behind Cade and lifted his eyebrows. "Ready to go, sweetheart?"

Abby frowned in Cade's direction. "Sounds good to me," she said and rose from her bar stool. It took every bit of her concentration not to look at Cade. "G'night," she said, without meeting his gaze, and hooked her arm with Austin's as she strutted out of the bar.

As she and Austin stepped into the cold night, she sucked in a clean breath of air. "I'm not sure that worked."

Austin chuckled. "Well, I think you showed him what he's missing."

His sense of humor lifted her spirits. "Thanks for being a good soldier."

"It wasn't so bad. It's not like I have anyone waiting for me," he said.

She studied his eyes, trying to read him. "I would almost think there was someone you want waiting for you."

"Don't worry about it," Austin said, opening the passenger door to his SUV.

"Hmm," she said, wondering if Austin could have a crush on someone. And for whom would he be pining?

Austin drove her home and she stepped outside the car. "Thank you for indulging my craziness," she said.

Austin shrugged. "We're all crazy in our own special way."

Abby laughed. "Thanks. You make me feel a little better. I think you may have been right from the beginning. This wasn't a great idea."

"You never know," he said. "He might surprise you."

"I won't count on it," she said. "But thanks, anyway."

She watched as he pulled out of her driveway then reluctantly turned toward her home, wondering if she could make it to her bedroom before any of her family saw her because they would give her a hard time for dressing so out of character. The house wasn't well lit. Abby suddenly recalled her mother mentioning something about a Brunswick-stew dinner being held at the local Knights of Columbus. Her father loved Brunswick stew and, if the dinners were cheap, she suspected the rest of her family was chowing down, too. Her mother must have been thrilled to skip meal preparation tonight.

She stomped through the frozen snow to the front door of her home and opened the door. She waited in silence, listening for signs of her family. Nothing. Thank goodness. She breathed a sigh of relief then suddenly heard a tap at the door.

Wincing, Abby eyed the peephole and got the shock of her life. She blinked to make sure she wasn't dreaming. It was Cade.

Taking a deep gulp of breath, she swung open the door. "Forget something?" she asked.

He narrowed his eyes at her. "You okay?"

"Of course I'm okay," she said, unable to conceal her impatience and a bit of witchiness.

His gaze fell over her. "I was worried about you," he muttered.

"Why?" she asked, leaning against the doorjamb.

"The way you were dressed. I didn't want your date to take advantage of you," he said.

"He was a perfect gentleman," Abby said.

"Yeah, well—" He sighed, his gaze falling over her. "You gonna invite me in?"

Surprised, Abby stepped backward. "Sure. Come on in."

The foyer was dimly lit by a lamp.

Cade stepped toward her and lifted his hand to her hair. "You don't need all this makeup and gunk clouding your natural beauty. What were you thinking?"

Abby swallowed over a lump of emotion. "Natural beauty?" she echoed.

"Yeah," he said and stroked her hair. "Why would you mess with this?"

She opened her mouth and stared at him. "Umm." She shrugged her shoulders. "I don't—"

His mouth descended onto hers.

Abby gasped, trying to swallow her shock.

"You're hot without all the makeup," he told her, and she felt her world turn upside down.

Somehow, the two of them stumbled to the couch in the den. She fell backward and he followed her down. His weight was the sexiest thing she'd ever felt in her life. She closed her arms and legs around him.

Cade devoured her mouth and slid between her legs. His hardness meshed against her, making her wish the clothes between them would dissolve. She wanted him inside her. There was no such thing as close enough.

He rubbed and she arched. His tongue tangled with hers. *Give me more,* she thought. *Give me all of you.*

Cade swore under his breath, but continued to kiss her. He kissed her as if she was the most important thing in the world. Abby was hot with want and need. She'd wanted him so long, so very long.

His hand slid to her breast and she stopped breathing. He rubbed her nipple. Abby arched toward him. He groaned into her mouth. The sound was so sexy she couldn't stand it.

"I want you so much," she whispered desperately.

"I want you," he muttered and thrust against her.

Abby heard, felt something in the room, but Cade overpowered her senses.

The sound of a gasp took her slightly away from Cade's spell. "What?" she murmured.

"Oh, my God. How perfect is this."

Abby blinked, hearing her sister's voice. She tugged her mouth from Cade's and felt him look in the same direction.

Laila smirked. "This really is perfect. Why didn't I see it before?"

Mere breaths later, he rose from Abby and stood. He glanced from Laila to Abby, but his gaze lingered on Abby. "Crazy," he said. "This was crazy. I can't explain it. I'm sorry. I should go," he said and left.

Abby stared after him, trying to compute everything that had happened. Why had he kissed her? She wondered what would have happened if Laila hadn't interrupted them. Abby felt a rush of frustration and met her sister's gaze.

"Oops," Laila said. "It could have been worse. Everyone else is on their way back from the Brunswick-stew dinner."

Abby rose from the couch. "Why don't I feel better?"

"It's not my fault I walked in on the two of you. It's not like you sent up a warning flare," Laila said.

Abby could have screamed. "Do you have any idea what it's like being your sister?"

Laila blinked. She winced. "That bad?"

"Beauty queen a gajillion times over, super successful. Worse, there's Cade."

Laila bit her lip. "How long…"

Abby shook her head. "Longer than you want to know."

Laila gave a slow nod. "Sorry," she said.

"Yeah," Abby said and rose from the couch.

"I gotta ask. What's with the outfit?" Laila asked, waving her hand toward Abby's leather skirt and tight top.

"It was an experiment," Abby said, not wanting to linger on her so-called makeover.

Laila laughed. "Bet you knocked Cade on his ass."

Abby bit her lip because she wasn't sure what Cade would do tomorrow. "I'd appreciate it if you wouldn't broadcast what you interrupted tonight," Abby said. "G'night."

Cade drove his SUV to his place outside of town. He was torn between arousal and the overwhelming feeling of insanity. What had he been thinking?

He had not been thinking. That was the point.

He'd seen Abby dressed like sex on a stick, felt protective and chased after her, then gave in to some insane urges. He was still hard from kissing and holding her. He had definitely gone insane and he needed to bring himself back to sanity, no matter how painful it was.

Pulling into his long driveway, he sucked in a deep breath and pulled to a stop. He cut the lights of his SUV and felt a sense of loneliness at the thought of nothing going on inside his house with no one waiting for him.

A sliver of Dominique slid through his mind like a

ghost. He remembered her black hair and her laughing black eyes. He'd hoped she could heal him, but he hadn't been sure. When he'd finally gotten around to deciding to ask her to marry him, she'd died in an automobile accident. That seemed as if it had been a lifetime ago. Years earlier, his mother had died and his family was trying to dig their way out of their grief.

After Dominique he'd just closed the door on his emotions. It had been the easiest route. Then, Laila had seemed just like him. Emotionally closed off. After dating her off and on for years, it had made sense to Cade for them to marry. In many ways, they were the same. They were getting to the place where they should go ahead and do the baby thing, so perhaps he and Laila should get married.

In retrospect, it had been a crazy idea, and he deeply regretted pursuing the possibility. Cade wanted a family of his own, and he hated that he wanted it. Life would be so much easier without that strong desire. He could work at his family's furniture shop, build his motorcycles, contribute to the community, take a woman friend every now and then and his life would be fine.

Right?

Or not.

Cade swore under his breath and raked his hand through his hair. He'd just made out with Laila's little sister. How screwed up could this situation be? Shaking his head at himself, he stepped out of his truck and walked into his lonely-ass house. The dog greeted him at the door. Thank goodness for man's best friend.

Strolling to the refrigerator, he grabbed a beer. The sound of his footsteps echoed on the wood floor of his foyer and kitchen. Is that what he was going to hear for the rest of his life? The sound of his boot heels on his own kitchen floor?

What was wrong with that?

He took a long swig of his beer and headed for the den, his dog, Stella, trailing after him all the way. Cade found the remote and turned on his giant flat-screen TV. He flicked through a few channels. Thank goodness there was a college football game. He didn't care who was playing.

Sinking down on his leather couch, he took another long swig of beer then sucked in a deep breath. He stared at the big-screen TV and waited for the game to anesthetize him. The thought of Abby's lips against his slid through is mind. The sensation of her lips, soft, silky, swollen, slick.

Her breasts had felt so good against his chest. Her nipples against his chest, his palm. Lower, lower, he'd rubbed against her. She'd arched against him.

He'd given in to the urge to slide his hands lower, to seek out her secrets. He'd felt her damp arousal.

Then Laila had walked in.

Cade swore under his breath. He didn't want to think about this anymore. He should focus on the game and his beer instead.

An hour and a half later, he woke himself up with a snort. He blinked, staring at the screen. The game was over. An infomercial about an exercise machine was playing.

Cade stared at it for a few minutes then flicked off the TV. A soft lamp kept the darkness from completely enveloping him. In the past, the darkness had been comforting. But now...

Now he wanted more and now he wanted Abby. And that was insane. Super insane.

His body grew hard too quickly and he swore again. Rising from the couch, he headed for the shower. Cade turned the water on cool, stripped off his clothes and stepped inside. A hot shower would have felt a lot better, but he needed to get away from his need for Abby. A cold shower should cure him. That was all he needed to knock some sense into himself and Abby out of his mind.

Chapter Four

Cade did what he'd always done when he was bothered about something. He threw himself into his work. It was good timing because between the approach of the holidays and some new high-dollar custom orders, Pritchett & Sons were slammed.

He sanded a bed head in preparation for stain. A man had commissioned this piece for his wife for their tenth anniversary. It would be a nice piece when he finished it, Cade thought, feeling a nip of envy over the customer's good luck of having a woman and children in his life.

Narrowing his eyes, he refocused on the work at hand. A family just wasn't in the cards for him. At least, not now. Cade heard his brother using the electric screwdriver on a table he was making and glanced over at him. Dean was good company because he didn't talk all that much. Cade couldn't have abided much chattiness at the moment. He was too busy trying to quiet his own mind.

Dean met his gaze and nodded in the direction of the bed head. "That's looking good."

"Yeah, I think Mr. Winston will be pleased with it. Hopefully Mrs. Winson will, too," he said wryly. He'd learned through the years that women often didn't see things the same way men did.

Dean nodded and gave a low chuckle then got back to work.

Cade continued sanding. He found the rhythm of woodworking both soothing and absorbing. From an early age, when his father had taught him the basics, Cade had envisioned little touches he'd wanted to add in the pieces on which he'd worked. His father hadn't discouraged him, and although Hank was more focused on producing solid, basic furniture, Cade had taken an artistic bent.

Within the past few years, people had sought him out for his one-of-a-kind pieces, even asking for his signature on the finished furniture. At first, it had seemed silly to Cade, but the request for his signature had become so frequent, it was now almost a routine.

Nearly finished with the sanding, Cade heard the shop door open and glanced up to see their regular courier, Mike Jones, loaded down with boxes. "Hey, Mike, let me give you a hand with that," Cade said, rising from his bench.

"Thanks. I've got more in the truck."

"I can help," Dean said.

Cade took the boxes into the back room to sort them out later. Seconds later, Dean and Mike brought in more. "You can tell it's the holiday season just by the number of packages," Cade said.

"For darn sure," Mike said, pulling out his electronic gizmo for Cade's signature. "Unfortunately, holidays can bring out the wackiness in people." He shook his head. "I just made a delivery to the Tattered Saddle and Jasper demanded that I wait while he opened the packages. He tore through them and apparently didn't find what he was looking for. I was waiting for his signature, and he called somebody on the phone yelling about some missing package. And then, I must not have heard correctly, but the old man said something about how the Rib Shack may not be as easy to take down as expected."

Clearly rattled, Mike shook his head again. "Gotta run. More deliveries. See you guys later and thanks for being *sane*."

The courier ran out the door, leaving a rush of cold air in his wake. Cade looked at Dean and saw the same mixture of alarm and confusion written on his brother's face that he felt. "What the—"

Dean lifted his shoulders in confusion. "I've always thought Jasper was odd, but I can't believe he's behind the problems at the Rib Shack. What would he have to gain?"

"You got me," Cade said. "Maybe it's like Mike

said and he didn't hear the old man right. Jasper's been known to mutter and mumble."

"Hmm," Dean said, the sound short and full of suspicion.

Cade shrugged it off. "We need to get back to work."

"Yeah. Same for me if I want to make that poker game tonight," Dean said, heading back to the table.

"Just be careful who you're playing with," Cade said.

"I know better than getting in a game with a bad crowd," Dean said with a scowl.

"Just a reminder from someone who's bailed you out a couple of times," Cade said.

"Three years ago," Dean said.

"Some things you don't forget. Like being woken up at 3:00 a.m. because your younger brother has been left in the snow wearing only a pair of underwear and his socks because he bet more than he had."

"Three years ago," Dean repeated with a sigh. "Thanks for coming."

"There was never a doubt I would do anything else."

Dean nodded and they returned to work, but Cade felt his mind turning to thoughts of Abby. He didn't like surprises and he was damn surprised that he'd acted like he had with her. He'd always viewed her almost as a little sister or cousin. She was his little buddy, he'd thought. Not a woman with whom he wanted to share a bed. Now she was someone who made him feel so worked up and *hot*.

Irritated with his distracting thoughts, he tossed his brush aside and stomped to the back room to get a cup of coffee. It may as well have been tar since he'd made it this morning. Sipping it, Cade grimaced and walked out the back door of the shop, hoping the cold air would clear his head and cool his body. A couple minutes later, he walked back inside and returned to his bench.

"You okay?" Dean asked.

"Yeah," Cade said, taking another sip of terrible coffee.

"There's a lot of talk about Laila and Jackson getting married. It's enough to get on anyone's nerves, let alone—"

Cade swore under his breath. "I'm okay with Laila marrying Jackson. I wish them well. Laila isn't who's bothering me."

Dean's eyebrows rose in surprise. "Then who is?"

Reluctant to discuss the subject with anyone, Cade shrugged. "Nobody is. It's just work. I have a lot of work to do. So do you."

"Yeah, whatever," Dean said. "You aren't usually this much of a pain in the butt to deal with just because you've got a lot of work to do."

Cade sighed at his brother's words. He'd been trying so hard not to think about Abby that he hadn't realized he'd been hard on everyone else. "It's not Laila. It's Abby."

"Abby?" Dean echoed. "Abby who? The only Abby I know of is Laila's little sister." Dean must have seen the conflicted expression on Cade's face. "Really? Abby Cates?"

"I'm not sure how it happened. I saw her crying a

few weeks ago and offered to buy her a hot chocolate. Somehow we ended up at the Hitching Post instead. I drove her home, and she kissed me."

"Whoa, that must have caught you off guard," Dean said. "It's always awkward when you have to tell a woman you're not interested." Silence followed. "You did let her know you weren't interested, didn't you?"

"Yeah, but then I saw her out with some guy, and she was dressed for trouble. I was worried about her, so I followed her home and we stopped talking and started—" He broke off. "Anyway, it's crazy. Abby's not my type. I can't see myself in a long-term relationship with her."

"Hmm," Dean said. "You don't think she's some kind of rebound fling for you, do you?"

"No," he snapped. "I wouldn't do that kind of thing to Abby. She's too good to be treated that way. And besides, I'm over Laila. I was never in love with her."

Dean lifted his hands. "Okay, okay. I'm on your side. Remember?"

Cade frowned. "Yeah, I know. I'm gonna take a walk. I'll be back in awhile."

In a town as small as Thunder Canyon, Abby was sure she'd run into Cade sooner or later, but it was as if he'd vanished. She knew he was putting in long hours at the shop, but still, she would have expected to see him out and about at one time or another. During the past week, she'd completed two papers, babysat for one of her ROOTS girls and endured hours of wedding-planning discussions from her mother and Laila. The good news was that her mother had started to set out snowmen and Santa figures inside the house. Abby could only hope the holidays would provide at least a slight reprieve from wedding talk.

Since she had walked in on Abby and Cade, Laila had tried to overcompensate by constantly remarking on how pretty and smart Abby was. Although Abby appreciated the sentiment, she wasn't interested in the extra attention. She really didn't want the rest of her family knowing about her unanswered quest for Cade. It was bad enough that Laila knew.

One of Abby's friends, Rachel, invited Abby to join her at the Hitching Post for a girls' night out. Ready for a break, she accepted. Although she didn't tease her hair like the girls at ROOTS had done, she realized she wanted to look more like a woman than a high-school girl, so she put on some mascara and lip gloss, changed into a sexy shirt and wore some high-heeled boots with her jeans. She looked in the mirror and shrugged at her reflection. No one would accuse her of being a beauty queen, but she supposed she looked a little better than usual.

"Abby," her mother called from the kitchen. "Rachel's here."

Grabbing her jacket, she headed for the front door where Rachel stood. Her father was sitting on the couch reading his paper. "Don't get into any trouble," he said.

Abby planted a kiss on his cheek and laughed. "Now, when have I ever caused you any trouble?"

"Hmmph," he said. "It's not too late. You be careful."

"You, too, Daddy. Too much bad news is bad for your health," she shot back with a cheeky grin. "Let's go," she said to Rachel and the two of them ran down the front steps to Rachel's six-year-old Ford Explorer. "Thanks for inviting me out," Abby said. "I need a break from everything," she said.

Rachel nodded. "Me, too. I turned in a ten-page paper this week."

"Multiply that times two," Abby said.

"At least you're getting near the end," Rachel said. "I'll have to take some courses in summer school to wrap everything up."

Abby knew Rachel and her boyfriend had recently decided to take a break and Rachel was very upset about it. "Heard anything from Rob lately?"

Rachel frowned. "Just some texts and Facebook messages."

"You could 'unfriend' him," Abby said.

"I'm not ready yet, but we're not going to think about Rob tonight. We're going to have fun. Jules and Char are meeting us there. How's the wedding planning going?" Rachel asked.

Abby groaned. "Can we put that in the same category as Rob tonight?"

Rachel laughed. "Fine with me."

The Hitching Post was hopping with business. With a football game playing on several of the flat-screen TVs, the bar area was crowded with guys rooting for their teams. Abby skimmed the bar/restaurant for Cade, and felt a pinch of disappointment when she didn't see him. *Get over it,* she told herself.

Jules and Char waved them over from a table on the far side of the room. "Woo-hoo," Char said, lifting her beer. "The chicks are out of the coop tonight." She lowered her voice. "Plus we've got a hot server. I think I should order a round for everyone, don't you?"

"I'm a lightweight, so I'll take water to start," Abby said.

"Me, too. I'm driving, so I don't want to take any chances," Rachel said.

Char frowned. "Okay, but I don't think he's going to like the tip he gets from water."

"We can order some food," Rachel suggested, grabbing a menu. "The ribs look good."

"Not for me," Abby said. "Those are LipSmackin' Ribs and I don't want to have anything to do with that company."

"Such passion about ribs," the server said from behind her and gave her a once-over, twice. "You could give their waitresses some competition."

Abby felt her cheeks heat with color. "I'm not interested in competing with LipSmackin' Ribs's waitresses. I would, however, like a hot-fudge sundae with whipped cream and nuts."

"Cherry on top?" he asked, and she saw a look of sexual interest in his gaze. After her recent depressing experiences with Cade, it gave her a little thrill. At least some males found her attractive.

"Yes, thank you," she said.

"What else can I get you lovely ladies?" he asked and took their order. "I'll be back," he said, looking deliberately at Abby.

"Ooh, he's definitely interested in you, Abby," Jules said. "And he's cute. Maybe you should hang out with him."

Abby felt conflicted. "I don't know. I'm really busy right now with school and ROOTS. This probably isn't a good time."

"When *is* a good time?" Rachel asked. "Come to think of it, you hardly ever give a guy a chance. Unless you're still holding out for—"

Abby shot Rachel the look of death, which thankfully caused her to close her mouth.

"Oops," Rachel said.

"Holding out for what?" Jules asked.

"Or who?" Char said.

A friend since junior high school, Rachel was one of the few people in the world in whom Abby had confided about her crush over Cade, and since Laila had started dating him, the two had made a deal not to discuss him unless Abby brought up the subject, which had been nearly never.

The server returned with their drinks and orders. He set her ice-cream sundae in front of her along with a piece of paper. "Text me," he invited, then turned to the rest of the group. "Anything else I can get you?"

"Three more just like you," Char said, flirting outrageously.

He chuckled. "I'll see what I can round up," he said and went to another table of customers.

"You have to text him," Jules said. "He's cute and I bet he would be a lot of fun. You could use a little fun."

"We'll see," she said. Maybe Jules was right. Maybe she shouldn't be spending all her time waiting for Cade. It's just that no other man had come close in her eyes.

"Speaking of fun, is anyone leaving town during the holidays?" Rachel asked. "I'm stuck here."

Abby shot Rachel a look of gratitude for taking the focus off of her, and the women discussed dreams of a trip to the Caribbean. It was all in fun. Abby visited the restroom and when she came out, her gaze collided with Cade's. Her heart immediately slammed into her ribs.

His gaze traveled up and down her and he gave her a slight nod before he turned back to the football game. She felt a shot of something like humiliation travel through her at his muted, unfriendly response. He might as well have snubbed her.

Indignation rose within her and she refused to let him get away with it. The last time she'd been with Cade, he'd been practically making love to her and she wasn't going to let him forget it that easily.

Stiffening her spine, she sauntered toward him and tapped him on the shoulder. "Nice to see you. How you been lately?" she asked and deliberately licked her lips.

"Okay," he said, barely sparing her a glance. "Been busy at the shop."

"Yeah, it's that season," she said. "It must get terribly *frustrating* being cooped up in that shop all day and night. I don't know how you do it."

"You do what you have to do," he said.

And she would, too, she told herself, taking her courage in her hands. "That beer looks good. You mind if I have a sip of yours?"

He glanced at her. "I thought you didn't like beer."

She shot him what she hoped was a seductive look. "I might like yours," she said.

He gave a muffled sigh and lifted the beer toward her. She lifted her hand at the same time and between the two of them, the mug was jiggled and cold liquid spilled onto her chest.

Abby gasped. She had not intended that to happen.

Cade swore under his breath. "Hey, give me some napkins," he said to the bartender. Seconds later, he was pressing them against her chest. "How the hell did that happen?" he muttered.

Abby's heart stuttered at his closeness, her body conjuring memories of how he'd caressed her and kissed her. "It's not the only thing that could happen again," she murmured.

He jerked his head upward and met her gaze. He looked at his hands and her chest for a long moment, then picked up one of her hands to give her the napkins while he backed away. "Go away, little girl."

His insistence on calling her a girl made her crazy. "You know very well I'm no little girl."

"This isn't going to work. Do you realize that I baby-sat for you once?" he asked.

Abby felt another wave of humiliation, but she pushed it aside. "That was one time and it wasn't really babysitting. It was a swimming camp and my mom asked if I could stay late because she had to take one of my sisters to the doctor."

"Close enough for me," he said. "You're too young and immature for me. I need a woman, not a girl."

Abby felt her anger explode like a Fourth of July firecracker. Straight through the roof. Her heart hammered like a shotgun that wouldn't stop. She narrowed her eyes at Cade, picked up his half-spilled beer and dumped the rest of it. In his lap.

His eyes widened. "What the—"

"That's what this woman does when she is roaring mad," Abby whispered. "Maybe you can remember the cold feeling down below when you start thinking about the fact that you want me more than you're willing to admit." Turning on her heel, she strode to the table where her friends were chatting and drinking.

Rachel glanced at her and her brow furrowed. "You okay?" she whispered.

"Never better," Abby said, adrenaline still coursing through her veins.

"You're lying," Rachel said, looking over Abby's shoulder. "What happened?"

"I just did something a sweet, good little girl wouldn't do," Abby said in a low voice, taking a sip of her water and wishing it was a martini.

"And that is?" Rachel asked.

"I poured half of Cade Pritchett's beer in his lap." The revelation was more satisfying than she could have ever expected.

Rachel gasped, then laughed—then laughed again. "You didn't?"

"I did," Abby said.

"Oh, I wish I could have seen that." Rachel lifted her hand for Abby to give a high five. "You just kicked butt. I can only hope I'll have enough guts to do the same thing to Rob."

"I didn't plan it," Abby said, feeling a sliver of guilt.

"Of course not," Rachel said.

"What are you two whispering about?" Char asked.

Abby paused a half beat, then manufactured an excuse. "I didn't want to tell everyone I was pooped. It's embarrassing."

"Hey, we're all overbooked with exams and papers," Char said. "We understand. Plus we can always insist you give a rain check. And maybe you can bring that server and a few of his friends with you."

For the first time in a long time, if not forever, Abby considered taking a chance on someone other than Cade since Cade was rejecting her completely. She didn't know how much humiliation she could take. Even now, she felt a twinge of regret for dumping Cade's beer in his lap. It wasn't her nature to be so impulsive and, well, aggressive.

Abby rubbed the piece of paper with her server's contact information between her fingers, wishing it were a lucky charm that would release her from her passion for Cade. "You never know," she finally said. "Anything is possible."

Cade couldn't believe sweet little Abby had dumped his beer in his lap. He stared after her as she returned to her table.

"Need some more napkins?" the bartender asked innocently.

"Yeah," Cade muttered. He didn't want to leave the bar with his pants so wet.

"And another beer?" the bartender asked as he gave Cade some napkins.

"Not right now," he said then swore under his breath. *Women.* Who would have thought Abby could be so impulsive? So emotional? So passionate and hot…

A slew of images and memories conspired against him, making him want to take her to his bed for at least a night. Or thirty nights.

All wrong, he reminded himself as he forced himself to remember that he had once been her babysitter. He had once been involved with her sister. Cade knew Abby would want more from him than he could give. Unlike Laila, Abby would want all of him. His mind, body and heart, and Cade had no intention of giving away all of himself to any woman.

A few days later, Cade walked toward the diner to get a decent cup of coffee since the coffeemaker at the shop had taken its last gasp. He ended up getting an extra cup for his brother Dean and headed back to work. Passing by the community center, he heard the sound of children singing. He remembered that the kids were preparing a Thanksgiving program and wondered if this was part of it.

He'd successfully avoided Abby since the incident at the Hitching Post. Her words, however, grated on him. It still wasn't acceptable for him to get involved with her. Abby had a soft heart and he would hurt her. Hell, he already had.

He hated himself for it, but he missed seeing her. He'd spent a lifetime not thinking about Abby, and now thoughts of her crept up in his mind at the oddest moments. Cade should just continue on his way back to the shop. No detours.

Or he could stand in the back where no one would notice him. Just to see if the props from Pritchett & Sons were working out okay. Sipping his coffee, he stepped inside the center and nodded at the woman at the desk as he made his way to the gymnasium.

It must have been a dress rehearsal because the kids were in costume. He had to admit they looked cute. A bunch of little pilgrims stood on the bow of the faux ship singing their little lungs out. One of the pilgrims pulled off her hat and started playing with it. In front of the ship, a group of mini–Native Americans wearing headdresses squirmed and wiggled. One little Native American started tugging on his neighbor's headdress.

He spied Abby stepping toward the tugger and shaking her head. The boy immediately stepped in line.

He chuckled. The boy must have learned, as Cade was learning, that despite her sweet smile and nature, Abby had a kick to her personality. The song about making friends and sharing ended, and Abby and the director applauded the children's efforts.

Cade knew that most of these preschoolers came from disadvantaged homes. Their time at the community center provided a hot meal, early education and exposure to learning all kinds of things they might never experience otherwise. With all her other activities, he had to admire Abby for helping the children.

As she bent down to untie a headdress, the children swarmed around her like bees to a flower. No surprise that she was good with kids. He felt the dark longing for his own family yawn inside him again and tamped it down. Maybe someday, but not with Abby. He would only hurt her.

Chapter Five

Between school, her work at ROOTS and filling in at the community center, Abby's schedule switched into high gear. In theory, she was too busy to think about Cade, but that's why theories were only theories. Real life was something else. The good news, however, was that she was too busy to be overly bothered with Laila's wedding. Sure, she felt a twinge every now and then, but with her current demands, it was easier to push aside.

After one of her night classes, she grabbed a hot chocolate with marshmallows at the diner while she sat in a booth and reviewed notes for an upcoming exam. A shadow fell over her and she glanced up to see the server from the Hitching Post looking down at her.

"You didn't call or text me," he said.

"I've been crazy busy with school and other things," she said.

"Too busy for a little fun?" he asked, sitting across from her.

"Too busy for any fun," she said.

"You don't remember my name," he said.

She searched her memory. *Started with a D.* "Daniel," she managed.

He raised his eyebrows. "Well done."

She shrugged, knowing she'd just gotten lucky and tried not to squirm at the way he studied her.

"I'm not just a waiter for the Hitching Post," he said. "I'll be studying law in the fall."

"I wasn't judging you," she rushed to say, although she was somewhat surprised.

"But you couldn't be less interested," he said.

She was impressed by his perceptiveness. "You're good," she said and pushed a strand of her hair behind her ear. "The truth is I'm cursed," she confessed.

His eyebrows lifted. "Cursed? That sounds a bit dramatic," he said.

"Well, it is dramatic, and I am, indeed, cursed. I fell head over heels for a man when I was a teenager, and even when I tried my very best not to care for him, I did. I failed at ignoring him. I failed at not thinking he was the best man in the world."

Disappointment flitted through his gaze. "Oh. Damn. How come no one like you went crazy for me as a teenager and couldn't be seduced away?"

"Ha, ha. I'm sure there were plenty of girls falling

for you. You just probably didn't notice them because there were so many. You're not exactly hard to look at, and you're full of charm."

"Not enough charm to turn your head," he said.

Abby sighed. "I'm just sick. It's a sad thing, but I'm sick."

"You should give me a chance," Daniel said. "Maybe I could cure you."

She laughed, wishing she felt remotely tempted, and shook her head. "Maybe not me, but I could refer you to at least eight of my friends if you promised not to break their hearts."

"Eight at once and no hearts broken? That's a tall order," he joked.

She laughed, again wishing her heart were as free as it should be. Free enough to enjoy and exchange interest with another man. Darn Cade Pritchett. Why had he captured her heart if he would never return her feelings?

The weather forecast was wicked bad. Blizzard coming. Fifteen inches. Zero visibility. Abby thought about Mr. Henson. She'd packaged several meals from the Cateses' freezer and taken them to him several days ago, but she hadn't checked on him recently.

Guilt slashed through her. She should have visited him. She should have… Well, no more should haves. She would go check on him now before the storm hit full force.

Abby drove her VW Beetle as the snow was flying.

She pulled in to Mr. Henson's driveway with more food and rushed up the steps to knock on his door.

"Coming," he called from inside.

Abby waited impatiently, glancing at the snow pouring sideways.

Mr. Henson opened the door and smiled. "What are you doing here?" he asked, his grumpy tone at odds with his expression.

"I wanted to make sure you're okay," she said. "A blizzard is coming and I brought you some more food."

"I like your mama's cooking," he said. "Yours isn't too bad, either," he added, waving her inside. "You shouldn't have come out in this weather."

Abby stepped inside. "I was worried about you."

"No need to worry about me. I'll go when I'm supposed to and—"

"—not a day before," she finished for him. "I just don't want you rushing things."

He met her gaze. "Why is that?"

"I like you."

His lips lifted in a small, craggy smile. "You shouldn't get too hung up on me. My Geraldine told me I was dangerous to women. I never believed it, but—"

Abby stifled a laugh, but smiled. "Geraldine was right. How's your ankle?"

"Damn slow healing," he said as he shuffled toward the kitchen. "If I was just a few years younger, I'd be better fast, like that," he said and snapped his fingers. "This one is taking a while. Gotta say the ice and meds help a little. A *little*," he added with emphasis. "It's no miracle."

"I hope you'll turn a corner soon. I'm glad you're not hurting quite as much. In the meantime, I want to make sure you're ready for this blizzard headed our way."

Mr. Henson lifted his head as if he were offended. "I've lived through more blizzards than years you've been alive, missy."

"I'm sure you have," she said. "But I'm a neurotic whippersnapper who wants to make sure you make it through this one, too."

He stared at her for a long moment. "This younger generation is strange."

A knock sounded at the door, startling both of them. "I'll get it," she said and strode toward the door. She opened it, stunned to see Cade staring back at her. Her heart felt as if it lodged in her throat.

"What are you doing here?" she and Cade said at the same time.

Abby blinked, reining in her heart, mind and soul. *Oh, not soul,* she told herself. Not soul. That was too much, too deep. "I'm here because of the blizzard."

"So am I," Cade said. "You shouldn't be here. It's already started."

"My car is good in the snow," she said, lifting her chin.

Cade gave a short, humorless laugh. "In this weather? I don't think so."

"It is," she insisted. "I wouldn't have come out here if my car couldn't have made it."

"Yeah, well, good luck making it back. The visibility is already shot," Cade said.

Abby frowned. Now she was dealing with two grumpy old men.

Cade walked past her. "You need some wood? What's your flashlight and candle situation?" he asked Mr. Henson.

"What's wrong with you two? I've been through blizzards before. I can do it again," he said.

"But your ankle," she said.

Cade glanced back at her. "What about his ankle?"

"He sprained and bruised it. I took him to the doctor last week."

"It's nothing," Mr. Henson said. "But the ice and meds helped. I'm fine."

"Why didn't you tell me?" Cade asked.

"You weren't talking with me," she retorted. "I'm too young to know anything. Remember?"

Silence fell over the room. They could have heard a pin drop.

"Hmm," Cade said and turned back to Mr. Henson. "Let's double-check your supplies, heat and cell phone. I need to make sure Abby gets home okay."

"I'm good. You get your woman home," Mr. Henson said.

Abby groaned.

"*My* woman?" Cade echoed. "She's not my woman."

"Well, she would be if you had any sense," Mr. Henson said. "Do you know what a good cook she is? She's brought me some meals."

Cade shrugged his shoulders. "I didn't know. Glad she's been feeding you."

"You know, it's a mighty fine thing when a woman can cook like she does. That's part of what makes a good wife. Plus she's doggone pretty. Have you taken a good look at her? She's—"

"Mr. Henson," Abby said, feeling her cheeks blaze with embarrassment. "We really do want to make sure you're going to be okay during this storm." She cleared her throat. "Batteries," she said. "I'll check the batteries."

Within a few moments, she and Cade had Mr. Henson armed and prepared for the storm. "Now, you take care and I'll check on you again. Call if you have any problems," she said, squeezing the elderly man's shoulders.

"I won't have any problems," he told her.

"Then call for any reason," she said. "I should go." Resisting the urge to meet Cade's gaze, she pulled on her gloves and strode out of the house.

Cade had been telling the truth about the weather. The white stuff was pouring down with a vengeance. She adjusted her cap and swiped the snow out of her eyes as she stomped to her car. Her VW started up with its usual dependability and she flipped on the windshield wipers to the fastest setting. Putting the car into gear, she pushed the accelerator and slowly moved forward.

The visibility was terrible, but Abby figured if she went slow and steady, she would be okay. Fishtailing up Mr. Henson's driveway didn't build her confidence, but she soldiered on. It was only about twenty miles between Mr. Henson's house and her home, she told herself and kept a light foot on the accelerator.

Soon enough, she saw Cade's SUV in her rearview mirror. Certain she was moving too slowly for him, she opened her window and waved her hand for him to pass, but he didn't. Of course not, she thought. He had to look after her the same way he would look after his little sister. Having him at her backside just made her more edgy, especially when her little VW pulled left when she was holding the steering wheel straight.

Moving at a snail's pace, she wrapped her hands around the steering wheel with a death grip. Suddenly another car appeared out of nowhere and headed straight for the driver's side of her VW. Her heart raced and panic rushed through her. Abby swung the steering wheel to the right and mashed on the accelerator. The snow was so thick she was driving blind. She felt it the second her car lost traction with the road and pitched downward, then collided with something that brought her car to a halt, her seat belt jerking her tightly against her seat. She held her breath and squished her eyes together, waiting for the air bag to slap her.

When it didn't, she slowly opened her eyes and took a careful breath and did a quick physical evaluation. She jiggled her arms and legs and—

A thump sounded on her window, scaring the bejeezus out of her. Abby looked out the window into Cade's concerned gaze. Her heart turned over. Blast it.

"Are you okay?" he yelled.

She nodded. "Fine. Really," she called in return. "I can handle it. I'm okay."

He shook his head and motioned for her to roll down her window.

"I'm fine. Really," she repeated as she lowered her window. "I can handle this."

"You're in a ditch," he said.

"Oh," she said. "Oops."

"Unlock the door. I'll help you up to my car," he said.

She didn't like the put-upon sound in his voice. "I could call my father," she said.

"There's no need for him to come get you when I'm here," he said.

"I don't want you to feel obligated," she said. "You feel obligated to rescue everyone. I don't want you to feel obligated about me."

"Open the door," he said. "It's damn cold out here."

"Charming," she muttered under her breath, but did as he said. He extended his hand and she accepted it, wishing he was reaching for her in entirely different circumstances. That was a dream that wasn't going to come true anytime soon.

Pulling her hand from his, she climbed up the side of the ditch. She tripped once and he reached out his hand, but she ignored it. She trudged upward and made it to the top where Cade's SUV blinked its emergency lights at her in an almost mocking way. Abby resisted the urge to stick her tongue out at the vehicle, knowing her attitude was ridiculous.

Cade led the way to the passenger side of his vehicle and opened the door. She stepped inside, reluctantly grateful for the warmth. Cade climbed into the driver's seat.

"You shouldn't have gone out to old man Henson's house in the middle of a blizzard," he said.

"It wasn't the middle of a blizzard," she retorted. "It was the beginning."

"Same thing," he said. "Why didn't you call me?"

"Why should I?" she asked. "You told me I was too young. That means nothing I say is valid."

"I didn't say that," he began.

"Same thing," she countered and crossed her arms over her chest.

Silence followed, and she refused to fill it, though she wondered if it would kill her. This was going to be the longest ride of her life.

He could smell her perfume. It wasn't strong, but soft and flowery with a hint of spice. Cade told himself he should ignore it, but his nose must have thought differently because he inhaled more deeply. Lord, she smelled good. He stole a sideways glance at her and immediately caught the stubborn set of her jaw so at odds with her soft, overly full mouth.

Her lips could conjure wicked images in a man's mind. Not his, of course, he told himself. Abby was the equivalent of his second little sister. Off-limits.

He saw her lick her lips and his gut tightened. Those wicked images began to seep through his brain like smoke through a keyhole. Cade gritted his teeth and focused on the road.

"I would listen to you about Mr. Henson. I know you've got a good head on your shoulders," he said.

"Hmmph."

"Really," he said. "Look at all you're doing for the community center and ROOTS. You're close to graduating." He paused and took a breath. "You're an intelligent young woman."

She shot him a gaze full of doubt.

Cade tore his gaze away from her sexy mouth. "You are," he insisted and took a deep breath. "You and I just shouldn't get involved."

"And why is that? If I'm an intelligent young woman?" she asked in a quiet voice.

"Because—" He bit his tongue to keep from saying she was too young and inexperienced. "Because underneath it all, I'm a heartless sonovabitch and I'll hurt you."

Her shocked silence was so thick he could have cut it with a knife.

"I find that difficult to believe," she finally said. "I've known you for a long time and I don't know anyone who would call you a heartless sonovabitch."

"You don't know anyone I've ever fallen in love with, do you?" he challenged, tightening his hands on the steering wheel.

Another silence stretched between them. "Laila," she finally said.

"No. Laila and I were never in love. I haven't been

capable of love for a long time, Abby. You're not rough and hard like me. You should have someone who can love as freely as you can."

Abby didn't say anything in return as she appeared to digest his words. Instead of talking, she turned on his radio to a classic-rock station and turned up the heat in his SUV a notch.

Aeons later, he pulled into her driveway. Abby turned to him. "You wouldn't want me to make decisions for you. Don't make decisions for me," she said in a soft voice. "And I'm sorry I poured that beer in your lap the other night. It was impulsive, even though you kinda deserved it." She leaned toward him, close enough to kiss him.

He felt a crazy, wicked expectancy swell inside him and waited. And wanted.

"Thanks," she whispered, pulling back and getting out of his car. He looked after her, swearing at himself because he was hard with wanting her. Forbidden fruit was a pain in the butt.

He had warned her off. If anyone was advising Abby, they would say to stay away from Cade Pritchett, but her thoughts gravitated toward him despite the fact that she was crazy busy. He should have been the last thing on her mind, but he wasn't. Abby did her best to make sure he wasn't the first, but he was right up there.

Even though he'd warned her away from him, she'd seen the way he'd looked at her mouth. He'd almost wanted her to kiss him. Almost. So, he *was* attracted to her. She had to keep reminding herself because he'd discouraged her every time she'd approached him. Every time she'd tried to seduce him. Which had felt like a joke because she didn't know anything about seduction. The only thing Abby knew was that she had wanted Cade as long as she could remember.

But she wasn't sure she could put herself out there again. It was so humiliating wanting him to notice her as a woman, wanting him to want her just half as much as she wanted him. She'd seen the spark, though, and a part of her couldn't help but hope that spark could turn into a fire between Cade and her. If only the two of them could get together again with no one else around. Just the two of them and maybe, just maybe she would get the chance she'd been waiting for since forever.

Abby waited several more days, hoping she would run into Cade, but that didn't happen. At this rate, it looked as if she would have to seek him out if she was going to see him before next year. Taking matters into her own hands, she headed for Pritchett & Sons near closing time. Just before 6:00 p.m., she walked into the display area and found Cade putting holiday decorations into the window.

He met her gaze then looked away. "Hey," he said.

Abby shoved her hands into the pockets of her jacket at his cool tone. She had her work cut out for her. "Hey to you. Bet you've been busy lately," she said and walked toward him.

"Always busy this time of year," he said, carefully placing a nutcracker on the middle shelf.

She nodded. "Yep." She bent down and picked up another nutcracker. "My mother loves these. She collects them."

"I know," he said.

Of course he knew, she thought. He'd dated Laila for several years that had included several Christmas seasons. "I think there's something creepy about them."

He glanced at her in surprise. "Really? Why?"

"I think it's the combination of inanimate eyes and a jaw that can crack nuts. It reminds me of Chucky in that horror movie *Child's Play*."

"They're not that spooky," he said and bent down to put another nutcracker on the shelf.

"Easy for you to say," she said. "Did one of your older sisters ever whack you on the head with one of them?"

He shot her a sideways glance. "Not Laila," he said.

"Yes, Miss Perfect Laila," she said, revealing a bit more bitterness than she intended.

"She's not perfect," he said in a mild voice. "That wasn't why I proposed to her."

"You proposed because she was the most beautiful woman in Thunder Canyon," she said.

"Most beautiful is relative. I proposed because I thought she was strong enough to deal with me. You know, despite getting whacked with a nutcracker, you're lucky you have your family. Especially when the holidays come around."

"I guess," she said and picked up an ornament that resembled a snow-covered church. She giggled as she held up the ornament.

"What?" Cade asked.

"Do you remember when Reverend Walker's mother blew up her kitchen just before Christmas?"

Cade nodded with a smile. "She was making moonshine."

"My mother didn't stop talking about that for months," she said and giggled again. "I love Christmas."

She felt his gaze on her and looked up at him. He glanced away. "What about you?"

"It's a mixed bag," he said with a shrug. "I have some happy memories, but ever since my mother died, it's hard. Sometimes it's just a day to get through."

Abby's heart twisted at the pain in his voice. "That's got to be difficult."

"That's why I said you're lucky. You still have your family intact."

Grabbing hold of her courage, she took a quick breath. "You could have your own family if that was what you really wanted. You just have to reach out for it."

Cade met her gaze for a long moment, and she saw the hunger in his eyes, the same hunger she felt for him. He leaned toward her and lifted his hand, then pulled back at the last second as if coming to his senses.

"You don't know what you're talking about. I'm not right for you," he said.

Frustration roared through her, making her want

to stomp her foot and scream, which she suspected wouldn't help her cause. "Says who? Shouldn't I get a say in the matter? I'm starting to wonder if you're afraid of how you feel for me."

"I'm not afraid," he said in a low voice, but she saw something different flash through his gaze. A strong flicker of passion she hadn't seen before. Abby took a step closer, then another and lifted her hand to his arm, sliding it upward to his shoulder. She gently pressed her chest against his and watched him close his eyes and take a quick, sharp breath.

"Doesn't this feel right?" she whispered and lifted her other hand to his other shoulder.

Moving in achingly slow increments, he slid his hands around her, pulling her into his arms. Her heart pounded in her chest and her lungs refused to work. Cade's stormy gaze met hers and she could tell he was still fighting his feelings. "I shouldn't be the one to take your innocence."

"You won't be. I'm more grown-up than you think," she assured him and lifted on tiptoes to press her mouth against his. She slid her tongue over the seam of his lips, and he immediately took her mouth in a hungry kiss.

It was as if a dam inside him broke loose. She felt his hands on her hair, against her back, pushing her into his hard crotch. Breathless, hot and filled with need, she matched him kiss for kiss, caress for caress.

He pulled back slightly and swore. "Are you sure about this?"

"Yes," she said before he could finish the question.

He took her mouth again in a quick, hard kiss that promised so much more. "I'd better lock the door."

Chapter Six

Cade cut the lights and led her to a room in the back. "We can have some privacy here," he said and closed the door behind them. A big sofa faced an old television, and at the far end of the room sat a small table and chairs with a refrigerator and microwave. "This is where we rest when we're pulling all-nighters," he said.

Her heart skipped as he laced his fingers through hers and guided her toward the sofa. She couldn't help hoping they would be pulling a different kind of all-nighter tonight.

He slid his fingers through her hair and she automatically lifted her mouth to his again. He kissed her deeply, and the fire between them flared again. Now that he was so close, she couldn't get enough of him fast enough. She tugged at his shirt, pulling the buttons free, dipping her open mouth against his throat to catch a breath. His ragged breathing was music to her ears.

With his assistance, she finally peeled off the layers covering his upper body and slid her hands over his muscular chest. He was all man. She wanted to feel all of him against all of her. She rubbed her chest and mouth over his bare skin and he shuddered.

Unable to fight her impatience, she pulled off her sweater and tossed it over her head. When she reached to remove her bra, his hands replaced hers and that barrier was gone in seconds.

She moaned in pleasure at the sensation of her bare breasts rubbing against his chest. His groan joined hers. "You feel so good."

"I'm gonna make you feel good, too," she promised and slid her hands down to unbuckle his belt and undo his jeans. She filled her hands with him and he whispered another oath.

"Where did you learn—"

She pressed her mouth against his and began to stroke him. Now was not the time for questions. Now was the time for pure pleasure. The heat between them built so quickly she would have sworn it was summertime. When he grazed her nipples with his thumbs, she felt a corresponding tug low between her thighs.

She bit her lip at the sensations ripping through her. "I want you."

"Not too fast," he said. "Not too—"

She stroked him intimately again and he sucked

in another sharp breath. "What are you trying to do to me?"

"The same thing you do to me," she said. "Fast isn't fast enough."

With a rough groan, he stripped off the rest of her clothes and nudged her onto the sofa. He stood directly in front of her and she pushed his jeans and underwear down then gave him an intimate kiss.

It didn't last long. Seconds later, he followed her down on the couch, pushing her legs apart with his thigh. He dipped his fingers into the place where she was aching for him.

"You're already wet," he said in approval as he caressed her and made her more restless for him. Each stroke made her a little more crazy.

"Inside," she whispered. "Come inside."

Three more delicious, mind-bending strokes and it seemed he couldn't wait any longer. He thrust inside her and she arched toward him. She felt his gaze fall over her like liquid fire. The want in his eyes nearly pushed her over the top. When he began to move, she moved in return. The sensations inside her built and she clung to him. He thrust again and she felt herself spin out of control. A heartbeat later, she felt him stiffen with his own climax and she relished the fact that for this moment, this night, he was finally hers.

Cade stared at the lithe temptress in his arms while he tried to catch his breath. Little Abby Cates. Who would have known she was wild in bed? She met his gaze and her lips lifted in a sensual smile that reminded him of a cat who'd just licked a bowl of cream. Her hands slid over his skin with sensual strokes that indicated she wouldn't be adverse to going round two with him.

Cade, however, wanted to get control of himself and he was curious as hell about Abby Firecracker Cates. She was a lot more experienced than he'd expected and not at all shy about going after what she wanted. It made him wonder how many men… A shot of jealousy burned through him, taking him by surprise. He shifted, sitting up slightly, and pulled her onto his lap.

"You took me by surprise," he said, sliding his fingers through her hair, which skimmed the top of her breasts. Gazing down her naked body, he thought about everything he still wanted to do to her.

"How is that?" she asked.

"Well, I don't know. I didn't think you'd be so—" He broke off. "I though you would be more shy. Not so experienced."

She licked her lips. "Are you saying you didn't like—"

"Hell, no," he said and raked his hand through his hair. "I just— How many guys have you dated, anyway?"

She smiled. "Oh, well I've been out with a lot of guys, but I've only really been with one other guy. First year in college. One time," she said and turned her head away as if she embarrassed to discuss it.

"One time?" he echoed, incredulous. "You didn't

make love with me like you'd only done it one other time."

Abby sighed and looked at him, sliding her hands over his chest in a way that made him begin to get aroused again. "Okay, I'll tell you my secret," she whispered and rubbed her mouth against his. "You inspire me."

A ripple of pleasure raced through him like lit gasoline. No one had ever said anything so sexy to him in his life.

An hour later, after they'd made love again, Cade knew he would sleep well tonight. In fact, he could fall into a half coma given half a chance.

"I should take you home," he said, sliding his hands through her hair. He could get addicted to the silky sensation.

"No need. My car's parked down the street," she said.

"I can't let you drive home by yourself," he said, his innate sense of protectiveness rising to the surface.

"That would be crazy since I have my car," she said, rising and beginning to put on her clothes. "But it's a nice thought."

Cade felt a strange combination of feelings. He didn't want her to leave, yet he needed to get himself together. This had been a wild few hours that he hadn't expected.

"This doesn't seem right," he said, pulling on his own clothes.

"It's okay," she said, then paused and a flicker of vulnerability flashed through her eyes. "Is this a one-night stand?" she asked in a low voice.

Cade paused. It should be a one-night stand, he thought. But it wouldn't be. Abby had burrowed her way inside him and he couldn't let her go. Right now, anyway. "No," he said standing. "It's not a one-night stand."

Relief trickled through her expression, and he could practically feel the tension ease from her frame. "Then everything's okay," she said and pulled on her boots. "And I, um, guess I'll see you when I see you," she said, meeting his gaze with a smile.

She was fully dressed and somehow much more grown-up to him than she had been mere hours ago. She was a woman.

"I'll walk you to your car," he said and pulled on the rest of his clothes. He grabbed his jacket and led the way out the back room, then out of the shop. The frigid air hit him like a slap in the face.

"Whoa," he said. "It's doggone cold."

"Can't disagree," she said, snuggling inside her coat.

He reached over and put his arm around her. "Sure you're okay driving yourself home. This doesn't seem right."

"I'll be okay," she said.

"So, you wanna get together Wednesday?" he asked.

"Not good for me. I have a study group that night."

"Thursday?"

"Babysitting for my ROOTS mom Lisa," she said.

"Well, can you squeeze me in on Friday?" he asked in a half-mocking voice.

"Maybe," she said, fluttering her eyelids in a flirty way.

His gut clenched. Frowning, he wondered where that sensation had come from. "Friday," he said firmly.

"Where?" she asked.

"My house," he said. "And I"ll pick you up."

"It would be better if I drive. That way I won't get any questions."

"I can handle questions," he said.

"There's no need right now," she said and before they knew it, her orange VW was in sight.

"You should be driving a more substantial vehicle," he grumbled.

"My car gets me around," she said.

"And into ditches," he said.

"One ditch," she corrected. "Durring a blizzard. I've never gotten stuck before."

"If you say so," he said as they stopped beside her car. He lifted his hands and cradled her hand between them. "I'll see you Friday," he said and lowered his mouth to hers. Her lips were swollen from their passion. They quickly grew warm. He did, too. He slid his hand lower to the small of her back to draw her against him where she made him ache for her. Even after all their lovemaking.

That kiss went on and on, and he would have extended it longer if he hadn't needed oxygen. He drew back and they both gasped for air. Cade laughed uneasily. He couldn't remember the last time a woman had affected him this way. Had Dominique?

"All righty," she finally said in a sexy, husky voice. "I guess I should go."

"Yeah," he said, but still held her in his arms.

"I don't really want to," she confessed in a whisper.

"That makes two of us," he said. "I'll get my SUV and follow you home."

"Not necessary," she said.

"It is for me," he said and gave her a brief, firm kiss and pulled back.

"G'night," she said softly, and he helped her into her car.

Jogging back to the shop, Cade got into his SUV and quickly caught up with Abby on her drive toward her home. As he drove, he remembered all the other times he'd taken this same route to get together with Laila. That seemed centuries ago. Although Cade had never been in love with Laila, Abby had completely wiped Laila out of his mind.

He turned onto her street and watched as she pulled to a stop. Lowering her window, she peeked outside. "See you soon, Cade," she said with a wave.

Cade waved in return, feeling a little crazy.

Abby sauntered into the warm kitchen of her home where Laila and her mother were making lists and looking at photographs of bridesmaid dresses. Humming under her breath, she tried to withhold her giddiness over the evening she'd shared with Cade. Plus, she would see him again soon. She was so happy she almost couldn't contain herself, yet at the same time, she wanted to keep the fantastic news to herself a bit longer.

"Hey, Abby," Laila said. "What do you think of this bridesmaid dress? It's not too fussy, is it?"

It was horribly fussy and the color was hideous. "Oh, it's pretty."

"What about this one?" she asked, pointing to a pink dress with lace.

"Oh, that's pretty, too. Is there anything around here to eat?"

"You didn't have any dinner, did you?" her mother asked, frowning. "Where have you been, sweetie?"

Abby felt her cheeks heat and swiped at her hair. "Regular thing. Studying."

Feeling Laila scrutinize her, Abby turned away. "I'll just fix myself a peanut-butter-and-jelly sandwich."

"There's some chicken potpie in the refrigerator," her mother said.

"The wind must have picked up outside," Laila said. "Your hair's a mess."

Her hair was a mess because Cade couldn't keep his hands out of it, she thought, remembering how he'd tugged at her hair to draw her mouth against his. She bit her lip and began to make her sandwich. "It always gets difficult to manage when I wait too long to get a haircut. I should make an appointment."

"Hmm," Laila said. "Hey, do you mind taking a look at just one more dress and telling me what you think."

"No problem," she said, licking a dot of grape jelly

from her finger. She looked over Laila's shoulder at the photo where's Laila's perfect fingernail pointed at a putrid green dress with rainbow-colored lace and a bustle. It was one of the most hideous dresses she'd ever seen in her life. *But who cares?* she thought. She'd be happy to wear a burlap sack as long as Cade held her the way he had tonight. "Pretty again," she said and took a bite of her sandwich.

Laila shot her a look of complete suspicion. "What have you been smoking? That dress is awful."

Abby shrugged. "I hear it's bad luck to disagree with the bride."

"And what is your honest opinion?"

"My honest opinion is that this is your wedding and you should be happy with all of it," Abby said. "I'm going to grab a glass of milk and hit the sack soon. I'll see you later," she said and kissed her mother on the cheek.

Her mother sniffed. "Is that a new perfume you're wearing? I can't quite place it."

Abby felt a nervous twist and giggled. "Eau de *pbj?* G'night. Love ya."

Abby gulped down her sandwich and milk, then washed her face and brushed her teeth. Stripping out of her clothes, she put on her pj's. She picked up her shirt and inhaled, smelling a hint of Cade's scent—a delicious combination of aftershave, leather and pure man.

Her bedroom door swung open and Laila stepped inside, studying her. "What are you doing?"

Abby glanced away. "Smelling my shirt to see if I can get another day's wear out it. What do you think?"

"I don't know," Laila said. "There's something about you. I can't quite put my finger on it. You're practically—hmm—glowing. What's going on?" she demanded.

"Nothing. How are you doing? You seem to be making progress with your wedding plans," Abby said.

Laila furrowed her brow. "Don't change the subject." She frowned then her eyes rounded. "You've been with Cade. *What* have you been doing with him, Abby?"

"Nothing terrible," she said, because it had all been wonderful. "Why do you care? It's none of your business. You don't want him anymore. You never did," she said, her stomach clenching nervously.

"I care because you're my sister." Laila crossed the room and sat on Abby's bed. She lifted her hand to push a strand of Abby's hair from her face. "I know I said it was perfect if you and Cade got together, but I hope you won't move too fast with him. Or expect too much from him."

"What do you mean?" Abby asked, feeling a yucky sensation in her stomach.

"I mean, you're not that experienced."

"Oh, don't you start with that, too," Abby said, pulling back and rolling her eyes.

"Ah, so Cade has said the same thing," Laila said.

"I'm really tired," Abby said, not wanting to hear what her sister had to say. She'd had a magical evening, the most wonderful evening of her life, and she didn't want anyone, especially Laila, to spoil it. "I need to get some rest."

"Just be careful," Laila said. "Cade is a wonderful man, but when it comes to his heart, it may as well be locked up in Fort Knox."

"How would you know that?" Abby asked. "You never really took him seriously, anyway."

"But I've known him a long time," Laila said. "Like I said, Cade's a good man, but I don't want you to get hurt."

Abby sighed and put her hand over Laila's. "You had your chance with Cade and you didn't want him. Maybe that's why he never really opened up his heart to you. You didn't love him as much as—"

Laila's eyes rounded. "Oh, Abby. You may have a bad case of hero worship, but you can't be in love with him. You're too young."

Abby's frustration ripped through her. "I realize you're in love, but that doesn't make you an authority on my feelings, or Cade's." She smiled. "Be happy for me. I am. Just please don't tell anyone else. It's still too new," she said and sank back onto her pillow.

"What does *too new* mean?" Laila asked.

"Exactly what I said. Can you please keep it to yourself?" Abby asked.

"Yeah," Laila said in a reluctant but gentle voice and stroked Abby's head. "Just be careful with your sweet heart. And remember you deserve a man who can give you all of his heart, too. G'night, sweetie," she said and turned off the lamp beside Abby's bed.

In the darkness, Abby closed her eyes, wanting to close her mind to everything Laila had said. Laila may have dated Cade off and on for several years, but their relationship had never been deep. Abby shoved her sister's warnings out of her mind and focused on how Cade had felt in her arms, and how much he had wanted her. Surely, that had to mean something. With all his reservations, Cade wouldn't have given in to his feelings for her if those feelings weren't strong. Abby clung to that thought, but her sister's voice played through her mind like a song she wanted to forget.

Cade's fingers itched to call Abby several times during the next few days. He was torn between wanting to get together with her before Friday and telling her that the two of them together was not a good idea. He held off until Friday when his father came down with a virus, which wouldn't have been a big deal if a reporter for a major decorating magazine wasn't coming to town to interview his dad.

At the last minute, Cade was stuck answering three thousand questions from a snap-happy journalist. In the back of his mind, he noticed the time passing, but the journalist was fascinated with their specialty pieces and the stories behind them. At six o'clock, the journalist/reporter, Ellie Ogburn, offered to take him to dinner. Cade sent a text to Abby canceling their date, telling her he had a big work issue.

At the Hiching Post, Ellie continued to interview him. She was a lively, confident woman in her late twenties with an inquisitive mind. "So, how did you become such an artist? From my initial phone interview with your father, he said you were artistic from the beginning."

Uneasy with the woman's flattery, he scrubbed his chin with his palm. "My dad was being kind. In the beginning, my creativity didn't always mesh with functionality."

"Yes, your father encouraged you. So he must have seen a spark of genius?"

Cade winced. "I think *genius* is pushing it. You need to remember my family is all about hard work. All of us show up every day to get the job done."

"But you're the one in demand now. You're the one who makes the specialty pieces that everyone wants signed. Why?" she asked.

He shrugged. "I can't explain it. I just listen to the stories of why these clients want specialty pieces, and then I go to work. Sometimes it's about family. Sometimes it's about work, but it always involves some kind of passion. I think about the personalities of the people who are requesting these specialized pieces. The woodworking is important to them or they wouldn't be seeking me out. If you want something basic, you can go to a big-box store to take care of it. There's nothing wrong with that. This economy is squeezing all of us. But if you come to me asking for a customized piece, then I'm going to do my best to give you something unique that fits you and your needs."

Ellie smiled. "That's pretty impressive. You mentioned the word *passion*. Where's the passion in your life? Do you have anyone special that inspires you?" she asked, batting her eyelashes at him.

Her flirty response gave him a jolt, and his mind slid to thoughts of Abby. He couldn't help remembering when she'd told him that he inspired her. "I keep my personal life private," he said and just let his statement sit there. He could deal with the silence, but he'd learned that many other people couldn't.

Ellie nodded and finally said, "Okay, well, is there a Mrs. Cade Pritchett?"

"Not gonna discuss my private life," he said firmly.

"That's just a status," she protested. "Single or married."

"Last time," he said. "I'm not discussing my private life."

"That's a shame. Any chance you'd like to come to New York for a long weekend?" she asked.

"I wouldn't want to cloud the article you're going to write from this interview," he said.

She pursed her lips. "You're no fun."

"True," he said. "Ask anyone. I'm no fun."

"Why do I think that's a front?"

He shrugged, his mind sliding toward Abby. "No idea."

An hour later, he escorted Ellie to her hotel, but left before she entered the lobby. He drove home and entered his too-silent house. His dog greeted him with a bark and a wag then followed him as he walked to the kitchen to grab a beer. If things had ended out differently, as he'd planned, he wouldn't have spent the evening alone. His body warmed at the thought. She would have gotten him hot and taken him up and down and all around. She would have made him needy, but left him satisfied.

She was nowhere close, right now, though. He checked his cell phone for the tenth time for her response, but there was none. He wondered why she hadn't replied and decided he should shrug it off.

Cade took a beer from the fridge, popped it open and took a long gulp. What a day. He felt as if he'd been probed and prodded every which way. In any other situation, he would have walked away, but this had been business. This article could bring in big business. He especially hadn't liked it when the discussion had veered toward his personal passion. Cade didn't spend a lot of time thinking about personal passions. In fact, he avoided anything or anyone that got him too worked up. He'd fallen in love once, and that woman had died. On top of that, the woman who had made family happen for his brothers, sister and father, had died suddenly, taking away the whole concept of family happiness with her. Since then, Cade had felt half-dead inside. He'd still longed for his own family, but without the terrible pain he'd experienced when he was younger.

He checked his phone one more time. No messages, text or voice, from Abby. Maybe it was for the best.

Cade worked all day with his brother Dean on Saturday to make up for the time he spent with the reporter on Friday. The two of them finally took off for a late dinner at the Hitching Post after seven.

"I'm getting too much of this place," he said. "I'm going to DJ's for some good ribs next time I eat out."

"You didn't like Ellie?" Dean asked. "I thought she was hot."

"She was tiring," Cade said, sipping his beer and surveying the bar. "I'm glad you and I made good progress today. Her interview really cut into my time yesterday."

"Man, you're getting old if you think she was tiring. I wish you would have handed her over to me," Dean said.

"That interview could mean a lot for us. I wouldn't want you cluttering it because you wanted a good time. You can get a good time with a lot of women. No need to piss off this one," he said.

"And you think you didn't piss her off?" Dean asked, starting his second beer. "She looked like she wanted more than dinner with you."

"I dropped her off at her hotel and went home. I'm not a complete fool," Cade said.

"Tell the truth," Dean said. "You wouldn't have minded going up to her room, would you?"

The truth was Cade hadn't been at all interested, but he wasn't going to tell Dean that. "You gonna come into the shop tomorrow after church?"

Dean blanched. "I gotta go to church?"

Cade laughed. "Leona Moseley was asking about you the last time I went."

Dean groaned. "No way. She's been after me for two

years. Why do you think I don't go to church without someone to protect me? It's enough to make a man lose his religion."

Cade laughed again. "We all have to take turns. I took a turn two weeks ago. Dad is sick, so someone else needs to step up."

"Have some pity, Cade," Dean said. "I don't want to face Leona."

Cade groaned, but heard the sound of a familiar laugh from across the room. He tilted his head then searched the room. Nothing. Nothing. Noth— Cade's gaze collided with the sight of Abby with a group of girls and a guy with his arm wrapped around her waist.

A wicked twist of jealousy wrapped around his gut and throat like a python. What the hell was she doing here? What the hell was that guy doing touching her like that?

Chapter Seven

Abby forced herself to laugh at everyone's jokes. The sound she made was hollow to her own ears, but she focused on being amused instead of heartbroken. She laughed at another comment one of her friends made, although she couldn't repeat what made it so funny.

Daniel squeezed her waist. "You want to meet me after my shift?" he asked. "We could go out."

"That's too late for this schoolgirl," she said. "I have a ton of work to do."

"So you're blowing me off again," he said. "I could give you a good time."

"Maybe she doesn't want to have a good time with you right now. Or anytime," Cade said, taking Abby completely by surprise.

She dropped her jaw in surprise.

"Hey," Daniel said. "The lady can decide for herself."

"Well?" Cade said expectantly.

She narrowed her eyes at him for a long moment. How could he be so arrogant when he'd stood her up last night?

"You were pretty busy last night," she said then lowered her voice to a whisper. "With another woman."

"What did you say?" Cade asked, wrinkling his brow in confusion.

"You heard what I said," she hissed.

"I didn't," Cade said.

"Well, use your imagination. You were having dinner with a woman. One of my friends sent me a cell-phone photo of you enjoying a meal with a pretty woman last night when you told me you were working."

Realization flooded Cade's face. "That was the reporter. My father was supposed to handle this interview, but he got sick."

"Uh-huh," she said, unable to conceal her disbelief. "It must have been a real hardship to spend the evening with her."

"Hey, maybe I'd better take Abby home," Daniel said. "She seems upset and you're not helping any," he said to Cade.

Cade's face hardened with anger. "Not tonight, or any night for that matter." He took Abby's hand in his and tugged. "Abby and I need to talk. Have a good night," he said and led her in a swift trot outside.

"That was rude," she sputtered as they stood a few steps outside the back door of the Hitching Post. "He was trying to look after me, which is more than you can say. Besides—"

Cade shut her off when he pressed his mouth against hers. She made an unintelligible sound of protest that turned into a moan, when he changed the tenor of the kiss and slid his tongue past her lips.

Abby sighed and lifted her hand to his shoulders. She pulled back and stared into his eyes. "What the hell were you doing with that woman last night?"

"Exactly what I told you. My dad got sick, so I had to take the interview. The reporter's questions were nonstop. She insisted on dinner. That was when I sent you the text."

"Hmmph," she said, still suspicious. "You could have called me after the interview ended."

"I thought about it, but I figured you might be busy with classwork and I didn't want to interrupt your sleep if you'd hit the sack," he said.

She stared at him silently.

"Why are we arguing when you and I both know we want to go back to my place and be alone?" he asked in a husky voice that touched her in secret places.

"Is that what you want?" she asked.

"It was what I wanted last night," he said.

Her heart tripped over itself. "Then let's go."

She got into his SUV with him, and at every stop sign he reached across the console to kiss her. Their stops grew longer and hotter. At the next-to-last stop, he gave her a long French kiss. It must have been a very long one because a car behind them beeped.

Cade swore under his breath and raced forward. He glanced at her at the next stoplight, but set his jaw as if he were trying to steel himself from kissing her again. Finally, he pulled into his driveway and stopped the car just outside his front porch. He jumped out of the driver's side of the car and rounded the vehicle to open her door. Then he helped her out and rushed her up the steps and inside his house, slamming the door behind them.

Pushing her against the wall, he tangled his fingers through her hair and took her mouth. "Who was that guy back there? Is he important to you?"

"No," she admitted. "He's just been asking me out for a week or so. I've turned him down."

"Except tonight?" he asked, and she could feel the tension in his strong body. The hint of possessiveness in his tone made her feel as if he'd turned her upside down.

She took a deep breath. "How would you have felt if you'd received a text photo of me having dinner with another man when we were supposed to get together?"

She felt him hold his breath then he released it. "I wouldn't have been happy."

"Well, I wasn't, either," she said, meeting his gaze dead-on.

"You didn't have anything to worry about," he told her.

"How was I supposed to know that?" she challenged.

"I'll show you," he said and took her mouth again. They tugged off each other's clothes, and soon enough she felt her naked skin against his. He kissed her and touched her as if he couldn't get enough of her. Abby could hardly breathe with the passion he expressed to her.

As if he could no longer wait, he pulled on protection and took her against the wall. Abby wrapped her legs around his waist and clung to him. It was the most exhilarating experience of her life. She almost couldn't believe it was happening, but then he thrust high inside her, groaning his release.

Abby had never felt so desired and so desirable. She'd dreamed of being with Cade, but the reality was so much more powerful than she'd ever thought possible. A burst of emotion rolled through her, stinging her eyes with its intensity and to her horror, tears began to fall down her face.

Trying to shield her tears from Cade, she turned her head away, praying she'd moved fast enough.

"What's wrong?" he asked, still holding her tightly against him. He slid his hand up to her cheek and felt the telltale wetness. "Did I hurt you?" he asked, sounding horrified.

"No, no," she insisted, swiping at her tears as he lowered her unsteady feet to the floor. "It's ju—just—" She sniffed, damning her emotions. "When I saw that photo of you with her, I thought the other night had been a one-night stand, after all, and—"

"It wasn't," he told her, cradling her against him. "I'm sorry you got that picture. You can check out the feature when it hits the stands. It was really important to the business."

Abby took a deep breath and tried to get herself together. She was appalled that she'd cried.

"I promise," he said, lifting her face to his. "Don't cry anymore. It kills me."

She made herself smile. "No more crying," she promised.

He lifted her up and carried her down the hallway into his bedroom. Placing her gently on his bed, he followed her down. "You are so beautiful," he told her. "You're so much more than I realized."

Her swollen, battered heart eased just a little with his words and she curled into him. "You can skip the condoms," she told him.

"Why?" he asked, looking intently at her.

"I'm on the pill for bad cramps and I'm pretty sure neither one of us has a social disease," she said.

He groaned in anticipation of pleasure. "You just made my day even better," he told her and began to make love to her again.

Two hours later, she pulled on one of his shirts and joined him in the kitchen. "Let me fix you some scrambled eggs and toast," he said. "I'd like to offer you more, but I'm running low on groceries because it's our busy season."

"I don't need any—"

"You're not hungry?" he asked. "Because I'm starving."

Now that he mentioned it, she pressed her hand to her stomach. "Scrambled eggs sound good."

He pulled bread from the freezer and popped four slices into the toaster while he turned on the gas stove. She watched him, naked from the waist up, as he cracked eggs into a bowl and beat them silly. After pouring a little oil in the skillet, he tossed in the eggs and stirred them. Minutes later, both the toast and eggs were ready.

Cade put the food on plates and nudged her to the table. "There," he said, setting a plate in front of her. "I'll have something better for you next time. And there will be a next time," he said, meeting her gaze as he bit off a piece of toast.

Abby took a tentative bite of eggs, surprised to find them cooked perfectly.

"What? You don't like the eggs?" he asked.

"Actually you did a great job with them, not over-cooked, not undercooked."

"You sound surprised," he said.

"Well, you're a bachelor carpenter. You haven't mentioned taking cooking classes," she said and scooped another mouthful.

"You thought I was completely useless in the kitchen?"

"I didn't say that," she said. "I just didn't think it was your forte," she said. "Delicious. You didn't even burn the toast."

He chuckled. "That's because it was frozen. You can probably cook circles around me, but I can fix a few things worth eating. Steak, barbecued chicken, fish on the grill."

She smiled. "If it involves fire, you're there. Right?" she asked.

He met her gaze and grinned. "Stop looking at me and finish your eggs before they get cold."

Abby bit her lip and looked at him, anyway.

He looked at her and his gaze held an irresistible mix of sensuality and Cade. "I mean it, Abby. Stop looking at me or I'm going to haul you off to my bed again."

"Would that be such a bad thing?" she asked.

He shook his head and scrubbed his hand over his face. "Finish your eggs. I don't want to be responsible for making you faint."

"Then you should have put on a shirt," she told him and ate her eggs.

Although they got a little distracted, Cade managed to help her get dressed and he bundled her up and led her to his car. "I don't want you having to answer a lot of questions about where you've been," he said and he drove toward her parents' house.

"I don't mind if people know you and I are seeing each other," she said. "Do you?"

"I don't like people poking into my business. I don't want either of us to have to deal with gossips. I just want us to be for us right now," he said and covered her hand with his. "Is that okay with you?"

Warmth flooded her. When he looked at her that way, she would say yes to anything he asked. Plus he made an important point. Even though she had known Cade forever, they hadn't shared an adult relationship very long. After what Laila had said to her the other night, Abby didn't want to hear the opinions of any detractors. She was glad Cade felt the same way.

He stopped in front of her house and pulled her against him once more. "You feel so good it's hard to let you go," he said.

Her heart skipped over itself at his words, and she sighed. "That makes two of us."

"It's supposed to be unseasonably warm for the next day or two. If the weather matches up with the forecast and you're caught up on your classes, maybe I could take you for a spin on my Harley."

"I'd love that," she said, remembering how envious she'd felt all those times Laila had ridden off with Cade on his motorcycle.

"You'll still need to dress warm," he warned her.

"Call me," she said, knowing she would be pulling a late night for her classes in order to make time for a ride with Cade. It would be worth it, she told herself. She could sleep some other time.

The following afternoon, Abby drove out to Cade's house to meet him for their motorcycle ride. The temps were supposed hit the mid-fifties. For Montana in the winter, that was considered a heat wave. She was so excited she felt like a kid at Christmas. He approved her warm clothing. "Good job with the ski mask and gloves. Just hang on and lean with my body on the curves," he said and put a helmet on her head.

She mounted his prized Harley behind him and wrapped her arms around him as he started the engine. "You ready?" he asked.

"I was born ready for this," she said.

He laughed and they were off. Cade steered the motorcycle toward the countryside. Although the roads were perfectly dry, some stubborn snow packs remained here and there. Abby knew this jump in temperature was just a tease. They would get snow again before the week was done. That knowledge made her all the more determined to enjoy the ride.

The moutains loomed with dramatic beauty over the plains, providing breathtaking vistas. A half hour later, Cade pulled into a small diner and parked the Harley near the door. He helped her off the motorcycle and Abby pulled off her helmet and ski mask. She was surprised to feel a little wobbly.

Cade must have noticed because he laughed as he steadied her. "Still feel like you're riding?" he asked.

She nodded. "I can still hear the buzz in my ears, too."

"You'll get used to it," he said. "You just need some practice. I figured we could grab a bite to eat here. If you're not hungry, they make good coffee and hot chocolate."

"Yes to the second," she said and shook her hair as they walked inside. "I bet my hair looks crazy," she said, raking her hands through it self-consciously, feeling it crackle with electricity.

He sat across from her in a booth and shook his head.

"You look beautiful. Your cheeks and lips are red and you hair reminds me of what it looks like after we—" He broke off as a waitress approached them.

"How ya doin', Cade?" the thirtysomething red-haired waitress asked with a wink and a smile. "It's been a while, but I guess you don't ride that Harley through a blizzard."

"It's true, Dani. I'll take a club sandwich and coffee. What about you, Abby?" he asked.

"Hot chocolate," she said.

"You sure like 'em young these days, don't you? Are you sure she's legal?" Dani asked with another wink.

Slightly irritated by the waitress's remark, Abby smiled. "I look younger than I am. Must be all that clean living. I guess I need to dirty up my lifestyle a little so I can catch up," she joked.

"No need for that," Cade countered.

The waitress laughed. "I like her sense of humor. Got a little kick behind that sweet face. Good for you. I'll get your coffee and hot chocolate," she said and walked away.

"You handled her pretty well," he said. "Dani's known for ribbing people."

"I have a feeling she's trying to get your attention. She looked at you like she wanted to gobble you up. I guess I can't blame her," she said with an exaggerated sigh.

He chuckled at her. "You keep surprising me. I just never would have expected sweet little Abby to have a wild bone in her body."

"I'm pretty sure I have more than one. I just haven't discovered all of them yet," she said.

He groaned. "Heaven help me. What do you think of the ride so far?"

Dani delivered their beverages and scooted to another table.

"It's glorious," she said. "We are spoiled with all these beautiful views and I think we see them so much we stop really looking at them. You can't avoid it when you're on the motorcycle. The mountains and hills and lakes are right there in your face."

"That's one of the things I like about riding. Nothing between me and nature," he said. "Did you get too cold?"

"No," she said, taking a sip of her hot chocolate. "You kept me warm."

His eyes darkened in sexual awareness. "You're asking for trouble again," he said. "Do you say these kinds of things to other men?"

"No. Why would I do that when it's you I want?"

Cade felt the need ripple through him at the look in her eyes. It was amazing how such an innocent girl—woman, he mentally corrected himself—could get him stirred up with just a side comment or the way she looked at him. Even the way she sipped her hot chocolate was sexy to him. Abby Cates was looking like a lot of trouble, but he didn't feel like running the other way. At least, not yet.

After he talked her into sharing a few bites of his club sandwich, they hit the road again. He slowed as they drew close to Silver Stallion Lake. The lake served as a recreation area for local families and visitors. He'd spent a few summers lifeguarding during the summers.

He pulled to a stop and cut the engine. "I have a lot of memories from here."

"Me, too. It was the first time you held me in your arms," she said.

He swung his head to look at her and pulled off his helmet. "What?"

"Yes," she said, pulling off her own helmet and the ski mask. She had an impish gleam in her eyes. "You were giving swimming lessons. Some water went down the wrong way and you rescued me," she said in a melodramatic tone.

Cade rolled his eyes.

"You don't remember?"

"I can't say I do," he said, racking his brain. "In my defense, I pulled a lot of choking kids out of the water. How old were you?" he asked, then shook his head and lifted his hand. "Don't tell me."

She laughed and swatted at his shoulder. "Feeling old?"

He thought of everything that had happened in his life since those carefree summers at Silver Stallion Lake and the truth was he did feel old. Between the loss of his mother and Dominique, and his work at the shop, he'd felt gutted and empty more often than not.

"You're not old, Cade. You just need to get out and have a little more fun," Abby said. "I can help with that," she offered in that sexy voice that made his blood heat. She squeezed her arms around him and he felt a surprising corresponding squeeze on the inside, somewhere near his heart.

"I might just take you up on it," he said and started the engine. "Get your helmet on," he said and followed his own advice. He accelerated, leaving the lake behind him, but he longed for that lighthearted young man he'd once been.

Abby sat on Cade's sofa wrapped in his arms. A fire blazed in the fireplace and they both sipped hot cider. She couldn't imagine anything better. She leaned her head against Cade's chest and stroked his hand. After several more moments passed, it occurred to her that Cade hadn't spoken for quite awhile.

"You're quiet," she said. "What are you thinking about?"

He sighed. "Nothing," he said. "Lots of stuff."

She smiled at his response. "I think I'll go with your second answer. What kind of stuff?"

"Oh, what things were like before my mother died. How quickly it all changed. My father changed overnight. My younger brothers went a little wild. I considered it, but I saw how much my dad was hurting. I didn't want to add to the pain. My sister, Holly, she just seemed lost. Dad doted on her, but for a while, there, he was a dead man walking."

"I know that was hard for you," she said.

He nodded. "It was," he said. "And the holidays were the worst. My mother was the one to make holidays happen, so when she was gone, we didn't know what to do. The holidays would hit and we didn't plan for them, so we would fumble around and throw something together." He chuckled. "I can't tell you how many cooking disasters we had. Lesson number one, you need to thaw the turkey."

Abby stroked his hand and studied his face. "Well, at least that's a funny memory."

His smile faded. "Yeah. One of the few."

"I bet there were some other funny ones," she said.

Cade nodded. "The gifts we bought. One of my brothers bought Holly bubble bath that made her break out. My father gave us savings bonds and stale chocolate my mother had bought a long time ago. He forgot to buy the new stuff, so he gave us the old chocolate. We all ate it, wanting to feel like we had when we were younger, when she was alive, but it didn't work."

"I'm sorry," she said. "I'm sorry she died."

"Yeah, I am, too. And then there was…Dominique," he said.

Abby's stomach clenched. She'd heard very little about Dominique, the woman who had stolen Cade's heart. Her family had lived in town briefly and she'd attended the same local university as Abby. Abby had heard Dominique had been a one-of-a-kind dark-haired beauty. A lot of guys had chased her, but she'd liked Cade best.

"You were serious about her," Abby said.

He nodded.

"Everyone said you were going to propose to her

when she returned from her trip to California," she added.

"Everyone was right about that," he said. "She took off between Christmas and New Year's to meet some friends in California. I figured I would surprise her when she got back. I'd bought the ring."

As much as she wanted Cade for herself, the thought of his loss stabbed deeply at her. "I can't imagine how horrible that must have been."

"Pretty damn bad," he said. "And her parents partly blamed me because I didn't propose before she left. They were convinced she would have never gone if I'd asked her first."

Her breath stopped in her chest. "They blamed you? That's horrible."

He shrugged. "Maybe they were right. I wanted her to have a break. She'd been working hard at school. She was looking forward to the beach."

Abby shook her head. "It's just wrong. You were being sweet and—" It was hard for her to say the words, but she swallowed back her own pain. "And loving. Couldn't they see how hurt you were?"

"They were devastated. They couldn't see past their own pain," he said. "I can't blame them."

"So all of this is why the holidays suck for you," she said.

He paused a moment then nodded. "Yeah, I guess so."

Abby took a deep breath and slid her hand to Cade's jaw. "I would if I could, but I can't bring back Dominique or your mom. I can't make things the way they were, but if you're open to it, I can probably make things happier than they have been."

He lifted an eyebrow at her. "You think?"

"Only if you're open to it. If you're not open, I can't do anything. I'm no Houdini."

His lips twitched. "And if I'm open?" he asked, lifting his hand to push a strand of hair from her face.

"I'll surprise you," she said.

"You've already done that."

"Well, I'll do it again."

Chapter Eight

The following night, Cade arrived home and was surprised to find a Christmas wreath hanging from his front door. *What the—* He opened his front door and smelled the delicious scent of something he definitely had not cooked. His dog greeted him with a wagging tale and anticipation of a few bites of whatever was cooking.

"I love you, darlin'," he said, rubbing her soft, furry head. "But the vet says you should only get dry dog food. And this smells so good I may not be able to share."

Cade walked farther into the house, noticing the sound of his television playing the sweet music of Monday-night football. "Hello? I hope you're not an ax murderer, but if you are, can I eat before you kill me?"

Abby poked her head from the kitchen doorway and smiled. "No plans to kill you," she said. "Unless you complain it's overcooked. Have you looked at the time?"

"You need to remember I had to make up for all the time I lost doing that stupid interview instead of my real work," he complained.

"Yeah, eating a meal at the Hitching Post with a pretty woman making eyes all over you," she said. "Pure agony."

"I guess I shouldn't have brought that up."

"I guess you shouldn't have," she said. "But we could change stations if you're interested in some beef stew."

"Do I have to beg?"

She gave a slow smile. "That's a tempting image," she said. "But I think I'll save it for another time. Come on and I'll pour a bowl. I have biscuits, too."

Cade's mouth drooled. He tried to remember the last time he'd had homemade biscuits and couldn't. Striding into the kitchen with the dog at his heels, he blinked at a turkey decoration, this one hanging from one of his kitchen lights.

"That's something," he said, pointing at the bird.

"Pull his foot," she said, arranging biscuits on a small plate.

Curious, Cade pulled it. Nothing happened.

"Other foot," she said as she placed his meal on the table.

Cade pulled the other foot and the turkey gave a *gobble-gobble* sound. Cade stared at the stuffed bird and couldn't resist pulling the leg again. The turkey gave another *gobble-gobble*.

"I don't know what to say," he said, tempted to pull the foot again, but the aroma of the beef stew called to him at a cellular level. He sat down at the table. "Where the hell did you find it?"

"Addictive, isn't it?" she said with a lone biscuit in front of her. "Seems silly, but it's hard to resist pulling the turkey's foot."

"Is that all you're going to eat?" he asked, his spoon poised over the stew.

She gave a gentle, crocodile smile. "I ate hours ago."

He growled then took his first bite. "Food of the gods," he said. "Who fixed this? Your Mom?"

Quicker than he could take his next breath, she pulled his bowl away from him and he realized he'd made a huge mistake. "Because you're too busy to cook. You have a wicked-crazy schedule. No time for cooking something this amazing." He paused. "Is this when I beg?"

She slid the bowl back in front of him. "Your habit of underestimating me is getting a little old. Even old Mr. Henson tried to tell you I was a good cook."

"You're right," he said, taking another bite and swallowing a moan of pleasure and satisfaction. Cade was a bachelor, all too familiar with frozen dinners and restaurant meals. A home-cooked meal was a thing of wonder to him. "I will never underestimate your cooking again."

"That's good to know," she said, as she leaned her

chin on her palms and watched. "Is that the only way you won't underestimate me?"

Cade thought of how she'd made love to him and desire thudded through him. "No, but I won't finish this meal if you keep reminding me."

She smiled. "So, are you rooting for the Eagles?"

He met her gaze and felt his heart lift at her effort to let him enjoy the meal she'd prepared for him. It occurred to Cade that with the exception of that turkey hanging from the light in the kitchen, he could get used to Abby greeting him with a hot meal and a welcoming smile. Tension eased out of him. She kept surprising him, and he wasn't inclined to ask her to stop.

After he finished his second bowl, he built a fire and they watched the game. In a manner of speaking, anyway. Cade couldn't tell you the score at halftime because he'd been too busy taking off Abby's clothes and making love to her. He pulled her on top of him and she rode him, bringing herself and him to climax. He watched her smooth, creamy skin shimmering in the firelight. Her face glowed with arousal. The expression in her eyes called to him. At the same time, it frightened the hell out of him.

A half hour later, he cradled her in his arms.

"I should head home soon," she said. "It's getting late."

"It would be nice if you could stay all night," he said, brushing his mouth over her soft jaw.

She gave a soft sound of pleasure. "It could be arranged, but it would take some planning."

"Oh, really," he said. "How's that?"

"I've pulled all-nighters with study groups before. I've gone out of town on girl trips."

"If you stayed overnight with me, you wouldn't be studying schoolwork, I can promise you that," he growled.

She laughed. "No, I would just say something along those lines to my parents."

"I don't like the idea of you lying to your family about me," he said.

"Well, you want to keep it on the down low. And I'd just as soon not get grilled about it, either." She sighed. "Maybe I can figure something out. But I should head out now."

"See you tomorrow night?" he asked reluctantly, standing with her, pulling on his jeans as she got dressed.

"No. Tomorrow night I'm with my ROOTS girls. During the day, I'm helping with the community-center Thanksgiving production. Thank goodness, they'll be giving their performance soon. Then they'll be out on break. That reminds me, I should stop by and check on Mr. Henson, too." She glanced up at Cade. "So tomorrow I'll be slammed. Do you want to try for lunch on Wednesday or is that too public for you?"

"I can do lunch on Wednesday," he said, but was surprised at his eagerness to spend more time with her. Maybe it was the sex. Lord, he hoped so because a big part of him wanted to occupy all of her free time.

"You'll have to keep your hands off of me," she

warned him with a sexy tilt of her lips. "You'll have to pretend we're just friends. Are you sure you can do that?"

With the way she was looking at him, he suspected it might be more difficult than he would have expected, but Cade had a long history with self-restraint. "I guess I'll just have to buck up and do my best," he said, pulling her back into his arms. "We'll make up for it some other time."

Cade insisted on following her home. It didn't feel right to have her drive home by herself. If they'd been officially dating, he would have always walked her to her door. As she got out of her car, she waved at him and walked into her family home.

Cade stared after her. She was so young, tender and sweet. He knew she was stronger than he'd originally thought, far more of a woman, but he still feared that he would hurt her. He couldn't help believing that eventually Abby would want all of him, and Cade had lost part of himself a long time ago, and that part would never come back.

Abby helped at the community center and spent the afternoon in class. Afterward, she squeezed in some time at the university library. Since she'd been spending so much time with Cade, she was really having to maximize her study time. Sipping a bottle of water, she made notes for yet another paper she was writing.

"One of your friends told me I might find you here," a male voice said.

Abby glanced up to find Daniel looking down at her with a smile. "Uh, hi," she said, completely surprised. "Who—"

"Char," he said and sat down next to her. "You disappeared the other night at the Hitching Post. I was concerned about you. That guy looked pretty intense."

"Cade?" she said. "Cade would never hurt me. No, I've been crazy busy and I can't talk now because I need to work on this paper."

"Rain check?" he asked and, when she paused, he covered her hand with his. "You gotta give me a rain check after I tracked you down."

Uncomfortable, she moved her hand away from his. "You really shouldn't have."

"I see a woman who makes me curious and I gotta find out more," he said. "But I can wait. Take care. I'll keep in touch," he said and strolled out of the library.

Abby frowned after him. She would definitely need to speak to Char about passing any further personal information on to this guy. The more often she saw him, the more uncomfortable he made her and he didn't seem the least bit discouraged. She shrugged off her uneasiness and refocused on her paper, wondering what Carl Jung would have to say about Daniel.

A half hour before her meeting with the ROOTS girls, Abby left the library and grabbed a fast-food burger and soda. She usually skipped caffeine this late in the day, but she could feel herself starting to fade. From her first visit at ROOTS, Abby had learned she had to be on her toes with the girls.

The group started out small and quiet, so she helped the girls with their homework. Since many of the girls came from such disrupted homes, it was often difficult for them to find a quiet place to concentrate. Thirty minutes into their meeting time Katrina and Keisha burst into the room.

"You have to report him. You have to. What if it gets worse?" Keisha asked Katrina.

"Shut up," Katrina hissed. "If I ignore him, he'll go away."

Abby stood, alarmed at the bruises she saw on Katrina's face. "Girls," she said.

Keisha looked at Abby and lifted her chin defiantly. "You talk to her. She won't listen to me."

"Katrina?" she said. "Would you like some water or hot chocolate? We can talk over there if you like," she said.

Katrina was a sixteen-year-old with bleached blond hair who did her best to make herself look tough with the black leather and kohl eyeliner she wore. Abby knew that beneath her tough exterior, the girl had a mother who was rarely at home and Katrina was struggling to stay away from a bad crowd at school. She'd been suspended for smoking in the girls' room.

"It's no big deal," Katrina said as she swiped her damp face with the back of her hand. "It's my mother's new boyfriend. He's been staying over and he gets pissed when I spend too much time in the bathroom. I'll just spend the night with one of my friends. He'll cool down."

Abby didn't like the sound of this at all. She handed Katrina a cup of hot chocolate. "Does your mother know?"

Katrina shrugged, but her hand was shaking as she held the cup. "She's too busy. She's working three jobs. He says he was laid off," she said, but her tone suggested she didn't believe him.

"How long has he been around?" Abby asked.

"A couple months. He was okay in the beginning, but once he started staying overnight, he thought he could tell me what to do when my mom wasn't around. He really likes his whiskey. Seems like he drinks a bottle every day."

"I'm so sorry you've had to go through this," Abby said.

"Don't feel sorry for me. I can take care of myself."

Abby nodded. "If Keisha was in this situation, what advice would you give her?"

Katrina gave a short laugh that almost sounded like a sob. "Keisha wouldn't be in this situation. She would kick his butt out of the house."

"Okay. What about Shannon?"

Katrina paused. "Shannon's different."

"What would you tell her?"

"As much as it sucks, I would tell her to rat on him. It's such a pain to deal with child protective services. If only we were eighteen," she said. "Everything would be easier."

"Not so much," Abby said. "But that's not the point. I want you to give an official report. I could do it, but

I want you to care enough about yourself to do it for yourself."

Katrina sighed. "I'll have to stay with some super strict people I don't know," she said.

"Maybe not," Abby said. "Plus it wouldn't be forever. Do you really think your mother would keep this guy around if she knew he was hitting you?"

Katrina shrugged. "She doesn't want to deal with it."

"Which means you have to," Abby said. "You deserve to live in a situation where you are not abused and neglected. If I've helped you learn anything, you've learned that."

"I don't want to be with people who are always telling me what to do. You know I'm not used to that," she said.

"It's temporary," Abby said. "That's what you have to remember. You're a strong young woman and this is one of those times when you need to be your own best friend. I'll go with you to make the report."

Katrina swore under her breath. "You really think I have to do it?"

"You've been around here long enough to see what happened with other girls in this situation. You are a very smart, very capable young woman. I think if you end up with someone who wants to know where you are and when it may not be fun, but it will be a lot better than worrying about whether you'll be beaten. And I repeat, it won't be forever."

Katrina sighed. "Okay, okay. Can we do it now? Believe it or not, I don't want to miss school tomorrow. I have an exam."

"Let me take a few more minutes with the other girls, then you and I can head out," she said.

Abby talked to the other girls while Keisha walked over to give Katrina a big hug and shook her finger at the girl. Abby felt a surge of warmth at how the girls were supporting each other.

Hours later, Katrina was safely tucked in bed at her temporary foster parents' home while her mother's boy-friend was brought in for questioning and would soon be charged with assault on a minor. Before that, the drama had intensified: Katrina's mother arrived in a sad state, apologizing profusely to her daughter and promising to do a better job.

Although it was nearly 2:00 a.m. when Abby arrived home, she felt a sense of temporary relief that she knew Katrina was safe, and she was so proud of her ROOTS girl for choosing to stick up for herself. These girls came across as tough, but many of them had been abused, and one of Abby's biggest goals had been to help them grow away from a victim mentality.

Abby said a little prayer, and just before she drifted off to sleep, she thought of Cade. She wished all of those girls at ROOTS could find a man as strong and gentle as Cade.

Cade met Abby at DJ's for lunch on Wednesday. He arrived a couple minutes early and ordered coffee for himself. He didn't mention that anyone would be joining him, but sat in one of the booths at the back of the restaurant. He saw her open the door and glance around, pushing her hair behind her ear. Instead of waving, he simply stood, and within an eye blink, she saw him and moved toward him.

"What a surprise to see you here," she said in a mocking voice and gave him a far-too-quick hug before she sat down. "Nice to see you," she said.

He drank in the sight of her, noticing the dark circles under her eyes and the slight pallor of her skin. "Did you sleep at all last night?"

"Why?" she asked. "Do I look like a hag?"

"I would never call you a hag," he said.

"Well, something must have made you say that," she said.

The waitress showed up then. "Lunch ribs with coleslaw for me," he said. "What about you?" he asked Abby.

She gave a quick glance at the menu and shrugged. "Barbecue sandwich and fries. I need some grease."

"And to drink?" the waitress asked.

"A chocolate milk shake," she said.

The waitress smiled. "Excellent choice. I'll be back soon."

"So I look like a hag," she said to Cade.

"I did *not* say that. You just look very tired. Circles under your eyes, your skin is pale—"

"I need to get better with concealer. I think it's a required skill. Think about it. If you can hide dark circles, then no one will know that you spent the last night with a girl who'd been beat up by her mother's boyfriend."

"Oh, my God. Who's the girl?" Cade asked. "Who's the guy? If you want me to talk to him—"

She finally smiled, and it was like the sun broke through. "I knew you'd say something like that. That's one of the reasons I—" She broke off. "One of the reasons I like you."

Warmth spread throughout his chest, but he tried to shrug it off. "Is the girl okay?"

"For now," Abby said. "I had to talk her into reporting the incident and the guy. I stayed with her thoughout the whole experience and the poor girl was put through the ringer. The temporary foster parents seem pretty nice if they can deal with her independence. She's used to doing everything for herself, which means she's not used to taking orders or filling anyone in on her whereabouts."

"That's a rough way to live," he said. "You do a good job with those kids at ROOTS."

"Sometimes I wonder if they do more for me. But I have to tell you when someone has been physically abused, it really draws the line about what needs to be done. Her sweet face was bruised all over. I was just glad I could be a tiny part of getting her to a safe place."

"I bet you're a much bigger part than you think you are," he said, wishing he could take her hands in his, pull her against him so she could relax for a little while.

She shrugged. "What's important is that Katrina is safe. I hope things will continue to be on the upswing for her. I'll be watching, that's for sure."

"Hmm," he said.

She shot him a sideways glance. "What does that mean?"

"It means you're always talking about me having a hero complex. I'm starting to wonder if you don't have the same problem," he said.

Her lips tilted again. "Very funny," she said.

"I'm not being funny," he said.

"Sure you are," she said and the waitress delivered their food. "Thanks," she said to the woman.

"My pleasure," she said. "You two let me know if you need anything else, okay?"

Both of them dug in to their food, creating a comfortable silence. Abby took a few sips of her milk shake. "Brain freeze," she said, squeezing the bridge of her nose then shaking her head. "How have things been at work? Any more gorgeous reporters?"

"No more reporters at all. It's back to me and the wood. Sometimes I make art. Sometimes I make furniture. I do a lot of knocking, sawing and sanding, but no one needs to call the police because of it, thank goodness."

"That's a funny thought," she said. "You sawing on a piece of wood and a bunch of wood specialists come in and arrest you."

"Very funny," he said, clearly disagreeing with her. "But the truth is it's pretty satisfying. I'm sure it's not as big as having a kid, but it's been good for me. You really look like you could use a nap. If I were in charge, I would take you off to bed so you could get some rest."

"I'll survive. I'm a young college student. We exist on adrenaline, right?"

"If you say so," he said. "I'd still like to drag you off and make you take a nap."

She paused a half beat, studying him. "I may not wake up for a long time if you did that, and today, I've still got a long ways to go."

"Don't burn the candle at both ends too long. Mother Nature has a way of kicking you on your butt if you push her too far."

"Sounds like you're speaking from experience," she said and swallowed more of her shake.

"Unfortunately," he said in a wry voice.

The waitress delivered the check and when Abby glanced up, Cade noticed she cringed and sorta hunched down. As soon as the waitress left, he studied her. "What's up?"

She lifted one shoulder, glanced over it then looked back at Cade. "Probably nothing. It just seems like this guy keeps showing up everywhere I am. It's like he has a GPS on me or something."

His sense of protectiveness shot up inside him. "Who is he?"

"He's a server at the Hitching Post. He was flirting with my friends and me the night I was out with them, but I wasn't all that impressed. I think he's one of those guys who is attracted to a girl because she's not interested. I think he sees it as a challenge."

"What's his name?"

Abby lifted her gaze as if she were searching her brain. "Um. *D* something. Daniel."

"Daniel what?"

She shook her head. "I have no idea."

"Is he the guy who was hitting on you the other night? Do you think he's stalking you?" he asked, his gut tightening. He didn't like the idea of anyone bothering Abby.

She paused a half beat and shook her head again. "No, he can't be. It's just that he showed up at the university library and he doesn't even go there, so that creeped me out a little. It's probably nothing. I'm probably freaking out because I need sleep," she joked. "Don't worry."

But he would. If he didn't worry, he would think about it. "Let me know if he pops up anywhere else during the next few days."

"It's really nothing," she said.

"Then it won't be a big deal for you to tell me if he shows up," he said. "Deal?"

Her lips lifted in a slow smile. "Deal." She took another sip of her milk shake through the straw and gave a quick, soft sound of approval that reminded him of… *No need thinking about that,* he told himself.

"Where are you headed? I'll walk you to your car," he said.

"Are you sure you want to do that? People may talk," she said, her eyes glinting with flirty challenge.

"I'll keep my hands to myself," he said, barely containing a growl.

"Well, darn," Abby said and stood, and Cade was treated to the sight of the sexy sashay of her sweet, round bottom as they walked from DJ's.

Friday couldn't come soon enough, Abby thought as she sat in the diner waiting to meet two classmates to discuss their presentation for class the following Tuesday. In charge of the Jung presentation, she filled out a few more note cards as she waited.

"You never stop, do you?"

Abby's stomach knotted at the voice that was becoming all too familiar. She reluctantly glanced up. "Daniel. What a surprise," she said.

He smiled. "It's not that big of a surprise. I know you like this place and you frequent it at night. You know I'd like us to spend more time together."

His smile was a little too practiced. It bothered her. "I hate to be blunt, but us spending more time together? It's not going to happen."

"Sure it is. You'll catch a break soon, be ready for some entertainment." He bent his knees and braced himself on the table so his face was level with hers. "I'm more than ready to provide it."

"No," she said, wishing she didn't have to be even more blunt. It was as if he'd completely forgotten the other time she'd turned him down. "You don't understand. I'm not interested in having a relationship with you."

He shrugged. "No problem. We can start out having fun."

Abby was tempted to scream, but she swallowed the urge. "You know how there are girls who say no and mean yes?" she asked. "I'm not one of those girls."

Chapter Nine

"**I**'m on my way," she said after Cade picked up his cell phone. "Can we have some sort of fabulous take-out for dinner?"

"Such as?" Cade asked.

"Lobster, filet mignon, asparagus, au gratin potatoes, chocolate mousse, followed by some time in a hot tub and maybe one of those martinis you got me at the Hitching Post. Nothing too complicated," she said.

He chuckled. "Right."

"Pizza and soda. I hardly ever drink soda, but tonight I want to be bad."

He laughed louder. "If soda is your version of bad..." he began.

"Don't mock me. At least I kept it simple."

"I'll see what I can do," he said. " Stella will be glad to see you when you get here."

"Anyone else around there who'll be happy to see me?" she asked.

"Me," he said.

Twenty minutes later, she pulled into Cade's driveway, stopping as she drew close to his porch. Normally, she would jump out of her car and bound up the steps, but she was seriously dragging tonight. She hoped she didn't embarrass herself by falling asleep unexpectedly. It didn't help that just as she left the community center this morning, Daniel had been waiting in front of the building. She hadn't said anything to her friends yet, but she thought she was going to have to have a conversation with Char. Her friend probably was just trying to nudge her into giving in to a fun time with a hot guy. Char had no idea that Abby was involved with someone else.

Frustration nicked at her. In one way, she chafed at the idea of keeping her relationship with Cade secret. In another way, she agreed with him that she didn't want to endure anyone else's thoughts or assessments of her and Cade. So, for now, she just had to be evasive. Not her best talent.

Sighing, Abby got out of her car and stretched. The wind whipped over her, reminding her that it was still winter. The warm day last weekend had been a quick little treat and it was gone now. Bundling her collar upward, she climbed the stairs and knocked on the door.

Stella barked, and within seconds Cade opened the

door. "Well, look what the wind blew in. Very nice," he said, tugging her inside and pressing his mouth against hers. "You're cold," he said.

"That's why I mentioned a hot tub," she said and glanced behind him. "You have one in your back pocket?"

"Very cute," he said. "I don't have a hot tub, but I have a tub filled with hot water. If you're interested," he said.

She stared at him in disbelief. "Really? A tub? For me? A bath? Omigosh, I can't believe it. An early Christmas gift."

"It's just a tub," he warned, guiding her toward the hall bathroom.

"Haven't you noticed how many sisters I have? Do you know how often I get to take a bath? Take a guess," she said, staring at the steaming water. It was all she could do not to instantly strip and jump in the tub.

"Not often. Go ahead. Get in. Just don't drown," he said.

She smiled and squeezed his arm. "Oh, I won't drown. I had an excellent swimming teacher."

He shook his head. "Shut up and take a bath."

"Really? Are you sure I don't need to wait for the pizza?" she asked.

He shook his head again. "No need," he said. "But don't fall asleep."

Abby shut the door behind him, stripped out of her clothes, twisted her hair into a knot on top of her head and put her foot in the steaming water. It was *hot*.

Which made it perfect. She eased the rest of her body inside the tub and leaned her head against the back of the tub. Abby was in heaven. Her long showers rarely lasted over eight minutes, so soaking in Cade's bathtub felt like the most indulgent luxury possible.

She felt the muscles in her body relax, tendon by tendon. From some point in her brain, she thought she heard Cade's doorbell ring. Pizza? she wondered, but couldn't find it in herself to move more than a millimeter. Had her bones turned to butter? She hadn't felt this relaxed in…how many years?

Mentally playing a jazz song, she closed her eyes and just floated.

Seconds later, she heard Cade knocking on the door and instantly sat up, startled. "What?" she asked, wondering when the water had turned cold. She shivered at the temperature. It had been so lovely and hot, like, two minutes ago.

"Abby, I'm starting to get worried. Answer me. Are you conscious?" Cade asked from the other side of the door.

"I'm here. I'm awake." Beginning to shiver, she stepped out of the tub. "Is the pizza here?"

"In a manner of speaking," Cade said, opening the door and extending a terry-cloth robe in her direction. "You want this?"

"That would be perfect," she said, grabbing the robe and clutching it against her.

"Don't drag your feet. I don't want the pizza to get cold," he said.

"Okay, okay," she said to herself then spoke louder as she towel dried herself. "I'll be out in a minute."

She pushed her hands through the sleeves of the robe, tied the sash and bent over to pull the plug out of the drain of the tub.

Stepping out of the bathroom, she headed down the hall to the kitchen and found a table spread with steaks, shrimp, baked potatoes, *asparagus*—she noted in shock—and bread. She looked at Cade in surprise. "I thought we were having pizza," she said.

"You don't want it?" he said.

"No," she said. "Of course I do. I'm just so—" She was both amazed and touched. "How did you do this?"

"A little help from my brother. I couldn't pull off the lobster. This time," he added, rubbing his chin thoughtfully.

Unable to stop herself, she threw herself against him and wrapped her arms around him. "I can't believe this. Aren't you Mr. Hotshot?"

He squeezed her against him. "You get this excited about a nice meal?"

"It's not the meal. It's the fact that you would go to trouble to make me happy," she said. As soon as the words were out, she feared she should have kept them in.

"It wasn't that much trouble," he insisted, clearly uncomfortable.

"It was nice. Very nice," she said. "Thank you."

She lifted her lips upward, and he paused a half beat,

then kissed her. The pause bothered her, but then he kissed the bother out of her.

Cade pulled back. "I can't let you distract us from eating this meal."

"Even if I tried my very best?" she said, sliding her fingers down the neck of the robe to the belt.

"Stop," he said. "Or Stella will get this while I'm hauling you off to my bed."

He pulled out a chair for her and she took the seat, reveling in his attention. Abby and Cade ate the steak and vegetables, nibbled on the bread. She sipped a fruity martini he'd concocted for her and poured into a beer mug. "This is fabulous. I haven't had a meal like this in—" She broke off. "I can't remember when I had a meal like this."

"I'm glad you asked for it," he said, nodding. "I should do this more often."

"I didn't ask for it," she said. "I was joking. I told you I was joking. I never expected you to actually to do this."

"So I surprised you?" he asked, a wicked glint in his eyes.

"Yes, you surprised me," she said. "And it's all wonderful, but I'm so full I don't think I can eat one more bite."

"Better make some room," he said, taking another bite of his steak. "There's something chocolate in the fridge."

Surprised again, she shook her head. "You're joking."

"Not me. I guess I can let you take a little break if you need to. Want to sit in front of the fire?"

"As long as you promise to keep me awake," she said.

"Burning the candle at both ends again," he said. "I warned you about that."

"It's temporary. My schedule should ease up soon. Besides, I have to ask you, what time do you get up and go into the shop?"

"That's different," he said. "I'm used to getting up at 5:00 a.m. I've been doing it since…" He shot her a dead-serious look. "Since you were ten."

"You are wicked and horrible. People don't know," she said. "They all think you're this super amazing, wonderful upstanding citizen, but I know the truth."

"And what is the truth?" he asked, his eyes glinting with the devil again.

"You are quite simply the devil," she said. *And I'm falling out of my crush on you and into love with you.* She bit her tongue to keep from saying the words. She'd always known she had a crush on Cade. In her more melodramatic moments, she'd insisted it was a lifelong passion. But real forever love? Oh, no, this wasn't good.

Cade's hand shot out to grip her arm. "Are you okay, Abby? You look a little squeamish. Did the food bother you?"

Abby shook her head. "Not at all. It was wonderful, and you know it. Thank you for arranging such a fabulous meal. I'm very touched," she said, feeling her throat grow swollen with emotion. Oh, heaven help her, she couldn't cry. "I'm also very full, so I'd like to take you up on that offer to sit in front of the fire." She stood. "Let me help you clear the table first."

Moments later, he linked his hand through hers as they walked into his den. It was Friday night, so there wasn't much on television. Abby sank onto the sofa. "Oh, what a day and now what a wonderful night."

"Rough day?" he asked.

"Just busy. Went to the community center, visited Katrina, took an exam and got fitted for a bridesmaid dress." She winced when she realized what she'd said. "I'm sorry. Really sorry."

"It's okay," he said. "I'm happy for Laila."

She searched his gaze and saw that he was telling the truth. A sliver of ease slipped through her and she sighed. "That is really good."

He nodded and pulled her against him. "Anything else?"

"Not really. My car is working great. I'm not behind on my papers. I have a group presentation next week, and I'm ready for my part." She paused. "Um, I guess I should tell you this. I don't have to stay tonight, but I told my mom I might be staying overnight with a friend."

"I don't want you lying to your family about us," he said.

"But you also don't want me telling them the truth about us, either," she pointed out, lifting her hand to his chin. "That makes it kinda tough, so I told her the truth when I said I might be staying with a friend. You are my friend, aren't you?" she asked, leaning toward him and pulling his head down to hers. "A very, very good friend, right?" she asked and he kissed her.

Abby fell asleep just before ten o'clock, which told him she was continuing to burn the candle at both ends. He'd have to wake her up to fuss at her, though, and she looked so tired he couldn't bring himself to do it. He picked her up and carried her to his bed. She semi-awakened then immediately fell back asleep. Cade slid into the other side of his bed and tried to remember the last time a woman had spent the entire night. His house was his private domain, so he rarely invited a woman to stay longer than an evening. He looked at the outline of her feminine form beneath the covers and knew she was naked underneath. It wouldn't take much for him to want to wake her and make love to her. He knew she wouldn't protest, either. He couldn't remember a woman who had matched his sexual appetite, but Abby did.

He couldn't explain it and sure as hell didn't want to overthink it, but he liked seeing Abby in his bed. She was the last thing he saw before he fell asleep and the first thing he saw when he awakened the next morning. Sometime during the night, she'd snuggled up against him. Her legs were laced through his and one of his arms was curled around her waist. Her eyelids were fluttering and she blinked as her eyes opened as if she weren't sure where she was.

"You're here with me," he said. "In my bed."

"I was getting there," she said. "I'm not always speedy quick in the morning. I don't remember coming into your bedroom," she said, lifting her head to glance around. "I haven't spent a lot of time here before, so I was curious…"

"You didn't get here under your own steam. I carried you," he said.

She looked at him in surprise. "Well, darn, I wish I hadn't missed that." She gave a sheepish smile. "I must have fallen asleep very early. Sorry."

"It wasn't that early," he said and lifted a finger to her nose. "If you're nine years old."

She swatted his hand away. "Thanks a lot. I was a regular box of Cracker Jack last night, minus the popcorn and the toy."

He laughed. "You made up for it before," he said and pulled her against him. "And today you're all mine."

When Abby finally looked out the window, she saw that it had snowed several inches during the night. So much for another motorcycle ride. Not today. They still managed to share a glorious day without leaving Cade's property. After breakfast, she joined him in his workshop as he tinkered with the motorcycle of a friend who had asked him to pimp it out. During the afternoon, he watched part of a college game while she put the finishing touches on her brief PowerPoint presentation. Afterward they went outside and tossed the ball with Stella. The dog couldn't get enough of the game.

When it began to turn dark, they went inside and ordered pizza.

"You're quiet," Cade said after a few moments of silence. "And you're not eating much of the pizza."

"I hate to see the day end," she admitted. Her stomach was clenching at the prospect of returning home and having to pretend that she still wasn't involved with Cade. Plus, the day had been so wonderful and they hadn't done anything monumental. They'd just been together.

"Me, too," he said. "But it will be easier this way if we don't have other people knowing our business."

"I guess," she said.

She saw him stiffen slightly. "You don't agree?"

"Well, I'm one of six children. My mother is all wrapped up in planning Laila's wedding, so I'm not sure she has any time to think twice about who I'm dating as long as he's not a recently released convict."

He chuckled. "I guess I could pass muster on that one. I just don't want to deal with the gossip and uninvited opinions. I don't like people talking about my private business."

"Except when you asked Laila to marry you in front of the whole town," she said, because it popped out of her mouth before she could bite her tongue. She bit her lip instead—way too late.

"That was strictly a moment of insanity invoked by a combination of a stupid discussion with my brothers, whiskey and the fact that I'd recently turned thirty," he said.

Abby gaped at him and covered her mouth. "You were having an age crisis?"

"I figured she probably was, too, since she's the same age as me. I figured I need to start a family sometime. May as well be sooner than later."

Cade could start a family with her, Abby thought, but although he had come around to seeing her as a lover, he didn't seem to view her as a viable option as a wife. The knowledge stung, but her ego had taken a beating more than once with Cade. "So that was a phase," she said. "You're not interested in having a family anymore."

"I didn't say that, but it's got to be the right time with the right person," he said.

A stab of pain shot through her. She'd already hinted that Cade could have what he wanted with her, but he seemed determined not to hear her. She refused to beg. "I hope you find exactly what you're looking for."

He blinked at her response. "What does that mean?"

"Exactly what I said. I think people get into relationships to meet different needs. We all have to figure out who can really meet our needs and who can't," she said and picked up her slice of pizza and prayed she would be able to swallow the bite she took.

Cade seemed more thoughtful than usual during the next hour. He watched her carefully. "I'm thinking you're going to have another busy day tomorrow since you played hooky today."

"You're thinking right," she said, mentally reviewing her insane schedule.

"How's Monday since you'll be busy Tuesday night?" he suggested.

She was impressed that he remembered her standing ROOTS commitment, but didn't allow herself to get too worked up over it. "Monday is better. What did you have in mind?" she asked.

"I'll come up with something better than Monday-night football. Will that work?" he asked.

"Yes. I love surprises," she said.

"It's a good thing one of us does because I hate them," he muttered, then pulled her against him. "What's going on in that pretty head of yours?" he demanded.

"You mean you can't read my mind? I would have sworn that was one of your superpowers," she joked.

"You must have me confused with someone else," he said.

"Nope," she said, shaking her head. "I would swear it was you."

"Well, you're wrong, and I've noticed you still haven't told me what's going on in your brain," he said.

"Good for you," she said, still not revealing her thoughts and feelings. "Observant, too." She lifted her hands to his shoulders and sighed. "When are you going to stop talking and kiss me?"

Between the impending holidays, her cousins' upcoming double wedding and Laila's wedding planning, things at the Cateses' household were moving at a fever pitch. Her sisters were busy with their jobs and social lives, and it always seemed as if one or two of them were moving in or out of the house. Her brother, who still lived at home, provided ample companionship for her father since they were both football freaks and her brother would choose to root for the team opposing her father's choice just to up the ante.

All the busyness made Abby wonder if anyone would really notice if she were gone for a few days, or more. A tempting thought when she daydreamed about taking a trip with Cade... As if that would happen. Maybe in her next life.

On Sunday, her mother encouraged all the kids to go to church. "It won't hurt you. You may even learn something," she'd always said.

Abby often enjoyed the worship service on Sunday morning. It was a quiet slice of time that offered her the opportunity to calm down and remember what was important. Today, however, as she sat with her mother, father, Laila and Jackson, she found herself checking her watch and resisting the urge to squirm. Just two weeks away from Thanksgiving, the sermon topic focused on sharing with both friends and those less fortunate. The pastor pointed out that even though our friends may not seem to need anything, many of us keep our vulnerabilities hidden. He also said that we should especially keep people in mind who have suffered losses during the holidays.

Abby couldn't help thinking of Cade. People thought of him as the man on whom everyone could depend. He was, but Abby had caught a glimpse of the pain of loss he suffered, pain he rarely let anyone see. It frustrated her that he would only let her so close when she was certain she could make some of his pain go away.

Even though he clearly had passion for her, she knew he didn't view their relationship as long-term, and that hurt her every time she thought about it. Something inside her kept her from giving up just yet. During the last hymn, she thought about how to help Cade through the holiday season. Christmas was right around the corner and she wanted him to feel joy instead of dread.

After church, she helped her mother put a big Sunday lunch on the table. Roasted chicken with vegetables, mashed potatoes and biscuits. Her entire family, along with Jackson, made it for the meal.

Abby's father gave a quick grace, and a second after he said "Amen," her brother was reaching for the mashed potatoes.

"I'm glad all of you were able to join us for lunch," Abby's mother said. "I'm sorry you missed church. The minister gave an excellent sermon. Don't you agree, Abby?"

Abby hated being put on the spot, especially when her mother was using her as the example, especially when she was not the least bit perfect. "Very good sermon. The minister reminded us to be generous and thoughtful to everyone because we don't always know when people are suffering. Mom, you and Dad have been such good examples in this area, I'm sure the rest of us will be thinking about this." She searched for a change of subject and glanced at Laila. "How are the wedding plans coming?"

"I can't believe all the details," she said. "It's not just choosing my dress. It's also choosing the bridesmaids' dresses and what the men will wear, the decorations for the church, what the theme will be."

"Vegas sounds like a great theme to me," Jackson muttered. "Eloping."

Abby's mother gasped. "Don't you dare think of it."

"Too late for thinking," Jackson said. "But don't you worry, Mama Cates. I want everyone to know Laila is off the market."

Everyone at the table except Abby laughed. Jackson's comment was in stark contrast to Cade's determination to keep his relationship with her a secret. One more little stab, but Abby brushed it aside.

Speed-cleaning the dishes and kitchen after the meal with a couple of her sisters, Abby mentally planned her afternoon and evening.

"You sure are quiet," Jordyn, one of her sisters, said as she dried a pot.

"And you're cleaning like a bat out of you-know-where," Jasmine agreed, as she dried a pan. "What's the rush? Aren't you gonna hang around for the football game?"

"Not today," Abby said. "I have too much to do. I'm behind on my schoolwork."

"Well, don't work too hard," Jordyn said, shooting her a look of concern. "You're looking a little thin and rough. Circles under your eyes."

"If it were anyone but you, I'd wonder if you were lovesick," Jasmine said just as Laila walked into the kitchen.

"Lovesick?" Laila echoed. "Who's lovesick?"

"No one," Abby said firmly. "I've just got a lot of schoolwork to do. Add that to working at the community center and ROOTS and I'm swamped."

"Hmm," Laila said, clearly unconvinced.

"Like I said," Jasmine repeated. "I'd think you were lovesick if I didn't know you better. You've always been more into your grades than dating."

"And you've always been more into dating than anything else," Abby said with a laugh.

Jasmine swatted at her with the towel, but Abby successfully dodged her sister. "I gotta run. Hope you guys win your bets this time."

"Fat chance," Jordyn said with a mock scowl. "Brody almost always manages to win."

Abby headed for her bedroom to gather her laptop and books. Just as she turned around, Laila appeared in the doorway. "Lovesick?"

Abby's stomach sank. She really didn't want to have this discussion. "Not me," Abby said. "I don't have time to be lovesick."

"But Jazzy had a point. You look like you've lost weight and you have circles under your eyes," Laila said. "I can't help thinking Cade is responsible."

"Cade is not responsible. You know I have a crazy schedule," Abby told her, grabbing her coat from the back of her chair, mentally scolding herself for almost forgetting it. She needed to get her head together. She was far too distracted.

"I also know you're crazy for Cade," Laila said.

"So what if I am?" Abby tossed back at her sister. "You don't quiz Jazzy about all her boyfriends. Why me?"

Laila hesitated. "Because you're different," she said. "Your heart is softer. I'm afraid you could really get hurt."

Her sister's concerns slid past her defenses and Abby fought the sting of tears in her eyes. She dumped her stuff on the desk and wrapped her arms around Laila in a hug. "I'm lucky to have a sister who cares so much about me, but you can't stop this. You can't keep me from getting hurt. This isn't the same as when I was learning to ride a bike and I scraped my knees. I can't turn away from the most amazing man in the world."

Laila groaned. "Oh, no. You really do have it bad."

Abby pulled back and forced a tiny laugh from the back of her tight throat. "Well, it's about time, isn't it?" she asked. "However it turns out, I'll survive. I've got the backbone of a Cates."

Laila sighed. "That's true. I just hate—"

"Stop," Abby said. "Be happy for me. When I'm with Cade, I'm happier than I ever dreamed possible."

Laila gave a slow nod. "But if you need anything from a hug to a place to stay for the night, you let me know."

"I will. Thanks," Abby said. "Now, I've really got to go."

"And don't forget to eat," Laila yelled as Abby flew out the door.

* * *

That night at the library, Abby typed notes on her laptop for two more papers with a deadline before Thanksgiving. She took a sip from a bottle of water as she scanned one of her research books for more facts pertinent to her topic. She'd been so distracted by her time with Cade that she'd slipped up and forgotten about these papers. Plus she'd checked on Katrina today just before her mother showed up for a parental visit. That situation was looking up since Katrina's mother had kicked her boyfriend out of her house and life.

She scratched a note on her notebook and decided to look for another reference. Glancing at the time on her cell phone, she winced. The library closed at midnight and it was already ten-thirty. She searched for a couple more titles that looked promising and headed back to the section that held those books. "Not that, not that, not that," she murmured then found one of her books. "There you are."

"Exactly. There you are," a male voice said from behind her.

Abby swung around to find Daniel standing just a few feet away from her. "Oh, you startled me."

"Gotta keep a girl like you off balance to keep you interested."

Except, she had never been interested, she thought, irritated, as she turned back to the bookshelf. "I really can't chat tonight, Daniel. I've got to find one more book to make some notes."

"You're always busy, Abby. You need to take a break.

You know what they say. All work and no play is bad for your health."

"My health is fine. It will be a lot better when I get through this semester," she muttered as she surveyed the shelves.

Daniel stepped between her and the shelves she was searching. "C'mon, Abby. I've been chasing you for weeks. What's it take to get your attention?"

She noticed the smell of alcohol on his breath and her irritation intensified. "Daniel, I told you I don't have time for this tonight. I don't have time for this at all. I'm not interested in you," she said bluntly. Surely that would make him leave.

"Why not?" he asked, moving toward her, so that she backed against the opposite shelf. "Your friends tell me you need to get out more. You're not involved with anyone." He lowered his head. "I think we could be good together. Very good," he said as he lowered his mouth.

Shocked, Abby turned her head and tried to step away, but Daniel closed his arms around her. "You ought to give me a chance. Just one. I could change your mind."

"Let me go, Daniel," she said, her heart beating with a combination of surprise and fury.

"You smell so good," he said. "I've had dreams about you."

"Daniel!" she yelled, not wanting to alert the entire library over his foolish behavior, but he had crossed over the line.

He slid his mouth over her forehead.

"That's it. I warned you," she said and jerked her knee sharply upward into his groin.

Daniel yelped in pain and doubled over. His whimper made her feel sorry for him, for about a half of a second then her anger came back full throttle.

"What the hell did you do that for?" he asked. "I was just trying to give you a little kiss."

"I didn't want a little kiss," she told him. "I didn't want any kisses from you, and if you ever put your paws on me or anyone else I know in the future, I'm calling the police. When I say no, I mean no. And here's a news flash, that goes for all women. Do you understand me?"

He looked behind her, still grimacing. "Yeah, me and everybody else," he said and limped past her.

Abby whirled around and found at least twenty students, along with the librarian, staring at Daniel, then her. Her face flamed with embarrassment. She made a habit of not calling attention to herself, and to have everyone observing her in this situation was, oh, humiliating. She cleared her throat. "Sorry for the interruption. I, uh, need to get back to work."

Chapter Ten

Another jam-packed day. Abby worked with the kids at the community center, went to two classes, worked more on her two papers and squeezed in a little surprise shopping for Cade. She would have been more excited about her purchases, one of which was burning a hole in her pocket, if she hadn't gotten a late start for his house because her mother had phoned her cell to ask her to pick up some groceries.

She pulled into his driveway and bolted out of the car. Before she could make it up the steps to his porch, he opened the door and leaned against the doorjamb. "Well, well, well, if it isn't the nutcracker herself."

Abby blinked at him and her mental to-do list fell into a pile of dust. "Nutcracker?" she said. "What are you talking about?"

"I'm talking about your new nickname," he said.

Confused, she walked up the steps, noticing a couple sleds propped against the house. Her gaze was drawn back to Cade, and she lifted her shoulders. "What do you mean?"

"As of last night, there are stories going around that a young man named Daniel Payne suffered bodily injuries that you inflicted," Cade said. "Stories I'm certain are not true. Because you would never let a guy get to the point of no return in the college library."

Anger soared through her. "He walked into that library past the point of no return. He'd been drinking. I told him I wasn't interested and never would be, but he wouldn't stop. Crowded me against one of the bookcases. I yelled. I warned, but he wouldn't listen. There was only one thing left to do."

"Did it occur to you to call me?" he asked, something dark flicking through his blue gaze.

"I didn't have my cell phone on me when I was reaching for the book on abnormal psychology. It was very embarrassing. By the time I stopped yelling, a crowd of people were watching and listening. For a minute there, I was afraid I might get banned from the library, but this was not my fault. I have *not* encouraged that guy in any way."

"You still should have called me," he said, scowling at her.

"I told you I didn't have my phone," she said.

"Afterward. You should have called me afterward.

You had to be shaken up and I could have paid this guy a visit to make sure he didn't bother you again," he said.

She felt a rush of warmth at Cade's protectiveness. "That's nice of you," she said softly. "But I don't think there's any danger of him coming anywhere near me again."

"He better not or he's going to have to answer to me," Cade said, pulling her inside his foyer. He opened the closet door and grabbed a hat.

"There's no need to get physical, Cade. You're a lot bigger than he is. You could squash him with one of your feet," she said.

"Look who's talking about not getting physical, *nut-cracker*," he said. "And I've rarely needed to resort to violence in my life. I'll just reason with the guy."

Her stomach began to lurch. Abby had tried not to think about the incident, but down deep it really had bothered her. She knew, based on her studies, that she would have to work through it sooner or later, but later just sounded better to her right now.

"Can we talk about something else? It's not a happy subject for me," she said.

His gaze softened. "Sure, and I have just the thing to take it off your mind," he said, pulling on the hat he held in his hand then following up with his gloves. "We're going sledding."

"Now?" she asked, the idea appealing to her in a surprising way.

"Now," he said. "The hill behind my brother Dean's place is perfect."

"Aren't you worried he'll see us and ask questions about you and me?" she asked.

"Dean knows about you and me," he said, guiding her out the door.

She gaped at him. "He does?"

"Yeah, I told him about it a couple weeks ago. He knows not to discuss it," he said and grabbed the sleds.

Abby was so stunned she didn't know what to say, until a thousand questions entered her mind. *Exactly what did you tell Dean? How much does he know? Two weeks ago? You were still saying I was too young then. Did you tell him you've fallen desperately in love with me and can't live without me?* She rolled her eyes at the last one because she knew the answer to that. *No and no.*

Within an hour, she felt seven years old again. Flying down a snow-covered hill shrieking with joy. Cade dared her to race him. She won once. He won the second time. Then he double-dared her to ride down the hill on his back. Unable to resist, she joined him and they took a tumble in the snow.

"Are you okay?" he asked, his voice anxious as he rolled her from her front side to her back in the snow. "I must have hit some ice."

"I'm fine," she said and started to laugh. "I'm going to be so wet by the time we get back to your house." She laughed again. "And it's all your fault because you are a reckless sled driver."

He frowned with consternation. "I'm not reckless. I just hit some ice. Are you sure you're okay?"

"Fine except for all the snow that's gone all the way down my neck to my back. I never dreamed that perfect Cade could be reckless," she teased.

He looked as if he were trying to be stern with her, but her giggles must have gotten to him. "Sit up, so you don't get any more snow down your sweater," he said, pulling her up. "Look at you. You've got snow all in your hair. You're a mess," he said, shaking his head.

"All your fault, Mr. Reckless," she said and smiled up at him. "I have an early Christmas present for you."

He looked at her in confusion. "Christmas? We've got a whole month to go," he said.

"You wouldn't know that by your display window at Pritchett & Sons," she said.

"True," he said. "So what's this Christmas present? A lump of coal?" he asked with a wary expression.

"Nope," she said and pulled a mistletoe packet out of her pocket. She lifted it above her head. "Oops. Kiss me quick or it's bad luck."

He shook his head and snatched the mistletoe from her. "Trust me, you don't need mistletoe for me to kiss you." He lowered his head and his warm lips took the cold away from her within mere seconds. As he deepened the kiss, her temperature heated up and she wrapped her arms around his neck. She loved his strength. She loved his wisdom and sense of humor. Being with him made her feel so much more than happy. She couldn't think of one word to describe all the ways he affected her. Abby kissed him with all her heart and passion.

Cade responded. A moment later, he finally pulled back, his eyes dark with wanting. "We'd better head back to the house or I'm going to strip you and we're going to give my brother an eyeful. And I would never hear the end of it."

Cade led the way back to his house and they both stomped the snow from their boots before they stepped inside. He glanced at Abby and spotted her teeth chattering and her blue lips from the cold and swore.

"Why didn't you tell me you were freezing?" he asked, pulling off her gloves and coat. "Hold on to me while I help you ditch these boots."

"It wouldn't have done any good. We still had to walk back to your house. It's no big deal. I'll warm up. By next week," she said, smiling through her chattering teeth.

He chuckled despite himself. He didn't like being responsible for her getting this cold. He was surprised at how protective of her he felt. When he'd heard about that Daniel guy molesting her at the library, he'd wanted to go after him but, from what he'd heard, the guy was planning on leaving town for a while. Good riddance, Cade thought and gave up on pulling off the rest of Abby's soggy clothes in the foyer. She needed warm water. He ditched his own jacket and boots.

"Here we go," he said, picking her up in his arms and carrying her down the hall.

"What are you doing?" she asked.

"You need a hot shower," he said, carrying her into

the bathroom. He turned on the jets to the shower then pulled off the rest of her clothes and his. "Ready?" he asked, already distracted by her naked body. It felt as if it had be aeons since he'd made love to her.

He hauled her into the shower and she shrieked. "Are you trying to scald me to death?"

Cade dialed the temperature back a little bit and pulled her against him. She was still cold. He pressed his mouth against her shivering mouth and she put her arms around him as she sank into the kiss. He felt a couple of chatters, but he knew he'd knocked off the worst of the chill when she sighed against his mouth. Her sigh said so much. If her sigh could talk, it would say she trusted him and wanted him. Her sigh said she was already feeling pleasure, but there was more to come. That sigh coupled with her naked body against his was the most wicked and wonderful sensation he'd ever had.

"You can turn up the water temperature now," she said.

He liked the way she heated up, he thought, and he had every intention of making her blood boil with pleasure. Lowering his mouth to her again in a deep, wet kiss with the water streaming over them, he lowered his hands to her breasts, focusing on her responsive nipples.

Abby made a sexy sound and wriggled against him, making him stiff with wanting her. This time, he wanted to make her want and wait. This time he wanted to make her crazy. He lowered one of his hands between her silky thighs and found her warm and wet. He continued to stroke and she began to wiggle against him.

"Cade, I want you," she whispered. "I want you inside me."

"Soon," he promised and dipped his lips to her breasts, taunting her nipples then sliding lower and lower.

Mere minutes later, her body flexed and she climaxed, letting out a high-pitched moan of satisfaction. Taking her with his mouth had nearly put him over the edge. The ability to wait burned to cinders. He picked her up and with her back propped against the tile wall, he took her.

Her sexy gaze burned into his with each stroke he took and somehow in the middle of taking her, he felt as if she had taken him.

After they got out of the shower, Cade wrapped Abby in his big terry-cloth robe and pulled on a pair of jeans and a sweater. "Soup and sandwiches okay with you?" he asked as he pulled from the refrigerator the premade deli sandwiches he'd bought from the grocery store on the way home.

"Perfect. You want me to heat the soup?" she asked, walking into the kitchen. She pulled the foot of the turkey still hanging in his kitchen.

"Gobble, gobble, gobble," said the electronic voice.

Then she pulled it again. "I didn't want him to feel neglected," she said to Cade.

"He hasn't been," Cade assured her. "His foot is

pulled every morning and every evening when I get home from work. Whether he needs it or not."

She gave a low chuckle. "Glad you're taking care of him." She glanced through his cupboard and pulled out a can of soup and poured it into a pot on the stove. "You really do cook like a bachelor, don't you?"

"How's that?" he asked, unwrapping the deli sandwiches and putting them on paper plates.

"I mean you don't cook anything like chicken or soup or stew," she said.

"I cook barbecue pork. Does that count?" he asked.

"On the grill?" she asked.

"Yeah."

"If it's on the grill it doesn't count for real cooking. The grill is great, and I love food cooked on the grill, but sometimes you have to turn on the oven," she said.

He glanced down at the petite woman with wet, mussed hair and big brown eyes who was trying to give him instructions on cooking. He knew that she could cook circles around him. "That's when I turn on the microwave," he said.

"Good for you," she said and laughed.

A few moments later, the soup was heated. She served it with some crackers she found and they sat at the table. "Bean 'n' bacon soup. Excellent choice," he said.

"It's not rocket science. You could have done the same thing," she said. "All it takes is a can opener, a pan and a stovetop."

"That's two steps too many for me," he said, lifting another spoonful of soup to his mouth.

She laughed. "Well, I'm glad I could help out."

He looked into her amused brown eyes and watched her take a bite of her sandwich and felt something inside him ease. What was happening to him? When had canned soup and deli sandwiches felt like a gourmet dinner with Abby sitting across from him.

She met his gaze and glanced away then back at him. "What's wrong? Is there mustard on my chin or something?"

"No. I was just thinking how pretty you are," he said.

Her cheeks flushed. "Thank you. After being hounded by my sisters for looking too thin and having circles under my eyes, that's very nice to hear."

He frowned and studied her. "Now that you mention it," he began.

She shook her head. "Don't you start," she said. "The circles are temporary because of the increased schoolwork at this time of the semester."

"Plus there's the matter of you spending all your extra time with me. I don't want to keep you from your schoolwork," he said.

"Oh, please do," she joked.

"Really, Abby. You're too close to let anything get in your way. Including—" He broke off when his house phone began to ring. "That doesn't happen very often," he said. "Everyone who knows me calls my cell." He paused for a moment then let the call go to voice mail. "What were we talking about?"

"The Jacuzzi you're planning to install," she said.

He chuckled, although the image of Abby naked in a tub of bubbling water was all too appealing. "I've actually thought about it, but never got around to it…"

The phone rang again and he frowned. "Maybe I should check it," he said, rising from the kitchen table. He glanced at the caller ID and felt as if he'd been punched. He immediately picked up the phone.

"Cade Pritchett," he said and waited.

The silence stretched for one, two, three seconds. "Cade, this is Marlene, Dominique's mom."

"Hello," he said. "How are you?"

"Bill and I are doing well. We're actually in Montana visiting some relatives. We wondered if we could drop by and see you tonight," the woman said.

Cade nearly choked on the next breath he drew. "Tonight?" he asked, glancing at Abby, sitting at the table in his robe. She shot him an inquiring glance.

"I know it's short notice, but I think it's important. We won't stay long," she promised.

Hearing the twinge of desperation in the woman's voice, Cade felt compelled to respond. "Okay. I'm finishing up dinner. When do you think you'll be here?"

"In fifteen minutes or less. And we've already eaten, so you don't need to feed us. See you soon," she said.

Cade hung up the phone and stared at it.

"Can you give me a vowel?" Abby asked after a long moment of silence.

"Dominique's parents are coming. They'll be here in less than fifteen minutes."

Abby gaped at him and dumped her spoon in her soup. "Oh, wow, I need to get out of here," she said, rising form her chair. "But we forgot to put my clothes in the dryer, didn't we? Darn," she said. "I could borrow something from you if I wrapped it around me twice."

He chuckled at the image. "Not necessary. You can stay here. We'll throw your clothes in the dryer now."

"I'm not greeting your former girlfriend's parents in your robe," she told him.

"I wasn't suggesting that. You could finish your sandwich in my robe and watch the television in there."

"Oh, hide out in your room," she said. "That could work."

"There's no need for you to hide," he said, frustrated that their evening was being interrupted by people who had held him responsible for the death of their daughter when his biggest crime had been loving her. "If you want to meet them, I'm fine with it."

"I'm not," she said and picked up her plate. She pressed her lips together and looked at him in sympathy. "Good luck, Cade," she said and gave him a kiss. Then she skedaddled toward his bedroom and closed the door behind her.

Cade raked his hand through his hair, wondering why the Gordons had chosen this time to visit him after all these years. His appetite gone, he dumped his soup in the sink and put the remainder of his sandwich in the fridge. He threw Abby's clothes in the dryer and the doorbell rang. Stella barked and ran to the door. Cade brought up the rear and opened the door to the mother and father of the woman he had once planned to marry.

"Hi," Marlene said and timidly stepped inside. "I'm sorry this is such short notice."

Bill extended his hand. "Pritchett," he said with a nod. "Nice to see you. You're looking good."

"Thanks, Bill. Come on in, both of you. Can I get you something to drink?"

"Oh, we won't be staying that long," Marlene said, making him curious as hell. The Gordons looked a little worn around the edges considering their age. Cade supposed he couldn't blame them. They'd had two children and one had died way before she should have.

"How's Bill, Jr.?" Cade asked.

"Doing very well," Marlene said. "He's working for a computer company about an hour away from here. He got married two years ago and he and his wife had a baby six months ago. She's gorgeous."

"Looks like Dominique at that age," Bill said.

Cade's gut tightened. "That's gotta be great for you two," Cade said. "Come into the den."

The two Gordons did as he asked and sat gingerly on the sofa. Silence stretched between them for a long moment.

Bill cleared his throat and adjusted the collar of his coat jacket. "The reason we wanted to see you is because Marlene and I realized we were hard on you when Dominique died."

"We weren't just hard on you," Marlene said. "We weren't fair."

"Dominique was determined to go to California during her break and nothing was going to stop her, even you," Bill said. "You probably knew that. Even if you didn't, you knew what kind of nature Dominique had. She needed to travel every now and then. It was in her blood. She probably got it from me. I went into the air force to see the world."

"We would have done everything to keep her alive, and we believe you would have, too, but who could have predicted that terrible accident?" Maureen asked with a shudder. "We'll never get over the loss, but holding you responsible was wrong and cruel. You were grieving for her, too."

"But we couldn't see that because we were hurting too much," Bill said, lacing and unlacing his fingers.

"So, we're here to apologize," Maureen said. "We were wrong to blame you. We hope you'll forgive us. More important, we hope you don't hold yourself responsible for Dominique's death."

Cade was stunned by all the Gordons were telling him. "I don't know what to say except that I still miss Dominique's presence in my life."

Maureen bit her lip and reached out to pat his hand. "We know you do. Because of that, we'd like to give you the necklace she wore. I believe you gave it to her," Mrs. Gordon said as she pulled a small box from her purse and handed it to Cade.

Cade opened the box to the diamond-accented sparkler pendant he'd given Dominique all those years ago.

He'd told her she was a firecracker and that she lit up his life. The memory squeezed his chest again.

"This was a perfect example of her personality. She was a dynamo. That's one of the reasons we felt such a void when she died," Bill said. "I couldn't stand it. So we moved back to California and tried to make ourselves feel better."

"In some ways, it helped to move away," Marlene said.

"In others, it didn't. How do you explain to people you're meeting for the first time that you had the most beautiful daughter in the world and she would have accomplished amazing things if she hadn't died way too young?"

Cade nodded. "I hear you," he said, his mind suddenly flooded with images of Dominique.

Bill took a deep breath. "We'll never stop missing her," he said.

"Never," Marlene agreed. "But Dominique wouldn't want us to hold a grudge. She would want us to get as much out of life as possible. She would want the same for you, Cade."

Cade felt jolted by Marlene's last comment. "I'm living. I miss her like you do, but I'm living."

"Did you ever get married?" Marlene asked gently.

"Marlene," Bill said. "That's none of our business."

Marlene extended her hand to Cade's again. "Well, I just want to tell you, Cade, that I hope you will find another woman to love. You have a lot to offer and it shouldn't be stuck in the past." She took a deep breath.

"That's all I have to say except to thank you for being so good to Dominique. You were a solid, stable force that made her feel safe enough to fly. You were exactly what she needed at that time in her life."

Cade took in Marlene's words, but he would have to digest them later.

"We should leave now," Bill said to Marlene. He stood and helped his wife to her feet. "Thank you for seeing us. Thank you for being a good man to our daughter and to us," he said and shook Cade's hand again.

"God bless," Marlene said and threw her arms around his neck. "God bless and good night," she said and the two of them left his house.

Cade stared after them, looking at the tire tread marks their vehicle left in the snow. The words from both of the Gordons felt as if they jumbled together in his head. What did all this mean? Did it mean anything? He rubbed the necklace he'd given Dominique all those years ago between his fingers. He felt his lungs constrict. What was he supposed to do with this? As much as he'd loved Dominique, he didn't carry anything of hers around on a daily basis. Nothing material, that is. Her attitude about life had often haunted him. He'd been more practical. She'd enjoyed the unexpected. She'd looked for the magic. Cade didn't believe in magic. But surprises—lately he was changing his mind about those. Or maybe it was Abby who was changing his mind.

The dryer buzzed, signifying the end of the cycle,

and Abby stepped outside the bedroom. "All clear?" she asked in a hushed voice.

When he nodded, she walked toward him, searching his face. "Did it go okay?"

He gave a slow nod. "Yeah. Better than I expected," he said and rubbed his fingers over the pendant in his hand.

Abby glanced down at the necklace. "Did that belong to her?"

"Yeah. I gave it to her when we were dating. They wanted me to have it," he said, still stunned by the conversation he'd had with her parents.

Abby lifted her eyebrows. "Sounds like they had a turnaround."

"Yeah." He paused a moment. "They apologized for blaming me for her death."

"Wow," Abby said. "That's huge." She smiled. "And wonderful. Even though you knew you weren't responsible, it's got to feel great knowing they don't resent you anymore."

He thought about that for a moment. Practically speaking, he'd known he wasn't responsible, but some part of him had thought there must have been something he could have done to prevent Dominique's death. "Sometimes I've wondered if I could have done something to keep her safe. It was my job. It felt like my job, anyway."

"Ohhh," Abby said. "Your superhero complex coming out again. You have the power to save everyone and everything?"

He shot her a sideways glance at her light jab. "It's more that I felt responsible for her."

She nodded. "You were responsible for keeping her safe," she said. "Twenty-four-seven even though you weren't with her and your superpowers are unfortunately limited." She sighed and wrapped her arms around him. "As happy as I am to be with you now, I'm sorry you've had to suffer such a terrible loss."

Her words felt like soothing water on a sore place inside him. He held her close and felt comforted in a way he couldn't remember. Her sweet honesty made a tightness inside him ease. Cade couldn't help wondering if Abby was the one with superpowers.

Chapter Eleven

When Cade went to work the next morning, he felt like a different man. The trees looked prettier, the snow was beautiful, the crisp air felt good to breathe. He hummed along to the country music tune playing on the radio in his SUV. He waved a car in front of him at an intersection. The sun was shining. He would see Abby tonight. Anticipation hummed through him. Today was going to be a good day.

He pulled into the parking lot and got out of his car, ready for a hard, productive day at work followed by an evening with Abby.

"Hey, Cade," his brother Nick said as he walked into the shop. He gave a broad wink. "I hear you've been busy robbing the cradle with another Cates sister."

Cade blinked. Where had Nick heard about him and

Abby? Nick had been on a hunting trip for the past ten days, so this was the first time Cade had seen his brother in a while. Wondering if his other brother, Dean, had been talking, he called for him. "Dean!"

Dean poked his head out from the back room and held up his hands. "It wasn't me. I didn't tell him anything. He went to the Hitching Post last night and apparently the gossip has already started." Dean shot him a sympathetic look. "Sorry, bro."

"I'm not robbing any cradles. Abby's twenty-two." He walked toward the back room. "Welcome back," he added as an afterthought, his mood plummeting. Cade was a private man and hated being the subject of gossip. He was just getting past the fallout from his public proposal to Laila Cates and sure as hell didn't want to stir up anything else.

"So you really are seeing her?" Nick asked, following him to the back room. "It's none of my business, but this isn't a rebound thing because of Laila, is it?"

Cade turned and shot Nick a deadly glance.

"Hey, it's wasn't my idea. One of the waitresses said she wondered if that's what's going on since you lost out on Laila," Nick said.

A month's worth of his patience shot in five minutes, Cade ground his teeth. "Here's a news flash. I don't feel like I lost out on anything with Laila. I'm glad she and Jackson are happy together."

He could tell by his brother's expression that he wasn't convinced. "You've known me a long time. Am

I the kind of man to go out with a woman for the sake of a rebound?"

Nick paused then pressed his lips together in a slight wince. "Sorry. I was just surprised to hear it. Are you serious about her?"

Cade clenched his jaw again. His feelings were nobody's business but his own. "I'm not about to get serious with a woman after two weeks."

"Sure," Nick said. "That makes sense."

Cade sighed and put Nick out of his misery by changing the subject. "So, how was the hunting?"

"Oh," Nick said. "You wouldn't believe the rack on the elk I bagged."

The subject of Abby was blessedly dropped. Cade worked in complete silence without stopping until after lunch and decided to get a breath of fresh air and a cup of coffee and a sandwich to go at the diner. Old man Henson waved at him from a stool as he ate a piece of pie.

Cade placed his order then walked toward him. "How's that ankle?"

"Pretty good. I'm getting around good. Mildred here at the shop has been dropping off some goodies for me after she gets off work. I think she's sweet on me," he said in a lowered voice. "But she's a nice woman. A bit young for me but my Geraldine would approve of her."

Cade smiled. "Good for you," he said.

"I saw your little lady in here this morning. She loves her hot chocolate, doesn't she? Won't touch the coffee. I asked her about you and she said she had seen you a few times." Mr. Henson gave him a nudge. "I knew you would come around. Pretty, sweet and can cook. What's not to like about that?" he asked. "She's a looker and a cooker. You'll do good with her."

"Abby and I aren't serious, so there's no need to be thinking about the future," Cade said.

Mr. Henson shook his finger at him. "Don't you wait too long to get her in your corral. I'll tell you there's plenty of other young bucks right behind you."

Mr. Henson's hearing wasn't the best, so he tended to speak loudly. Cade felt the small crowd in the restaurant watching him. The whispers would start any minute, he realized, and his gut began to churn. "How's that pie?" he asked, pointing toward the pastry on the old man's plate.

"Oh, it's good," Mr. Henson said. "But you know everything here is good."

"How's your truck?" Cade asked. He wanted to provide everyone who was listening with a mundane conversation, so they would turn their attention elsewhere. Away from him.

"Order for Pritchett," the waitress at the register said.

"That's mine," he said to Mr. Henson and slapped the man on the back. "You take care of yourself."

He paid for the order and picked up the bag. "Thanks," he said.

"You're welcome. We all love Abby here. You're a lucky man," the waitress said shyly, then whispered, "I gave you a piece of pie."

Cade clenched his jaw and nodded then left the diner.

* * *

After helping at the community center and going to one of her classes, Abby paid a visit to Katrina since she had just been returned to her mother's apartment. "Everything okay?" Abby asked, sitting across from her on a couch in the modest room.

"It's all good. The foster family was really nice, and they invited me to stop in anytime."

"So you got some new friends out of this," Abby said. "Not bad. You think you would ever visit them?"

"I might," Katrina said, nodding. "They really were nice to me. They always wanted to know where I was, but they were nice."

"And no sign of your mom's boyfriend, right?" Abby asked.

Katrina's eyes darkened. "Ex. My mom's ex. He's gone for good. She promised, and I think she means it. She's talking about dropping one of her jobs so she can spend more time with me."

"That would be great. You know I'm so proud of you, don't you?" Abby said and pulled Katrina into a big hug.

Katrina resisted for half a second then returned the hug. "Yeah. It wasn't fun, but it had to be done. I like that you didn't *make* me do it. You just made me think I deserved to be treated better."

Abby gave her another squeeze then pulled back. "Never, ever forget that," she said.

Katrina met her gaze. "I won't. See ya tomorrow night?"

"I'll be there," Abby said and stood. "Call me if you need anything."

Katrina nodded. "I'll do that."

After going to another class, Abby received terrific grades on an exam and a paper she'd turned in two weeks ago. She was flying high by the time she was scheduled to meet Cade at DJ's for a quick early bite. Just as she entered the eatery, her cell rang. It was Cade.

"Hey," she said. "Everything okay?"

"I decided to pick up ribs and bring them back to the house. Is that okay with you?" he asked.

"Sure, sure," she said, but wondered about something she heard in his voice. "I should be there in about fifteen minutes."

"See you then," he said and hung up.

His tone bothered her, but she had no idea what was wrong. She would ask when she got to his house. The important thing was that they would be together. She'd been looking forward to seeing him since she woke up this morning, she thought, smiling to herself.

Pulling into his driveway, she bounded up the steps, knocked on the door and stepped inside. Stella immediately came to greet her, wagging her tail. "Welcome me here, darlin'," she called. "I've had a crazy-good day and it's just gonna get better."

Cade appeared in the doorway with an inscrutable expression on his face. "What happened during your crazy-good day?" he asked in a subdued tone.

"Are you okay?" she asked, studying him.

"Tell me your good news," he said.

She rubbed Stella's soft, furry head and stepped toward him. "Where do I begin?" she said and looped her arm in his. "I got As on my exam and one of my major papers. Katrina moved back in with her mother and that's looking good. And the best thing is I get to see you." She stood up on tiptoe and pressed her lips against his.

He gave a brief response. "Good for you. Congratulations."

She looked at him in confusion. "Something's wrong. Tell me," she urged.

"Some things happened today that made me start thinking," he said.

"About what?" she asked.

He took a quick breath and narrowed his eyes. "About us."

"What about us?" she asked, his expression making her stomach knot. "Have you been happy when you've been with me?"

"Yeah," he said. "I've been happy."

"That's good, because I've been unbelievably happy. The only thing that would make me happier is if we didn't have to keep it a secret. My feelings for you seemed to be growing exponentially every day. Every time we're together, I feel closer to you. I—" She bit her tongue, but could no longer hold back the words. "I love you, Cade. You're such an incredible man. Being with you is a dream come true for me."

Cade looked at her for a long moment then looked away.

Her heart fell at his lack of response. *Oh, please, Cade, don't bail on me now.*

He lifted one of his hands and cleared his throat. "Sweetheart, you may think you want me. You may think you love me, but you haven't been around me enough to really know that."

She stared at him in disbelief, then shook her head. "Yes, I have. I've known you forever."

"You haven't known me as a man," he said. "Even you would say you've been carrying around a heavy dose of hero worship for a long time."

"And it was valid. You've been a hero to a lot of people. You've been the man that so many people knew they could depend on, especially if they needed help," she said. "I could meet a hundred other men and it wouldn't make any difference to my feelings. I know my own heart."

"Just listen to me. I think we need to slow things down," he said, meeting her gaze.

Shock rushed through her. "Slow down? Now?" She laughed in disbelief. "It's too late for that. I'm in love with you, Cade." She paused and the silence that followed was deafening.

She shook her head. "You can't say it, can you?" She felt as if her world had been turned upside down. "You obviously have feelings for me, but you can't say them. It's just you, me and Stella, and you can't say anything about what I mean to you."

He clenched his jaw and she could see he was wrestling with something inside him. But it looked as if she wasn't on the winning side.

Insidious, ugly doubt crept inside her. Her sister's words of warning played through her mind. Maybe Cade didn't really love her. Maybe he couldn't.

She bit her lip as her chest twisted so tightly it hurt. "I don't know what to say. You can stand up in front of hundreds of people and ask Laila to marry you, but you can't give me any words at all. None," she said and waited through another agonizing silence.

"I need to go," she said, feeling the pressure of tears build behind her eyes. She ran for the door. She stumbled down the steps and blindly climbed into her car. The first sob racked through her and she tried to keep another at bay as she started her car. If she could just get away from his house, off his property, away from him...

She barreled down the driveway, tears falling heedlessly down her cheeks. She swiped at them so she could see to turn onto the road. Abby felt as if her heart was being ripped from her chest. She couldn't remember hurting this much, feeling this much pain. Her throat ached from holding back her sobs. She pulled into a church parking lot and killed the engine of her little car and cried until she wore herself out with her grief.

Gutted from her emotional outburst, she knew this wouldn't be the last time she would cry. Putting her car into gear, she began to drive and hated that Laila's prediction had become true. Cade, her beautiful, wonderful, caring Cade, wasn't capable of giving his heart anymore. Abby had come into his life too late.

Instead of driving home, she found herself heading for Laila's apartment. She couldn't face her family. She really didn't want to face anyone right now, but she thought Laila might understand her feelings. Laila's heart had never been broken, but she'd seen Abby's broken heart coming from a mile away.

She closed her eyes and sighed. Was there any way she could have prevented this? It would have been the same as trying to prevent a blizzard. She debated going to Laila's apartment. Her sister might not even be there. Jackson could be there. Abby almost decided to drive away, but punched her sister's cell-phone number. One ring. Two rings. Three— Abby lifted her finger over the stop button.

"Hey, Abby, what's up?" Laila said.

"Are you busy?" Abby asked.

"No. I was going to meet Jackson for dinner, but he has a special conference call. You want to go somewhere for dinner?"

"I'm not very hungry," Abby said, cursing the waver in her voice.

"Abby, are you okay?" Laila asked, concern threading through her voice. "Where are you?"

"In your parking lot," Abby said, her voice caught between tears and laughter.

"Get your butt up here right now," Laila said. "Or I'll come out there and get you myself."

Her sister's scolding warmed her heart. "Okay. I'm coming, but it's not gonna be pretty."

She made her way to her sister's apartment, and Laila was holding the door open before Abby even arrived. Laila scooped Abby into her arms and ushered her into her apartment. "What happened, sweetie?"

Unable to bear the sweet worry in her sister's gaze, Abby looked down. "You were right," she said, the terrible knot growing in her throat again. "You were right. Cade can't love me," she said and began to sob again.

"Oh, Abby," Laila said and guided her to the sofa and just held her while she cried.

Abby finally felt her tears wane. "Sheesh," she said, taking a deep breath. "You would think I wouldn't have any more water left in me."

Laila gave a soft smile. "Let me fix you a cup of tea."

"I don't really like tea," Abby said.

"You will right now. I'll add a little honey and booze. Lean your head back on the sofa and take some deep breaths."

While Laila made her tea, Abby closed her eyes and felt as if the room were spinning. Laila gave her a cool, damp washcloth for her face then doctored her cup of tea and brought it to her.

"Wait a moment or two then just sip it," Laila said and pushed Abby's hair from her face. "I was so afraid of this happening. You never got involved in the games with guys. You weren't interested in stringing along a bunch of guys just for the fun of it. You were saving your heart for the real thing. I knew that when you decided to love someone, you would love with all your heart. When I first saw you and Cade getting involved, I thought it could be good for both of you. But the more I thought about it, the more I became afraid, because you're so emotional and Cade is not."

"But he is," Abby said. "That's the thing. He's very emotional. He's talked with me about losing his mom and Dominique."

Laila widened her eyes in surprise. "Whoa. Dominique? That surprises me. He was always a clam when it came to that subject."

"He is an emotional man," Abby said. "But I'm afraid you're right that he can't give his heart again." She felt the terrible sensation of tears backing up behind her eyes again and groaned. "Not again. I don't want to cry again."

"Sip your tea," Laila said.

Abby did as Laila instructed.

"And another," Laila said.

Abby took another sip. "This isn't bad."

"The honey and the booze help. Keep on sipping. I wish I could tell you that it's a magic drink and you'll never cry again, but I would be lying," Laila said. "You love too hard for it not to hurt a lot when it doesn't work out. But listen to me," Laila said, dipping her head to look straight into Abby's gaze. "You deserve a man who loves just as hard as you do and nothing less."

"I'm not sure such a man exists," Abby said hopelessly.

"You don't have to think about whether he exists or

not tonight. You just need to know that you deserve a man who can give you all his heart. Now, I'm going to call Jackson and tell him not to come over."

"Oh, no, I don't want to interrupt—"

"You're not interrupting. I can see Jackson tomorrow. You and I will drink spiked tea and watch something stupid on television." She gave Abby another hug. "I'm glad you came to me. It means a lot. Now let me put on some more tea."

Laila provided a much-needed diversion from Abby's misery, and after another cup of tea, Abby had no trouble falling asleep the second her head hit the pillow. When she awakened in the morning, though, her pain hit her first thing. Her impulse was to pull the covers over her head, but she knew she couldn't.

Forcing herself from bed, she took a shower and the water felt like a healing spray on her face and body. Afterward, she walked into the kitchen where Laila was fixing eggs and bacon. "There you are. Good morning, sunshine," she said.

"Yeah, sunshine. That's me," Abby said. "Impressive breakfast."

"Feel the love. You better eat it," she said spooning the food onto a plate. "Orange juice? Coffee? Oh, that's right. You don't drink coffee."

Surprised, Abby took a bite of bacon. "I'm surprised you knew I didn't like coffee," Abby said, sitting down at the kitchen table.

"Why wouldn't I?" Laila asked, joining her at the table. "You're my sister."

"I'm one of six. You can't know the preferences of all of us," she said.

"You'd be surprised. You may think no one notices you, but we're all proud of you. We know you make straight As. We talk about you behind your back and wonder if you're going to be the first one to get an advanced degree."

"I've got to get this one first," she said. "But it's nice to know you're rooting for me even if it's done in secret."

"Right. Now you're going to need a strategy so you don't burst into tears every other hour," Laila said. "You need to keep busy, but also take lots of naps."

"How do you know about this? You've never had a broken heart," Abby said.

"I've gotten close a couple times, but I've nursed a few friends through some terrible breakups. And," she said, putting her hand on Abby's arm, "I couldn't stand it if Jackson and I broke up now. The very thought of it makes my heart stop. It would be too terrible."

Abby nodded, the yawning sadness stretching inside her.

"But you don't have to do it alone. I want you to call me anytime. If you don't call me, I'll harass you. And remember, you have the Cates backbone," Laila said. "Now eat your breakfast. You need nourishment."

Abby left Laila's apartment and went home to change clothes. Thank goodness she had a busy day. She worked at the community center, gave her presentation for class, finished a paper and forced down a sandwich before she left for ROOTS. The girls were wired tonight because Thanksgiving was less than two weeks away. They sorted donated food into bags for families in need. By the end of the evening, all of them were pleased with how much they'd accomplished.

"You guys did great," Abby said. "Tell your parents what you did tonight, and if they could use a bag because growing teenagers eat food like they have holes in their legs, send them over. We're still collecting food."

"You'll be here next week, right?" Katrina asked.

"Absolutely. Wouldn't miss our before Thanksgiving get-together. But I have to tell you I've got a ton of work right now with my classes. So you won't get much sympathy from me if you're not staying on top of your schoolwork," Abby said.

There was a collective groan. "Whatever happened with that guy you liked? When we fixed your makeup and hair so you could get his attention?" Keisha asked.

Abby felt a sudden stab of pain and took a quick breath. "Didn't work out. I guess he wasn't the right one."

"Stupid guy," Keisha said. "You're the best."

"Thanks," Abby said. "I needed that."

Abby successfully made it home, made a cup of herbal tea with a heavy dose of honey and let it cool while she took a shower. She took a few sips and climbed under her bedcovers and cried herself to sleep.

Cade worked around the clock on Tuesday through Wednesday. Work was a solace. He felt as if he'd smashed a butterfly. Every time he closed his eyes, he saw Abby's hurt face. The devastation he'd seen in her gaze, heard in her voice, made him feel like the worst human being on the face of the earth. The truth was that he did have feelings for Abby. The truth was also that he couldn't give Abby what she needed. He'd known that from the beginning and it had only become more clear with each time he'd shared with her.

He never should have given in to his feelings for her, but she'd made him greedy for her passion and lightness. She'd made him want what he hadn't had in too long, maybe what he'd never had.

"Take a break," his father said. "We're all going to the community center to watch the kids do their little show."

"I'm not in the mood," Cade said.

"Well, get in the mood," his father said. "We have to be good examples. The director invited us, so we have to go. You look like hell. Brush your hair, wash your face. Do something to yourself, then come over. It won't last that long."

Cade washed his face, brushed his teeth and tried to avoid looking in the mirror. He had done what he was determined not to do. Hurt Abby.

Pulling on a jacket and putting a hat on his head, he walked over to the community center. It was a cold night and the scent of oncoming snow was heavy in the air. The merchants were mixing Thanksgiving and Christmas lights and decorations in anticipation of the holiday season. As usual, he felt no joy at the season.

Abby would, though. She would find a way to get him to smile, use something like that dang gobbling turkey still hanging in his kitchen or hold some mistletoe over his head.

He tried to shake off the thoughts as he stepped inside the community center to the sound of children singing. Standing in the back, he watched the kids perform their well-practiced show. One little pilgrim forgot his words and he heard Abby give a prompt. His gaze automatically flew in her direction.

The room was more dark than not, so he had to focus to find her, but he did, standing on one side in the front, encouraging the kids. She would be a great mother, he thought. Loving and fun-loving, she would make growing up an adventure, just as she would make marriage an adventure for the right man. She would find him, he knew. The knowledge brought a bitter taste to his mouth.

He stayed through the rest of the show, but left as soon as the audience applauded. He needed to get home. With his mind being tortured nonstop, he needed the escape that sleep could provide.

After arriving home, he turned on the TV to drown out the silence, then downed a peanut-butter sandwich and a glass of milk. The TV quickly annoyed him, so he turned it off. Stella watched him wander around from the den to the kitchen and back. Little bits of Abby mocked him. The turkey hanging in his kitchen, mistletoe she'd hung in three different doorways. It was more painful for him to look at that turkey than it was for him to look at Dominique's necklace.

Craving the need to escape his thoughts of her, he took a shower, praying it would wash thoughts of Abby from his head. He went to bed and tossed and turn then finally fell asleep.

Cade heard the collision and the crunch of metal and glanced behind him. What he saw filled him with horror. Abby's cute little VW was a twisted mess. A truck had ran into her little car just outside his driveway.

His heart pounding in his chest, he raced to help Abby. She had to be okay, he told himself. She had to be. He got to her car and saw her slumped in the seat, unconscious. A trickle of blood slid down the side of her cheek.

"Abby," he yelled at the top of his lungs as he beat on the VW's window. "Abby!"

The sound of his own voice awakened Cade. His body drenched in a cold sweat, he shook his head, still locked in the terrible nightmare where he couldn't get to Abby, where he couldn't help her.

Sucking in deep breaths of air, he blinked his eyes and turned on his bedside lamp. It had been a dream, he told himself. A dream. Still, he reached for his cell phone and his finger hovered over the speed dial for her phone number. He just wanted to hear her voice, to make sure she was okay. That was all he needed.

Reality finally began to penetrate his brain, and he

scolded himself. He needed to get control of his emotions. He was totally out of hand. He was going to have to work harder at reining in his feelings. When he'd let his heart get away from him in the past, it had always led to pain. This time was no different.

On Thanksgiving morning, Cade went to DJ's along with what seemed like everyone else in the community to pack up turkey and rib dinners for the less fortunate. He walked into the diner and nearly walked straight into Abby.

He reached out to steady her, but Abby put up her hands and stumbled backward as if she would do anything to keep him from touching her. The knowledge stabbed at him. "Hey," he said. "How are you doing?"

She bit her lip and didn't meet his gaze. "I'm okay. Busy as usual. Oh, look, there's Austin," she said, gesturing toward a familiar-looking young man.

Cade studied the guy for a few seconds and realized this was the young man who had taken Abby out that night she'd been dressed to thrill. He felt a twist of jealousy even though he knew he had no right.

Abby glanced at one of several sheets of paper she held in her hand. "Austin," she called. "Rose," she said to the Traubs' sister and waved them toward her. "Do you two mind riding together to deliver the dinners? We want to start making deliveries as soon as possible because they're all spread out." Abby paused a moment then gave a slight smile. "Oops, maybe you two haven't met."

"I can take care of that," Austin said and extended his hand. "Austin Anderson. I've seen you around, but was never lucky enough to meet you."

Rose smiled. "Rose Traub. I believe my brothers are better known than I am," she said wryly.

"I can't imagine why," Austin said. "They can't be nearly as pretty."

Rose glanced at Abby. "Thanks for putting me with someone who has a sense of humor. It will make the day go faster."

"Have fun," Abby said to both of them and gave them a sheet of paper. "Here are the names and addresses for your deliveries. Thanks so much for your help."

Cade forced himself to move away from her even though he wanted nothing more than to be close to her, even in this room full of other people. Spending the past week without her had been pure hell. But necessary, he told himself as he joined an assembly line putting together the food boxes. He loaded a box of ribs into each package of food.

The room was full of conversation and purposeful activity. He heard a few people chuckling and wondered when he would feel like laughing again.

Suddenly an unfamiliar young woman approached Zane Gunther, the country music star who had made Thunder Canyon his home and recently fallen in love. "Mr. Gunther, I'm Tania Tuller. Ashley was my sister."

The whole room turned quiet because everyone knew that Zane was fighting a lawsuit over a fan dying at one of his concerts. The tragedy had apparently forced Zane to reconsider his career in the fast lane. The poor guy had been horrified that such a thing could happen at one of his concerts.

"Mr. Gunther, if there's one thing I've learned from my sister's death, it's that none of us knows how long we have here to live our lives. That means we've got to go after our dreams and make the best out of the time we're given. Holding grudges is a waste of precious time. Ashley died going after her dream of seeing her hero. You were her hero," Tania said, her voice breaking.

Zane stepped toward Tania and put his arm around her to support her. Tania leaned against him. "My parents' lawsuit is an idea. Ashley would be horrified by it. Your music was the light of her life. I'm going to try my best to talk my parents out of this lawsuit, and I really believe I can."

Murmurs spread throughout the room like wildfire. Cade watched Zane speak quietly with Tania, but he found Tania's words sticking him like needles. Almost everything she said could have been directed at him. Life is short. He might not be holding on to a grudge, but holding on to fear was just as bad or worse.

He looked at Abby, who was struggling to put on a brave face, but he could tell she was miserable, and he was the cause of it. An overwhelming wave of realization swept over him. Abby was the woman of his dreams. She made him feel as if anything were possible. Being with her gave him the deepest sense of peace and happiness he'd ever dreamed possible.

Hard facts slammed into him. Fear had been holding him back. Fear might be why he wasted so many years dating Laila. Deep down, he knew that spending time with her was safe. He was so scared he would lose Abby that he was pushing her away before he could get hurt. Cade couldn't wait one more minute to talk to her.

Striding across the room, he stood directly in front of her and looked into her sad brown eyes and wanted to kick himself. "I've been a fool," he said. "You've misunderstood my reaction to you and I've been fighting my feelings like a bull in a china shop. I love you so much it freaks me out."

Abby blinked in surprise. "What?"

"Yeah, and I think deep down you suspected it. When I wanted to back off, I confused you. I'm so sorry for that," he said, shaking his head. "I love you so much that the thought of losing you scares me to death."

"But you didn't lose me. You pushed me away."

"I didn't lose you, but I've lost others. What I feel for you is stronger than anything I've ever known before. What if I lost you, too?" he asked, the sound of his voice gruff to his own ears.

"Oh, Cade," she said, stepping into his arms. "I wish you had talked about this with me before. I never want you to suffer like this. Never."

The sensation of her body against his was so sweet he had to catch his breath. "I've been a total hard-headed fool. You're everything I've ever wanted. I just hope you can forgive me."

She bit her lip as if she wasn't sure she could trust

him. That possibility tore at him and he was determined to regain her confidence in him.

"You know that people will talk about us. Are you sure that's not going to bother you? Are you sure you're not going to change your mind?"

"Not in a million years," he said. "Let them talk. The most important thing in the world to me is you."

Cade wasn't given to wild impulses, but Abby brought out all kinds of surprising things inside him. He climbed on top of a table. "Listen, everybody. I love Abby Cates."

A heartbeat of silence passed before the room exploded with applause. Cade jumped off the table and pulled Abby back into his arms. Her face was full of shock and happiness. "Cade?" she said in surprise.

"Better get used to it, Abby. This is the effect you have on me," he said and took her mouth in a kiss for all the world to see.

Epilogue

Abby experienced the most thankful Thanksgiving day in her history. Every time she thought about Cade standing up on that table in DJ's to profess his love for her in front of everyone, she pinched herself to believe it was true. Of course, it helped that everyone in Thunder Canyon wanted to replay the scene with her over and over. Old man Henson chuckled over it every time she saw him, and the servers at the diner thought it was the most romantic thing they'd ever heard. Even her ROOTS girls wanted to hear the story over and over like a fairy tale from when they were little girls.

Her parents had always loved Cade, so they were thrilled, and Laila was pleasantly surprised to hear that Cade had stepped up the way he should. After Thanksgiving, the days passed with the speed of light and suddenly it was time for the Cateses' double wedding.

Cade was taking her to the wedding, of course. They'd spent every possible moment with each other, and both freely admitted, every possible moment just wasn't enough. Abby followed in her mother's footsteps by putting Christmas decoration in every room of Cade's house, including the bathroom. At first Cade had thought it was ridiculous, but she'd heard him humming the Christmas song from a music box she'd placed in his bedroom on more than one occasion.

Although her friend Austin Anderson had originally planned to escort her, he'd graciously bowed out and Abby had heard he was taking Rose Traub.

Abby wore a navy velvet dress in honor of the holiday season, curled her hair and applied her makeup with care. This was the event of the season but, more importantly, she wanted to impress Cade. She wondered if there would ever be a time when she didn't want to impress him and just couldn't imagine it. At the same time, though, Cade made her feel as if she were the most beautiful woman in the world even if it was the end of the day and she knew she looked as tired as she felt.

"Abby!" her father called. "Cade's here."

Abby grabbed her coat and walked into the living room where Cade stood in a dark suit that set off his light hair and blue eyes. All she could do was stare.

"You look amazing," he said.

She laughed breathlessly. "I was just thinking the same thing about you."

"All right, you lovebirds, get on your way. I'm going to have to push my wife out the door soon. Never seen so much primping in my life," her father said. He'd been ready for a half hour.

"What do you expect, Daddy? It's a double wedding in a ballroom. We all want to look our best," Abby said and pressed a kiss on her father's cheek. "We'll see you there."

Cade led her to his SUV and helped her into the car. They talked during the entire ride about how they'd spent their morning. Soon enough, they arrived at the wedding. A line of guests formed, waiting to be seated for the ceremony of two of Thunder Canyon's most beloved couples. Abby could feel the excitement and anticipation in the air.

"Oh, look," she said. "There's Zane Gunther with Jeannette. She looks so pretty."

"Did you hear that the Tullers dropped their lawsuit against Zane?" he asked.

"No," she said. "That's wonderful news."

Cade nodded. "He's started a special foundation in Ashley's honor and he's naming it The Ashley Tuller Foundation."

"He's a good guy. It's amazing how fast he and Jeannette got together. They're already engaged."

"When it's right," Cade said, looking into her gaze, "you know it. And there's no need to waste time."

Her stomach dipped and she squeezed his hand. She stood on tiptoe and whispered in his ear. "I love you more than anything, Cade Pritchett."

He snuck a quick kiss and sighed. "This may be bad timing, but—"

"What?" she asked, confused by the nervous expression on his face.

"Come here," he said, pulling her away from the crowd. He led her to a quiet, private place on the other side of the building. The wind fluttered through his hair, making her want to touch it.

"I had wanted to wait to give this to you for Christmas, but I can't. Everything is right with you. You make me feel more complete, more at peace, more happy than I have in my entire life. I don't want to wait another minute without taking the next step," he said.

Her heart beating like a helicopter's propeller, she stared at him. "What are you talking about?"

Abby watched as Cade knelt down one knee and pulled a small velvet box from his pocket. He opened it and lifted it for her to see a beautiful diamond ring. Abby gasped at the sight of it, but she couldn't keep her eyes off of Cade. Was this really happening? She was certain she was having an out-of-body experience.

"Abby, I love you with all my heart and soul. You are my true soul mate. There is nothing that would make me happier than to spend the rest of my life with you. Will you marry me?"

Abby's hands began to shake. She couldn't believe this was happening. Yes, she'd had a crush on Cade for as long as she could remember, but her crush had grown into a woman's love. Knowing that he wanted her to be his was so powerful she nearly couldn't comprehend it. "Could you repeat that last bit?" she managed in a husky whisper.

Cade stood and pulled her into his arms. "I love you, darlin'. Say you'll be mine forever."

With his arms around her, the reality set in. Cade Pritchett had just asked Abby Cates to marry him. "Yes," she said. "Yes, I will."

Cade placed the ring on her finger and sealed their promise with a kiss that sent Abby around the world. She knew she and Cade had found the love of a lifetime, and they would always cherish each other.

* * * * *

"Yeah, Red. I want you, too."

Austin took a strand of her hair and rubbed it between his fingers. "Pretty much from the moment we met, I knew we were heading in this direction."

"You did?" Heart pounding, Rose stared up at him, the flames in the hearth highlighting the intensity on his face. His brown eyes went almost black. "Even though I refused to go out with you?"

His mouth turned up at the corners. "I knew it would be all the sweeter. What comes too easily isn't cherished as much as what we have to work for."

"And why did you persevere?"

"Because I couldn't not pursue you." He cupped her cheek in his hand. "I couldn't walk away from you. I couldn't stop wanting you."

HER MONTANA
CHRISTMAS
GROOM

BY
TERESA SOUTHWICK

First published in Great Britain 2013
by Mills & Boon, an imprint of Harlequin (UK) Limited,
Eton House, 18-24 Paradise Road, Richmond, Surrey TW9 1SR

© Harlequin Books S.A. 2011

Special thanks and acknowledgement to Teresa Southwick for her contribution to the Montana Mavericks: The Texans are Coming! continuity.

ISBN: 978 0 263 90149 8
ebook ISBN: 978 1 472 00540 3

23-1013

Harlequin (UK) policy is to use papers that are natural, renewable and recyclable products and made from wood grown in sustainable forests. The logging and manufacturing processes conform to the legal environmental regulations of the country of origin.

Printed and bound in Spain
by Blackprint CPI, Barcelona

Teresa Southwick lives with her husband in Las Vegas, the city that reinvents itself every day. An avid fan of romance novels, she is delighted to be living out her dream of writing for Mills & Boon.

Special thanks to Susan Litman
for her support and guidance through the fictional
world of Thunder Canyon, Montana

Chapter One

Rose Traub hadn't wanted to get naked with a man since moving to Thunder Canyon, Montana. That was kind of a problem if you wanted to get married, and she wanted it bad.

"Rose?"

Austin Anderson's deep voice scraped over her nerve endings and snapped her out of it. "Hmm?"

"You okay?"

"Of course." She looked over at him, sitting in the driver's seat of the old truck. The two of them had just finished delivering Thanksgiving dinners to the town's invalids and people a little down on their luck this year. They'd left with the meals from DJ's Rib Shack and Austin had brought her back to pick up her car. "Why would you think I'm not fine?"

"You got quiet. I was afraid tryptophan fumes from all

those turkey dinners put you to sleep. That's easier to be-lieve than…"

"What?" she asked.

"That I bored you into a coma."

She laughed and shook her head. "You're great com-pany, Austin, and you know it. Now you're just fishing for compliments."

"Busted." Lights in the empty parking lot illuminated the interior of the truck and his grin was clearly visible. "So you're not sorry about being stuck as my partner today?"

"Nope. It was fun."

He nodded. "Any regrets about moving to Thunder Canyon?"

"Nope."

She was only sorry Austin didn't fit her male fantasy profile because he was, by far, the most interesting guy she'd met. He was also very cute, in a Ryan Reynolds, sex-iest-man-alive sort of way. If only… But wishing for what could never be was a waste of time and that was something she didn't have.

"Any regrets?" she mused.

Glancing out the truck window at mounds of white that had been plowed to the sides of the lot, she remembered the first snowstorm several days ago. It was beautiful but cold. Shivering, she pulled her knit hat more securely over her ears. "I'm not in Texas anymore. Living in the cold and snow is very different from reading about the seasonal range of temperatures online."

"You get used to it," he assured her. "Take it from me, snow is a lot better when you're inside with a big fire going."

"I've got a fireplace in my apartment. I'll have to learn how to use it," she said.

"I've lived here my whole life, except for going away

to college. That translates to lots of experience. So if you need any help with that fire, you know who to call."

Was he suggesting something? Her heart skipped a beat, which was just plain stupid, and to read something romantic between the lines, more than a little pathetic. It was an involuntary reaction that smacked of desperation.

"I guess snow is the price one pays for living in the Montana mountains and I do love them. Thanks for showing me the ropes today, Austin." She started to reach for the door handle. "I should probably go—"

"How's the new job?" he asked.

She looked back at him, grateful for the excuse to stay a little longer. "It's good. Working for the mayor is great. Bo Clifton is enthusiastic and energetic. I almost feel guilty taking a paycheck for doing publicity and communications for his office because he makes it so much fun." She met his gaze. "Just between you and me, this is the first job I've had that wasn't for my family. Don't get me wrong, I learned a lot at Traub Oil, but it feels good to know I have actual marketable skills and my family wasn't just feeling sorry for me."

"No, now I have a job with your family's company and they feel sorry for *me*." He laughed. "Seriously, working for Traub Oil Montana is a terrific career opportunity. I'm grateful to your brother Ethan for taking a chance on me."

"He's the lucky one. To find a hometown boy with an engineering background, a doctoral student researching green energy alternatives…" The complexity of what he did boggled her mind. According to Ethan, he was brilliant, innovative and passionate about this new technology. Not just a pretty face, she thought. "Ethan is really excited about the possibilities."

"That makes two of us."

Was she imagining that his gaze lowered to her mouth

when he said that? Probably. Desperation did strange things to a woman.

"I'm glad things are going well with my brother because he can be focused, intense and demanding."

Austin's expression was ironic. "You just described practically every guy I know."

"Me, too," she said, laughing. "And I know a lot of guys, what with having five brothers."

"Lucky you," he said with mock envy. "I've got two sisters."

Rose had met the younger one, Angie, earlier at DJ's Rib Shack as the holiday volunteers had split into teams. Rose had already been assigned to ride along with Austin, a newbie learning the ropes from someone more experienced. Her attraction to him had been instantaneous, and she'd asked his sister a few questions. She almost wished she hadn't, but it was probably better to know up front that it wouldn't work. Still, the disappointment had not made her things-to-be-grateful-for-on-Thanksgiving list.

"Seriously, though, Ethan is a great boss. And I owe him for giving me a start." He rested his wrist on the truck's steering wheel. "We're definitely on the same page. Protecting Thunder Canyon and the environment is important to both of us."

She nodded. "I haven't lived here long, but I can certainly understand that this is a special place. Part of what drew me is that the town takes care of its own. I'm grateful to be a part of it."

"Remember that at dinner when everyone has to say what they're thankful for."

She laughed. "Does your family really do that?"

"Oh, yeah. It's tradition." His dark eyes were warm with humor. "Are you cooking or going somewhere for dinner?"

"I'm not cooking for which my family is thankful," she

answered. "Ethan and Liz invited me to have dinner with them. What about you?"

"As far as cooking, I could *engineer* the heck out of trussing a turkey, but I'm not sure it would be fit to eat. It's going to be a quiet dinner, just me, Angie and Haley. But we're having dessert with the Cates clan because she and Marlon can't bear to be separated for too long. The two of them decided to have this one last holiday with their families. A quiet one because the wedding is day after tomorrow."

"I can understand that."

"Why?"

"Duh. It's a double wedding." Marlon Cates was marrying Haley Anderson and his twin, Matt, was marrying Elise Clifton. By all accounts it would be a fabulous affair. "I hear it's going to be the Thunder Canyon social event of the year. By the way, you'll look great in the family pictures."

Was it okay to say that? He'd never be her boyfriend, so it wasn't flirting. Just the truth.

"You think so?"

"Yes. And you're fishing for compliments again."

"Busted again. You'll be there, right?" he asked.

"Yes. Elise is the mayor's cousin and he asked me to take notes for the press release from his office."

"Just part of your job?" he asked.

"That and the Traubs have been friends with the Cates family for years." She shrugged.

Austin studied her intently and there were questions in his eyes. "Double wedding. Social event of the year. Yet you don't sound excited about it."

"It should be great." She hoped he didn't see through the phony enthusiasm. "Are you looking forward to it?"

"Wearing a tux? Smiling until my face hurts? Being nice to everyone?" He shrugged. "Should be fun."

"Now who doesn't sound excited?"

"Who's your lucky date?" he asked.

The question didn't surprise Rose. She had gone out with more than a few guys here in town and earned a reputation as a "dating diva" which made her all the more pathetic for going solo to the wedding. But she couldn't tell a lie. Even if she was tempted, he'd know when she showed up alone.

"I'm not going with anyone."

"Then I'll take you."

Oh, God, he felt sorry for her. It was a pity invitation, but seriously nice of him. And that was such a problem. She'd seen him in action today and liked what she saw. He was funny, not scary-looking but scary-smart, and she'd spent a lot of time wondering if he was a good kisser. She could tick off at least five of her man-must-haves. Ironically it was number six on the list that was a problem. It was the same number that took him out of consideration. His sister Angie had told her how old he was and that made him six years younger than she was.

She'd always dated men at least five years older. It was the perfect age difference and part of her fantasy since she'd been a four-year-old flower girl at her first wedding. Going out with Austin wouldn't put her in cougar territory, but definitely within growling distance as far as she was concerned. And that was unacceptable.

"I'm sorry," she said, truly meaning that. "But I really can't go with you."

Austin was pretty sure that was regret in her big blue eyes. Rose. A beautiful, sweet name for a beautiful, sweet girl. Her hair was just dark enough to call auburn, but in the sun it was red. The freckles on her turned-up nose were extremely cute which was a contradiction to her voice. It was grit and gravel and gumption that scraped across his nerve endings in the best possible way. She was an intriguing combination of fire and ice that made him want to know her better.

"Why?" he asked.

"Why what?"

"Can't you go with me?"

"Because I'm too old for you."

Austin stared at her and figured if she hated his guts and would rather take a sharp stick in the eye than go out with him she could have come up with a better lie than that. He'd been lied to before, a betrayal so personal it left a mark that would never go away.

"How do you know how old I am, Red?" he asked.

"Someone mentioned it in the context of how much you'd accomplished for a guy your age."

"So, what are you? Twenty-five? Twenty-six?"

Her full mouth pulled tight before she answered. "Just turned thirty."

She looked like a college kid with her blue knit cap pulled low on her forehead and long, silky strands of red hair spilling over her puffy jacket.

"No way," he said.

"Unfortunately it's the honest-to-God truth."

"Why unfortunate?"

"Because I thought I'd be married and a mother by now." She sighed, a sound full of frustration and disappointment. "Back in Texas I knew a lot of women who wanted to get married but couldn't find a guy. Men have it so much easier. They can snap their fingers and have women coming out of the woodwork."

Austin disagreed. Not every girl was dying to get married and he'd showed the poor judgment to pick one of those. After that, getting serious was the last thing he wanted, although he was all in favor of having fun. He liked women. He liked Rose. Giving back through volunteering was something he did, but hadn't expected it to be so much fun. He'd actually had a great time today. And he wanted a second helping.

"Go with me," he urged. "What have you got to lose?"

"The title of cougar for one thing."

"It's not that big an age difference."

"It is to me."

"So you'd rather go alone?"

"Yes." But there was no conviction in her voice.

He wanted to see Rose again because she was fun and the wedding would be more interesting if he could hang with her. But there was a stubborn set to the mouth he'd spent the better part of the day resisting the urge to kiss. He had to come up with a strategy to change her mind.

Life had thrown him some big curves, personal and financial. In spite of it all, he'd gone to college and become an engineer. He was really into taking things apart to figure out how they worked. Or building something new that had never existed before. There must be a way to use his skills.

Rose was in public relations for the mayor's office. Spin was her business. She'd said straight out that she was looking for a guy, so that's where he'd start.

Behind the steering wheel he angled his upper body toward her. "It's easier to find a man when you're with one."

"What?"

"Think about it. They say it's easier to find a job when you have one." That hadn't sounded as lame in his head. "If you're alone at the wedding, a girl as pretty as you, the available guys there are going to wonder what's wrong."

"You mean like dandruff, halitosis or snorting when I laugh?"

"Yeah." He frowned. This wasn't going quite as he'd hoped. "Sort of."

"Look, Austin—"

"Hear me out." He held up a hand to stop her words. "If you're seen with me, you get the Thunder Canyon seal of approval and *men* will come out of the woodwork."

One corner of her mouth quirked up. "So that's been my problem since moving here this summer? The great and powerful Austin Anderson hasn't anointed my social life with his presence?"

"Well said." He tried to be serious but couldn't help laughing. "Seriously, tell me you didn't have fun today."

"I didn't have fun today," she said automatically.

"You're lying."

"Yes, to save you from yourself. It's very sweet of you to ask me. Really. And I do appreciate the offer, but… No."

"I don't accept that."

"You have to."

"That's where you're wrong."

"What part of no don't you understand?" she demanded.

"Pretty much all of it. Never have." Losing his mother when he was sixteen had made him want to give up and he had for a while. But folks in Thunder Canyon hadn't given up on him and made him see that if a door closed you went around it. One foot in front of the other to get what you want. "If I did, I wouldn't be an engineer at all, let alone doing a doctorate program in green energy or working for Traub Oil Montana." He took a breath and met her gaze. "Therefore, I have an alternate suggestion."

"And that would be?"

"You're looking for a serious relationship, but I don't meet your criteria. I'm only looking to have fun—at my sister's wedding. Nothing permanent. You told me I was great company today. Did you mean it?"

"Of course, or I wouldn't have said it."

"Then it's official. As my Thanksgiving volunteer partner you passed the Austin Anderson friendship test with flying colors. There's no reason we can't attend the Thunder Canyon social event of the year in that capacity."

"Friends?"

"Yeah." And if it turned into friends with benefits, who was he to complain?

"You're serious?"

"Completely."

"We did have fun today. And I don't want to go alone." There was determination in her eyes even as the doubts refused to dissolve. "But if even one person makes a crack about robbing the cradle…"

"You'll just have to whip out your ID and prove you're at least twenty-one so no one thinks I'm perving on you."

"Oh, please—" But she laughed, then pointed at him. "Okay, I'll go with you, but only as friends. No strings attached."

He wouldn't have it any other way.

Rose walked into the three-story lobby of the Thunder Canyon Resort on the arm of Austin Anderson. People looked at them, but no one pointed and laughed, which was a relief. Still, when he'd taken her hand and slipped it into the bend of his elbow, it felt more than friendly. She'd opened her mouth to call him on it, but his disarming grin had taken all the bite out of her protest.

This was like dieting with a box of doughnuts in her hand. One touch and all her willpower went out the window.

"Wow," he said. "Look at this place."

When she did, her breath caught. She'd been to the resort a few times, but this evening it was transformed into a romantic holiday wedding scene. Two groups of chairs with a white runner separating them were set up on the gleaming inlaid floor and facing the huge stone fireplace. The mantel was draped with lighted green garland and trimmed with red bows. Individual poinsettia plants were arranged in the shape of a tree on either side of a raised dais. Hanging crystals reflected firelight, candles and small twinkling white lights.

Rose stared in wonder. "Just breathtaking."

"I know what you mean."

There was a huskiness in Austin's voice that made Rose look up at him. He was staring at her and the gleam in his eyes made her heart skip.

"I was talking about the decorations," she clarified.

"I wasn't."

In that instant two days of fretting over an appropriate outfit dissolved as it passed a test she hadn't realized existed. She'd chosen a long-sleeved black dress with velvet sleeves and bodice and a full skirt fashioned from lace. Her peep-toed pumps were velvet, too. Then there was the problem of what to do with her hair. It was a cold, damp evening which made the priority all about control.

She'd done a soft side part, then pulled it sleekly back from her face and tucked the mass into a knot behind her right ear. The way Austin was looking at her, a hairstyle would be all she had any chance of controlling.

People were moving past them and the room was quickly filling up.

"I better go sit down." The words came out a sort of husky whisper that she hoped he didn't notice.

"Right."

They moved to the chairs and Rose was about to take one in the back row.

"Not here." Austin walked around the outside formation

as the aisle was blocked off for the ceremony. He led her to the front row on the bride's side.

"But this is reserved for family," she protested.

"I'm family and you're my— You're with me." He winked, then glanced at his watch. "I have to go do a thing. The wedding planner has us on a tight schedule."

"What happens if you're late?"

"I don't want to find out." He shuddered, then touched her arm. "I'll be back in a little while. Don't run away."

Rose nodded, sat and blew out a breath. Her face was hot, but that had nothing to do with the flames snapping and popping in the fireplace and everything to do with Austin.

She should have turned down his invitation, but he'd caught her in a weak moment, when she was feeling sorry for herself about attending this high-profile event all alone after being a high-profile dater since relocating here. It would be a lie to say that she wasn't really glad he'd walked her in, but everyone was bound to talk. No doubt tomorrow it would be all over town that she was officially desperate enough to poach from a younger dating pool.

So be it. The damage was done, but there wouldn't be more fuel for the fire because she and Austin weren't an item. This was a one-shot deal. Just friends.

In the row of chairs just behind her people took their places. Then someone touched her shoulder and she turned. Her brothers Ethan and Corey bookended Liz Landry, Ethan's fiancée. All three smiled at her.

"Hey, little sister." Ethan took Liz's hand and linked his fingers with hers.

"You look beautiful, Rose," Liz said. "I love your dress."

Corey leaned forward and said, "How did you score the best seat in the house?"

It really wasn't. She was several seats from the aisle

where the brides would pass. Those empty chairs were probably reserved for family. She was just a... What did she call herself? Not a date.

"My *friend* Austin, brother of the bride, asked me to go with him. He sat me here."

Rose could see that all of them had questions, but a quartet started to play chamber music and she was saved by the strings. The sweet notes of the musical instruments soothed her nerves. Not that it mattered. This event was about two brides and two grooms who'd found true love and soon would pledge their lives to each other. She truly envied them.

When Frank and Edie Cates, parents of the twin grooms, took their seats on the opposite side, it was clear that the time line was progressing. A few minutes later, Betty and Jack Castro came down the aisle. They were Elise's biological parents but hadn't raised her. Last year she'd learned that she and Erin Castro were switched at birth and taken home by the wrong families. It had been a shock to both women, one that Rose couldn't imagine. But Rose's brother Corey had helped Erin come to terms with the past and now they were happily married.

Next down the aisle was Helen Clifton who'd raised Elise, the woman she would always call "Mom." Once the parents were in place the pace picked up. The music stopped and a gray-haired man stepped to the middle of the dais with a Bible in his hands. A clue that he'd be administering the vows. Then the twin grooms appeared beside him with their best men, Marshall and Mitchell Cates. The unmistakable dark hair, eyes and similar features marked them all as brothers.

The minister said, "If you'll all please rise."

The guests did as asked and the musicians played a processional. First down the aisle was Erin Castro Traub. Rose stole a look at her brother Corey who was smiling proudly at his wife, the love of his life. Next was maid of honor Angie Anderson, stunning in a simple red silk strapless dress and carrying a bouquet of white orchids.

When the two attendants were in place, the traditional wedding music cued Elise Clifton. She came down the aisle on the arm of her brother, Grant. Her long dark blond hair was a cascade of curls held in place by a diamond head band. She looked like a Greek goddess in a one-shouldered satin beaded gown. Matt beamed at his bride, eagerly taking her hand.

It was time for bride number two and Rose looked back just in time to see Haley kiss Austin's lean cheek, then put her hand in the bend of his elbow. She looked like a princess in her strapless, full-skirted organza gown. Her floor-length veil flowed from a diamond tiara that held her upswept brown hair in place. Rose glanced at Marlon Cates who couldn't take his eyes off the woman who would shortly be his wife.

As he placed his sister's hand into her groom's, Austin said, "She's always taken care of Angie and me. Now my sister finally has someone to take care of her. Don't let her down, Marlon."

"Never."

Rose felt a double dose of emotion lump in her throat and not only because it was a doubly happy moment. A wave of sorrow washed over her. Neither bride's father was there and Rose didn't know why. She only knew that someday when she got married, her father wouldn't be there, either. No giving her away. No father-daughter dance. Charles Traub had died when she was only two and she had no memory of him. Her brothers had always talked about him as if he walked on water and she envied their recollections. She was sad for what was lost to her, for once-in-a-lifetime memories that could never be made.

And then Austin was standing beside her. He leaned down to whisper, "My work here is done."

Suddenly there was no room in her head for anything but him. He was movie-star handsome. He smelled good and cleaned up pretty nice. But did any man look like a toad in a traditional black tux? She thought not.

Still, a wicked grin and a nice suit didn't make her any less too old for him. The magic of the wedding venue with lights, flowers and brides in beautiful dresses couldn't erase the difference in their ages. More memories that could never be made. She forced herself to focus on the now, details swirling in her head for the mayor's press release.

The ceremony moved quickly in spite of double vows and rings, but there was twice the applause and cheers when the twins kissed their new wives. Rose was sure the four of them were relieved. In their shoes she would be. But when this part of the evening was over, she would have the reception to worry about.

It was being held in the Gallatin Room, the fine-dining restaurant at the resort. She would breathe easier when it was okay to mingle on her own. That didn't mean she wasn't grateful to Austin for walking her in, but the less time they spent together the better. No point in needlessly firing up Thunder Canyon gossip.

But after the two newly married couples led the recessional down the aisle, Austin grabbed her hand before she could strike out on her own.

"The formal part is over, now it's time to have some fun. Stick with me and I'll show you a good time."

That's just what Rose was afraid of.

Chapter Two

Austin nodded to his boss, Ethan Traub, as he led Rose back the way he'd come from walking his sister to her groom. He envied Haley. Marlon was a great guy and the two were deeply in love. Now they had their whole lives ahead of them. It was everything Austin had once badly wanted.

The Andersons had been a traditional family before his father walked out. Austin still remembered being a little boy and blaming himself because he'd done something bad. His mom made him see it wasn't his fault and they moved on. Then she died and Haley took over, missing out on her chance to go away to college. There was nothing conventional about that, but his sister did a great job with all the responsibility.

Still, he had vivid memories of that short time when he'd had a father and mother. And he'd wanted to have a family of his own, but the dream died when Rachel ran out on him. Now he just wanted to have fun.

With Rose.

Her hand was tucked in the bend of his elbow and he put his fingers over hers, then glanced down. She was eyeing the people filling the chairs they passed as if they were going to accuse her of something bad. Rose didn't know it yet, but he was the one with increasingly *dis*honorable intentions. Did she really not know how badly he wanted to kiss her?

She was so beautiful. The other day he hadn't noticed the dimples in her cheeks when she smiled. Or the way her eyes turned down slightly and crinkled at the corners when she laughed. Don't even get him started on the way she filled out her dress. The velvet bodice clung to her curves and the lacy skirt was all sugar and spice and everything nice, equal parts sweet and sultry.

But she was hung up on the age difference. While he appreciated her honesty, to him it was just a number and numbers held no mystery. She, on the other hand, was a puzzle he couldn't wait to solve.

He bent down and whispered in her ear, "Have I told you how beautiful you are tonight?"

The look she gave him was sassy, saucy and sexy. "Are you taking that line out for a spin to see how well it works?"

"Actually, no. I've used it often without a microgram of sincerity. But this time I really mean it."

"So you're not practicing on me hoping to reap the benefits of my vast experience?"

"For a mature woman," he teased, "your manners could use some fine-tuning. It's customary when a man pays you an honest compliment to simply say thank you."

"Thank you," she repeated automatically.

They stopped in the crowd of people who were filling the open lobby area. "A reciprocal compliment would be nice, too."

She looked him up and down, then moved around him to, presumably, inspect the rear view. Completing the circle, she said, "You'll do."

"Wow." He whistled. "Praise like that could turn a guy's head."

"Oh, please. Excluding my brothers, there might be one, maybe two men in this room better looking than you. I can't believe your ego needs massaging."

"It's just fine, thanks." He put his arm around her waist and drew her to a protected corner as the guests waited to file into the dining room for the reception. It was with great reluctance that he removed his hand. "I'm surprised at you. With five older brothers you should recognize teasing when you see it."

Her expression turned thoughtful. "Did you tease your sisters?"

"Still do. Every chance I get."

"And yet you were on your best behavior when you walked Haley down the aisle."

He could see the question in her eyes, why him and not Haley's father. But Rose was too polite to ask. "My father abandoned the family when we were kids. Haven't seen him since."

"Oh."

Austin saw the sparkle in her eyes fade to sadness and wished he could take back the words. Maybe put the sass back in her smile. "Sorry, didn't mean to be a downer."

"You're not." She glanced past him. "Looks like they're letting people in to the reception. I think I'll get in line, too."

When she started to walk past him, Austin put a hand on her arm. "Not so fast. Are you trying to ditch me?"

"Because we're here as friends with no strings attached, 'ditch' seems harsh. I thought I'd just mosey on in and watch single guys swarm around now that I have the Austin Anderson stamp of approval and they don't need to be afraid."

He'd set those parameters. It seemed the only way he could get her to go with him. But the idea of a bunch of guys hitting on her made him want to put his fist through a wall.

"Tell you what," he said. "There's a receiving line. We'll say hello to the bride and groom and the bride and groom and then I'll buy you a drink."

"Done. Except I'll buy my own."

"It's an open bar."

"Big spender," she teased.

Austin rested his hand at the small of her back, urging her to the end of the line. It didn't take long to reach the couples of the hour standing just outside the double doors leading into the Gallatin Room.

Rose hugged Matt Cates, then his new bride. "Congratulations. You look stunning."

"Thanks," Matt answered.

Elise smiled radiantly. "She meant me, although you do look fairly spectacular, husband."

Austin had been a couple years behind the twins in school, but they all knew each other well. He shook hands, then hugged Matt's wife. "I suppose it's too late to talk you into running away with me?"

"Sorry." The pretty blonde shrugged. "It was too late a long time ago."

"If you change your mind…"

"Not a chance," she said.

Rose moved on and gave Marlon a hug. "Congrats. I wish you every happiness."

"Thanks, Rose. Hey, Austin— Or should I say 'bro'?"

"I answer to either." And he truly meant that. The connection was legal now, but he felt as if he did have a brother. He met his sister's gaze and didn't miss the spark of interest in his "date." "Haley, have you met Rose Traub?"

"No." The two women shook hands. "Marlon and I have been traveling and planning the wedding. But I heard you moved here from Texas."

"Yes." Rose smiled. "When I was here for my brother Corey's wedding I fell in love with Thunder Canyon."

"Who wouldn't," Haley said. "But I don't understand what you're doing here with my brother."

"What?" Rose looked like a kid who just got caught cheating on a test. "Why?"

"Because he's an obnoxious jerk." Haley gave him a teasing smile. "But I love him anyway."

"Back at you, Hay." Clearly his sister was joking, but Rose had gone directly to the bad place and he wasn't sure how to get her out of it. He slid his arm around her waist. "Lets go find our table."

"With any luck it's in a dark corner behind a plant."

"You're overly sensitive. It's not that much of a difference. You just had a birthday." He decided it was best not to put a finer point on it with numbers. "And in two months I'll be a year older. See? We're practically the same age."

"Nice try. With hinky math like that it's a wonder you got into an engineering program at all." She shot him a rueful look.

Austin followed Rose, mesmerized by the sway of that feminine skirt. There were white cloth-covered tables three deep lining the perimeter of the room with the center open for dancing. Poinsettias in red and white with candles on either side made up the centerpieces. In the far corner, wedding gifts were piled up and there were two bars set up on either side of the room. Austin guided her straight to the closest one.

"I'd like a glass of chardonnay," she said.

The bartender, in crisp white shirt, red tie and black pants, had dark hair shot with gray. "May I see your ID?"

"What?" she asked.

"Identification," he repeated. "It's illegal for me to serve alcohol to anyone under twenty-one."

"I'm way over that," she assured him.

"Okay, but I need to see some proof of that." His tone was polite and professional.

"You're kidding, right?"

"No." He didn't budge.

"He's a friend of yours," she said to Austin, suspicion lurking in her eyes. "You put him up to this. It's a practical joke."

"I've never met him before," he assured her, giving the guy a what-are-you-going-to-do shrug.

She blew out a breath, then opened her tiny beaded black evening bag, pulled out her driver's license and handed it over.

The bartender checked the date and looked surprised. "Wow, I'm usually not that wrong."

"And I haven't worked that hard for an alcoholic beverage since... Actually ever."

"Did you even try to get a drink before you were old enough?" Austin asked.

"No."

"Good thing."

"Why?"

"Because you've probably always looked about twelve."

"Thanks, I think." She took a sip of the pale gold liquid.

"What'll you have?" the bartender asked him.

"Beer. Bottle is fine."

"Coming right up."

"Hey," she said to the bartender. "How come you didn't ask him for ID?"

The guy grinned. "Because I can tell by looking that he's legal."

Austin saluted a thanks with his bottle and they walked across the open dance floor to find their table. Rose was frowning and clearly in a snit.

"What's bugging you, Red?" he asked.

"Like you don't know," she grumbled.

"I've always looked older." He shrugged. "It's why I was able to get a tattoo when I was under age."

"No way."

"Yeah." He took a sip of his beer. "It's a beaut, too."

"Where is it? Show me."

"That would require undressing—"

She slid him a wry look and shook her head.

Too bad. He would very much like to undress her and see if she had more freckles on the curvy body under her lace and velvet dress. She was really stubborn about the age thing and if he was as smart as everyone thought, he'd throw in the towel. The problem was, he liked her. She was a real firecracker and it had nothing to do with the color of her hair.

Austin was inclined to hang in for a while and see if he could fire her up.

After dinner, Rose sat alone at the table watching couples on the dance floor. Until a few minutes ago she and Austin were one of them and she'd really liked the feel of his arms around her. Then his sister Angie had commandeered him for the chicken dance. What wedding was complete without that?

Everyone seemed to be having a great time. What was not to like? The whole event had lived up to its advance billing as the social affair of the year. It was completely enchanting. This room looked as magical as the resort's transformed lobby with twinkling lights wrapped around bare white branches and the poinsettias added a touch of red. The brides were perfect and perfectly happy with their hunky, handsome grooms.

It was the ultimate romantic fantasy and Rose was having serious doubts about her own ever coming true. Of course her brother Jackson chose that moment to sit down beside her. His fiancée, Laila Cates, pulled out the chair next to his.

"Hey, sis."

"Hey, yourself. Hi, Laila."

"Hi, Rose." The other woman smiled. "Love the dress."

She appreciated the compliment, but it didn't lift her spirits. How she longed to rest her head on her big brother's strong shoulder, but he wouldn't understand. Besides the fact that he was a guy's guy, he'd found the love of his life. Blonde, blue-eyed and beautiful, Laila looked like she'd stepped off a page of *People* magazine. And handsome Jackson, with his dark hair and eyes, could be in the movies if he wasn't doing community outreach and public relations work for Traub Oil Montana.

"You look really pretty tonight," Laila added.

Rose smiled at the woman who would be her sister-in-law. "I might have had a shot at mildly attractive until you sat down."

"Oh, please." She waved off the compliment.

Jackson's dark brown eyes glowed with pride and love when he looked at her. "My sister is right."

"About what?" Rose demanded. "That I have to wear a bag over my head?"

"No, that the woman I plan to marry is as beautiful as she is sweet and caring."

"Yeah." Rose nodded grudgingly. "If she wasn't, I could take great pleasure in hating her guts."

Laila laughed and like everything about her, the sound was beautiful. The least she could do was snort. "That's probably the highest praise and most sincere compliment I've ever received."

"But true." Rose sighed. "Darn it."

"You're not happy for me?" Jackson glanced at his fiancée. "For us?"

"Of course I am. Truly."

"What's wrong?"

"Everything's fine." If she pretended long and hard enough, maybe that wouldn't be a lie.

"Look, Rosie, you ought to know by now that fooling me isn't going to happen. So why won't you tell me what's up with you?"

"Because you really don't want to know."

"Yes, I do. We do," Jackson said and Laila nodded her agreement.

Rose looked at the happy, perfect couple and loneliness sucked her in further. This room was filled with happy, perfect couples and that was hard to look at when you weren't part of one. Especially when she'd worked so hard to make it happen. She'd dated a lot of guys, but not one of them was her prince and a happy ever after wasn't looking hopeful.

"I think there's something wrong with me," she finally said.

Jackson frowned. "What are you talking about?"

"It would be easier if I could blame my singleness on

a lack of men. But no one would buy that excuse because I've dated more than any girl in the history of Thunder Canyon."

"We noticed." Her brother's tone was wry.

"Don't start on me. The thing is, you'd think out of all those men there would be a spark, some chemistry, some hope, but not so much. There's no magic. No zing. No lightning. No sizzle."

Except with Austin Anderson.

It was proof that fate had a bizarre and warped sense of humor. From the moment he'd picked her up for this wedding, her skin had tingled. Being near him made her chest feel tight and don't even get her started on the zing and sizzle when he'd held her in his arms on the dance floor.

Rose met her brother's gaze. "The guys I've met are all great, so the only possible conclusion is that there's something wrong with me. Maybe my standards are too high."

"Maybe you're afraid." Jackson's gaze never wavered.

"Of what?"

"Being hurt. You haven't had a long-term relationship since the jerk in college."

Rose was surprised that, not only had he been paying attention to her romantic life, but that he had also remembered. And the memory shouldn't still sting, but it did. She wanted very much to change the subject, but blowing off the question gave the past more power than it should have.

She looked at Laila. "When I was in college there was this pre-med student. We were together over a year and I was in love with him. Graduation was coming up fast for both of us and it was time to fish or cut bait. He cut bait."

"Why?" Laila glanced at Jackson who nodded.

"He fell into the poor-but-proud group. I believed that love was all we needed." She shrugged. "He chose medical school over marriage."

"That's too bad." Laila's blue eyes brimmed with sympathy. "Sounds like the timing was just off."

Apparently that was Rose's fatal flaw—attraction to ill-timed men. The only one who interested her was born too late. Or she was too early. Either way that made him too wrong.

"Will you two excuse me?" Laila squeezed her fiancée's hand. "I'm going to the ladies' room."

"I'll be waiting." There was love and longing in Jackson's eyes as he watched her weave through the crowd to the door.

Rose felt equal parts of envy and pleasure that the two had found each other. She loved her brother and wanted him to be happy. "She's a keeper."

He nodded. "You and Austin Anderson looked pretty cozy out on the dance floor."

The words snapped her back to attention even as she wondered if Jackson Traub had turned into a mind reader. She wasn't sure what annoyed her most: that he'd noticed her with Austin or that he was right about the cozy part. If he'd noticed, surely other people had, too. That's just what she'd wanted to avoid.

"What are you talking about? Cozy?"

"Laila mentioned it."

"What?" she hedged.

"That you and Austin seemed to be having a good time," he answered. "She hoped that's a sign that things are looking up for him."

"For Austin? I don't understand."

Jackson shrugged. "Apparently he had a bad experience with love."

Surely he'd misunderstood Laila. It was hard for Rose to believe that someone as handsome, sexy and smart as Austin wouldn't have women falling at his feet.

"What happened?"

"Not a clue. It was before I moved to Thunder Canyon."

Rose tried not to be curious about Austin's past. It was none of her business. Because she'd scratched him off her list, whatever had taken place would not impact her. They were nothing more than friends. But friends cared about each other. And confided their concerns. It would help to know the details of his bad luck.

"Laila probably knows his story," she suggested.

"Probably," he agreed.

"You should ask her."

"Why?" Jackson's look was skeptical.

Rose couldn't meet his gaze. She glanced away and saw the man in question coming toward them with a beer in one hand and a glass of white wine in the other.

"No reason," she said. "He's a nice guy and I can't imagine what woman in her right mind would dump him."

"Maybe that's it."

"What?"

"She probably wasn't in her right mind," Jackson suggested.

"You should ask Laila."

His dark eyes narrowed. "You seem awfully interested."

"Not really." She willed herself to look indifferent when every nerve in her body was quivering with questions. "It's just that we're friends."

"Okay."

"So you'll find out what happened?"

"I'll ask Laila."

"Promise?" Rose said.

"You want a pinky swear?"

She did, but the words would never pass her lips. "A solemn brotherly promise is sacred enough for me," she teased.

Jackson glanced at the doorway, clearly looking for Laila. "I think I'll go find my lady."

"Sounds like a good idea."

He stood, then tapped her nose. "There's nothing wrong with you, Rosie. If anyone says different, I'll beat him up."

"I'd like that," she agreed laughing.

"Seriously, if you need me, I'm there."

"I know."

She watched him walk away and meet his love at the door.

"Who is Jackson beating up?" Austin put the white wine in front of her.

"Guys with tattoos." That was something else about this particular man that tweaked her curiosity.

It was nothing more than being nosy. Curiosity was better than feeling sorry for herself. And how stupid was that? She had a great job. A family who loved her. And Traubs didn't give up. She wasn't a couple today, but tomorrow? Anything was possible. Still, she felt the tiniest twinge when Austin set the glass of wine in front of her, shades of regret that he could only be her friend.

"Thanks."

"So you're sure I can't talk you into looking at my tattoo?"

She laughed and realized how much easier it was to share in the joy of this beautiful evening when he was around. With luck, the romantic magic would shift in her direction. If it held, she wouldn't have to kiss too many more frogs before one of them turned into a handsome prince.

Chapter Three

And another frog it was.

There was no way Rose would kiss Harvey French. With her elbow on the wooden table, she rested her cheek in her palm and tried to look interested in what the guy was saying. Two days ago she'd been at the wedding with Austin and now, with her tush perched on the red vinyl seat in a booth lining the big room at Lipsmackin' Ribs, she was missing him more than she could say.

Harvey was an attorney she'd met in the mayor's office that morning and he'd asked her to dinner. Note to self, she thought, when a guy asks you to dinner, be sure to find out where. This place was a big clue that would, as Mr. I'm-the-best-attorney-on-the-planet say, go to character. And his was as repulsive as the short, tight, blue-and-white, belly-baring T-shirts this restaurant made its waitresses wear.

It was a big red flag. Not only was this place competition for her cousin DJ, there'd been some weird stuff going on between the competing restaurants.

As far as a kiss transforming this guy, in the fairy tale it was all about looks and Harvey was already handsome. He was blond, blue-eyed and broad-shouldered. The gray suit and red silk tie he wore were expensive. And yet…

Kill me now, she wanted to say. A direct meteor strike would be sudden and painless, unlike this never-ending, excruciating date. And they hadn't ordered yet, just drinks. But there wasn't enough liquor in the world to improve his personality.

"I really took them apart in court," he was saying. "It wasn't even a contest."

"Oh?"

"It cost them a bundle to defend against my client's cause of action. I buried them in paperwork, tied up the legal team answering motions in court. It was a beautiful thing to behold."

"Really?" Rose kicked herself. The single word would signal encouragement to continue, which was the last thing she wanted. He was probably black and blue from patting himself on the back. If she heard one more party-of-the-first-part, fiduciary duty or jurisprudence, she'd scream. Or choke him.

"They were forced to finally settle out of court. I was making it too expensive for them to continue defending against it. Although, just between you and me, there was no merit to my client's lawsuit."

Rose stared at him. It was lawyers like him who gave every attorney who'd passed the bar a bad reputation. Time to change the subject to something neutral. Like her new hometown. The weather.

"Thunder Canyon is a great place to live," she said. No "I" anywhere in that sentence.

"I've lived here all my life. Did I mention I played football?"

By her count he'd mentioned it four times. She remembered because she'd responded the same way three times and this made number four. "In Texas we take our football seriously."

"So you said." Harvey sipped his whiskey and soda.

Color her surprised that he'd noticed. She'd hoped that bringing up Thunder Canyon would segue into his asking why she'd moved. How she liked Montana. Did the cold bother her? Was it true that the best way to ride out a snowstorm was in front of a fire? She remembered Austin offering to help her build one and just the memory had her sizzling.

Rose flashed back to how handsome he'd looked in his traditional black tux at the wedding. She remembered delivering dinners with him on Thanksgiving and his joking about boring her into a coma. No danger of that happening. He was fun. Unlike the buffoon sitting across from her.

The buffoon continued, "In high school, I was quarterback of the football team when we won our division and went on to state."

"Is this a colder winter than usual in Montana?" she asked.

"No, I remember football practice and games in the snow. Although our season went longer because we were always in playoffs when I was the quarterback." The ice in his empty glass clinked when he swirled it. "It was good training for practicing law. Everyone tries to knock you down, but you dig in and don't let them."

"Words to live by." That was as close to neutral as she could get.

She studied him. Good-looking. Smart enough to become a lawyer. From a nice family. On paper he was everything she wanted in a man if you left out the boring and self-centered part. He hadn't asked her anything and apparently didn't care how she was adjusting to her new life in town. Call her perverse, but she let the awkward silence drag on because everything that popped into her mind to say would only lead him into another topic about himself.

"I'm pretty good on a pair of skis," he said. "But there's nothing like the adrenaline rush of snowboarding."

"Oh?" She couldn't resist. "I bet that's good practice for a career as a lawyer, too. Fall down, get back up."

"Smart girl. I decided on a career as an attorney because knowing the law gives you power. And the money's good, too." He grinned and winked.

Dear God, did he really just wink at her? She barely held back a shudder. "So I've heard."

"I've got the mayor's ear." He lowered his voice as if he was sharing a national security secret and all the families eating ribs in booths and wooden tables around the room were spies. "If your brother Ethan needs local legal counsel for Traub Oil, I'm his guy. Or if he's looking to merge the legal departments of Texas and Montana under one roof, I could help with that, too."

The "aha" light came on and all became clear to Rose. This blowhard wasn't attracted to her any more than she was to him. He had an ulterior motive for asking her out. If Harvey hadn't picked her up at her apartment, she'd have walked out right that second. But her place was a long hike in the cold and she was wearing heels.

She stood up suddenly. "Excuse me, Harvey. I'm going to the ladies' room."

Before he could answer, she turned and hurried through the place. She passed waitresses wearing short, tight blue shorts and a big red lip imprint on their T-shirts feeling as exploited as they probably did. Following the back wall, she finally found the alcove with doors that said "Men" and "Women" staring at each other. She pushed open the female door and blew out a long breath, grateful that it was quiet and she was alone.

"That pompous windbag. Conniving, underhanded, self-absorbed jerk. How dare he use me to get Ethan's legal business?"

There must be a way to cut this abomination of an experience short. It wasn't practical to simply walk out and she couldn't insist he take her home immediately. Working with him could get awkward if he wasn't exaggerating the truth and really did have access to the mayor.

Bo Clifton had probably known Harvey a long time. There could be press releases with critical wording that might require legal tweaking, to keep the mayor out of hot water because of unfortunate phrasing. How could she gracefully end this horrid encounter before committing justifiable homicide? It would be self-defense because if it lasted any longer, Harvey French would bore her to death. But if she choked him, there could be jail time involved. That would upset her family and she didn't think she'd do well in jail.

Although she was sick of Harvey, pretending to come down with an illness was problematic. Her acting skills weren't that good. There was only one thing to do, what she always did when she was in trouble.

She pulled her cell phone out of her purse and brought up her contact list, then hit Jackson's number. The last thing he said to her at the wedding was that if she needed him he would be there. Time to put up or shut up.

Rose worried her lip as the phone rang three, four, five times. Darn it. He wasn't answering. Just when she was afraid the call was going straight to his voice mail, Jackson finally picked up.

"What?" He sounded crabby and breathless, as if he'd been running, or…

Oh, no. Shoot, shoot, shoot, she said to herself. With caller ID, he already knew who was calling, so she had to say something. "It's Rose."

"Are you okay?" The words were laced with alarm.

"Fine, physically. I have a date, but—"

"You called to tell me you have a date? What am I? Your BFF? That's not breaking news. It's business as usual for you."

"No, Jackson, listen. I'm with him right now—"

"Why is your voice echoing?"

Rose leaned her shoulder against a tile wall. The mirror and sink were beside her. She stared at her reflection, the desperation on her face, and hoped it was as clear in her voice. "I'm hiding in the restroom, so technically he's not here now. He's waiting for me at the table."

"I don't need a play by play—"

"Stop yelling at me and listen. You have to get me out of here."

"Are your legs painted on? Just walk out."

"He picked me up, I don't have a car. The thing is, I met him at work. There's no graceful way for me to handle this and it could get awkward at the office."

"Rose—" Annoyance grated in his voice.

"Please, Jackson. I wouldn't have bothered you if there was any other way. I'm begging you to get me out of here. Think of something so he won't be offended. He's got an ego on him." She added the final argument. "I'm at Lip-smackin' Ribs."

"Traitor."

"It wasn't my idea," she protested. "He surprised me. But do you see what I'm up against?"

There was a long silence before he finally said, "Give me fifteen minutes."

"Thanks, Jackson."

Rose reapplied her lipstick, then went back to the table. "All freshened up."

He looked a little miffed. "The waitress was here to take our order, but I didn't know what you wanted."

That surprised her from the man who thought he knew everything. On the other hand, she didn't want him to be on the hook for food she had no intention of eating.

"We've been so busy blathering away that I haven't had a chance to look at the menu." She gave Harvey a bright smile, something it was possible to do now that help was on the way.

It was actually closer to twenty-five minutes before Jackson finally showed up. He stopped beside the booth and scowled. "I've been looking for you."

"Jackson?" She put as much surprise as possible into her voice. "I'm on a date here. Harvey French, this is my brother Jackson Traub."

"Nice to meet you." Harvey put out his hand and they shook.

"What are you doing here, Jackson?" Her performance wouldn't win any awards, but it was the best she could do.

"Your cell phone is off. There's urgent family business and I'm here to get you."

"Can't it wait until Harvey and I have dinner?"

"No." There was a dangerous glint in her brother's dark eyes and she wondered if she'd pushed it just a little too far.

"Jackson wouldn't be here if it wasn't important." She pretended regret when she looked at Harvey. "I'm so sorry, but it looks like I have to cut our evening short."

"Only if I get a rain check," Harvey said.

"Only if…" That wasn't an outright lie. She stood and grabbed her coat and purse. "Thanks for the drink."

She lifted her hand in a wave, then turned and followed her brother outside. His new luxury SUV was parked at the curb, proof that he was settling down. Rose opened the door and got in. "You're a lifesaver."

"Yeah." He turned the key in the ignition and the dashboard came to life, highlighting his angry expression.

"I'll make it up to you."

"Good, because you owe me big time. Laila and I were just about to have a—romantic moment."

That's what she'd been afraid of. His hair was uncombed and looked as if Laila had been running her fingers through it. Beneath his sheepskin-lined jacket his shirttail was hanging out, as if he'd dressed in a hurry and didn't take the time to tuck it in. There wasn't much she could say, but she had to try.

"I'm so sorry. I feel terrible about that, but I was desperate."

"That's what you get for going out with someone from work."

"How else am I supposed to meet men?" she asked.

Jackson's only response was an angry look. In the silence that followed, she realized he was driving in the opposite direction from where her apartment was located.

"Where are we going?"

"You'll see."

A few minutes later her brother pulled up in front of The Hitching Post and turned off the car. "I didn't make up the part about urgent family business."

Rose narrowed her gaze on him. "What's going on?"

"Come with me."

"Do I have a choice?"

"No." He came around the car and met her on the sidewalk. The streetlight illuminated his features and there was a very real possibility that the glare on his face was permanent. Without another word, she followed him into The Hitching Post.

Unlike Lipsmackin' Ribs on Tuesday night, this place was quiet. Divided by a half wall, there was a restaurant on one side and a bar on the other. Rose was pretty sure they were going to the other.

Her suspicion was confirmed when she saw her brothers Dillon, Ethan and Corey at a table with the best view of the painting behind the old west-style bar. In the picture, a scantily clad and scandalous Lily Divine stared down at the men with a "come hither" challenge in her eyes.

"Bet she didn't have any trouble getting a man," Rose grumbled.

And that's when she saw Austin Anderson on the restaurant side sitting at a table with his sister Angie. Family night at The Hitching Post, just her luck. They saw her and waved and she lifted a hand in response. For a second she thought about breaking rank and joining them because it was clear Jackson had mobilized Traub reinforcements for some reason.

All her brothers were there except Jason who was still in Midland, Texas. Whatever the four in Thunder Canyon had to say was probably not something she wanted to hear. And she really would rather Austin didn't have a front row seat. He'd already seen her get carded and a stern talking to by the Traub tribe was not another humiliation she wanted him to witness.

"You know, Jackson, I think I'm going to skip this family reunion," she said.

"If you take one step toward that door, I will put you over my shoulder." It didn't seem possible that his fierce look could intensify, but the angry stare got angrier and stopped her cold.

"Okay, let's get this over with."

"My sentiments exactly. Laila's waiting."

Rose moved around him and with head held high, walked to the table where her brothers waited. All of them were at least six feet tall, broad-shouldered and dark-haired. She'd told Austin they were the best-looking men at the wedding, but right this minute she would take back those words and substitute annoying.

She took the last open seat at the table for four. The three of them had beers and there was a fourth that Jackson picked up. Nothing for her.

Dillon, the oldest, rested his forearms on the table. "Jackson called me after you sounded the alarm, Rose. I decided a family meeting was in order."

"Why?" This wasn't unprecedented, but it didn't happen very often.

"Consider this an intervention," he said, a very doctor-like thing to say. Because he *was* a doctor, the word choice made perfect sense.

The meaning? Not so much. "What for? I don't smoke, do drugs or drink too much."

"You're addicted to dating," Corey said.

"You're not serious," she scoffed.

"Yeah, we are." Jackson pulled over a chair from the adjacent table. "You date too much."

"Define too much." Her chin lifted a notch.

"So many men, so little time." Dillon took a pull on his beer. "Off the top of my head there's Nick, Dean and Cade Pritchett."

"Okay, so—"

"John Kelly," Corey added. "The mortgage banker."

"Yeah." Rose struggled to put a face with the name. "He was very banker-ish."

"You don't remember him, do you?" Ethan looked thoughtful. "Zach Evans. He's a rancher."

"Rob Lewis, chamber of commerce president." Corey turned his beer bottle.

They continued to add names to a list that became pretty impressive. She was amazed that her macho brothers had paid so much attention to her love life. Or, to put a finer point on it, her *lack* of love life.

"They don't even know about Harvey French." Jackson's eyes narrowed.

"Then I'll tell them," she said. "He's a lawyer and asked me out because he wants to get Traub Oil Montana's legal business. And possibly the Texas stuff, too."

"Jerk," Ethan muttered.

"My sentiments exactly. That's why I called Jackson," she defended. "So if we're done here—"

"Not so fast," they all said.

Ethan nailed her with a look. "You've got to stop, Rosie. Take a break."

"I can't do that." She folded her arms over her chest and looked at each of them defiantly.

"Yeah, you can. Get your head on straight," Corey suggested. "Decide what you're looking for. Separate the wheat from the chaff."

"What does that even mean?"

If this was a job, they'd be telling her to work it, put in the hours, make herself indispensable. This was even more important. It was her life, her happiness. Why should finding love require any less dedication than her career?

Jackson leaned forward, rested his elbows on his knees. "Some soul searching couldn't hurt, Rose. You need to figure out why no guy is generating sparks."

That wasn't completely true, she thought. There were enough sparks with Austin to start a fairly frightening forest fire. She glanced over at him and saw he was looking at her. The expression in his eyes set off a fireball in her belly, proving her point. She grabbed Ethan's beer and took a drink to put out the blaze.

This *thing* with Austin was nothing. It couldn't be.

"Jackson's right," Corey agreed. "Time-out."

"Since when are you guys the dating police?"

"Since always." Dillon met her gaze. "It's what big brothers do."

They were also men and didn't get it.

"I'm a grown woman. You can't ground me," she protested. "Don't think I don't appreciate all you do, but—"

"No excuses. Cold turkey." Jackson took a sip from his bottle. "I bet you can't go a month without a date."

That touched a nerve, but she pushed down the competitive streak. "A woman of my advancing years can't afford to sit on the sidelines that long."

"Don't talk to me about piling up the years." Dillon, the oldest sibling, shook his head. "You're just a baby."

"Hardly," she said. "And you don't understand. You all found love without even trying."

The four of them stared at her, then started laughing.

"What's so funny?" she demanded.

"It's never as easy as it looks." Amusement still lurked in Corey's light brown eyes. "Jason is the last unattached Traub brother and he's still in Texas. Maybe it's something about Thunder Canyon."

"That's what I'm trying to tell you," she said. "And I've got to keep myself out there—"

"No." Jackson shook his head. "That's what we're trying to tell you. Time-out, for Pete's sake. I double dare you to put the brakes on the dating wagon for thirty days."

Double dare? Rose gritted her teeth. He knew her too well. She never turned down a double dare, darn him.

"You're going straight to hell, Jackson Traub." She glared at him and figured the expression was just as fearsome as his.

He looked completely unimpressed. "A brother's gotta do what a brother's gotta do."

Frustration knotted inside her when they all nodded in agreement.

"And if any one of us catches you on a date before time is up, it's back to day one, plus two weeks," Jackson warned.

"A month and a half?" she cried.

"Double dare," he reminded her. "Technically I could double the stakes, but I'm cutting you some slack."

She blew out a breath. "Done."

"And remember, this isn't Midland." Jackson pointed a finger at her. "Thunder Canyon is a small town and word spreads real fast, so don't be trying to pull anything. We've got eyes and ears everywhere."

"I'll get even with you. Every last one of you," she warned, treating each of them to the Rose Traub double dare stare. "You won't know where or when, but payback is coming."

"Yeah, we're scared." Dillon stood and the others followed suit.

He patted her head. Ethan tapped her nose. Corey ruffled her hair. Then the three walked away, leaving her with Jackson. As Rose watched their backs, her gaze drifted to Austin. He was frowning at his sister and it reminded her that her brother was supposed to get her information about him.

Rose watched Jackson shrug into his jacket. "So," she

said, "what did Laila say about Austin? Did you get details about why his love life has nowhere to go but up?"

"You're not dating for a month." Jackson stared at her as if she had two heads. "What do you care?"

"I don't."

That was a big, fat lie.

Even worse than lying to her brother, she couldn't stop thinking about Austin Anderson.

Chapter Four

Austin supervised a group of teenagers who were putting lights on the Christmas tree at ROOTS. He could have helped, made suggestions about spacing and symmetry, but it was their tree and they didn't need adults butting in. That was part of the philosophy here. Supervise for safety, advise only when asked. Watching the kids joking and laughing, talking and teasing, he wished there'd been a hangout like this when he was growing up. It had been Haley's dream and she'd pulled rabbits out of a hat to make it happen.

The mural she'd painted of teens playing sports, using computers and texting on cell phones filled the wall that faced Main Street. She'd found an old couch, a recliner that no longer reclined, ugly lamps and scratched tables that the kids could use without worrying about messing anything up. They came to talk, vent, do homework and have fun.

Thanks to a long list of volunteers, there was always an adult on the premises.

Tonight he was that adult.

If only Rose Traub saw him that way. Somehow he was going to change her mind about him, although so far he didn't have much of a plan about how to make it happen. Last night he'd seen her at The Hitching Post with her brothers who appeared to be pulling rank. He recognized the big brother body language and remembered how young and defiant she'd looked. Austin recognized that body language. He'd gotten an advanced degree in young and defiant.

Angry voices in the corner around the tree got his attention and he moved to defuse the situation. Three girls watched the two boys as arguing turned to shoving. Understanding from personal experience how a flood of testosterone could drown a guy's common sense, Austin quickly moved in to separate them.

He pushed his way between the teenagers who were both skinny and shorter than he was. But a stray punch thrown was always a concern.

"Break it up, guys," he said. "Use words."

"He already did that." The shaggy-haired blond had fire in his blue eyes. "He was talkin' trash about my sister."

"No, dude—I said she was fine." Black hair and eyes along with low-slung jeans screamed bad boy.

The image attracted girls for some reason and Austin should know. Growing up, he'd excelled at that phase and never lacked for attention from the opposite sex. Then his luck with girls ran out. About the time he'd graduated from college, he'd thought he was grown up enough to have his own family, but the girl he'd asked had easily resisted him.

The bell over the front door dinged, but before he could

see who came in, the two combatants lunged at each other again. Austin put his hands out to keep them apart.

"Knock it off, Evan," he said to the blond. "Looking out for your sister is a good thing, but I guarantee she won't thank you for punching out the dude who's giving her a compliment." He gave the tough guy a hard stare. "It *was* a compliment right, Cal?"

Rebellion crackled in the dark eyes, then backed off a notch, signaling a truce. Full surrender would take time. And maturity.

"Yeah," the kid finally said. "I didn't mean anything."

"Didn't think so." Austin dropped his hands. "Take five, guys, and grab a soda. Cool off."

In the back room there was a refrigerator with fruit, cold drinks and water. A pantry was full of crunchy snacks. Not only could teenage boys consume unbelievable quantities of food under normal circumstances, sometimes kids also weren't getting enough to eat at home. There were families in financial need because of job loss in the recent recession. Austin hoped the green engineering process he was working on would create employment opportunities for some of them.

"Is it always this exciting around here?"

Austin knew that voice belonged to the redhead on his mind. There was a wide grin on his face when he turned.

"Rose."

She lifted a mitten-covered hand. "Hi."

"It's usually pretty quiet in here," he said, glancing at the doorway where the teens disappeared. Their voices drifted in from the back room.

"I know it's wrong to condone fighting, but—" She smiled. "A brother protecting his sister's honor."

"It's what we do." He'd stepped in to defend Angie when Haley had brought home a teen in trouble. Although it turned out he'd misinterpreted the situation. But Rose wasn't talking about him. "This is a pleasant surprise."

Not his smoothest dialogue. Maybe he should pull out his bad boy alter ego and see if it still worked magic.

"How are you?" she asked.

"Good. You?"

"Fine." She was bundled up in a puffy jacket, navy cashmere scarf, matching hat and mittens. Black slacks and boots completed her winter look. "How's Angie?"

"Busy. Between college classes and work, she's got a lot on her plate."

"Sounds like it." She pulled off her jacket and mittens which meant she wasn't in too big a hurry to leave. "I saw you with her last night."

"Yeah." When Rose had walked in, he could hardly keep his eyes off her. "We stopped for a quick burger."

"The Hitching Post has pretty good ones."

"Arguably the best in town," he agreed. "Is there something you wanted? Not that I'm pushing you out the door, but—"

"Right, I'm not the typical demographic for ROOTS."

"We specialize in rebellion, group therapy for angst-related issues and anger management. It's a lot about healthy, positive ways to channel hormones."

She laughed. "What a diplomatic way of saying I'm too old to be here."

"Not from where I'm standing."

They were in the middle of the room with no convenient place to hang mistletoe, but he'd never wanted some of that twig more in his life. It would give him an excuse to kiss her. And he badly wanted to which was becoming a chronic problem. Every time he saw her, the urge to take her in his arms was stronger.

With every lamp and overhead light on in the room, he

knew the pink that crept into her cheeks was a blush and not from the cold outside. That was good, right? At least it was some reaction to him.

"I just walked over from the mayor's office to deliver some Christmas cheer in person," she said.

"You walked?"

"It's only a couple of blocks and the night is gorgeous and clear."

"Not too cold?" Austin asked skeptically.

"I bundled up."

He could see that. While the Eskimo look was cute, he did like her in the black lace dress that was like sex in motion when she walked. "So what's the news?"

"As you know, I handle public relations and communications for the mayor's office."

She seemed a little nervous, and from his perspective, just happened to be the cutest communicator he could imagine.

"The mayor hasn't decided to revoke the ROOTS permit, has he?"

"No," she said quickly. "Just the opposite. Sort of. I mean I'm not here with another permit. You don't need two. But Mayor Clifton and the town council believe this place has proved to be beneficial to the teenagers. There's been a definite drop in nuisance-related complaints since it opened. He's allocating funds for tutoring and more computer equipment."

A sudden burst of laughter from the other room told him the boys had let go of their anger as boys usually did.

Austin grinned. "That's great. Haley's on her honeymoon, but I'll let her know when she gets back. She'll be really happy to hear about that."

"The press release is going out tomorrow, so I wanted to stop by for a minute and deliver the good news."

"I'm glad you did." And not just because the equipment and scholastic help were so badly needed. "Some kids don't have a computer at home and they're not likely to broadcast that by using the ones at the library. It's an academic disadvantage without access at home. Plus, this place has become the cool place to hang out. Putting a subtle emphasis on study might make schoolwork a little cooler, too."

"I see what you mean." She smiled. "This is the best part of my job."

The kids drifted back into the room and after a curious glance at the newcomer, they resumed stringing lights on the tree.

Austin looked back at Rose. "Actually, by showing up you saved me a phone call."

"Oh?"

"Yeah, I was going to ask you out, but now I can do it in person."

"A date?"

The distressed expression on her face meant this was not starting out well. "When a guy invites a woman to dinner, by definition it's called a date."

"I was afraid of that."

"Afraid? Why is it a problem? Because I'm not your ideal age?"

"No." She hesitated. "I mean yes, you're not. But that's not the only thing."

"What else?"

"I'm on a dating diet."

That was pretty close to the lamest excuse he'd ever heard. He could see the headline now. *Former bad boy crashes and burns. Reputation on life support.* Irritation chipped away at him and he didn't want to set a bad example for the kids.

"How about some coffee?"

"No, thanks."

He took her arm anyway and led her into the back room. This discussion wasn't for curious teenagers to hear.

Austin folded his arms over his chest and stared down at her. "Now tell me what you really want to say."

"I just did."

His eyes narrowed. "Dating diet? Really? If you don't want to go out with me, just say so."

"I actually did that and you wouldn't take no for an answer."

"Then explain to me the dating diet."

"It's actually the result of a double dare." Her expression was completely honest, which was refreshing. She answered in her characteristically straightforward way. "My brothers told me that I need to take a break from dating."

"They do realize you're in the market to get married?"

"Yup." She held her jacket close to her chest. "But it didn't matter. I told them what to do with the suggestion, then Jackson bet me I couldn't go a month without a date."

"So you took the bet?"

"Not until he double dared me," she explained. "He knew I couldn't resist that. So now I'm stuck. If I go out with you, I have to start from scratch and add two weeks. I can't afford to be off the market that long."

"I see." That was what her brothers had been pulling rank about. He knew she was absolutely serious, but it was hard not to laugh. And she completely charmed him. "We could do something together that in no way resembles a romantic rendezvous."

"You're not serious."

"I have never been more sincere in my life."

"Okay, here's a test." She looked skeptical. "What about stuffing Christmas card envelopes for the mayor?"

"You're on," he answered, jumping at the chance.

"How do you feel about watching the snow melt?" she asked suspiciously.

"It's a dirty job, but someone has to do it. And there are other options, including but not limited to cleaning graffiti off the public walls in town. Or I could use help decorating the house for Christmas."

"Seriously?"

"Haley is married and Angie's too busy."

"So you're saying you need a woman?"

If she only knew how badly. "It's not a sexist thing."

"Really? How about washing my car? Or…" A very cute, yet evil look slid into her eyes. "I know. You could help me *shop*. It's that time of the year. I have lots of Christmas presents on my list. Mention the *s* word and a girl can separate the men from the boys every time."

He hated shopping as much as the next guy, but if she was there, it would be fun. "The noble yet manly thing would be to carry the bags. Therefore, I'd be happy to help spend your money," he offered generously.

"As long as you're not spending money on me and it couldn't be in any way, shape or form defined as a date…" She tapped her lip thoughtfully. "No way I'm losing this bet."

"You really are competitive."

"Yeah," she said with a "duh" inflection. "What was your first clue?"

"That gleam in your eyes that says your brothers are going down. Plus…" He lifted a strand of her hair spilling out from underneath her hat. The soft, silky, sexy feel shot a flash of desire straight through him and he struggled to hide it.

"What?" she asked.

"Hmm?"

"You said plus," she reminded him.

"I think that determination turned your hair a shade brighter. Is it an urban legend that redheads are more stubborn than the average woman?"

The corners of her mouth turned up and her dimples winked at him. "I couldn't say about redheads in general or the average woman in particular, but when *I* make up my mind about something, it's not changing."

Because she'd made up her mind that the age difference between them was a deal breaker, Austin knew he had his work cut out for him.

The bell over the front door dinged and he heard the teens call out greetings to someone they knew. He was kind of enjoying having Rose to himself and wanted that just a little longer.

"So, this is your first visit to ROOTS. What do you think of it?"

"I think if those boys hadn't been here under your watchful eye, one or both would have black eyes and fat lips. Now they're having a good time. Great place for them to come and be supervised. I'm sure their parents are pleased, too."

"The feedback has all been positive," he agreed. "Kids come here to talk about whatever is bothering them. Real life happens even though they're not grown up. It's a safe place to get all those feelings out."

"I noticed the embroidered sampler on the wall in the other room. Tell me about it."

"My mother made that." He wasn't sure when remembering Nell Anderson changed from pain to a soft warmth. She'd been there for him until he was about the age of the kids in the other room and he would always miss her. He quoted the words he knew by heart. "There are but two lasting bequests we can give our children—roots and wings."

"That's really lovely." Rose smiled. "And so true. Very wise."

"It's why Haley dedicated the Nell Anderson ROOTS Teen Center to our mother. She was taken from us too soon, but her spirit goes on in this place."

"What happened to your mom?"

"Car accident," he answered. "I was sixteen."

"Oh, Austin…"

He was stating a fact, not looking for sympathy, but didn't turn down the comforting hand she settled on his arm. "It was a long time ago."

"How did you get through it?"

"Not gracefully. Tried to grow up too fast." Maturity couldn't always be calculated in years put in and he should get extra credit for a lot of emotional miles. "There was some rebellion."

"The tattoo?"

"Yeah. Wanna see?"

"There are minors in the other room," she scolded, even as the corners of her mouth curved up.

"Another time."

And there would be, he vowed. She wasn't the only one who could get her stubborn on when her mind was made up.

As they stared at each other, the sweet haunting sounds of a guitar drifted to them from the teen center's main room. Rose tilted her head, listening, then went to the doorway. He moved behind her, close enough to feel the warmth of her body through his cotton shirt. He swore there were sparks.

"That's Zane Gunther, the country singer." Her voice had the awestruck excitement of a fan.

The country star was sitting on the old couch in the center of the room with the teens clustered around him.

Austin was used to seeing the guy and that feeling of awe had worn off.

"Yeah, he comes in a lot and hangs out with the kids. I think he's trying to redeem himself for what happened."

Rose looked up at him. "You mean the teenage girl who got caught in a crush of people asking for his autograph and died."

It wasn't a question. Anyone who didn't know the story of Ashley Tuller's death was probably living under a rock. A star of Gunther's caliber couldn't dodge the publicity from something like that no matter how hard he tried. And he'd tried pretty hard. It's why he'd become a loner and eventually turned up in Thunder Canyon. He'd met a local single mom who had pulled him out of a deep hole and put the sparkle back in his eyes.

They watched the singer hand the guitar to Cal and show him where to put his fingers on the strings to play a chord. The bad boy tried to act cool, but excitement chased away the sullen indifference he usually wore like armor. A blonde girl, Emma, asked to try and giggled when Zane demonstrated how to strum the instrument.

Rose looked up. "He's really good with them."

"Yeah." Redemption at work.

Emma handed back the instrument. "You play something, Mr. Gunther."

"It's Zane," he said.

Austin couldn't see his face but knew there was regret in the green eyes as the former country star hesitated. He'd worn a scruff of beard when he'd first started coming by, but was clean-shaven now. He never went without a black cowboy hat and always wore a snap-front Western shirt tucked into worn jeans. Boots finished off the look that played down his star power.

Finally Zane nodded and took the guitar from the girl.

He started strumming and the melody was upbeat with strains of emotion running through it. The lyrics were a story of love lighting a torch in the dark. When he was finished, the teenagers enthusiastically applauded. Rose clapped as she walked into the room and around the couch.

"That was a beautiful song, Mr. Gunther." She held out her hand. "Rose Traub. I work in the mayor's office."

"Nice to meet you." He shook her hand, then looked past her. "Hey, Austin."

"How are you, Zane?"

"Okay," he said, nodding as if that still surprised him a little.

"I'm a fan of your work. I know all your music," she said. "But I don't recognize that tune. Is it new?"

"Yeah, I'm still fiddling with it."

"So you're writing music again?" she asked.

"Yes." He held the neck of the guitar in his left hand and let the other wrist dangle on the curved edge of the body.

"It's been a while since you've had a song out," she said gently.

"Things on my mind sorta shut me down."

Rose nodded. "What happened to that teenager was horrible, but it wasn't your fault."

"Still hard to let it go. Helps when a good woman believes you're a good man."

"Jeannette?" Rose shrugged at his surprise. "She works part-time with me in the mayor's office. Women talk."

"That's a fact." Zane smiled for the first time. "And I love that woman. Between that and settling the lawsuit, it feels like a weight has lifted. Sort of opened up the creativity."

"That's great to hear." She looked around at the kids who were hanging on every word.

"It's the last song for my new CD," he explained.

"Your fans will be glad to hear that," she said. "I know I am."

"Us, too." Emma looked around at the other kids who were all nodding. "It's really awesome. He wrote a song about ROOTS."

"Really?" Rose looked impressed.

"Yeah." The guilt in his eyes was unmistakable. "I've got a platform most people don't. A way to make a difference for these guys in some way."

This was news to Austin. "Haley will be very excited to hear about that."

"Anything I can do for the kids." Zane shrugged. "I'm thinking about starting a foundation in Ashley's memory. Figuring to donate the profits from the song and then a percentage of profits from the CD to get it off the ground."

"That's awfully generous of you," Rose said.

"It's the least I can do. Make something positive out of what happened."

"Definitely." She looked distracted for a moment. "You know, Mr. Gunther—"

"Please call me Zane."

"All right, Zane. I just got a really crazy idea."

Austin looked at her. "Sometimes those can be good. Maybe. What are you thinking?"

"If you really want to get the foundation up and running with sales from a CD you need advance publicity."

"The look on your face says you've got a suggestion for that," Austin said.

"I do." Her blue eyes sparkled with excitement. "What about a concert?"

"First off, there needs to be a venue," Zane pointed out.

"What about the fairgrounds?" Austin said. "It's an indoor arena. It's not being used Christmas Day. I bet we could get them to donate it for the good PR alone."

"What a great idea." Rose looked at him as if he'd hung the moon.

"That's a tall order in a short time." Zane looked from one to the other.

"It can be done." Enthusiasm brimmed in Rose's eyes. "I can help with the publicity. There's no doubt in my mind that Mayor Clifton will get behind it. With his connections and endorsement, I'll have the green light to use contacts through his office to get the word out. Mobilize volunteers to sell tickets. Advertise on the radio. Get a story out to the local TV affiliate."

"We can help, too," Emma said. "Christmas vacation starts soon and we'll have time to get fliers out all over town."

"Before school gets out," Cal interjected, "we can spread the word. Lori, you're teacher's pet, right?"

"You're such a toad." The brown-eyed brunette huffed out a breath. "I'm involved with student council. And I can see where he's going with this. If we make an announcement at school, we can let a lot of people know."

Zane looked at the kids and grinned. "You guys are awesome. I like it."

"Okay," Rose said. "We need to get the okay from the venue and go from there."

Austin looked at the man who'd been to hell and back. If the love of a good woman had lifted the weight, the generous heart of another woman was heaving it clear of him. Rose Traub was something else. Enthusiastic. Smart. Funny. Straightforward, and yes, stubborn. Definitely the total package, inside and out.

It had been a long time since he'd felt this kind of pull. The strength of the attraction made him put on the brakes and really think about this. Maybe it was just as well she wasn't into him. He was all for fun; anything more was a risk. But she'd said straight out that she wanted it all. Past humiliation made him cautious of giving it all. Besides, she'd made no bones about being hung up on the age thing.

There was no harm that he could see in enjoying her company. Getting the redhead going was more fun than he'd had in a long time. She didn't know it yet, but he planned to get her going as much as possible.

In Austin's opinion she was thinking too much. If he could get her to let her guard down, they could have a good time together.

No strings attached.

Chapter Five

Rose couldn't believe she'd just met Zane Gunther. He was one of her favorite singers and she was going to help him with a Christmas concert. These teens were amazing, she thought, looking at the five remarkable young people she'd just met. They'd enthusiastically jumped right in to help. The warm feeling stealing over her was convincing proof, yet again, that she'd made the right decision in moving to Thunder Canyon, even if her love life wasn't as successful as she'd hoped.

Watching Zane play guitar while the kids sang along, she stood shoulder to shoulder with Austin. The manly, spicy scent of him fanned the flames of that warm feeling into something else. Something off limits.

It was way past time to get the heck out of here.

Rose touched his arm and angled her thumb toward the door behind her. "I have to go. Work to do before heading home. I wasn't kidding about the mayor's Christmas cards."

"I'll walk you back. What?" he said at her look. "I wasn't kidding about helping you with them. Besides, it's dark outside."

"Oh, please. This is Thunder Canyon. The town hall is only a couple of blocks. What could happen?"

"Famous last words." His dark eyes were teasing. "Just before the serial killer grabs the unsuspecting plucky heroine off the street."

"So I'm being stalked by a deranged lunatic and that's why you have to walk with me?" She shook her head. "You can do better than that."

He thought for a moment. "No, I really can't. And I don't need an excuse. I'm not letting you walk by yourself, so get over it."

"But you've got all these kids here."

He glanced at the group, gathered around Zane. "They've got a superstar singer. Do you really think they're going to care? They wouldn't notice me unless I was bleeding or on fire. Maybe not even then. Give me a sec."

Rose watched him speak quietly to the singer who grinned and nodded.

"You kids tired of me yet?" Zane asked.

When the teens answered "never" and "no way," Cal put two fingers to his mouth and whistled loud enough to shatter glass. Austin looked at her and his expression was somewhere between I-told-you-so and you're-stuck-with-me.

Stuck. Right. Maybe if he was Harvey French. She shuddered and Austin noticed.

"Are you cold?" he asked. "I can drive you back to your office—"

"I'm fine. It's a nice night."

A night for huddling and snuggling and sharing body heat if… Sometimes she really hated "if."

Austin grabbed his sheepskin-lined jacket from the back room, then joined her by the door. He took her coat and held it while she slid her arms into the sleeves. The courtly gesture set off the best kind of shivers and when he settled his big hands on her shoulders and squeezed gently, she wanted to sigh and close her eyes. But she had to keep them wide open and free of stars.

"Ready?" he asked.

Not even close, but she said, "All set."

When Rose and Austin walked outside, strains of the song "Rockin' Around the Christmas Tree" filled the room behind them, then grew fainter as they turned up Main Street. Austin moved around her and made sure he walked on the outside of the wooden sidewalk, closest to the street. Be still my heart, she thought. And she was begging here.

Rose zipped her jacket up against the cold because there wasn't going to be any snuggling or cuddling to keep her warm. Then she slid her hands into her pockets and gripped the mittens stashed there. If her arm brushed Austin's, it would be tempting to link her fingers with his, and hard to believe she was that comfortable with a man she'd known only a short time.

They strolled down Main Street without touching, but at Nugget Way he put his palm at the small of her back, guiding her across the street. She swore the warmth of his touch burned through every layer of clothing she had on.

Say something, she thought. Break the spell.

"I really like that the town has kept the Western flavor." Better a stupid statement than the charged silence arcing between them. She glanced up. "This cover over the wooden sidewalk makes me want to play gunslinger and the schoolmarm."

When Austin laughed, the cold turned his breath into a cloud. "I'd be pleased to audition for the gunslinger role."

She wasn't taking the bait. "Seriously, can't you just picture this place over a hundred years ago? Wagons rolling up and down. The creak of leather from saddles. People on horseback."

"Animal waste in the street," he said drily.

"You have no romance in your soul, Austin." She was pretty sure just the opposite was true.

"I'm just practical," he defended. "It's an engineer thing. Take the town hall, for instance." They were approaching the building. "The stone facade is original, but the other three walls are made of brick to replace the wooden part that burned in a fire. Practical."

"Yes, but the front was preserved and keeps the feel of those days gone by. Inside, too."

She fit her key into the main door as it was after hours and everyone with an actual life had gone home. In addition to the mayor and his staff, the building housed the DMV and court. In the reception room the floor was made of old, well-polished wood. A desk sat in the center for Rhonda Culpepper who answered questions and directed people where to go. To the left, just inside the double-door entry, there was a stairway with wooden spindles, tread and handrail leading up to the second floor. On the opposite side of the foyer there was an elevator for general accessibility.

"I always take the stairs up to my office," she said.

"It shows. You're in good shape."

She turned and found him looking at her legs. His shrug told her he didn't mind at all that she'd caught him staring. And she didn't mind that he liked what he was staring at. She was so going to hell.

On the second floor there was a landing that opened to a wood floor, walls and a big open ballroom with built-in wooden benches along the sides. In the middle of the floor there were stacks of boxes marked "X-mas."

"The housekeeping staff pulled that stuff out of storage. We've got volunteers scheduled to come in all week to put up the holiday decorations for the annual children's party on Saturday. Santa will be here," she explained. "My office is down this hall, next to my boss's."

She led the way and their footsteps echoed on the floor. Just beyond the door marked Mayor Bo Clifton, Rose turned the brass knob and opened the door to her work area.

"Here it is."

Austin looked around and she tried to see it through his eyes. The walls held framed black-and-white photos of Thunder Canyon from fledgling frontier town to current day. She'd hung Traub family pictures around, too, even one of the father she'd never known. It was obvious where her brothers had come by their good looks.

Her desk and computer were in the center of the room with filing cabinets behind it. On the flat surface was a stack of cards and envelopes that she'd arranged before going to ROOTS to deliver the good news. Maybe part of her had hoped Austin would be there and another part had been procrastinating. She'd offered to do this for the mayor, but it was going to be a tedious job. She sneaked a look at Austin and thought, maybe not as tedious now. At least the view was good.

"Let's get started." Austin shrugged out of his jacket and put it on one of the wooden chairs in front of the desk. "So what do you want me to do?"

Oh, boy, was that a loaded question. She swallowed once, then said, "Do you want to stuff or lick?"

He didn't comment on the suggestive wording, but his wide grin said he hadn't missed it.

"What I meant to say... The cards are all personally signed by the mayor and the envelopes are addressed. We just have to put them inside and seal the flap."

"I actually knew what you meant. I'm an engineer," he said again.

"Oh, good. So I don't have to show you a diagram, schematic or use visual aids."

"No, but you're pretty funny. I like that."

The compliment started her glowing like the star on top of a Christmas tree. "You're pretty funny, too. But the real question is, are you all flash and no substance? Do you know your way around Christmas card preparation?"

"I think I can handle it. Let's get this job done."

Her sentiments exactly because the more time she spent with him, the harder it was to think straight. "You really don't need to help. It's way beneath your pay grade."

"Yours, too. But if you can do it, so can I. We'll get it done in half the time." He walked to the desk and picked up a card and envelope. "I'll stuff."

"By process of elimination, I'll seal."

He met her gaze and she swore his settled on her mouth and somehow she knew he was thinking about licking. She ignored the tingles dancing through her and moved beside him. They went to work and quickly got a rhythm going. It wasn't long before she wished for an alternative source to moisten the glue on the envelope flaps. Taking a breather, she arranged the cards ready to go in the lid to a box of computer paper.

"You're falling behind," he challenged.

"It's called a break. I'm running out of spit."

The words hung in the air between them. Their arms were a millimeter apart and she could almost feel him go completely still. Austin looked down at her and she looked up at him. It seemed like time stopped. Then suddenly he moved and his mouth was on hers.

His lips were soft, seeking and he smelled so good. The voice in her head said back away now and no one will get hurt. It was good advice, but there was one problem. Her hormones were having too good a time to listen. Before the thought completely formed in her mind, her hands were sliding up over his chest and around his neck. And he kept kissing her while pulling her snugly against him.

The touch of his mouth, the width of his shoulders, the feel of his hard body to her softer one was so good. Pressing as close as she could get with clothes on, she immersed herself in the spicy, crisp scent of him that was comforting in its masculinity. Why did he have to smell so darn good? She had the strangest feeling that she belonged right here.

She opened her mouth and he instantly accepted the invitation and slipped inside. Their tongues darted and danced, a tempting duel that whirled and tumbled her already-spinning senses. The contact fired up friction in every nerve ending in her body. He nipped her bottom lip, then sucked, producing a sensation that was pure pleasure and handfuls of heaven.

Then he pulled back and whispered, "You taste like a Christmas card."

The ragged tone sent her breathing from zero to sixty in half a heartbeat and she cupped his cheek in her hand. The skin was scratchy from his five o'clock shadow and her palm tingled. She'd tried so hard to tell herself that he was hardly more than a boy, but this kiss was all man.

And she wanted him.

It was tempting to ignore the voice inside saying this was fifty kinds of wrong, but now she did listen. Breathing hard, she backed away.

Say something, she thought. Something to let him know she hadn't meant it even though she had.

She swallowed hard. "Break is over. I need to finish up these cards. Gotta get home. Don't want anyone to see us and mistake this for a date."

How stupid did that sound? He'd kissed her, for Pete's sake and she'd kissed him back. Technically she hadn't violated the terms of the bet, but at the very least what she'd done breached it in spirit.

"Right, and I have to get back to ROOTS." Austin blew out a breath and ran a shaking hand through his hair. "So are you going to DJ's tomorrow to help with the Holiday Presents for Patriots project, the gift boxes going to military personnel overseas?"

She licked an envelope but couldn't look at him. "I signed the volunteer list."

"Then I'll see you there," he said, eyes twinkling. "But it's not a date."

Maybe not, but he'd seemed very interested in her answer. She couldn't believe how worried she'd been about touching him on the walk over here. A kiss had not been on her radar. She hadn't seen it coming and now couldn't make the memory go away. Once you'd been *ohmigod* kissed by Austin Anderson, there was no way to *un*-kiss him.

Even more troubling, there was no way to not want more.

Rose left work at five-thirty the next evening and drove to the Thunder Canyon Resort where DJ's Rib Shack was located. No matter how hard she tried not to, she was anticipating this volunteer event more than the Thanksgiving one and that was all about Austin. She knew him much better now. Kissing had a way of doing that. Her lips tingled just thinking about him because it had been a spectacular kiss. Award-winning.

She pulled into the parking lot and knew it was time to get her focus back where it belonged. That resolve only slipped slightly when she parked beside his truck and permitted herself one last little flutter of excitement. Now it was time to make sure the media she'd arranged was in place. This was a holiday effort for soldiers serving their country, a noble undertaking. But sometimes they also served who stayed behind and DJ was doing that.

After getting out of the car, she spotted the van with the logo for the local television affiliate and a banner for the radio station. The producer she'd talked to said they would broadcast live inside. Both would give her cousin's restaurant some positive publicity for a change. With all the wonky rivalry stuff between the Rib Shack and Lip-smackin' Ribs, DJ could use some good press.

She walked in the back door and checked out what was going on. Her cousin had closed the restaurant for the evening and she'd made it clear to both media producers what a big gesture that was. The wooden chairs that normally held customers were pushed against the walls beneath sepia-toned pictures of cowboys, ranches and a hand-painted mural showcasing the town's history. Long wooden tables, where families normally sat, were pushed together.

Volunteers—male, female, old and young—were wrapping and packing food, toiletries, gifts and books. All the items and packing supplies had been donated by Thunder Canyon businesses. Radio personality Drew Casey was sitting with a microphone at a table set up in the corner and it looked like he was interviewing DJ. The film crew was moving around to the different work stations, getting lots of footage and sound bites for the six and eleven o'clock news. Everything was going as planned. Holiday Presents for Patriots was rocking the Christmas spirit.

Rose spotted Austin across the crowded room just as the reporter—Kimberly Roman—gestured to the cameraman to cut filming. When the bright lights went off, she reached up to hug him. A warm hug. Really, really friendly.

No matter how much she wanted to, Rose didn't mistake the jealousy pooling in the pit of her stomach. It was dumb and inappropriate, but it was definitely there.

"Hey, Rose." Angie Anderson stopped beside her. "Did you just get here?"

"Yeah. You?"

"I was working my shift here at the resort, so I didn't have far to go." The pretty brunette followed her gaze across the room. "Oh, wow, Kim is here."

"Kim?" Rose hoped her voice sounded curious instead of edgy and jealous.

"She went to high school with Austin."

"Really?" Of course she did. That would put her in the right age group.

"Yeah. They dated off and on when they were both around."

"She's prettier in person than on TV." Younger-looking, too. And thinner. Darn her.

"She's nice," Angie said. "But it didn't work out with them."

Watching the two chat and laugh, Rose agreed, "It looks friendly."

"Yeah. I don't know how my brother does it, but he somehow manages to stay friends with all his exes."

Rose snapped her gaze away from the couple. "*All* of them? Is it like tissues? He uses one, then throws her away?"

"Not in a bad way."

"Is there a good way?" Rose knew the effort to appear teasing was a dismal failure when Angie's smile faded.

"Austin just wants to have fun. Nothing serious."

And there was nothing wrong with that, Rose thought. It just highlighted another of the differences between them.

She forced a smile. "Good for him. A man who knows what he wants."

Angie nodded. "Yeah, he's a good guy.

"He is a very good guy." And off-limits to Rose. "It was nice to see you, kiddo. I think I'll go see where they need an extra pair of hands."

She wanted to disappear but that was the coward's way out. The next best thing was disappearing into the crowd. At one of the tables she spotted a gray-haired bear of a man who was somewhere in his mid-fifties. On the wooden table in front of him was a stack of electronic items and a roll of Christmas paper. He had a barrel chest and big hands, not anyone's idea of a present-wrapping sort of guy.

She walked over and said, "I'm Rose Traub. You look like you could use a woman's touch with those gifts."

Pale blue eyes took her measure. When he spoke his voice was deep and hinted at a zero tolerance for attitude. "Ben Walters. My wife used to do all the gift wrapping."

"Used to" could mean anything from divorce to disability to death. "Used to" paired with the sadness in those eyes that saw too much couldn't be good and she wasn't sure what to say.

"She passed on a while back." The tone was a little gruff, but obviously he'd sensed her uncertainty.

"I'm sorry for your loss."

"Me, too." He held out the tape. "Here you go, Rosie. I could use the help. Can't get the hang of holding the dang paper *and* gettin' tape off that confounded thing to make it stay together."

She grinned and took the dispenser. "Okay, then."

For the next fifteen minutes they chatted while they worked at paper cutting, putting it around music players, electronic games or DVDs, then sealing it up. She was on the last item and so engrossed in the effort that the tap on her shoulder was startling.

"Hi." Austin grinned down at her. "I see you met my good friend Ben Walters."

"Yes." The groan just barely stayed inside, but didn't that just figure. Of course she'd pick his good friend. Although probably everyone in Thunder Canyon was his good friend.

Austin shook the other man's hand. "It's good to see you, Ben."

"How you doin', son?"

"Great. Busy."

"Figured as much, what with not seeing you around town."

"I'm working for Traub Oil." He nodded down at her. "As a matter of fact, Rose's brother Ethan is my boss. In my spare time I'm writing my doctoral dissertation on extracting oil from shale in a way that doesn't harm the environment."

Ben grinned and shook his head. "I always knew you were something special, too smart for your own good. Otherwise you wouldn't have been so much trouble."

Austin met her gaze. "It's thanks to Ben and other people here in Thunder Canyon who took an interest in me that I have any future at all. They helped me mature and see the error of my ways. I was pretty screwed up in my teens."

"Does Mr. Walters know about the tattoo?"

"Yeah." Austin looked puzzled, a clue he'd noticed the coolness in her tone.

"It's a beauty," Ben said.

"So I hear."

Austin glanced at the wrapped stack. "Looks like you're finished here. I could use some help sealing the shipping boxes."

"I don't know. We might have more—" Rose looked at the older man for a way out but didn't get any help.

"You go on with Austin, Rosie. DJ has a spread set out for us volunteers in the kitchen. I'm gettin' some before it's gone. You young folks go make yourselves useful."

Before she could say anything, Austin took her arm and led her to a table where the assembly line ended and everything was placed in boxes. There was wider tape in a big dispenser suitable for securing the heavy cardboard flaps. She held them together while Austin slapped on the tape and moved the boxes into stacks in the corner.

They worked in silence because she didn't want to talk. She couldn't help thinking that the title of the song should be "*Guys* Just Wanna Have Fun."

"You're really quiet," he finally said.

"Nothing to say."

"Since when?"

On her knees, Rose met his gaze. He was bending over and the position put his face far too close to hers. She hated that knowing what she knew about him did not shut down that funny little skip of her heart. It was so darn annoying.

"So," she said, "you think I talk too much?"

"That's not what I meant."

"It was implied."

"No." He squatted and rested a forearm on his thigh, a blatantly masculine posture. "What I implied is that something's bothering you."

"And you'd be wrong." She shoved the sealed carton aside and pulled over another one.

"It's about that kiss last night, isn't it?"

She looked up, surprised that he was spot on. But it was more than that. This flirtation had more problems than a leaky row boat. Answering his question would lead to a discussion that was a waste of time.

"That's so not true."

"Then tell me what's on your mind," he insisted.

"There's nothing to tell."

"I know you're into dares." He frowned at her, met her stubborn and raised her one. "I double dare you to deny that you enjoyed kissing me as much as I enjoyed the hell out of kissing you."

Double dare? Really? Whatever had possessed her to confess that she was competitive with her brothers? She wanted the words back in the worst way because everyone knew a double dare was sacred.

"I can't deny it," she finally said.

"I thought so." Satisfaction slid into his expression. "Then what's the problem?"

"Why are you hanging out with me?" she challenged.

"I like you."

"But why? Is it for kicks? Bragging rights to the town dating champion? Give her the Austin Anderson stamp of approval?"

"That's not what I'm doing."

"No? Because word on the street is that you date as much as I do. The difference between us is that you're not looking to get serious."

The shadowed look was back and hinted of dark things. "What's wrong with that?"

"Not a thing," she admitted. "You're young and have lots of time to settle down. But here's where I have a problem with you kissing me. It leads to intimacy. In my opinion sex has to mean more than just having a good time. Unless a man and woman are emotionally committed, a session between the sheets shouldn't happen."

"Someone's been reading too many fairy tales."

There was an edge to his voice, hinting of hurtful things. She didn't have details, which shouldn't matter anyway. Something or someone had sent his love life into the Dumpster, but she couldn't afford to let that tug at her heart.

"Clearly you think romance is foolish. Good to know." Rose stood. "I think I need a break."

Before he could stop her, she turned and walked away. Knowing he was into quantity instead of quality was good information, a wake-up call. But it had the effect of a snowball down the back of her shirt and chilled her clear through. Her warm, dewy, wide-eyed anticipation to see Austin froze and died an ugly death.

Her romantic ideal was what it was. She wanted what she wanted. A prince of a guy who would love her forever, marry her and raise a family. It wasn't negotiable, so there was no point in wasting her anticipation on a man who didn't fit her romantic ideal.

Even if that man's kisses made her want a session between the sheets.

Chapter Six

It was finally Friday of a long week that Austin acknowledged was in the top five of long weeks. The truth was, only a couple days had passed since Rose brushed him off.

Someone's been reading too many fairy tales.

He wanted those words back more than any words had ever been wanted back in the history of man.

Surely he'd aged years since that night which might work in his favor, *if* she would ever talk to him again, he thought darkly. More than that, he didn't want pleasing her *or* talking to her again to be so damn important.

Ethan Traub had requested a face-to-face with Austin before lunch and he was in his office just waiting for the word that his boss was free. Concentrating was a challenge and he wasn't getting much work done, so he looked out the window.

The headquarters of Traub Oil Montana was located in a three-story brick building on State Street, in Old Town, one block off the square. Austin was an engineer working in Research and Development and had his own office with a desk, computer and a couple of chairs. Just a few months in the company's new Thunder Canyon center of operations, the furnishings were spartan, but he worked on the third floor and the view was pretty good from up here. Especially for a guy some people in town had predicted wouldn't amount to spit. There was a lot of satisfaction in proving them wrong and he'd feel smug about it once the Rose problem was put into perspective.

Word on the street is that you date as much as I do.

Those words kept playing over and over in his head. Word on the street? Who had she been talking to? And what exactly had they said to her about him? It couldn't have been flattering because clearly Rose had been ticked off. The behavior was a complete one-eighty from the night before when he'd made her laugh, then kissed her and made her want. She'd kissed him back and neither of them had been thinking of anyone else they'd dated.

His intercom buzzed and he pressed the button. "Yes?"

"Austin." It was Ethan's secretary. "He's free to see you now."

"Thanks, Kay." Then he had a thought. "Does he want to see any of my research data?"

"He didn't say, so I'd guess no," she answered.

"Roger that. I'll be right there."

On the way to Ethan's office, just down the hall, Austin wondered a little uneasily if this impromptu meeting had something to do with Rose. Had she told her brother about that kiss? Probably not, what with the pending wager she'd made. But the downside of having the hots for your boss's sister was not knowing if the request for a face-to-face was business or personal.

He pushed open the double doors and walked into the

outer office. Kay Bausch, an experienced secretary who'd relocated from the Midland, Texas, branch of Traub Oil, looked up and smiled. She was a blonde in her mid-fifties and very attractive. Blue eyes hinted at a sense of humor and keen intelligence. She was a widow. It occurred to him that she should meet Ben Walters. What was he? Cupid? Austin couldn't even manage his own love life. Bad choice of words. Not love. Not again.

Austin stopped in front of the desk. "How are you, Kay?"

"Great. You?"

"Also great," he lied. "Have you got big plans for this weekend?"

"I do if you define big plans as staying home with a good book." She smiled. "How about you?"

"My big plans include sorting research data to include in my doctoral dissertation." God, that sounded dull. He was a geek. No data required to support that theory.

"That's pretty impressive. When you're finished, do I have to call you Dr. Anderson?"

"Not if you want me to actually answer," he said.

The phone interrupted her laugh. Before answering, she said, "Go on in. He's expecting you."

Austin walked past her, knocked once on the closed door, then opened it. The man who was spearheading Traub Oil Montana sat behind his desk. "Hi."

Ethan looked the part of a spearheader—tall, handsome, powerful. He closed the laptop on the desk. "Austin, have a seat."

Noting that the other man didn't look particularly upset, Austin breathed a little easier when he took one of the chairs facing his boss. "What's up?"

"I had a meeting yesterday with the accountants and they've increased the R&D budget."

"Wow." Excitement poured through him. "Really?"

"Thanks in part to you, that town meeting in October went a long way toward easing some of the locals' misgivings about extracting oil from shale."

"Me? How? I just answered questions for people as honestly as possible."

"For now that was enough. We bought land leases from some and extraction rights from others, but every last one of them was concerned about the environmental impact of this project on the area around Thunder Canyon."

"So am I."

"It showed," Ethan assured him. "They were impressed with your answers and it meant even more coming from someone they consider one of their own."

"This is my home and I wouldn't be a part of anything to hurt it," he said simply. "All I did was tell them the areas of concern. The support activities generate wastes that require disposal. I'm doing my doctoral dissertation on in situ conversion processes that may reduce the impact."

"You have an emotional stake in what happens and it runs deep." Ethan nodded. "I've been reading your reports carefully. It's pretty technical stuff. Hard to understand."

Not as hard to understand as your sister, Austin thought. But that was information best kept to himself. "Basically, water is an issue. I'm working on a process of filtering and recycling."

"To eliminate toxins and reuse water which would be especially effective in arid regions where water consumption is a sensitive issue." Ethan's grasp of the reports was right on.

Austin was impressed. "Above-ground processing utilizes between one and five barrels of water per barrel of produced shale oil. In situ, below ground," he explained, "uses one-tenth as much water and I'm trying to mini-mize that."

"What else are you working on?" Ethan asked, clearly interested in this aspect of the operation.

"I'm looking at a process to refine carbon capture and storage technology in order to reduce the extraction pro-cess's footprint on the environment."

Ethan laughed and held up his hand. "I'm going to stop you right there. My eyes are glazing over. I try to keep up, but I'll have to take your word on the research part."

"Okay." Austin nodded. "But a bigger budget will really make a difference in improving our technology capabili-ties. Thank you."

"I'll pass that along to the number crunchers." Ethan leaned back in his chair. "The discussion you had with the Thunder Canyon High School science teacher was par-ticularly effective, by the way. Talking to the kids in class about what's going on is generating conversations with their parents. All the reaction is very positive."

"Glad to hear it." So all was good on the career front and should have made Austin a happy guy. *Should have* being the key words. He started to stand up. "Thanks for letting me know—"

Ethan held up a hand. "Before you go—"

"What?" he said when the other man hesitated.

Hopefully it was something more about business, but Austin didn't think so. There was a protective-older-brother look on Ethan's face that was a dead giveaway.

"You're under no obligation to answer. This is com-pletely unrelated to your work which is impeccable. I couldn't be happier with what you're doing here at Traub Oil."

"But?" Definitely about Rose, he thought grimly.

"Jackson mentioned something and I was wondering—"

"This is about your sister," Austin said. No point in dodging the issue.

"Yes."

"What about her?" He wouldn't volunteer anything that would give her brothers even a technicality win in the wager. He also didn't want to dig himself into a hole by opening his big mouth.

"I saw her with you at the wedding. And I'm told you've been spotted around Thunder Canyon together. Hanging out at ROOTS. At DJ's. The Holiday Presents for Patriots project."

Small-town life. Austin knew from firsthand experience that it was both a blessing and a curse. People were there for you and they were *there* for you, whether you wanted them or not. And they talked.

"About the wedding," he started. "We were both going alone, so—"

"A date?"

"No." The word came out more forcefully than Austin intended even though the wedding was before she'd made the wager. "Just friends."

"Are you dating?"

The double-dare bet. Austin wouldn't rat her out, no matter what tension there was between them. But Ethan's motivation for asking had nothing to do with a silly bet, Austin realized. The expression on the other man's face was all about brotherly concern.

"No, I'm not dating Rose."

"You're sure?"

His boss was pushing a bit and Austin pushed back. "Are you asking about my intentions?"

"No. Yes." Ethan dragged his fingers through his dark hair as irritation registered in his brown eyes. "Maybe. She's my baby sister."

"I understand."

"Look, Austin, I know as your employer that I've got no right to interfere in your personal life, but I'm kind of accustomed to looking out for her. No offense intended."

"None taken." Austin stood. "You can stand down. I've got a baby sister, too. And I'd never treat a woman badly."

Especially because he knew how it felt to be on the receiving end of bad treatment. As he walked back to his own office, Austin figured that it was probably for the best that Rose no longer wanted to see him.

Mixing business and personal was never a good idea, especially since he and Rose had very different ideas on dating.

"Really, Rose? The Tottering Teapot?" Jackson stared across the table after glancing at the female-oriented café's menu.

"I love this place," Laila said. "It's completely charming."

"Every woman in town loves this place," he said.

After shooting him a triumphant look, Rose said, "I'm glad you like it, Laila, because this lunch is all about apologizing to you for spoiling your evening the other night."

"*Her* evening? What about mine?"

"You already got your revenge," Rose reminded him.

She had another reason for picking up the lunch tab today, a favor to ask her brother. It occurred to her that The Hitching Post with arguably the best burgers in town might have been a better place to get on his good side.

"I've never eaten here," she said. "I wanted to try it."

"The portobello mushroom sandwich is so good," Laila told her. "This place is famous for its vegetarian sandwiches."

"No wonder I'm the only man in the place." Jackson blew out a long breath. "There's no meat here."

"Not true." Rose looked up from the menu. "They have free-range chicken and grass-fed beef."

"Oh, that makes it better," he said sarcastically. "The smell of candles and tea is sucking out all my testosterone. Just kill me now."

"Oh, for Pete's sake. Why did you agree to come here then?"

"Because Laila wanted to."

Rose nearly sighed out loud because of the way Jackson was looking at the woman who'd tamed his notorious bachelor's heart. You could practically touch the love arcing between them and she was completely envious. It's what she wanted—a man who would sacrifice testosterone to be with her at The Tottering Teapot.

The café was located in Old Town on Main Street near Pine. In addition to the menu, everything about the place was female-friendly. The tables were covered with lace tablecloths, no two the same. Food was served on thrift-store-bought, mismatched china. In deference to its name, there was an endless variety of teas, both herbal and otherwise.

Two thoughts came to mind simultaneously. Had Austin ever brought a date here? And she really hoped her brother didn't want coffee.

A young woman in her late teens or early twenties stopped at their table, pad and pencil in hand. "Hi, my name is Flo. Are you ready to order or do you need a minute?"

"A minute won't change the menu," Jackson grumbled. "I'll have a hamburger."

"We have veggie or turkey in addition to grass-fed beef."

"Beef," he said without hesitation. To his credit he didn't shudder at the other choices.

"Would you like a spring mix salad on the side?"

"No fries?" he asked.

"Sorry." With pencil poised above the pad, Flo shrugged.

"What's spring mix?" he asked skeptically.

"Different kinds of lettuce. Arugula, radicchio, red and green romaine—"

"Please tell me that's a Christmas thing."

"No, sir, it's organic."

"Girl greens—"

"He'll have the macaroni salad. It's delicious," Laila told him. "I'd like the portobello mushroom sandwich with salad. And peppermint tea."

"Make it two," Rose said.

When the waitress looked at him expectantly, Jackson sighed. "I'll just have water."

No one could accuse her brother of not adapting.

When they were alone, Rose said to him, "You're a really good sport."

"Maybe," he answered, glancing around the room crowded with women. "But if either of you tell anyone about this, I'll deny ever setting foot in the door."

"Good luck with that." Laila patted his hand. "You can't sneeze without everyone in Thunder Canyon knowing you've got a cold."

"It's true. You can't go anywhere without someone noticing who you're with." He nodded thoughtfully. "And you're right, Rosie. I am a good sport. The question is, are you? Because I think you lost the bet."

"Oh, please," Laila scoffed. "You're not really going to hold her to a month without a date."

"The heck I'm not. It's a double dare and she agreed to the terms. She's up to six weeks no dating now."

Their food arrived and Rose held back her comments until they were alone. "It would be hard to lose the bet since I haven't been out on a date."

Apprehensively, Jackson took a bite of his burger, then nodded appreciatively. After chewing he said, "More than one person has seen you with Austin Anderson."

"You're talking about the wedding, but that was before—"

"The bet," he interrupted. "I know. What about Holiday Presents for Patriots? You were with him there at DJ's. And before that ROOTS. That big window looks right out on the street where everyone going by can see. Someone saw you going into the town hall with him after hours."

"Oh, for Pete's sake. He helped me with the mayor's Christmas cards." The kiss wasn't something she planned to share. If only not remembering it could be that easy.

"A likely story." Hesitantly he took a bite of macaroni salad and nodded at Laila. "If this is fake pasta, please keep it to yourself. It's good."

"I wouldn't steer you wrong." She smiled at him. "Stick with me."

He winked at her. "Try and get rid of me."

This "apology" lunch was starting to feel like another interruption to their alone time and it was on the tip of her tongue to say "get a room."

"Seriously, Rosie, according to more than one eyewitness you're dating Austin Anderson."

"Not true," she said adamantly. "I went to ROOTS on the mayor's official business. Austin just happened to be there."

"And at DJ's? Presents for Patriots? He just happened to be there again?"

"Yes." She met her brother's gaze, telling herself he didn't need to know that Austin had made sure she'd be there right after giving her the hottest kiss she'd ever had.

"Come on, sis. You expect me to believe that he just happens to turn up everywhere you are?"

"I follow the rules. You can't lie on a double dare. It's wrong in so many ways." Stretching the truth, however, was different from an out-and-out untruth. "I can say in all honesty that our encounters did not contain the necessary components of a date. Nothing was prearranged with Austin and he spent no money on me. I swear."

He studied her for a moment. "Okay, then."

Rose and Laila had half their sandwiches remaining when Flo returned with to-go boxes. "Are you ladies saving room for dessert?"

Both of them declined. Rose looked at her brother. "How about you?"

"I checked it out." He shook his head. "You can't put carrots and zucchini in sugar and flour and call it cake. It's just wrong."

Flo laughed. "I'll leave the check, then. No rush."

"My treat." Rose grabbed it. "How was your burger?"

He glanced at his empty plate. "Surprisingly good."

Thank God, because it was time to hit him up for the favor. "So, Mayor Clifton is really looking forward to the kid's annual Christmas party tomorrow."

"I suppose he is." Her brother met her gaze.

"His little girl is turning one. It will be her first Christmas. First time seeing Santa." *If* she could get her brother to step into the role at the last minute.

"Homer Johnson has been doing it for years," Laila said. "He does a great job."

"I'm sure he does."

There must have been something in her tone and expression because Jackson gave her a hard look. "Don't go there, sis."

"What?" She put as much innocence as possible into her voice, but darn it, he knew her too well.

"I'm not playing Santa Claus tomorrow."

"What makes you think I'm asking—"

"I just know."

She sighed. "Homer called me this morning. He could hardly talk. It's the flu. He can't get out of bed let alone spread germs to all the kids. They'll be so disappointed."

"Don't turn those big blue eyes on me. It's not going to work."

"Why not? What have you got against kids? You're a good listener. All you have to do is ask them what they want for Christmas."

"Not going to happen."

"Why not?" Laila asked. "You love kids."

"Yes, I do, but what do I say when they ask how the reindeer pull the sleigh? Or how Santa can deliver toys all over the world in one night?"

"Just tell them it's magic," Rose suggested.

"What about the precocious one who wants specifics? And physics?" He shook his head.

Laila tapped her lip. "You know who would be good at that?"

"Who?" Rose asked. "I'm desperate."

"Austin."

Hadn't she just defended herself and all the time she'd spent with him lately? Now they were throwing him at her? As much as she'd enjoyed every minute with him, including that kiss, this was a really bad idea.

"I'm not sure he's mature enough to pull it off," she finally said.

"Of course he can." Laila nodded confidently. "He's got

that really deep voice. He looks much older than he is. And with the red suit and white beard as his disguise… Trust me, he'll be a natural at it."

Rose agreed with everything the other woman had said. The problem, and there was more than one, was that after the way she'd huffed out of DJ's the other night, she didn't think he'd speak to her, let alone help her out. And she wouldn't blame him.

"Can you think of anyone else?" she asked.

Laila and Jackson looked at each other, then said, "No." He looked at his watch. "And I have to get back to work."

"Me, too," Laila said.

When they stood, he helped her put on her jacket. Rose remembered Austin doing that for her and how the gesture had warmed her more than a coat ever could.

"Thanks for lunch, Rose," Laila said. "You didn't have to."

"Yeah, you did." Jackson grinned before escorting his fiancée to the door.

Rose waited for Flo to bring back her credit card so that she could sign for the charge. She couldn't think of anyone else to play Santa Claus and letting down the kids wasn't an option. She took her cell phone from her purse. Desperate situations called for desperate measures, she thought, pulling up her contact list. Austin Anderson was the first name. How ironic was that? After hitting the buttons, she heard the ring and he answered on the second one.

"This is Austin."

"Hi, it's Rose." Two beats of hesitation meant he hadn't looked at the caller ID. There was a short but incredibly awkward silence and she filled it. "Are you busy? Is this a bad time?"

"No, I'm not busy. Just got out of a meeting with your brother."

"How's Ethan?" Stalling. Procrastinating. Putting off his rejection.

"Good."

There was another awkward silence that was hers to fill because she'd called him. It was now or never. "Austin, I have a favor. It's really important. I wouldn't ask if it wasn't for the kids."

"What?"

She toyed with her teacup and the used bag on the saucer. "My Santa for tomorrow's party is sick. I can't find anyone and wondered if you'd be willing to fill in."

After two beats he asked, "Does Santa have a helper this year?"

"What?"

"I've been to the mayor's party. There's always someone to play the elf."

She hesitated because the answer was sure to be a deal breaker. "It's me. I'm the elf."

"I see."

This wasn't the best time to notice how really, really deep his voice was. And she wished he'd use it instead of leaving her hanging, twisting in the wind. "Look, it's really short notice. If you're busy—"

"Are you wearing the costume?" he asked.

"Of course."

"With the short skirt and tights?"

"Yes." She couldn't stop a smile.

"I'll do it."

Relief flooded her. "Thank you so much."

"There's a condition."

"What? It's not enough that I'll look like a fugitive from the toy shop at the North Pole?"

"My house needs decorating and I could use your help. Sunday night. Five o'clock." This time he filled the silence.

"It's not a date. Just a friend helping the friend who helped her."

Did she have a choice?

"Okay. I'll see you tomorrow, Austin."

"For two people who aren't dating, you and Austin are sure spending an awful lot of time together." Jackson picked up a red scarf from the seat of the chair where Laila had sat. Suspicion gleamed in his eyes.

Rose had been so into the phone call that she hadn't noticed her brother come up from behind her. "He agreed to be my Santa. Well, not *my* Santa. For the kids. It wasn't my idea," she reminded him.

But she was very grateful to Austin for bailing her out. Definitely a "white knight" moment.

And she was looking forward to seeing him in more than a friend-helping-out-a-friend kind of way. Anticipation was back with a vengeance.

Darn it all.

Chapter Seven

Austin had imagined how Rose would look in the elf costume, but the flesh-and-blood redhead in the short dress and green tights was so much better. It was worth wearing the hot suit, and he didn't mean that in a sexy way. The belly padding was bulky, the glue holding the beard on was irritating, he was already sweating and the party hadn't even started yet. After putting on the costume, he'd just walked into the big upstairs room at the town hall.

But the view of Rose's butt as she bent over the big Santa bags of wrapped toys made the discomfort so worth it. Then she straightened and turned. The holiday hat on her head had a bell on the end and there were two big round spots of color on her cheeks.

It was a Raggedy Ann does Christmas look and worked in a big way. Something tightened in his chest and he wasn't sure whether to be turned on, hang on to his heart, or both.

She walked over and gave him an assessing look from head to toe. "The suit is fantastic. You look great."

"So do you."

Self-consciously she touched her hat. "I feel really stupid in this get-up."

"I feel your pain."

"At least no one will recognize you. I'd rather be Mrs. Claus."

"So Santa can make an honest woman of you?" he teased.

"No, because of the long dress and age-appropriate character."

"Ah." He had her on a technicality. "Then one could assume if I'm age-appropriate enough to play Santa to your Mrs. Claus, that would make null and void your excuse for not going out with me."

She looked surprised. "You still *want* to go out with me?"

"Yes." Even though it was against his better judgment. "When your dating hiatus is over."

"Rose?" Rhonda Culpepper was calling her.

The older woman worked at the town hall reception desk during the week. She definitely got attention with her black hair and that dramatic white streak over the right temple. It was Saturday and she was one of the many volunteers who made this annual party a success.

Opposite the landing on the second floor, the big room had a raised stage where there was a big leather chair waiting for him. Austin suspected that it was borrowed from the downstairs courtroom. A tree with ornaments and white lights took up a whole corner. Decorations that had been in the boxes he'd seen the night he kissed Rose in her office now transformed the place into a holiday scene worthy of Dickens's *A Christmas Carol*. Downstairs there was the gift tree with names of needy kids and their wish list. Rose had told him one of the reasons for this party was to get higher-than-normal foot traffic through the building to make people aware that there were children who wouldn't have a Christmas without help.

Children.

Christmas was about kids. In a few minutes they would be telling Santa what they wanted most this year and he would do his best not to disappoint them. His gaze rested on Rose who was helping to line up the kids. If only telling someone he wanted her would make his wish come true. On his terms.

Rose left Rhonda and walked over to him. "We're on, big guy."

As they walked on stage to take their places, he said, "Aren't you supposed to say break a leg or something?"

"That sounds bad to me. Negative and bad." She smiled, but her nerves were showing. "This is going to be fun."

"So much fun." He blew out a long breath.

Austin took his place in the chair. When he was settled, Rhonda sent over the kids. First in line was Mayor Bo Clifton and his wife, Holly Pritchett Clifton, who was holding their one-year-old daughter. With their blond hair and blue eyes, they looked like Ken and Barbie, in a good way, a couple committed to family and community. Nothing phony about the Cliftons.

Bo had been a jeans-and-boots kind of guy before being elected and was still that way. He said a few words to the crowd, welcomed everyone to the party and wished all a happy holiday season. There was a photographer set up to take complimentary pictures of each child with Santa.

Then Austin had the little girl on his lap. Earlier he'd called Homer Johnson and asked for pointers. The man who could barely talk and had to cough his way through the conversation warned him that some of the kids got scared but not to take it personally. Some would tug on the beard to see if it was real. And then there would be skeptics with questions, but he was on his own to answer them.

Austin waited for Sabrina Clifton to shriek in fear, but she just looked curious. It was pointless to ask what she wanted for Christmas, so he directed the question to Holly.

"A doll and a tricycle," the mom answered.

"Has she been a good little girl?" Of course she was, he thought. How bad could a one-year-old be? But Homer had told him the question had to be asked. No exceptions. Carved in stone.

The mayor slid his arm around his wife and smiled at his daughter. "She's perfect."

Rose hunched down to Sabrina-level and handed her a pink-wrapped present. "Santa has a gift for you." Then she handed a candy cane to Holly and whispered, "If you want her to have it."

The couple reclaimed their daughter and it got really busy after that. Rose led the children over to him, then he lifted each one onto his lap. After the short conversation she handed each one a gender-appropriate gift and a candy cane. Teamwork kept the line moving steadily and all went smoothly until the two-year-old. Rose let his mother lead the wary child over.

"Do you want to sit on Santa's lap and have your picture taken?" Rose asked him.

The little boy shook his head, but mom pleaded. "I promised my mom I'd get pictures of everything. They can't be here this year because Dad got sick at the last minute. It's Santa, Colton," she pleaded, her own digital camera in her hand.

As soon as Colton's mom put the kid on his lap, the wailing commenced, loud enough to shatter windows. In

South Dakota. Colton wanted no part of this. Austin tried bouncing his knee, talking Santa to him and tickling, but nothing worked.

Rose leaned down and whispered, "You don't have a trick up your sleeve, do you?"

That gave him an idea. "Hand me a candy cane."

She did and Colton's crying slowed enough to show he'd noticed. Austin hid the candy in his sleeve, then made a great show of pulling it out of the kid's ear. He stopped crying and took the candy. With the other hand, he checked out his head, trying to figure out where it came from. The picture was snapped without a big smile, but there were no tears.

Rose smiled at him as if he'd hung the moon. "Ah, the magic of the season."

After that, he got the skeptic and beard-puller all in one. Blonde Sarah Swenson was about ten and followed instructions to smile for the camera after he'd lifted her onto his lap.

Before he could ask anything she said, "Are you real?"

"Yes," he answered seriously.

"Are those whiskers real?"

"Yes."

"Can I see for myself?"

"Of course." He braced himself and hoped there was enough adhesive to keep from blowing his cover. And when this gig was over, he really hoped he could get it off with most of his face intact. "Go for it."

She pulled and couldn't budge it but still looked skeptical when it stayed in place.

"What can Santa bring you for Christmas?" he asked in the deepest Santa voice he could manage.

"I went on an airplane trip with my mom and dad and it took forever to get there. If you're really real, how do you fly all over the world and leave presents for kids all in one night?"

"I'll tell you a secret."

"What?" Her look turned even more suspicious.

"The sleigh has a flux capacitor that makes it go really fast."

"What's that?" Sarah pushed the stray blond hair off her forehead.

"It's pretty complicated, but it gives the sleigh warp drive to make it go at the speed of light. It's something I invented a long time ago. But it wouldn't work without the special food for Rudolph."

"What kind of food?" Sarah looked interested now.

"At the North Pole, there are magic crystals in the snow. They're called dilithium and it makes his nose red so he can find the worm holes." Austin happened to glance at Rose who was grinning. But the laughter in her eyes told him she knew where he'd gotten this story.

"What are worm holes?" Sarah asked.

"Short cuts all over the world. When you go faster than the speed of light, time slows down. Sometimes I can make it stop if necessary. It's a physics thing. But I can pick up a lot of time that way."

"Okay." The little girl seemed to accept all that spin, but there was still something on her mind. "But how do you get in and out of the sleigh so fast and leave stuff? That takes a lot of time."

"It does," he agreed, as serious as she was. "But I have a trick. I wiggle my nose and beam the presents down the chimney. That really speeds things up."

"Can you make a two-wheeler bike go down the chimney?"

Pride goes before the fall. He was patting himself on the

back for all the spin and hadn't seen that one coming. But Rose happened to hear.

"Something magic happens when Santa wiggles his nose," she said.

"What?" Sarah asked, clearly interested.

"It's a process. He demolecularizes everything into a beam of light. When it's under the tree, it remolecularizes again." She met his gaze and her eyes were sparkling.

"In that case," the little girl looked back at him. "I would like a two-wheel bike for Christmas. Pink. With streamers on the handlebars."

"I can do that," Austin said seriously. "On one condition."

"What?" Sarah wanted to know.

"You can't tell anyone my secrets."

"Not even my mom?"

He glanced up at the little girl's mother who'd overheard everything and was doing her best not to laugh. "Not even your mother."

"Okay," she said solemnly. "And Santa? I'm sorry I didn't believe you."

"Sarah," he answered just as seriously. "Don't ever stop asking questions. Promise?"

"Yes."

He held up his hand and she gave him a high-five.

"Here's the suit."

Rose was in her office staring out the window and turned to see Austin in the doorway. It was late afternoon and the party was over, the room cleaned up and all the little ones gone. The building was eerily quiet after the noisy, festive, family-filled event.

She'd asked Austin to bring the Santa suit back to her, but could just as easily have requested that he leave the big box on her desk. The return didn't require her presence and she could have slipped away, but it was an excuse to see him one more time.

She stood behind her desk. It was probably best that she didn't get too close to him without being in costume. Watching him give magic to the kids had been a whole different kind of magic for her.

"Just set it inside the door."

Beside her elf get-up. More than once she'd caught him looking at her butt or her legs. It was hard to tell with the fake beard and wire-rimmed glasses, but she was pretty sure he'd liked what he saw.

He did as instructed, then slid his fingertips into the pockets of his jeans and leaned a shoulder against the wall. Apparently he didn't want to get close to her either, but probably for a different reason. And she owed him an apology.

"Seriously? Worm holes?" she asked.

"Give 'em the old razzle dazzle. I didn't think any suit could be more uncomfortable than a tux, but I was wrong." He glanced at the big box beside him.

"Austin, thanks for doing it. I mean that. You really saved my—" She shrugged and let him fill in the blank. "The engineer who rescued Christmas."

"Yeah, a real hero."

"I know you agreed because of the kids, not for me. Not after the way I left you at DJ's. It's a wonder you would even speak to me."

He met her gaze. "I was out of line with my comments. That was uncalled for."

Very gallant of him, but she should have let it roll off. "I feel as if I should explain my reaction."

"That's not necessary."

"Yeah, it is." She didn't come around the desk, but stood

her ground behind it. For an added layer of protection, she folded her arms over her chest. "When I was in college, I fell in love with a pre-med student. We were together for over a year and a half, moved into an apartment. The whole bit. Graduation was coming up and he'd been accepted to med school on the East Coast. Marriage was the next step and I was ready to work and support us while he went to school. I didn't want to take help from my family. We'd be poor but happy and both get what we wanted. Medicine and marriage."

"Did he propose?" There was an edge to his voice and darkness in his eyes.

"He picked med school over me. I was committed, he wasn't." She shrugged. "Not only did it take a long time to get over him, it was time I'll never get back. I apologize for being snippy the other night. You've been nothing but honest and didn't deserve that. I hope you understand."

Instead of answering, he asked, "You want to go get coffee?"

She did, but it wasn't that simple. Jackson was already getting suspicious. "What if someone sees us?"

"Good, that's not a no." He straightened away from the wall. "Is there somewhere safe from the Traub brothers?"

"I don't think they'll be going to The Tottering Teapot any time soon," she said wryly.

"That place doesn't have coffee and is probably closed now anyway because it's way past lunchtime."

She was impressed that for such a masculine guy, he was familiar with the female fortress of froufrou food. But he had two sisters and engineers were notoriously detail-oriented.

"You know what? Let's go across the street to The Daily Grind," she said, throwing caution to the wind. "You did me a huge favor and I'm buying coffee to say thanks. If anyone sees us and it gets back to my brothers, they can just ho, ho, ho it out their ears."

He smiled for the first time. "You're on."

With coats on, they walked down the stairs to the town hall foyer where Rhonda was saying goodbye to straggler volunteers.

The older woman smiled at them. "Austin Anderson, I never would have recognized you in that beard and suit and I've known you since you were a little guy."

"Thanks, I think."

"Next year Homer Johnson just might have some competition for the job."

"Not on my account. I was happy to fill in, but I hope next year he's hearty, healthy and Santa-ready." He stopped and picked the name of a needy boy from the lobby's Christmas tree and stuck it in his pocket before opening the door for Rose.

Rhonda stood by with a key to lock up after them. "You two have a nice evening."

Rose winced and started to say it was just a cup of coffee. There was no "you two." But protesting only fueled the rumor mill, making it a bigger deal than necessary.

Instead she said, "See you on Monday."

"'Night, Rose. Austin."

It was cold outside and a light snow was falling. She shivered at the change in temperature and Austin looked down, as if to make sure she was all right, but didn't say anything. In silence they walked across State Street. The Daily Grind, with the picture of a grinder and beans on the big picture window, was straight ahead. Again Austin opened the door and let her precede him inside.

The interior was a cozy combination of bistro tables, armchairs and displays of mugs for sale, some with Christmas designs for holiday gifts. There was a glass case with shelves of pastries, including scones, coffee cake and muffins. About a third of the tables were occupied, but Rose didn't recognize anyone.

A young woman, wearing an apron with The Daily Grind embroidered on it, smiled and asked, "What can I get you?"

Rose came here nearly every day since she worked across the street, but didn't recognize the teenager who probably worked weekends only. However, she knew the menu by heart and didn't hesitate.

"I'd like a creamy eggnog latte, nonfat milk."

"Whipped cream?"

The Monday-through-Friday group wouldn't have asked that question. "Oh, yeah."

"And you, sir?"

"I'm normally a black coffee kind of guy, but I'll have what she's having."

"And a pumpkin scone," Rose added.

He looked down at her. "Because you banked the calories saved with having nonfat milk and they're burning a hole in your pocket?"

She shook her head. "Because I burned those calories releasing my inner elf today."

When the coffees were ready, they found a table for two in the corner where it was quiet. She pulled the scone out of the brown bag and broke off a piece.

He shook his head when she offered him some. "I think we made a pretty good team today," he said.

"I don't know about me as an elf, but you did a terrific Santa. I had no idea you'd be so great with the kids."

"You sound surprised."

"I guess I am," she admitted.

"Why?" His eyes narrowed.

The dark expression was back, making him look older somehow. Sort of battle-tested.

"I don't know." Suddenly she wasn't hungry for her favorite pumpkin scone and turned the piece in her hands to crumbs. "Just connecting the dots, I guess."

"What dots would those be?"

"Kids would be part of a serious relationship and you're not looking for serious. Totally understandable. A guy like you—"

"Meaning a guy my age?" His voice didn't go up in pitch. If anything, it was husky, edgier, hinting at a deep pocket of anger.

Rose realized she'd never seen Austin really angry. Annoyed. Irritated. That's the side he'd shown to her snippy the other night. But this was very different.

"Age has nothing to do with it," he said. "There's no chronological connection to wanting kids and I did. I've always felt that way. In fact I was sure I'd be married and have one of my own by now."

"But I thought you were only interested in having fun. Playing the field."

"I am. *Now.*" There was a brooding look on his face as he turned his cardboard coffee cup. He hadn't taken a sip. Just kept turning it as the brood intensified.

She'd told him her story and clearly he had one, too. Maybe confession was in the air. She dreaded the answer but had to know. "What happened to you?"

"I asked a girl to marry me. Rachel." He met her gaze. "It was a couple years ago. She was a summer waitress at DJ's. I'd just graduated from college and was home for the summer. She was beautiful and outgoing and I fell—hard and fast. I thought she'd leave when the vacation crowds thinned out in September and I didn't want her to go."

"Did you propose?"

That was the same question he'd asked her earlier. It was pretty obvious that his story didn't have a happy ending either.

"At DJ's," he confirmed. "She was working. The place was packed. Someone overheard me pop the question and next thing I knew, everyone was cheering and clapping for me. For us. I put the engagement ring on her finger."

Rose had lived in this town long enough to know that kind of news didn't stop within the walls of the restaurant. The word spread all over Thunder Canyon that Austin was getting married.

"And?" she urged.

"I didn't realize until later that she never gave me an answer. It only felt like she'd said yes and I was getting the family I'd always wanted."

"What happened?"

"She left town. Disappeared without a word and took the ring with her. As failures go, a public one sucks."

He wasn't talking about his tattoo because that didn't show. But Ben Walters knew which meant he shared with people he trusted. Obviously, Austin got the double whammy for all to see.

At least the guy who'd hurt her had done it in private, but Austin hadn't been so lucky. It didn't matter that all of Thunder Canyon would take his side, Austin's humiliation was right out there for everyone to see.

"Oh, Austin—" Rose didn't think. She just reached out to touch him.

He pulled his hand away. "After that I decided to go for my doctorate."

Translation: He kept himself too busy for anything but shallow, uncommitted relationships. Nothing serious because that way he wouldn't get hurt.

The twit who'd run out with his ring had robbed him of

something even more precious. When she'd dumped a great guy like Austin, a guy Rose could really care about, she'd stolen his trust. Now Rose got really angry. What ticked her off was that kind of experience would leave a mark and it would be a long time, if ever, before he'd believe in anyone or commit again.

Now she knew all the gory details of his dark secret and almost wished she didn't.

She didn't have dilithium crystals or light speed to make time go backward and eliminate their age difference. And even if she could, he wouldn't risk getting serious again.

For her, that was a double deal breaker.

Chapter Eight

At five minutes to five Rose stood at Austin's front door waiting to ring the bell. The small stucco house where he'd grown up, where his mom had raised two daughters and a son, was outside of town and had a well-maintained yard. She supposed there was grass under the snow, but neatly trimmed bushes were definitely visible. His truck stood in the driveway, the only vehicle there, meaning Angie probably wasn't home. They'd be alone. For Pete's sake, the yard had a white picket fence.

Could it be more family-friendly? His salary as an engineer would certainly support a swinging bachelor pad, but he had a white picket fence, for goodness' sake.

Rose knew she should probably turn around and walk away but didn't for two reasons. The first being that she wasn't in the habit of breaking her word and she'd promised to help him decorate if he played Santa. Second, she couldn't run out on him without an explanation. She wouldn't be like the twit who'd dumped him and taken the ring. The thought of it made her mad all over again. No one would ever accuse her of doing something like that. If a man offered her a ring she wouldn't take it unless she was prepared to say yes.

So she was here to tell him she couldn't stay. After ringing the bell, she mentally rehearsed the reasons *why* she wouldn't be able to stay. The door opened before she was ready.

"Hi, Rose." Austin stepped back. "Come on in."

"Just for a minute."

"Putting up decorations will take more than a minute." When the cold air was shut out, he frowned. "Are you backing out of the deal?"

"That depends. Is Angie here?"

"No." He settled his hands on his lean hips. "She's working, then studying for finals with a friend."

That's what Rose was afraid of. She really wished there'd been more time for mental rehearsal. "It's not a good idea for me to be alone with you."

"We need a chaperone?"

She couldn't tell if he was angry or making a joke. Either way, honesty was best. "Yes."

"What if I promise nothing will happen?"

"I appreciate that, but what if I don't trust myself?" Her imagination had been in overdrive and he'd been the star of her fantasies ever since kissing her.

A smile curved up the corners of his mouth as he looked down at her. "I'm pretty sure I can protect my virtue and keep you in line."

She couldn't help smiling back. "How?"

"I'll throw you out if you get frisky."

"Promise?"

He made a cross over his heart. "Scout's honor. Okay?"

Rose knew it was a mistake not to turn around and walk right out the door. She knew it because of the delicious warm feeling she got just from looking at him, a feeling she had no business having. But she didn't turn around. She stayed and glanced at the inside of his place, getting the impression that it was just as family-friendly as the outside.

"This is nice. Homey."

"Yeah." He slid his fingers into his pockets. "Small but functional. Although it feels bigger since Haley moved out. I've gone up the food chain to the master bedroom. Rank has its privileges."

The kitchen was off to the left through a doorway. She got a glimpse of an oak table and chairs, soft yellow walls and white cotton curtains. Boxes were neatly stacked in the living room in front of the leather corner group. A simple oak coffee table was pushed aside. In one corner there was a flat-screen TV. The smell of fresh pine filled the room and mingled with something cinnamony.

In the other corner she saw the tree. She couldn't remember when, if ever, she'd been around a real pine. For years her mother had put up an artificial one, pretty but lacking the wonderful woodsy smell that no candle or aerosol scent could duplicate. The white lights were already on the tree and it was just waiting for decoration.

He followed her gaze. "Angie and I cut it down earlier today."

"Austin, you should hold off until she has time to do this with you."

"Not to worry. I mentioned you were coming over to help and she was grateful. If I waited for her it wouldn't get done until Christmas." He held out his hand. "So give me your coat and stay a while."

Rose handed him her things. When he disappeared with them into another room, she moved closer to the fireplace and warmed up. On the mantel there were framed pictures. In one there was a beautiful brunette flanked by two little girls and a handsome boy. The woman must be Austin's mother—gone far too young. Rose couldn't imagine how hard the tragic loss must have been on her children.

"Can I get you some coffee? Hot chocolate? Mulled wine?"

Rose turned and looked at him. "You do not really have mulled wine."

"Want to bet?"

"No way." She'd done enough wagering recently. Although she was beginning to realize that it wasn't the double dare that convinced her to go along with the dating hiatus. Deep down she'd known it was time to take a break. "Mulled wine it is."

"With a cinnamon stick?" he asked.

"You do not really have—" The wry expression on his face stopped her and she said, "Yes, please."

She followed him into the kitchen and noted that he had a nice butt. So sue her. If he could check hers out while she was bending over in an elf costume, she could do the same. Male butts were not created equal and she'd done a fair amount of observation research on the subject. Austin's worn jeans, showing the outline of his wallet, showcased to full advantage his superior posterior.

He stopped at the stove where steam was rising from a pot. Two snowman mugs stood on the counter beside it and he ladled the hot liquid into each. After inserting a cinnamon stick, he handed a cup to her.

"Smells good." She looked into the pot, then up at him. "You're an engineer, right? Not a mad scientist?"

"Yes. Why?" He leaned back against the counter and folded his arms over his chest.

"What's in this stuff? I saw oranges. And mulled wine?

Who thought that up? Mull means to contemplate. What could that concoction possibly be mulling over anyway?"

He picked up his cup and blew on it before taking a sip. "It's good. Trust me. Do you always go out of your way to make things complicated?"

"It's a gift." She took a small drink from her mug. "You're right. Good stuff. Just the thing for a cold winter night of decorating for the holidays. Which we should really get started doing. What do you want to do first?"

"Biggest job…"

"The tree," they said together.

"I have to get the ornaments out of the packing boxes," he told her.

She took several more sips of the warm, spicy drink, then set the mug down on the coffee table beside Austin's. The two were identical except hers had lipstick on the rim.

He pulled the top box from the stack and set it on the wood floor, then went down on one knee beside it and opened the flaps. Rose knelt next to him and looked inside. There were multiple packages of green, red, silver, gold and white circular ornaments in small, medium and large sizes. Beneath that were tiny boxes of collectibles with Austin's and Angie's names on them.

Austin saw her look and explained. "Every Christmas my mother bought each of us one special ornament. She said that someday we'd leave home and probably not have two pennies to rub together. The ornaments were a start for our own trees and our own lives. Roots and wings." He held up a little truck with a fir tree in the back. "She got me this the year I was fifteen and a pain in the neck about getting a tree. None of us ever thought she'd leave first, that she wouldn't be here to see us move out and get our first tree."

"That's why Haley's aren't here," Rose guessed. "She's putting up her very first tree with Marlon this year."

"Yeah."

Rose touched his arm. "Your mom is watching."

"Maybe."

"Trust me." When he smiled, she glanced in the box and saw what appeared to be handmade and dated decorations. There was a delicate round one with what looked like angel hair pulled over a thin, plastic circle with pasted on eyes and a black felt top hat. "It's a snowman face."

Austin smiled, but it was bittersweet around the edges. "My mother made that. Actually she made more than one."

"But I didn't see any others there."

"It was a school thing. When Haley started kindergarten, Mom initiated a PTA program to hand make ornaments. She organized parent volunteers, picked out the pattern and materials to assemble. The finished product was given to each kid in the class at the party just before the holiday break. She continued the project when I started kindergarten, then with Angie. We each have one dated ornament for grades K through six."

"That's such a wonderful tradition." Rose wondered if she'd ever have a child to start a tradition for. If so, she was definitely doing the ornament thing.

Austin's face showed pleasure mixed with pain, until he laughed.

"What's so funny?" she asked.

His dark eyes were full of a memory that made them dance with humor. He took the snowman from her. "I remember when she was making these. I got home from school and she was sitting cross-legged on the floor with an empty bottle of that white glue in front of her. The stuff was on her jeans and her fingers had that white hair stuck to them. It was everywhere but on the snowman's face."

"Do you know what it is?"

He nodded. "She unbraided white rope and combed it out, then stretched it over the round part, which is PVC pipe, by the way."

"An engineering marvel."

"Not as far as Mom was concerned. She got so frustrated, the glue bottle got heaved across the room. There were some colorful four-letter words muttered under her breath and I never told her I heard every one. Then she swore, without colorful adjectives, that she'd never do anything crafty again."

"But she did," Rose guessed.

"Every Christmas. She was determined that each of her kids would have one for every year in grade school. And we do."

"What a wonderful story, Austin. I wish I could have met your mom."

"Me, too."

"So." She stood, looking at the tree. "How do you want to do this? Showcase the special, one-of-a-kind decorations prominently in the front, then fill in with generic ornaments?"

"Sounds like a plan. I knew there was a good reason for luring you over here."

Before she could take that double entendre to a dangerous place, Rose carried an armful of decorations over to the tree and got busy. Austin did the same and they worked in silence. When she stood on tiptoe but couldn't reach the branch, he easily hung whatever she wanted wherever she wanted it. Every time he moved close to her and their fingers brushed, she felt friction and sparks and tingles.

Oh, my.

Had a man ever smelled so good? The temptation to bury her face in his chest was making her crazy. Finally,

Rose stepped back, pretending to survey full scope of the tree, but mostly to put a little distance between herself and Austin.

"Not bad. It looks balanced and all the really cool stuff is up front and in plain view." She turned as he was pulling green-and-gold garland from another box. "What's that?"

"The finishing touch." His eyes narrowed at the expression of horror on her face. "Something wrong?"

"I hope that isn't a family heirloom of your mother's."

"No, I got it on sale after Christmas a couple years ago."

"Thank God. And your sisters actually let you put it on the tree?"

"Truthfully, they looked a lot like you do right now. It must be a chick thing."

"No. Obviously both of them have excellent taste and saved you from yourself. But now's your chance. Haley's married and Angie's busy, so you get to defile a perfectly beautiful tree with cheesy plastic bristle. If you dare."

"That's harsh." The humor in his tone said he'd been busted and knew it.

"Not really. I was holding back." She put her hands on her hips. "I'm prepared to go to the mat on this. You'd better not dare. That abomination is not going on this tree. There must be something else."

"Suggestions?"

She rummaged through the boxes as she talked. "String popcorn. Beads. Ribbon—"

"Like this?"

Straightening, she turned. He held up a roll of red velvet ribbon sprinkled with gold glitter. "Perfect."

He hooked the end at the top of the tree in the back where it wouldn't show, then unwound the wide velvet down to a place where she could reach and finish the job. It was a classy substitute for the tacky garland. After several readjustments, loosening and tightening, she stood back to inspect the final result.

"What do you think?" he asked, moving beside her.

"It's the most beautiful tree I've ever seen."

"No way."

"Really." It was magical and meaningful. She looked up at him, then started to laugh. "You've got stuff all over your face. It looks like Tinkerbell exploded fairy dust all over you."

"Back at you, Red."

Rose reached up to brush the stuff off him. That was all she'd intended to do. One minute she touched him, the next his face was in her hands and she was on tiptoe, her lips searching for his. Then he pulled her close, his mouth moving over hers, and she realized he fit against her like the missing piece of a puzzle. They were pressed together from chest to knee and the touch set her on fire.

In spite of all that, she might have heard the warning in her head if his tongue hadn't touched hers and he hadn't made that low sound of male desire in his throat. It set off an explosion of hunger and need like she'd never known before. She couldn't get close enough and wanted him so badly. Their breathing was harsh and hurried and sort of desperate as they kissed and touched and strained together. He kissed her cheek, jaw and nibbled his way to her neck where he tasted the soft spot behind her ear.

It was like an electric jolt that seared its way clear to her soul.

"Oh, Austin, please—"

"Rose—" Her name was a whispered groan on his lips. Austin lifted his mouth from hers and cupped her face in his hands. "I swear this is going to kill me, but I promised—"

Promised what? Her brain was mush and she couldn't

drag enough air into her lungs to think straight. One heartbeat later she remembered what he'd said. If she got frisky…

Famous last words. If she'd really believed this could happen, she wouldn't have stayed. But she did stay and she'd crossed her own line. She took a step away from him, a step away from *sleeping* with him. If he hadn't ended the kiss, she would have gone to bed with the man. She would have followed him anywhere and regretted it later.

"Thank you, Austin—"

"Don't." He dragged a shaking hand through his hair.

"But it's the right thing."

"No, I'm not saying I think it's right. It's just what I promised to do. That's all." He blew out a long breath, then walked into the kitchen.

On top of everything else he was one of the good guys. That only made her want him more and that so wasn't fair. She had a well thought-out plan for her life and the man who would share it. If she ignored common sense and gave in to weakness, she'd lose herself.

And she didn't want to be any more lost than she already was.

"We're like Neapolitan ice cream." Perky Calista Clifton glanced at her two companions, big brown eyes bright with ever-present enthusiasm. "Blonde," she said, nodding at Jeannette Williams. "Brunette." She lifted a long, silky strand of her own hair. Then she looked at Rose. "Redhead."

"I suppose we are," Jeannette agreed.

The three of them were in Jeannette's office, huddled around a paper shredder. As the mayor's administrative assistant, Jeannette had been tasked with going through the files, but didn't have a lot of experience with the duties. To purge the previous city council's paperwork, she'd enlisted the other two for opinions and input on what to keep and what to toss.

Calista was a government intern and good-naturedly accepted "grunt work" as a stepping stone in her career. Rose had cleaned off her desk for the day and was happy to keep busy.

They'd started at the beginning of the alphabet and were going through each file, making a pile of paperwork for shredding. It was pretty much impossible to put three women in the same room without a conversation happening.

"So Zane is excited about the Christmas concert." Jeannette smiled happily. And why not? She was engaged to the sexy, talented singer after helping him work through his emotional demons. The foundation he was starting in memory of the girl who'd accidentally died at one of his concerts was the last step in his redemption.

Rose smiled at her. "It's all coming together quickly. The arena is reserved and I'm contacting different radio and TV affiliates for coverage."

"Jake and I are looking forward to it," Calista said.

Not a surprise. She looked forward to everything. And why not? She was so young. Just in Austin's age bracket, if she hadn't already fallen for hunky Jake Castro. He would have fit Rose's man-must-haves list if not already taken. Life was really weird that way.

Being called a redhead sent Rose's mind back to the previous evening at Austin's. Actually it didn't take much to make her think of him; he was on her mind all the time. But he called her "Red." No one ever called her that. She liked it; she liked him. She'd kissed him. If he hadn't come to his senses, there would have been a whole lot more kissing and she probably wouldn't have stopped there.

"Rose?"

"Hmm?" She looked up, not sure which of the women had spoken or what was said.

There were questions in Jeannette's blue eyes. "Is something bothering you?"

"No. Why?"

"You seem distracted. You've been looking through that file for a very long time."

She glanced down at the manila folder closed in her lap. "Just daydreaming, I guess."

"You guess?" Jeannette smiled sympathetically. "Is it Austin?"

"What makes you say that?"

Rose wondered how long it would take to stop being surprised that everyone in Thunder Canyon took her personal business personally. A blessing and a curse, she thought, remembering how Austin's proposal had gone from happy to humiliating.

"Zane told me he saw you at ROOTS to announce the mayor's decision to allocate funds for tutoring and computer equipment. And he mentioned that Austin left with you and that he was gone for a long time."

"Anything else?" Rose asked wryly.

"As a matter of fact…" Jeannette grinned. "He said Austin was preoccupied and distracted when he came back."

"And you're distracted now. Maybe you're both distracted about each other." Calista fed something into the shredder and when it was finished grinding said, "Austin doesn't strike me as the type to be distractible. He seems pretty focused."

"He is." Especially when he kisses, Rose thought with a shiver.

"So you know him pretty well?" Jeannette guided a

paper to the machine and waited for the jagged teeth to catch it.

Rose was getting to know him pretty well. It seemed the more she tried to tell herself he was off limits, the *better* she was getting to know him. "We've run into each other a lot lately."

"He did a great job as Santa. Jonah loved it. And the picture…" Jeannette reached over and took a frame from her desk that held a photo of her little guy sitting on Austin/Santa's lap. "Is this not the cutest thing ever?"

"It's adorable," Calista agreed. "Jake and I have one of Marlie. Of course she picked that moment to need a diaper change. Probably because she wasn't so sure about this guy in the white beard and red suit. But Austin was really good with her. A natural with kids of all ages."

"You should have heard his explanation for how Santa gets all over the world in one night." Rose smiled at the memory. "It was geeky physics stuff, some sci-fi spin and equal parts of sincerity and charm."

The other two women glanced at each other and then her with "aha" expressions on their faces. But it was Jeannette who said out loud what they were both thinking. "You like Austin Anderson."

"What is this? Junior high?" Rose looked at them, but there was no point in denying the truth. Although no one needed to know that her feelings were starting to tip into territory that was deeper than "like." "Of course I like him. He's a nice guy and really bailed me out at the kids' party."

"So you're just friends?" Jeannette put a document in the shredder.

"Yup." Rose nodded a little too enthusiastically. "Friends is all. Really."

"How can you be so sure it can't be more?" Calista asked looking disappointed.

"There's a maturity discrepancy," Rose explained.

"Maybe he's just waiting until you grow up enough for him," Jeannette teased.

Calista laughed. "I hope so because you two make an absolutely adorable couple."

"We're not a couple." And if her brothers heard even a part of this conversation, any chance of her winning the bet would be in serious jeopardy.

"That's too bad," the other woman said. "Because age shouldn't make a difference."

"Maybe not, but it does." Rose glanced through the file she was holding and shredded utility bills from the previous mayor's tenure.

"Love and commitment have no restrictions," Calista said earnestly. "There shouldn't be limitations on feelings because of hair color, weight or age. It's about attraction. Chemistry. Jake and I are twelve years apart, but we're soul mates. Abby Cates is eight years younger than Cade Pritchett, but they're great together. When it works, go with it."

Rose sighed. "I understand what you're saying. But this is where I point out that in both of those cases, the man is older. Socially that's more acceptable."

"There are some who might raise an eyebrow," Jeannette reluctantly admitted. She stood and took a stack of folders back to the filing cabinet and replaced them. "Unfortunately, where men are concerned there always seems to be a double standard."

"Maybe," Calista said. "But it shouldn't matter. The heart wants what the heart wants."

Even when the heart is wrong, Rose thought sadly.

"Darn it." Jeannette tugged on the bottom file drawer but it wouldn't come out all the way. "This one is so crammed I can't even open it."

"Maybe it's a sign that we should tackle the rest of this project another day," Calista suggested.

"Good idea. As the mayor's administrative assistant and lead on this assignment, I hereby say, go home."

Unlike her friends, Rose would cheerfully have continued until all the paperwork had been disposed of even if it took several more hours. Calista and Jeannette each had someone waiting for them at home. Rose had no one to notice whether she worked late. Sadly, there seemed no end in sight to that sorry, solitary situation.

Chapter Nine

Austin walked out of his boss's office grinning from ear to ear and couldn't stop. He wondered if too much smiling could hurt your face.

"It's Monday."

Sitting behind her desk, Kay looked up at him with a twinkle in her eyes. "Am I supposed to know what that means?"

Not much happened here at Traub Oil that she didn't know about, working as closely as she did with Ethan. So she probably knew what he'd just found out about.

"It means that I just got the best news of my life. News like this is supposed to happen on Friday because a guy needs the weekend to absorb the awesomeness of it and celebrate properly on Saturday, which is his day off."

"But it's only Monday," she agreed.

"The best first day of the work week ever," he agreed. "I will never, ever again say anything bad about Monday."

"I'm going out on a limb here." Kay stood and walked around her desk. "Ethan just broke the good news about your promotion."

"So you *were* in the loop."

She smiled. "I knew it was in the works even before he increased your budget. But I didn't have a clue when he was going to tell you."

"It was a good surprise."

"Again, going out on a limb… You're happy about it."

"Happy?" He shook his head. "Such a bland word for what I feel. Ecstatic, maybe. Thrilled. Elated. Delighted. Humbled."

Kay gave him a hug. "It's well-deserved, Austin. You're brilliant and you work so hard."

"From someone I respect as much as I respect you, that means a lot to me," he said sincerely. "But what's so cool is that it doesn't feel like work."

"Now you're starting to scare me."

He laughed. "I just love what I do."

"It shows." She leaned a hip on her desk. "I know it's Monday and you have to be back here bright and early tomorrow morning to earn your keep, but what are you going to do tonight to mark this momentous occasion?"

How he celebrated wasn't nearly as important as with whom. All he could think about was telling Rose.

"I'm not sure about the details, but champagne and dinner at the best place in town will definitely be at the top of the list."

"Good for you," Kay approved. "Ethan was wise not to share this information until quitting time. He knew you'd be walking on air and too distracted to get more work out of you today."

Austin's smile faded and he got serious. "He's given me a lot of power and with that comes a great deal of responsibility. I know that. He won't regret this decision. I won't let him down."

"Of course you won't. He knows that. Other than my late husband, Ethan Traub is the best judge of character I've ever known. If he didn't think you could handle the job, he wouldn't have given it to you. There's enough time to be serious. Tonight is for soaking up the reality of this career success and festivities to make it as memorable as possible. The good things don't seem to happen nearly often enough." There was a wistful sort of sadness in her eyes even as she was nudging him to live it up.

And that was probably what she meant. She'd lost someone too soon and was encouraging him to enjoy the moment and make it last as long as possible.

"Darn right I'll make it a night to remember," he promised, the grin back on his face. "I'll see you tomorrow."

"Yes, you will. And I want details on tonight's carousing, so take notes."

He tapped his temple. "All stored up here in the memory bank."

Back in his office, Austin plucked the cell phone from the case on his belt, then found Rose's number and hit Talk. She was the first person he wanted to share the good news with. Haley and Angie would be happy for him, but they could wait. It was best not to examine the emotional dynamic of that thought process too closely.

There was ringing on the other end of the line and it went on so long that he was sure the call would go to voice mail. When she finally answered, he figured this was the cherry on top of a really good day.

"Hello?"

She was breathless and the sexy sound scraped over his skin, then burrowed inside and settled in his chest. He got an instant mental image of her naked and running his fingers through her red hair as he spread it over his pillow.

"Rose?" The effort to keep his voice neutral took a toll. "Is this a bad time?"

"No, not at all. I just walked in the door. At home. With groceries I lugged upstairs. Then I couldn't find my purse, let alone my phone."

"So you're okay?"

"Yes, fine. You?"

"Good. *Really* good."

"You sound happy. What's up?"

There was genuine warmth in her tone, as if she was glad to hear from him. He wasn't sure after last night's kiss. He'd never know where the willpower to pull away had come from, but breaking a promise to her wasn't an option. The gesture bought him more time with her because she'd stayed to help finish decorating. If he had any positive credit left, he was hoping it would buy him time with her tonight.

"What's up?" He sat on the corner of his desk. "I've just had a great day. Possibly the best one ever."

"Care to share?"

"Celebrating was more what I had in mind." He took a deep breath. "I'd like to take you to dinner."

"What are you celebrating?"

"Why don't I tell you all about it at dinner?" he suggested.

"I'd really love to, but—"

He knew what was coming. "What?"

"The date-free month isn't up yet, Austin. I'm halfway to the finish line and I'd hate to risk losing the bet now." Her voice was definitely filled with regret which was something at least.

"Who's going to see us?" he asked. "It's Monday."

"What does that have to do with anything? Is all of Thunder Canyon deaf, dumb and blind on the first day of the week?"

"No, of course not." He laughed. It didn't take much to make him laugh, what with his good mood, but she could do that even when he was crabby. Just seeing her sweet face and basking in her even sweeter nature was all it took to snap him out of crabby. "The thing is, human behavior patterns would support the theory that more people are out to dinner on weekend nights. Therefore, it's statistically less likely that anyone who would rat you out to your brothers would see us."

"That might be true if we went to dinner anywhere on the planet but Thunder Canyon." There was rustling in the background, probably from unloading shopping bags. "So just tell me what this big news is. I'm dying of curiosity."

"Nope," he said. "It's so good that it must be shared in person. A basic rule."

"Is it that fantastic or are you that mean?"

"Both."

Good and fantastic didn't do the news justice. Ethan had given him more responsibility. More money. He could support a family, buy a house, have kids and put them through college without breaking a sweat. All of that was something he hadn't let himself think about for a long time. Not since Rachel.

"I can't believe you're doing this to me," she groaned. "I could call Angie."

"She doesn't know," he teased. "And before you say anything, Haley doesn't either."

"Oh, Austin." The "aw" in her voice said she got it that he was telling her before his family. "I'd really like to go out to dinner, but I can't take the chance that Jackson will hear about it. And before you say anything, not even a disguise would change my mind."

That had been his next strategy. Now he was down to his last option. "How about if I just drop by your place with a bottle of champagne. If you happen to be cooking dinner, I wouldn't mind an invitation."

There was a long silence on the other end of the line. He could almost see the wheels in her head turning, weighing the consequences of seeing him.

Finally she said, "You are too charming for your own good."

"I'll take that as a yes."

He ended the call before she could tell him he was wrong. This was turning into his best day ever and not because of his upward career mobility.

If that was all he cared about, he would avoid Rose Traub. If word got out that Austin lusted after the boss's sister, his career could hit a big speed bump.

But he couldn't bring himself to avoid her.

When Rose answered the knock on her door, she saw Austin standing there with a bottle of champagne and a bouquet of flowers. A man who showed up with champagne and flowers was romantic not mean. And the look of excitement on his face said more than anything that he was really excited about something.

It was so good to see him and her smile was automatic. "Hi. Come in out of the cold."

"Thanks. These are for you." He held out a bouquet of rust-colored mums and yellow daisies. "I stopped at Un-Wined for the champagne and got these on a whim."

"Thanks. They're beautiful. I'll put them in water."

Her apartment's living room had a fireplace and she'd arranged two love seats and a chair into a conversation area in front of it. A flat-screen TV was mounted on the wall above the mantel, courtesy of her brother Jackson. Like the rest of the place, the eat-in kitchen had light beige walls and white crown molding. The stainless steel sink matched the other appliances. Above the stove was a rack with copper pots hanging, again courtesy of her brother.

She wasn't sure what she'd have done about the manly things if he hadn't been there for her. Respect and gratitude for her brother's opinion might have factored into her taking the dating bet. If Jackson thought she needed a break, maybe she did. But it was awfully good to see Austin and it had been only twenty-four hours since she'd last seen him.

She filled a pitcher with water and put the flowers in, all the while watching Austin look around and wondering what he was thinking.

He shrugged out of his jacket and set it on the living room chair. "Nice place. You got firewood."

"Thanks. Yeah, I picked some up at the store but haven't had a chance to play with it yet." She set the flowers on the table she'd set for two. "So are you going to tell me the big news, or do I have to starve it out of you?"

After setting the champagne on the tile counter, he grinned. "You're looking at the engineer just promoted to be in charge of Research and Development for Traub Oil Montana. For the last few months I've been the only engineer. Now I get to hire more staff to be in charge of."

"Oh, Austin—" She threw herself at him and wrapped her arms around his neck, hugging hard. "Congratulations. That's so wonderful."

"And this is why I wouldn't tell you over the phone." He pulled her closer and rested his cheek against her hair. "Technology is great, but there's no substitute for a full-body contact congratulatory hug."

"That's true." She laughed, gave him one more squeeze, then very reluctantly stepped back. "And this just goes to show that my brother Ethan is a lot smarter than he looks."

"Not going there." Austin held up his hands in surrender. "That's a sibling thing and I refuse to get sucked in. He's my boss."

"Smart man." She lifted an eyebrow. "But can you open a bottle of champagne?"

"I'm an engineer." He made a scoffing sound, then untwisted the wire on the top of the bottle. The foil covering was next, before he pushed the cork with both thumbs. It came out with a loud pop and not a drop spilled.

Rose brought over the two Waterford crystal flutes she'd set out with the plates. On a whim she'd paid a small fortune for them when she moved to Thunder Canyon, thinking of the first toast at her wedding. The excitement and pride in Austin's face made her glad she had them for now.

He poured some bubbly into each glass, then handed her one. "To promotions."

She clinked with him and sipped. Then she added, "To continued success. I can't think of anyone who deserves it more."

They touched glasses again, then drank.

The timer on the oven dinged and she turned it off, then set her glass by one of the plates on the table.

"If I'd known about the promotion, it would be something better than salad and mac and cheese." She shrugged. "It's what I got at the store and I was shooting for comfort food."

There was a salad in the refrigerator and she pulled it out, then set it on the table. With mitts, she removed the casserole from the oven and set it on the hot plate beside the flowers.

"Dinner's served." They sat across from each other and she said, "Help yourself."

When they both had food on their plates, he said, "So why did you need comfort food?"

"Oh, you know." The question took her by surprise. "It's cold. And…"

"What?"

No way would she tell him that the mood had anything to do with him. That the conversation with her coworkers had made her ache with wishing things could be different. Jeannette and Calista were headed home to wonderful men waiting for them. When Rose pictured someone in her life, the man always had Austin's face. It happened while she'd been food shopping and that's when she'd reached for macaroni and cheese. If Austin hadn't called, there wouldn't be a salad. When a girl wanted comfort, filling up on greens wasn't going to happen.

"Does this dietary choice for mood alteration have anything to do with the holidays?" Austin ate as he waited for her answer.

"Why would you think that?" She could go with it. Better than telling the truth.

"There's not a single thing in your apartment to show that Christmas is just a couple weeks away. Talk to me, Red."

"Well, it's the first one not in Texas," she admitted.

He sipped champagne and nodded. "That's different for you."

"A change. But even one for the better is hard."

"And when it's not for the better, it's—" He shook his head.

"In your life you've had a lot that falls in the 'not better' column."

"Yeah." He moved the remaining mac around his plate.

"When my father walked out on us, I thought it was my fault."

"What?" Just starting to take a bite, Rose put her fork down. "Why on earth would you think that?"

"I was pretty young for one thing. You know how kids think the world revolves around them." One corner of his mouth curved up, but his eyes were dark with the memories. "But I remember him yelling at me. There was water everywhere and a nonfunctioning toilet because I'd taken apart the guts to see how it worked."

"How did you get that heavy lid off?"

"It was broken, I think." He shrugged.

"What happened?"

"He was really ticked off. Threw something. Said he wanted to be anywhere but there. The next day he was gone."

"I don't know what to say." Rose put her hand on his and tightened her grip when he tried to pull back. She remembered his telling the inquisitive girl on "Santa's" lap not to ever stop asking questions. "You do know he probably didn't leave because of you? That there was more to it? That it was about him and not a curious little boy?"

"I do now." He turned his hand over and linked his fingers with hers. "My mother explained things to me. I remember her saying that she was glad I'd said something so she could make sure I knew it wasn't my fault. She didn't want me to blame myself."

Tears stung her eyes. What an intuitive mom she'd been. "And then you lost her—" Emotion choked off the words.

"Myself, too, for a while after she died in that car accident. Haley had just started college and came home to take care of Angie and me. I didn't appreciate her sacrifice at the time, not until I went to school."

"It must have been especially sweet to see her and Marlon get married. Family is really important."

"I couldn't agree more." He released her hand and picked up his fork. "So that begs the question, why are you not going to Texas for Christmas?"

She chewed thoughtfully for several moments, then swallowed. "For one thing, everyone is here except my brother Jason, my mother and stepfather."

"Your mother will miss you for the holidays," he said.

"I'm not so sure." She met his gaze. "When my father died, it was as if I lost both parents. My mother had to take over running the business, but I only knew she wasn't there for me. Gosh, that sounds selfish and self-centered."

"Not if it's the truth. And you were a little girl. But if I learned anything from my mother, it's to get your feelings out there." He put his hand over hers and wouldn't let go when she tried to pull it away. "What happened to your father?"

"He died in an oil rig accident when I was two. I don't remember him at all, but my brothers do. Talk about your misdirected anger." She laughed and heard a trace of bitterness. "They talk about him as if he was an action hero in the movies and it just makes me mad that I have no memory of him and never will."

"What about your stepfather?"

"Pete Wexler," she said. "He married my mother when I was four and is the only father I've ever known. A good man. He's always been there for me."

"But?"

How did he know there was a but? It was as if he could see into her heart, mind and soul. Was that crazy? Or stupid? Or both?

"I've always felt as if there was something missing in my life," she explained. "That sounds so dumb. I've never wanted for anything, in material terms. It feels so greedy to want more. Is the crown too tight? Are the jewels too heavy? But there are things money can't buy. At father-daughter dances, my friends had their dads, but I had to put 'step' in front of the title." She sighed. "Go ahead and laugh."

"I'm not laughing."

"Not even on the inside?" she asked.

"Especially not on the inside. I can't help thinking—" He shook his head. "Forget it. None of my business."

"What?" She leaned forward. "I really want to know what's going through your mind."

"Okay." Intensity darkened his eyes. "This thing you've got about age, the reason dating older men is so ingrained in you, could have a lot to do with not knowing your real father."

Maybe, she thought. The more that idea rattled around, the stronger it took hold. "That's an interesting theory."

"It's worth what you paid for it." He shrugged.

"And yet, there could be something to it. I never really thought in those terms before."

"Not surprising. Just very human." His thumb moved softly back and forth across her knuckles. "It's a lot harder to see things in ourselves because we're too close, too emotional."

"And the whole world revolves around us?" she teased, thinking about him as a little boy.

He smiled. "Something like that."

"It occurs to me that you're a lot like your mother."

"Why do you say that?"

"It sounds like she was very intuitive and I can see for myself that you are."

Rose realized that he had the wisdom of a man far

beyond his years. She stared into his eyes and saw an old soul looking back at her.

"I take that as the highest of compliments," he said.

She smiled. "I'm glad."

"And to thank you for that flattering remark, I'm going to take you to get a Christmas tree."

"Now?"

He laughed. "Too cold. And dark."

"I'll grant you it's really cold, but the tree lots are lit up like— Well, like a Christmas tree."

"We're not going to a lot. Too civilized."

And the opposite was *uncivilized.* Rugged. That's when a shiver started deep inside that had nothing to do with cold and everything to do with this man. *Man.*

He was full of surprises and Rose could hardly wait for the next one.

Chapter Ten

On Saturday morning Rose cleaned her apartment. After putting away the cleaning supplies, she made herself a sandwich and a cup of tea, then sat at the kitchen table. As she ate, her gaze fell on the flowers Austin had brought. They were still as fresh as the new perspective he'd given her. There was no delicate way to phrase the "aha" except that missing her real father had narrowed her focus on men, excluding anyone who wasn't of a certain age.

It had given her a list of things to think about.

As always, Austin was at the top of the list. The bright, happy blooms made her smile. They also made her feel the lack of holiday spirit in her place. She looked around and it wasn't any more decorated than the night Austin had pointed out that it wasn't decorated. Somehow, he'd made her comfortable enough to bare her soul and she felt better for it. He'd also promised to take her for a Christmas tree, but not to a traditional lot.

She'd seen him every day that week. At ROOTS, she'd dropped in to talk with Zane Gunther about the concert on December 25 and ended up hanging out with Austin. Shopping at the mall had come up and he went with her the next night. He was at the town hall getting information on construction permits in connection with the processing facility for Traub Oil and dropped by her office. They'd had lunch together. But not once had he mentioned a specific date for taking her to get the tree.

She had gifts piled up in the other room and festive paper to wrap them. Stacking everything in a corner seemed wrong and it was time to change that. With chores finished and her tummy full, she'd just go take care of it herself.

After changing into a pullover sweater, jeans and boots, Rose ran a comb through her hair, then brushed on a little makeup. A girl just never knew who she'd see and if her luck held, that would be Austin.

She put on her hat and was about to grab her puffy jacket when her cell phone rang.

She looked at the caller ID and a happy little shiver danced through her. "Hi, Austin."

"Hey, Red. What's up?"

"Not much. You?"

"Well, it's the strangest thing." There was a teasing tone in his voice. "This old truck just sort of steered its way to your neighborhood. Kind of weird, really."

"Oh?"

"Yeah, because it was then I remembered you needed a Christmas tree and I promised to help you get one."

"That's right," she said. "I thought you forgot all about it."

"Why?"

"You never said another word. And it's not like I didn't see you during the week."

"There's a reason for that. I had to keep up appearances."

"Because?"

"I've been doing my level best to avoid any hint or appearance of a date. I don't want you to lose that bet on my account."

She was lucky to have him for a friend. Even as she thought it, deep down inside she knew there was a ripple of more than friendship. But that wasn't something she wanted to think about now.

"You're a good man, Austin Anderson."

"I'm glad you think so. And I keep my word. So…"

"Yes?"

"Grab a hat, gloves and jacket. You're going to need boots, too. We're going for a tree. I'll be there in ten minutes."

"Okay."

But Rose was way ahead of him. Great minds, same wavelength and all that. She decided to wait for him outside and opened her door, then shrieked. Austin was standing there, tucking his phone into the case on his belt.

And he'd surprised her again.

"Why didn't you just knock?" she asked.

"Well, you know, just in case…"

"I looked like something the cat yakked up?"

"No. Do you own a mirror? It's not possible for you to look bad. Ever."

Aww. Her heart melted just a little more even though it was freezing outside. "Then why?"

"I have two sisters. I know the drill. If one doesn't have prior arrangements, some lead time is required."

"And you thought ten minutes would do it?" she teased.

"You don't even need that." He grinned, but there was an intensity in his dark eyes that wrapped those words in absolute sincerity.

Keep it light, she thought. Don't go there. "You are a silver-tongued devil."

"I'm a hell of a guy."

Rose couldn't agree more, but wasn't prepared to say it. "Okay, let's get Operation Christmas Tree on the road."

"Your chariot awaits, my lady." He held out his arm and she slipped her gloved hand into the crook of his elbow.

They walked to the old truck and he opened the door, handing her inside. The interior smelled like him, spicy and masculine. It felt like being wrapped in his arms, a feeling she could too easily get used to.

He climbed in behind the wheel and they were driving out of her apartment complex and then onto Main Street. Before she knew it, they were passing ROOTS, The Hitching Post, Second Chances Thrift Store, The Tattered Saddle Gifts and Antiques, and Wander-On Inn, headed out of town on Thunder Canyon Road.

There wasn't a whole lot of civilization after they left the buildings behind. The passing scenery, with trees sticking up through the snow drifts, was breathtaking. And the farther they went, the more she felt a surprise coming on.

"So where are we going?"

"You'll see." With both hands on the steering wheel, he was concentrating on the curving road.

"This is going to be legal, right?"

"Why do you ask?"

"Besides the fact that you have a wild past and a tattoo to prove it?" She met his gaze briefly. "We're clearly not on our way to a lot where trees are displayed. A place where you pick and pay."

"I told you. We're not going to a lot." He grinned. "We're cutting one down."

"I've never done that before."

"No?"

"My mother always had an artificial one." This was exciting, but she couldn't resist teasing. "But what are the rules?"

Austin glanced over. "You're really hung up on regulations, aren't you?"

"Yes. I wouldn't want to trespass on private property and end up in the slammer. Or someone could set the dogs loose on us. Or shoot first and ask questions later."

"Sure can tell you're from Texas." He laughed ruefully. "No one will take offense if we cut down a pine tree."

"How can you be so sure?"

"Because I already talked to Ben Walters and got his permission. He's got a ranch outside of town where he runs cattle and horses. But it's a few hundred acres and a lot of it has trees. We've been getting ours there for years."

"Okay, then. I thought yours was wonderful."

And so was the kiss they'd shared beside it. With the scent of Austin surrounding her now, that memory was so real, it had pressure collecting in her chest until she could hardly breathe. She had never in her life wanted to kiss a man more than she wanted to kiss Austin Anderson right this minute. If he wasn't driving...

"We're almost there," he said, turning off the main road.

His voice snapped her out of the sensuous haze and she was grateful. The mission was to cut down her tree, nothing more.

He turned from the main road onto what was little more than a narrow passage carved into the thick forest. He guided the truck a short way in, then stopped and turned off the engine. The area was so dense with vegetation on both sides of them that the sun didn't shine through.

"I'll get the tools from the back."

"Okay."

She opened her door and slid down to the ground. It was so cold that her breath made clouds in front of her as she took in the scents of moisture, pine and fresh air.

Carrying an ax and handsaw, Austin met her on the passenger side and said, "Follow me."

"Paul Bunyan," she teased.

"He was big and burly, right?" Austin looked down, laughter sparkling in his dark eyes.

Her chest felt tight again, bringing back the urge to kiss him. "I believe so."

"Then he and I are like clones. Twins separated at birth."

"I was going to say…"

The funny thing was that if one didn't know anything about him, he could be a lumberjack. No one would necessarily peg him as an engineer with a scary-high IQ. He was tall and muscled in all the right places. She knew that from firsthand experience because he'd held her close to all those right places and made her want what she shouldn't want from him.

As soon as they left the trail, their boots sank in the snow and walking took all her concentration. There were trees all around them and the fragrance of pine was even more concentrated here.

"It smells so good." Rose stopped and looked around. "Any one of these would be beautiful. But it seems sinful to cut one down."

"If it makes you feel any better," he said, "in the spring we can plant a replacement. That's always been part of our agreement with Ben."

"I'd love that." And part of her did a happy little dance

that he'd said "we." She studied the plant life candidates closest to them with a critical eye.

"Remember, I have to carry it back to the truck."

"Okay, Mr. Big and Burly," she said laughing. "I get it. Size matters."

"Yeah, and keep in mind where it's going. In the wide open spaces it doesn't seem so big, but there will be height and width issues in your apartment."

"I see what you mean."

It took a while to find one with no obvious flaws in fullness that also met Austin's criteria for spatial limitations in her place. But after tramping around, he spotted the perfect pine. When she gave the thumbs-up with her mittens, he set about cutting it down.

After a few mighty whacks with the ax, he yelled, "Timber."

She stood behind him and watched it fall. With the handsaw, he cut through the last bit of bark and freed the tree. Then he grabbed the trunk and dragged it through the snow to where he'd parked. After stowing the tools, he lifted it onto his shoulder and gently set it in the truck bed.

"And the lady has a tree." He turned to secure the tailgate.

"The best one ever," she agreed.

Before stepping on the road, Rose looked at all the snow, then at Austin's broad back. The urge came out of nowhere, but she couldn't let such a tempting target go to waste. She bent and scooped up a handful of the wet, white stuff, molded it into a ball and heaved.

With a splat, it hit his neck just above the collar of his shirt and slid down inside it. "Bull's-eye," she shouted.

Hunching his shoulders, Austin turned and his eyes gleamed with challenge and retribution. "That was low."

"Devil made me do it."

With athletic grace, he successfully dodged a second one, then said, "This is war."

She expected him to bend over and go for the snow to make a ball and her plan was to get past him into the truck before he could retaliate. An inspired idea, but he surprised her and not in a good way. Instead of bending down, he came at her and grabbed her around the waist. He was too fast and too strong for her to escape, and a part of her didn't want to. Then his feet slipped in the snow and they both went down. He managed to twist his body so that she fell on top of him, but then he shifted over her.

His face was an inch from hers and they were both laughing. Then he suddenly stopped laughing and intensity darkened his eyes. It thrilled her all the way to her toes. She felt the cold as wetness seeped into her jeans and jacket but couldn't find the will to care. All she could think about was getting closer to this man.

"Oh, God, Rose," he groaned, his gaze skipping over her face. "You're so damn beautiful."

She cupped his cheek. "Austin, if you don't kiss me now, I'm going to—"

And then his mouth was on hers and she threw her arms around his neck, threading her fingers through his hair. He pulled her as close as the thickness of their jackets would permit but it wasn't nearly close enough. He nestled his knee between her legs and she trailed the heel of her boot down the back of his thigh, amazed that it could be so erotic even with all their clothes on.

Their lips touched and tasted and trailed fire, but the rest of her was starting to feel the cold. Her jeans were soaked now and she tried to hold back a shiver because she knew he would end this and she wanted it to go on forever. But the trembles wouldn't be suppressed and Austin knew.

He pulled back and looked at her. "I'm such an idiot. You're freezing."

"No, don't stop. I'm fine. I—" Want you, she almost said. She wanted him here and now. In the snow. Freezing her butt off. And she would have, too. Except for one thing. He was right. She was shaking from cold.

He stood and pulled her to her feet, then got her to the truck and lifted her inside. "I'm getting you home now."

When Austin drove into the parking lot at her apartment building, Rose's teeth were chattering and she could barely talk.

"The damn heater in this truck is useless. Go inside and get out of those wet things," he ordered.

"W-wow, you s-sure know how to s-sweet talk a girl."

"This is serious, Rose. Go take a hot shower and get warm. I'll handle the tree."

"B-but—"

"Now," he snapped. "I'm not arguing about this with you."

A violent shiver rocked her and she nodded. She slid out of the truck and couldn't feel her feet but managed to move her legs and get upstairs, leaving the door unlocked so he could bring in the tree before he left. In the bathroom she shed the wet jeans, sweater and under things, then got in the hot stream of water. Once she warmed up and the stinging stopped, it was replaced by a different sort of ache.

Wanting Austin.

Reluctantly, she turned off the shower, got out and dried herself off. After taking off the shower cap, she brushed her hair, then put on a gray fleece sweatshirt and matching drawstring pants.

She thought the yearning for Austin was a phenomenon of the forest. Hoped it was an aberration of the outdoors.

Wrong and wrong. Even back on her own turf she wanted him. But she'd told him straight out that intimacy should mean something. And given his emotional baggage, she wasn't sure it could for him. He wasn't likely to get serious after a public proposal and the subsequent humiliation.

It was her own fault that he'd unloaded her tree and then went home to get warm. That was a depressing thought. Not that he'd get warm. It was the going home part. The day had been so much fun. She had her first real, live Christmas tree. Then she'd hit him with a snowball and he took her down. They both got wet and cold. Now her very own lumberjack wasn't here to share a warm drink or anything else and her spirits took a dive.

Until she came out of her bedroom.

Austin was in her living room, squatting in front of her fireplace, poking at the blaze he'd started.

"Hey," she said. "You're still here."

He glanced over his shoulder and stood. "I wanted to make sure you were okay."

How sweet and chivalrous was that?

"I'm fine. Warm." She walked closer to the fire and held out her hands to the flames. "This is wonderful. Thanks."

"My pleasure."

She looked around the living room. "Where's the tree?"

"I hosed it off to remove any loose needles. And critters."

"Excuse me?"

"You know. Bugs. Woodland creatures. Stuff that belongs outside."

"The city slicker in me will be grateful to you forever."

"Don't mention it." He grinned. "Now the tree has to dry off outside for a while."

"Of course. That's basic Christmas tree setup, but I'm such a newbie. Seriously, Austin, thanks." She put her hand on his arm and felt the still damp material. His jeans and boots were soaked. He'd been rolling around in the snow, too, and probably got even wetter when he washed off the tree.

"You need to get out of these sopping clothes before you catch your death."

"I'm fine. I'll just head for home—"

"I'd let you go, but it's too far. And you're right. The heater in the truck is useless. You're already chilled and I won't have you getting sick. My conscience couldn't take it. I'm not taking no for an answer. Use my shower. I'll get you a fresh towel. And a blanket to use while your stuff is in the dryer. You'll be good to go in no time."

He took his wallet and keys out of his jeans, then set them on the coffee table. "Okay. I know when to pick and choose my battles with a redhead."

"And don't you forget it. Now scoot." Rose led the way down the hall and got a fresh towel out of the linen closet. For some reason she couldn't stop talking. "I'd give you a robe, but the color would be all wrong."

He grinned. "Not to mention it wouldn't fit."

"There is that." Then she backed out of the bathroom and shut the door. "Just throw your clothes in the hall and I'll put them in the dryer."

She set a blanket on the chair by the fire, then waited in the kitchen, wondering if he'd like tea or hot chocolate to warm him up. Or wine. She'd heard it dilated capillaries and increased blood flow to generate warmth. Brandy or cognac would be more sophisticated, but she didn't have the snifters or that kind of liquor. Wine she could do.

Nerves she could do, too. But seriously, what was there to be nervous about?

And then Austin was standing there with the towel knotted low on his hips. She couldn't take her eyes off his bare, broad shoulders and wide chest with the masculine dusting of hair.

"There's a blanket over there," she said, putting a fair amount of prim in her voice to mask how deeply the sight of him affected her.

The amused look in his eyes said he wasn't fooled. "I'm fine."

Yes, you are fine, she thought.

"How about some tea? Or hot chocolate? Or wine?" Anything so she could do something with her hands, keep busy. Ease the tension coiling inside her.

"Wine," he said.

"How about a pinot noir?"

"That works for me."

While she busied herself with opening the bottle, getting glasses and pouring, Austin used the fireplace poker to move the wood and stir up warmth. She brought over two wineglasses about a quarter full and set them on the coffee table beside his wallet. Straightening, she admired his wide shoulders and that's when she saw the tattoo on his shoulder blade that she'd spent far too much time wondering and fantasizing about.

It was a tree with roots, giving the illusion of growing deep into the ground. On one of the branches there was a bird with wings spread, preparing to take flight. She wasn't sure what she'd expected the rebellious, teenaged Austin would have chosen. Maybe something along the lines of "Live fast, love hard. The kid."

A tribute to his mother's philosophy on raising children had never occurred to Rose. This permanent tribute to the memory of the woman who'd raised him was testament to his depth of character and evidence of a maturity beyond his years.

Rose raised a hand and traced the roots. "I like your tattoo."

"I'm glad."

His voice was husky and his eyes gleamed with intensity when he half turned and encircled her wrist with his hand. He lifted her fingers to his lips and kissed each one. The want and need coiled in her belly exploded and surged through her. No way was she cold now.

"Austin—" The prim was gone and left pleading in its place. "When I insisted you stay and get warm, it's because I really—"

"Yeah, Red. I want you, too." He took a strand of her hair and rubbed it between his fingers. "Pretty much from the moment we met I knew we were heading in this direction."

"You did?" Heart pounding, she stared up at him, the flames in the hearth highlighting the intensity on his face. His brown eyes went almost black. "Even though I refused to go out with you?"

His mouth turned up at the corners. "I knew it would be all the sweeter. What comes too easily isn't cherished as much as what we have to work for."

"And why did you persevere?"

"Because I couldn't *not* pursue you." He cupped her cheek in his hand. "I couldn't walk away from you. I couldn't stop wanting you."

And then he pulled her against him. All that separated them was his towel and her sweats. Fleece had never felt so confining. He wrapped a strong arm around her waist, holding her close. Then he threaded the fingers of his other hand through her hair and lowered his mouth to hers.

Rose opened to him, giving him free access. He tasted like cinnamon, spice, everything nice and the kiss grew more urgent as their tongues tangoed and touched and teased. Her breasts were pressed against the wall of his chest and she wanted to feel her bare skin against his bare skin.

She pulled back and struggled to draw air into her lungs. Then she took his hand and said, "Let's go in the bedroom." He shook his head and disappointment flooded her. "I thought you wanted me—"

"More than you can possibly imagine. But here." He reached over and grabbed the blanket from the chair where she'd left it, then spread the thick softness in front of the hearth. His gaze never left hers as he traced a strand of hair that was falling over her breast, then finally curved his fingers into a fist around it. "I want to see the flames dance in your hair. I need to see the fire in your eyes when I make love to you."

Chapter Eleven

Rose's heart melted at his words. When Austin held out his hands, she put hers into his palms and they knelt on the blanket, facing each other in front of the fireplace. She could feel the warmth from the blaze, but that's not what made her hot. His eyes glowed with such breathtaking intensity that the snapping flames couldn't begin to duplicate the heat. It was a look that seared her skin and slammed straight to her soul. More than words ever could, the passion in his eyes said she was his.

He kissed her and no part of their bodies was touching except hands and lips. He just nibbled slowly, letting her get the feel of him until she wanted more. It wasn't long before she was overwhelmed by the need to feel her bare flesh pressed against his and he seemed to sense that exact moment.

Dropping her hands, he settled his fingers at the hem of her sweatshirt and tugged it up and over her head.

"Christmas came early this year," he said with a grin.

"Why?" Did that breathless voice really belong to her?

"Because you're not wearing a bra."

Her heart was pounding so hard that it was about to jump out of her chest. "Then you're really going to be happy when you unwrap the rest of the package."

He traced a finger over her collarbone and down the center of her bare chest. "You should know I like to enjoy one present at a time. Concentrate before moving on. Attention to detail…"

Because that's what an engineer did, she thought. A second later she couldn't think at all because he was tracing the tip of her breast with his finger, circling the nipple. Her stomach clenched and every part of her wept with anticipation. Between her thighs, tension coiled and twisted.

He took her breast in his mouth, flicking his tongue over the sensitive peak. Sexual current charged and sizzled through her, setting her on fire everywhere. Her head fell back, moving her chest closer to him, giving him free access to all of her. And he boldly took what he wanted.

He moved to her other breast, lavishing the sensitized skin with the same lazy, loving attention to detail. She couldn't hold back a moan and staying upright wasn't an option.

Rose sat and settled her hand on the smattering of hair over his wide chest. Feeling his heart hammering beneath her fingers, she smiled with delight. Her palms tickled and tingled until she touched his shoulders. Austin slid his arm around and lowered her to the blanket as her eyes drifted shut.

He kissed each of her eyelids, then whispered, "Look at me."

She did and her breath caught when she felt him slide her sweat pants over her thighs and down her legs until she could kick them off. Now she was as naked as the day she was born, on the floor of her living room with Austin.

"I see it now." His voice was deep and husky, as he stared into her eyes. "The fire. I knew it was there."

For him. She was burning for him.

And apparently he felt the same. His arousal was evident and somewhere, somehow he'd lost the towel. Christmas had definitely come early for her, too.

She couldn't seem to get enough air into her lungs but managed to say, "This isn't a date, right?"

"Not even close." His breathing was ragged as he slid his hand down over her belly and between her thighs. "But Christmas gets better and better."

"Fa la la la la," she said.

Then she couldn't have answered if her life depended on it. He found the incredibly sensitive bundle of feminine nerve endings and brushed his thumb across it. The touch sent jolts through her and she arched her back, pushing herself into his hand.

"Oh, Austin— Please—"

And then she couldn't say anything. Her whole body clenched, just before shock waves of pleasure rolled through her, pulling her apart. But Austin's strong arms held her together.

When she finally caught her breath, she looked at him, "I don't have the words…"

He touched a finger to her lips. "You don't have to say a word. Everything you're feeling is in your eyes."

He kissed her and it was like setting a match to dry kindling. She was going up in flames all over again and her only coherent thought was to feel him inside her. Again, Austin seemed to know what she needed even before she did. He reached over and grabbed his wallet on the coffee table, then pulled out a square packet.

Condom.

Mentally she smacked her forehead, even as what was left of her heart melted. Protection hadn't even crossed her mind, but Austin was taking good care of her. Then rational thought disappeared and all she could focus on was him.

He braced his hands on either side of her, taking his weight on his arms. Nudging her legs apart with his knee, he settled over her. The firelight turned his dark eyes to hot coals as he gently pushed inside her. The feeling was so good, so right as they became one.

Cupping his face in her hands, she pulled him to her for a deep kiss. He groaned and the sound of his surrender made her smile.

And then he was moving, slowly at first, letting her catch his rhythm. She matched him, stayed with him and they rocked together to a tune both could hear. The tension built until they were breathing hard, the sound beautifully harsh in cadence with the crackle of the blaze beside them. Without warning she felt her muscles clench before she shattered into a thousand points of light. Two heartbeats later, he went still, then thrust one last time before groaning out his own release.

He buried his face in her neck as his breathing slowed. Then he rolled to his side and took her with him, wrapping his arms around her. Rose had never felt safer and more protected or cherished in her life. She snuggled closer to him and his hold on her tightened.

"I want you again," he whispered against her hair. "In your bed. And my recuperative powers are pretty awesome, if I do say so myself."

Because he was the age he was. That thought brought all the doubts back because she was who she was. No man had ever loved her like that before, but the things standing between them hadn't changed. In terms of intimacy needing to mean something, she'd just made a huge mistake.

Now what was she going to do?

Austin saw the uncertainty creep into Rose's eyes. As she caught her bottom lip between her teeth and worried it, he felt her body go tight. He didn't have to read her expression to know why. But he did anyway. With his back to the fire he could see concern highlighted in her eyes. This was a bad time to realize he much preferred to see passion there.

God, they were good together and he craved more. It was entirely possible that he could never get enough of her.

He knew when she'd said she wanted him that there would be no keeping what he felt strictly in the fun column. But he wasn't prepared to quantify it any more than that. Still, what simmered between them could be better than good if she'd quit thinking it to death. He hadn't been lying when he said he couldn't walk away from her, that he wanted to make sure she was okay.

The need to protect her was stronger every time he saw her, although he didn't feel the need to define things, to put a finer point on it.

But a defining moment was here and there was no win in putting off the conversation. "What's wrong?"

"We need to talk," she answered.

And there they were. Four words that struck fear into every man's heart. Talk was the last thing on his mind with Rose in his arms. But talk is what they were going to do and he'd never before regretted so profoundly that he wasn't getting his doctorate in something to do with words.

"I was afraid of that," he said.

Rose reached for her sweatshirt, which was his cue that the conversation was going to happen with clothes on.

"My stuff is probably dry now," he said.

He found the laundry room and took everything out of the dryer. It didn't take him long in the bathroom, but he didn't rush. She needed a couple minutes. But the longer he spent in this room surrounded by the scent of Rose, her soap, her creams, the more he realized the truth. He didn't know what to say to her.

Finally he couldn't put it off and joined her in the living room. She was in front of the dying fire staring into the glowing embers. Her legs were pulled into her chest and she rested her chin on her knees.

He braced his hip on the chair arm instead of sitting beside her on the floor. If he sat too close to her, he'd pull her into his arms and no talking would happen. It would just put off the inevitable.

"I'm ready to talk," he said.

"Really?"

"Of course not. I'd rather walk barefoot over hot coals. But you're right, we need to." He blew out a long breath. "You start."

"First of all, I have to tell you that was probably the single most beautiful experience of my life."

That was not at all what he'd expected to hear, but as soon as he did the realization hit him. The hell of it was that he felt the same. All he could say was, "I'm glad."

"It can't happen again."

And that was unexpected, too, along with the way the words hit him in the gut and knocked the air out of him. "Why not?"

"For all the reasons we've already talked about."

"Tell me again."

She sighed. "You're only looking to have fun."

"Can you blame me?"

"No."

And still he felt the need to defend himself. "I used to

want a family of my own more than anything. My dad left us and my mom died. I was going to get it all back and do it right. Then I got my heart drop-kicked through the goal-posts of love and everyone in town knew that she'd made a fool of me." He ran his fingers through his hair. "Commitment means risking it all again."

"I understand," she said. "And I don't blame you."

"Okay." But he felt the blame. Felt the weight of what he couldn't say to her.

"But that's not the only problem."

In his mind it was, but he knew what she meant. "The rest of it is just your not wanting to commit. You've got your own hang-ups," he said.

It was on the tip of his tongue to add that he'd never hurt her, but he couldn't.

She sighed. "You're probably right about that. The thing is, I keep wondering what people would say about us. And in Thunder Canyon they'd have a lot of opinions. No one has ever accused this town of being shy about expressing them."

"So that's it, then?" He stood and watched her, the shadows that crept over her face in the fading light.

"I think so." But she wouldn't look at him.

Everything in him rebelled at ending things with her. He should have been relieved that she'd taken the risk off the table for him. The hell of it was, he *wanted* to keep the risk option open.

"Okay." The single word had more snap than he'd intended. "I'll back off. But think about this. It's not the years that turn a boy into a man but the mileage. And I've got so many miles on me you'll never catch up."

That should give her something to consider while he was doing God knows what.

* * *

In her office, Rose looked at the email message on her computer monitor one more time before sending. It was to another radio station requesting air time for Zane Gunther's Christmas concert. She clicked Send even though it wasn't her best work. It had been nearly a week since she'd seen Austin and without him, it seemed that nothing she did was her best.

That being the case, since it was quitting time, she shut the computer off, then grabbed her purse and coat. After taking the stairs to the first floor of the town hall, she stopped by the door to look at the Christmas tree in the reception area. All the kids' names were gone which was good news.

She thought about her tree. A neighbor had helped her get it inside her apartment and the wonderful smell came in, too. But that was a mixed blessing. Every time she took a deep breath, it brought her back to the damp, earthy fragrance of the dense forest. It brought back memories of being there with Austin and laughing with him about everything. That reminded her of kissing him in the snow. Not long after that he'd made love to her in front of the fire.

He was the kindest, gentlest and most sensitive, romantic man she'd ever known. But as he'd said, she had issues and so did he. Neither of them was willing to bend, so that was that.

At least the kids who need it most will have a good Christmas.

The thought made her miss her mother and stepfather. Maybe she should have gone to Texas and spent the holidays with them. Interesting that she didn't think of it as home now.

Rose felt a gust of cold air come inside along with an older man. He was carrying new, unwrapped gifts, one for a boy and one for a girl. He stopped beside her and put them under the tree along with the others that were waiting for volunteers to wrap them in festive paper.

The man looked familiar and when he straightened, she recognized him. Ben Walters. The friend Austin had introduced her to at DJ's when they'd worked on Presents for Patriots.

"Hi, Mr. Walters."

He met her gaze and smiled. "Rosie."

"You remember me."

"Hard to forget a pretty redhead. And call me Ben."

She returned his smile, but her heart wasn't in it. She hadn't heard from Austin which proved that he had no trouble forgetting her. Then she recalled that her tree had come from this man's property.

"I'm glad I ran into you," she said. "Thanks for the Christmas tree."

"Ah." The big man's blue eyes twinkled. "You're the friend Austin called me about who wanted to cut down a real tree."

There was a slight emphasis on the word *friend,* part statement, part question. She didn't know *what* Austin was to her. They'd started out friends, then lovers and now weren't anything. The thought of his not being in her life was really depressing.

"Something wrong, Rosie?"

"What makes you say that?"

He shrugged those big, wide shoulders. "Just a guess, but you look like you lost your best friend."

She sighed. That's what happened when you crossed the line and *slept* with your best friend. "I'm fine. Just tired." That part at least was the truth, she thought, staring at the tree's bright lights and colorful ornaments.

"You and Austin had a fight?"

Her gaze snapped up to his. "Why would you ask that?"

"Fine and tired are what women say when they're not fine at all and they don't want to talk about it."

He folded his beefy arms over that barrel chest and she had the most absurd thought. How did he find a jacket big enough to fit him? Then his words sank in.

"Women?" she asked.

"My wife, for one. And pretty much every lady I've known since she passed on."

Rose made a mental note not to underestimate this man. He saw way too much. "I really *am* tired."

"But you're not fine."

"No, and I don't want to talk about it."

"Might help," he said.

"I don't see how. It won't change anything."

"Get it off your chest. You'll feel better."

Touchy feely advice coming from this bear of a man just seemed wrong on so many levels. But there was a steely quality in those pale blue eyes, something that hinted he wouldn't take no for an answer.

"Did you go all stubborn on Austin when he was a kid?" she asked.

"I did. And from where I'm standing, he's still a kid."

"And that's my problem," she said.

"Don't see why. That kid is one of the best men I know. Bar none."

"Me, too." She slid her purse more securely onto her shoulder. "But there's a difference in our ages."

"You're too young for him?" The man looked puzzled.

"That's a joke, right?" She remembered being carded at the wedding and wondering if Austin had put the bartender up to it.

"A man doesn't live as long as I have and not learn one

very important thing." He met her gaze. "Never ever joke about a woman's age."

"Well, I'm not too young for Austin. Just the opposite, as a matter of fact."

"So you got a couple years up on him."

"More than a couple," she said grimly.

"I'm old, but for the life of me I don't see why you'd have any call to hold that against him."

"It's just my thing." Rose hugged her coat tighter to her chest. "A romantic notion, I guess."

"Notions are all well and good, but they don't keep you warm at night."

She nodded. There was no arguing with that statement. So far her ideas of romance had been a big bust. But this was the first time she'd ever hurt so much because of sticking to them.

"Ever since I was a little girl, I've had ideas about my perfect man."

"And Austin's not it?"

"In every way but one. I'm not sure I can let it go."

"Then I guess it's up to me to tell you how the cows eat cabbage, Rosie. Can't make you see that it's anything but the yammering of a lonely old man, but I'm going to say it anyway. And I expect you to listen good." He took a deep breath. "No man is perfect."

"I know. It's just—"

He held up a finger to stop her words. "No woman either. But some are more perfect together than others."

"There's more to consider than personalities. Austin only wants good times. No commitment."

"You're wrong. That boy wants a family so bad he can taste it. Made one mistake because of that and it was big. I kept my mouth shut when he had it bad for that waitress. Rachel." There was bitterness in his voice and the blaze of anger in his eyes was hot and bright. "I knew she wasn't playing fair with him. Knew she wasn't the right one and he'd get the stuffin' stomped out of him. I knew it and didn't say anything because he wouldn't have listened. I regret keeping that to myself a whole lot more than I can say. It might have spared him carryin' around all the blame."

"The fact is he does carry it," Rose said.

"Yeah." Ben rubbed a big hand across the back of his neck. "I won't make that mistake again. I'm going to say what I think and let the chips just fall wherever."

"You don't have to tell me I'm wrong for him."

"Don't put words in my mouth, Rosie. I think you're just right for him. The way he looks at you…" He shook his head. "That boy's got it bad. He might not want to and he might not know it. But he does."

Rose completely understood how that felt. From the very first moment she saw Austin, something was pulling her to him. She'd fought it with everything she had and here they still were. It was all a mess.

"Even if… Assuming that…" She looked up at him, helpless to find the right words.

"Spit it out, Rosie."

"But if we…" She met his gaze. "What would people in Thunder Canyon say?"

"Congratulations, probably. Everyone likes that boy and wants him to be happy. God knows he's had enough of the bad stuff in his life to deal with. He deserves to have some good and I think you are good for him." Intensity hardened his face, as if this was the most important thing he had to say. "But even if folks took exception to the two of you, it shouldn't matter. When one soul recognizes its other half, a birth certificate is just a meaningless piece of paper. Take it from me—foolishness is a waste of time." Sadness filled his eyes. "You don't know that till the one you were foolish over is gone too soon. The point is, if Austin makes you happy, well then, nothing else should matter a tinker's damn."

That made a lot of sense and she appreciated his words.

"Thanks, Ben." It occurred to her that he'd said things a father might say. "You've given me a lot to think about."

"Just don't think too long," he warned.

Chapter Twelve

Austin was miserable and angry. He'd been miserable and angry since leaving Rose's apartment almost a week ago. And with every day that went by, the misery and anger grew. It was December 23 and Ethan had thrown him out of the office a couple hours early to start his Christmas holiday. Austin had seriously thought about protesting that he'd much rather work because it took his mind off Rose, at least for a little while. But he figured it probably wasn't a good idea to air his romantic problems to his boss, especially when his boss was her big brother.

So here he was at ROOTS. With Angie. She was in a good mood, which made him even more miserable and angry and he hadn't thought that was possible.

The teen hangout was missing the teenagers that made it a hangout, but someone had to be there during the posted holiday hours in case a kid wandered in. He didn't have anything better to do. The two of them were sitting side by side on the old sofa facing the big picture window that looked out on Main Street. They'd wheeled the TV over and his sister used the remote to flip through the channels until she found the movie *A Christmas Carol*.

Austin knew the story and had always liked Scrooge's come-to-realize scene, the reaction of people who'd known him before he'd transformed into a decent human being. Right now Austin preferred the "before" Scrooge. The nasty one. It fit his mood.

He really cared about Rose. What ticked him off most was that there was nothing he could do about the problem. He was an engineer. Engineers fixed things, but there was no way to fix this. He couldn't change the age difference and Rose couldn't get over the fact that it was there. She kept reminding him that he was only interested in quantity, not a quality relationship.

She couldn't be more wrong. He'd been interested in having fun until he became interested in her. If she'd just bend a little, he would give up fun for her. Actually, he wouldn't phrase it quite that way if he got the chance, but that didn't seem likely.

At the movie's commercial break, Angie muted the TV. "I'm so excited about Christmas."

Austin glared at her, wishing he could crawl under a rock until the holidays were over. His New Year's resolution was to find a way to stop thinking about Rose. So his only response to Angie was a grunt.

"I'm so relieved that finals are over."

When she smiled, he realized how pretty she was. Her dark hair was straight and shiny and fell past her shoulders. Enthusiasm and excitement danced in her big brown eyes. By her own admission, she was finished with school until next year and wasn't working tonight. He was at ROOTS partly because if he couldn't be with Rose, there was nowhere else on earth he wanted to be. But what was his sister's excuse?

"Why are you here, Ange?"

"To help you supervise teens."

"Considering the fact that no one is here but you and me, why don't you have a date?"

"I've sworn off men."

He should ask why, but didn't want to know. He couldn't fix his own problems, let alone hers. "Okay. So why aren't you with kids your own age?"

"What are you? The wise old man? You're not that much older than me."

She was right, even though he felt ancient compared to her. "Why aren't you doing something fun?"

"I'd rather hang out with you."

One corner of his mouth quirked up even though he was nursing a pretty spectacular mad. "So spending time with me doesn't come under the heading 'fun'?"

"I didn't say that," she protested.

"But you walked right into it." He realized that they hadn't really talked in a long time. He'd been busy with work, writing his doctoral dissertation. And Rose. Angie had been involved with school and her job. "What's going on with you, kiddo?"

"What do you mean?" Her already dark eyes grew even darker with suspicion.

"I mean how is school? Did finals go okay? What do you want to be when you grow up?"

"My classes were easy and so were the tests. I've got a couple more general ed classes to get out of the way." She frowned. "I'm so far behind where I should be in college."

"It's hard when you only take a couple classes because of having to work." He stretched his arm across the back of the couch. "But money isn't a problem now. Haley and I can help you out."

"I know. It's just—" She clutched the TV remote, the movie obviously forgotten. "I don't know what I want to be and now it's time to decide. Fish or cut bait."

"What do you like?"

"Lots of things. Psychology. Sociology. History. English literature." Troubled dark eyes met his. "I'm not like you. I'm allergic to math and science. Serious hives. I'm not artistic like Haley. Can you believe we had the same parents?"

"You're right. Haley's artsy. I'm the family geek." Austin reached over and tugged on a lock of her hair. "But you're the one who got all the personality and heart."

"Aw shucks." She grinned. "You're just saying that because it's true."

"Did I mention humble? Because not so much on the humility." He knew now was the time for some insightful, brotherly direction and struggled for the right words. "I can't tell you how to focus your education. The best advice I've got is to study what you love. Somehow you'll turn it into a career. I promise."

"I'm holding you to that." She pointed a finger at him, then a sly look slid into her brown eyes. "What did you get me for Christmas?"

Just like that his two best friends, misery and anger, were back. "I don't want to talk about it."

"I know you got me something. I saw it under the tree."

"Bah humbug."

"Don't be such a Scrooge."

"Why?"

"Because I finally have time to enjoy the holidays and you should share in my spirit," she said.

"Again I ask, why?"

"It's the least you can do since I didn't get to help decorate the tree this year. Although you and Rose did a beautiful job." She tapped her lip. "Something tells me that was all Rose."

It was all Rose when he'd kissed her that night and when he'd made love to her by the fire. The two of them gave off enough sparks to light Thunder Canyon through the holidays and into next year. But she was too damn stubborn to admit how good they were together. Maybe if she wasn't an opinionated redhead. The hell of it was, he wouldn't change that even if he could. He wouldn't change anything about her. He'd...

Austin realized his sister was staring at him. "What?" he snapped.

The sharp tone didn't faze Angie. "I think I just figured out why there are no teenagers in here tonight."

"Because it's December 23 and they're shopping or doing family stuff?" His voice dripped sarcasm and he hoped it would be enough to distract her.

"No, you're scaring everyone away with that scowl. What's got your boxers in a bunch, big brother?"

"Nothing."

"Oh, please. This is me. I haven't been too busy to see you've been in a funk for the last few days."

"Maybe you should be a writer. You've got quite a flair for making stuff up and I understand that that's helpful in creating fiction." He slid lower on the couch, refusing to look at her because she might see how right she was.

"Not only that," she continued, "you've been brooding since we got here." Thoughtfully she tapped her lip. "I managed to pull you out of it for a bit. Then I brought up Christmas. And the tree. And Rose…"

He heard the "aha" in her voice. "What?"

"This is about Rose, isn't it? What happened?"

He'd made love to her and she brushed him off. At least she did it to his face and didn't split with no explanation. But he couldn't tell his sister any of that.

"There is no me and Rose."

"But you wish there was." Angie wasn't asking.

"Maybe you should go into law. This cross examination is pretty impressive." He glanced at her. "Or psychology."

"You're trying to distract me because I'm right."

He sighed. "Is there a possibility that you'll let this go anytime soon?"

"No."

"Okay, then." He looked out the window and focused on the building across the street with Christmas lights ablaze. "I'm deeply in like with Rose and she isn't interested."

"Why the heck not?" Angie demanded. "You're smart and funny. That is when you're not in a funk and being a jerk. I'll deny I ever said this, but you're pretty good-looking. She could do worse. What's her problem?"

"There's an age difference. And she wants a guy and a future. She thinks I can't be serious, that I won't commit because of…"

"Rachel." There was bitter anger in Angie's voice. Then her eyes went wide. "Oh, my God."

"What's wrong?"

"This is all my fault."

He sat up straight. "How do you figure? You're not responsible for when either of us was born."

"No." Guilt was etched on her face. "But I told her how old you are. When we were at DJ's on Thanksgiving. She was asking questions about you. And God knows why, but I'm proud of you. I was bragging about how smart you are and your degree and what you're doing now and you're only the age you are…"

"So that was you."

"Yeah, but there's more." The guilty expression intensified. "When we were at Presents for Patriots, I saw Rose when she walked in. She spotted you talking to Kim and mentioned that the two of you looked friendly."

"And?"

"I just bragged some more and said…" She caught the corner of her top lip between her teeth. "That you somehow manage to stay friends with all your exes."

"All?" No wonder Rose had frozen him out that night.

Angie nodded. "I didn't realize there was anything between the two of you. That was so stupid. She was interested right from the beginning and if I'd just kept my mouth shut, everything would have been fine."

Maybe. Maybe not. Probably it was best to have the truth up front. "Don't beat yourself up, Ange. It is what it is."

"I have to talk to her." She shut off the TV and stood.

"And say what? There's still an age difference."

"Which doesn't mean anything if you love someone. But I have to tell her that you don't use women like tissues."

"What?"

"You know—use them and throw them away."

He shook his head. "Don't talk to her. It won't do any good."

Angie twisted her hands together. "I know I've already done enough damage, but I have to try and fix it."

"You can't."

"Then *you* talk to her," his sister urged.

"I already have and it didn't make any difference." He rested his elbows on his knees.

"Look, Austin, the reason I'm not out having fun with my friends tonight is because I've been worried about you. Now I know what's been bugging you and it's all my fault. If she's the one you want, then go after her and don't give up. Don't let her give up. Andersons are made of sterner stuff."

He stood slowly, her words resonating inside him. Nodding, he said, "Maybe you should look into counseling. Or being a motivational coach."

"Why?"

"Because you're right. I'm going to convince her we're good together."

"That's the spirit." Angie grinned. "What's your plan?"

"I haven't worked that part out yet." He looked at his watch. "She's still at work."

"So call her. I'll cover ROOTS if you can get her to meet you somewhere."

"You're the best." He pulled out his cell phone. "But about that big mouth of yours— From now on, remember that silence is golden."

"Translation—shut my trap."

His only answer was a grin before he hugged her.

Rose looked at the calendar on her desk that said December 23 and wondered when she'd started counting the days by how many had gone by since she'd seen Austin.

The passage of time only did one thing that she could see. Every day just made her miss him more. The sun came up in the morning and set at night, but with every twenty-four hours that went by, her soul felt a little more empty until she wondered if it might wither and disappear completely.

She was cleaning off her desk before the Christmas holiday. Fortunately nothing important required her attention because pretty much all of it was focused on what Ben Walters had said.

When one soul recognizes its other half, a birth certificate is just a piece of paper. She was good for him.

Don't think too long.

That came under the heading "easier said than done."

"Rose?" Jeannette was standing in the doorway to her office. "Are you busy?"

"Just killing time before going home." And thinking too much. "Why?"

"I'm taking another shot at going through those old files. Calista and I are cleaning them out."

"Makes sense." Rose came around from behind the desk. "You're the mayor's assistant. The files are kind of a road map of what goes on in this office."

"It's certainly an education," the blonde agreed. "But I could use your help."

"Just tell me what to do."

"Nothing too involved. If we can get this done, it would be great to start the new year with lots of room in those file drawers. Out with the old, in with the new. We've just got a stack of stuff to shred."

"So you want me to perform the highly skilled job of feeding paper into a machine that turns it into confetti. I'm up to the task. I won't let you down."

"It's not national security." Jeannette grinned. "You joke, but it takes a lot of eye-hand coordination to keep your fingers out of those jagged jaws. And concentration."

"That's my middle name." Although, lately, her concentration had been mostly used up on a certain handsome engineer. The same one she'd stubbornly shut down. "I'm happy to help."

"Great. I can certainly use a hand."

"You just told me to be careful of my fingers and now you want the whole hand?" Rose continued to tease as they walked down the hall to the other woman's office.

"Figure of speech. And here you go," Jeannette said when they walked in the door.

Calista looked up from where she sat behind the desk, poring over a file. "Ah, reinforcements."

"At your service." Rose saluted smartly.

She looked at the mountain of papers on a corner of the desk and the shredder on the floor beside it. "That's an impressive pile and it will soon be gone."

"Good." With determination in her eyes, Jeannette walked over to the file drawer they'd abandoned because it was jammed during their last housekeeping session. "I'm going to get that one open if it kills me."

"Be careful," Rose cautioned. "I don't want to have to explain to Zane how you were attacked by a psychotic filing cabinet bent on your destruction."

Jeannette's look was wry. "I can see why you're so good at your job and writing public relations releases for the mayor. You've got a way with words to go along with that vivid imagination."

Calista grinned. "She does keep things lively around here."

Rose started feeding papers into the shredder one after the other, but even the steady noise couldn't keep the women from talking. Although Jeannette being on her hands and knees pulling and tugging files out of a drawer did tend to make the conversation somewhat two-sided.

"So," Calista asked, putting old town hall utility bills on the shred stack, "anything new with you and Austin?"

"Oh, well… You know." Rose shrugged.

The question had caught her off guard. Sex with Austin was definitely new, but it was so personal. She didn't know whether to answer.

"Hmm. Interesting." Calista was studying her. "Jeannette can't see your face, what with practically crawling into that drawer, but Rose is blushing."

"No, I'm not." The shredder buzz stopped when she pressed a hand to her hot cheek.

"Defensive, too," Calista said. "That means one thing."

"Rose slept with Austin." Jeannette's voice was muffled as she worked in the corner with file folders piling up around her.

"Even if you're right, which I'm not confirming you are," she added, "it doesn't change anything."

"You're wrong." Perky, pretty Calista who looked so impossibly young, now looked perfectly serious. "I've gotten to know you, Rose. Intimacy is a big step for you. If you took it, you're pretty serious about Austin. Whether you're ready to admit it or not."

Rose seemed to be getting messages from every direction that wisdom was not a direct result of years lived. Otherwise she would be wiser than she clearly was.

"She's right." Jeannette had yanked a file out of the drawer and was now sitting cross-legged on the floor.

"Not fair. Two against one," Rose protested.

"That doesn't make me any more wrong." Calista's expression was sweet and sure. "But this is all hypothetical anyway because you said *if* you'd slept with him."

"Right."

Rose started shoving papers in the shredder as fast as they'd go and the high-pitched grinding sound almost drowned out her thoughts. She almost couldn't hear herself telling Austin that in her opinion, intimacy had to mean something. It didn't happen unless two people were committed. And she'd committed to sleeping with him. Actions spoke louder than words.

Pieces fell into place and she was finished thinking. She just hoped it hadn't been too long.

"Jeannette," she said, "I need to take a quick break to…"

"What the heck is this?" The mayor's assistant was frowning over a file in her lap.

Rose walked over and looked down at the tattered manila folder. "That's seen better days."

"It was stuck between the drawers and that's why they wouldn't open."

"Is something wrong?" Rose asked, staring at the other woman's puzzled face.

"Good question. Among other things in here, there are bank drafts signed by former mayor Arthur Swinton to Jasper Fowler."

"My boss?" Calista sounded surprised.

"Who?"

"He owns The Tattered Saddle Antique Store where I work part-time."

"Why would the mayor have given him money?" Rose asked.

"Maybe that's a question our current mayor can answer," Jeannette suggested.

"He's still in his office, right?" Rose held out her hand for the file. "I'll go ask him. To shred or not to shred."

With the paperwork, Rose walked out into the hall and to the door marked Bo Clifton, Mayor. She knocked and heard him tell her to come in.

"Do you have a minute?" she asked, peeking around the door.

"A couple," he confirmed. "But Holly has some last-minute Christmas shopping and I promised to be home early to watch the baby."

Bo Clifton was a blond, blue-eyed muscular man who seldom wore anything more sophisticated than a Western snap-front shirt, blue jeans and boots. He dressed like the rancher he was, but when it came to Thunder Canyon, he was all business.

"I'll be quick." She showed him the bank drafts. "Any idea why a mayor would give money to a local shop owner?"

"Where Swinton is concerned, it would be easy to jump to conclusions, but that's not ever a smart thing to do." He frowned. "In my tenure as mayor I've had no business with The Tattered Saddle. Still, I can't say that Swinton didn't have legitimate reasons. Maybe something to do with Frontier Days."

"I see."

The phone on his desk rang and he looked at the caller ID. "It's Holly. We'll talk about this later."

"Okay. Thanks," she said, backing out the door.

She went back to Jeannette's office and announced, "He doesn't have a clue what this is about, but he mentioned that Frontier Days could be involved."

Calista leaned back in her chair. "It's possible. Jasper stocks a lot of Western antiques—guns, knives, saddles, ropes. Maybe Arthur Swinton paid him to borrow some of it for visitor displays and decorations to make it all more authentic."

"I could see that." Jeannette was still on the floor with files surrounding her. "He may have hired Fowler as a consultant, too."

It all happened before she moved to town, but Rose had heard about some very shady things occurring when Swinton was mayor. Then he'd been arrested for embezzlement, but the money was never recovered. This could be part of the story.

She slapped the file against her palm. "We'll probably never know what this is about since the former mayor died of a heart attack in jail."

"We can't ask him," Calista agreed. "But Mr. Fowler might know. He's weird, but more quirky weird. I could ask him why he accepted money from His Honor the Crook. In a good way."

Rose shook her head. "There's no diplomatic way to ask your quirky weird boss why he took money from a town official who went to jail. You could get fired. And I'm assuming you need the job or you wouldn't put up with Mr. Quirky Weird."

"Yeah." Calista nodded. "Definitely not doing it for fun."

"I'll go ask him," Rose said, looking at the other two women who didn't seem enthusiastic about the idea. "I guess I'm on a mission now. And you thought it was just about shredding. We need to get this job done. Out with the old, in with the new as soon as possible. Start the year with a clean slate."

"If you're sure," Jeannette said. "That would be great to tie up all the loose ends."

"It's just about quitting time."

"Thank goodness," Jeannette said. "Zane and I are going out to dinner tonight. By ourselves."

"A date," Calista said, sighing. "Every night with Jake feels like a date, but there's something about having a child that really makes you appreciate the alone time."

"Balance," Rose agreed. "So you guys have people waiting for you and I don't. I'll stop by The Tattered Saddle on the way home and see what I can find out."

Rose said goodbye before they could put words to the protest in their expressions, then went back to her office to get her coat and purse. And speaking of loose ends, she picked up her cell and looked at the contact list. Austin's name came up first and she was ready to hit the talk button when the phone rang.

"Hello?" She walked out of her office and headed for the stairs.

"It's Austin."

The sound of his deep voice filled her with such longing. "Hi."

"I need to talk to you." No flowery words. No beating around the bush. No small talk. "Just so you know, I'm not taking no for an answer."

Words to make a girl's heart go pitter-pat. She found the whole manly thing extraordinarily sexy and endearing at the same time. There was no way on earth she could turn him down.

"Isn't it handy, then, that I didn't plan to say no?"

"Yeah." The tension was gone from his tone when he said, "I'd like to take you to dinner. Why don't I pick you up—"

"Actually, I'm on my way to do an errand for the mayor's office. It shouldn't take more than a half hour. Why don't I meet you?"

"DJ's?" he asked.

"I'll be there."

"Me, too."

"Can't wait." Two words that weren't nearly enough to tell him what was in her heart. But in a very short time she would say everything in person and tell him straight out how she felt about him. "I'll see you soon."

After saying goodbye, Rose slid her phone in her slacks pocket. She was smiling from ear to ear because suddenly her world was as bright and shiny as the holiday season. At least it would be after she stopped at The Tattered Saddle.

Chapter Thirteen

Rose walked into The Tattered Saddle and felt a real sense of visual overload with a touch of claustrophobia thrown in for good measure. Every surface in the place was covered—floor, walls, ceiling and shelving. The tops of an ancient armoire and dresser were packed with old lamps, glassware and books. She knew there was a wooden floor underneath everything, but for the life of her she had no idea *how* she knew that because it was practically impossible to see with stuff everywhere.

And all the stuff was covered with at least one layer of dust, probably more. There were no charming Christmas decorations. Not even a tree, although there was no space for it. With a Western holiday theme, this could have been wonderful.

It was impossible to picture perky Calista working in this place even part-time. Harder still to believe she'd described her boss as quirky weird and not flat-out eccentric in a bad way. There was a TV series about hoarders that was truly frightening. She'd even seen an episode of a cop series where a body of someone who'd disappeared was discovered under a pile of junk. Usually a bad odor preceded the discovery. She sniffed and fortunately didn't smell anything but musty dust that made her want to cough.

Behind her a man cleared his throat and she whirled around, startled. She had been so caught up in the clutter that she hadn't noticed anyone else there.

He was behind a high wooden counter with a desk lamp illuminating his grizzled old face. His hair was white and icy blue eyes stared at her. Stranger yet, he didn't say anything. No "May I help you?" No "Merry Christmas." And no "Welcome to The Tattered Saddle, my name is…"

Apparently Rose was going to have to break the awkward silence. "Hi. You're Jasper Fowler."

"Yup."

She glanced nervously and held herself still, fearing the slightest vibration could start a chain reaction resulting in her getting buried and crushed under stuff or choked to death by the dust.

"You have an interesting variety of collectibles here."

"All old," he agreed. "Don't make stuff like they used to."

"Nope." She lifted a cream-colored ceramic vase with a three-dimensional pink rose. It was actually, surprisingly, quite lovely. "But they make computers now that they didn't make way back when."

"Hate them damn electronic gizmos."

From what she'd learned, Arthur Swinton was old, too, and if he shared the same computer phobia, it could explain the paper trail she and her friends had found. But as Bo had said, not a good idea to jump to conclusions. Still, paperwork was misplaced all the time. That file cabinet of old records could have been overlooked for years if the mayor hadn't tasked them with clearing it all out. And that's why she was here. Put it all to rest. Find out if there was a legitimate reason for those bank drafts. But blurting out a question didn't seem the best way to approach this standoffish man and get answers.

"How much is this vase? I don't see a price on it."

He came around the counter and took it from her. His hands looked surprisingly strong. "Ten dollars."

"I think I'll take it."

"Okay." He walked back to the counter but didn't go around. "Cash or check?"

"Do you mind if I browse? I have to get a couple of last-minute gifts for people who are really hard to buy for."

"Suit yourself."

Interesting sales technique, she thought.

Rose found a path of sorts through the maze and squeezed through furniture and free-standing shelves trying not to bump or break anything. She could hardly wait to see Austin, but if she was going to put this guy at ease and get him to talk, moving too fast wasn't a good idea. She glanced over her shoulder at his wrinkled, unsmiling face and suppressed a bad feeling. Quirky weird, she reminded herself.

That didn't reassure her much as she moved farther into the dark, crowded interior and it felt more like a little shop of horrors.

Toward the back there was a glass case with a lighted interior. Inside there were all kinds of weapons, different sizes and shapes. On a bed of black velvet, big guns and little ones were carefully arranged. Also there were knives with smooth blades and some serrated. Still another was wide, sharp and lethal-looking. All of them were well taken care of and there was no untidiness or disorder here.

This case was an anomaly compared with the chaos everywhere else.

She pretended interest and he was suddenly there, staring with pride at his collection.

"These look pretty old," she said.

"Older than me and that's sayin' something."

She met his icy gaze and shivered. "I'm Rose Traub, by the way."

"Any relation to DJ Traub?"

Maybe Fowler knew DJ and it would be sort of a bonding moment to lead into the conversation she wanted to have. "He's my cousin."

Cold eyes turned even colder. "I s'pose you're thick with all them Cliftons and Cates."

"They're friends, yes." She wasn't feeling the bonding. "They're part of the reason I moved here from Texas. I've only lived in Thunder Canyon for a couple months now."

Clearly this man made her nervous because she was nattering away like a moron. It was time to narrow her focus and get to the point. Her hand shook a little as she slid it into her pocket and curved her fingers around the cell phone there.

"Have you lived here long, Mr. Fowler?"

"Long time," he echoed, and there was a faraway look in his eyes. "There's a story going around that I drove my truck cross country with an empty coffin in the back."

Was he trying to creep her out? If so, it was working. "I hadn't actually heard that rumor." And she wished she hadn't heard it now. "Is it true?"

His only answer was a smile that was more grimace than anything else and not very reassuring.

"Thunder Canyon is a great town," she said.

"Used to be," he answered. "Way back when it was smaller. Before all the new things took over. Won't never understand why folks think old is no good. Don't like that it can't ever be the way it was."

"So," she said, drawing out the word, "I bet you like Frontier Days. Probably one of your favorite town festivals."

"One's the same as the next, if you ask me."

She looked at the array of weapons in the case again. "I just thought with your avid interest in antiques it would be a good fit with an event bringing in tourists to remember the good old days. The Wild West that Thunder Canyon once was."

"It's a day like any other." There was suddenly a glint of suspicion in his eyes. "You always this nosy?"

"Yeah, but I prefer to think of it as friendly."

"Nope." He didn't take his eyes off her. "Nosy. You got a point to make?"

"Yes." And a lesson learned: Never underestimate someone older than dirt. "I was wondering if former mayor Arthur Swinton paid you for the use of your collection in displays during Frontier Days. Or maybe he hired you to consult on the authenticity of some of the programs presented at the festival."

"Why would you think that?" He slid the glass door of the case open.

"No reason. Just curious. Nosy, I guess, like you said."

Rose couldn't look away from his eyes and knew he'd gone from weird to scary at the mention of Arthur Swinton. And she was officially scared when Fowler pulled a shiny old gun out and pointed it at her chest.

"It's loaded," he said. "And it works. Because I appreciate and take very good care of old things. Now, I'll ask again. Why do you think Arthur Swinton paid me to do anything?"

"Please put that gun away." Rose's heart was hammering so hard she was afraid it would jump out of her chest.

"First you tell me what you know."

She couldn't believe this was happening. It was like something out of a TV show and always happened to someone else. Not you, Rose thought. But how many murders made the news? How many times had she heard of someone killed by a friend, family member or acquaintance?

"I don't know anything." Lying seemed best under the circumstances.

Without taking the gun off her for a second, Fowler came out from behind the glass case and stood in front of her. "Then why are you asking questions about me and Swinton?"

It was on the tip of her tongue to ask who was being nosy now, but the gun was a big clue that if he'd ever had a sense of humor, that had changed when she brought up the former mayor.

"We found a file with bank drafts signed by Arthur Swinton to you."

"So who sent you?"

"No one. We just thought there could be a reasonable explanation." Because he was holding a loaded weapon on her, that seemed unlikely.

"Who's we?"

"Jeannette Williams. Calista Clifton. And me." She thought for a moment and came up with another name that was more official and might make him lower the weapon. "Mayor Clifton knows, too."

"I'm real sorry to hear that." His voice was deadly calm.

So many things went through her mind. Promise him she wouldn't tell anyone. Pretend that she wasn't aware what she'd found was proof that something illegal had transpired between the two men. Beg him to let her go to Austin because she so desperately wanted to feel his arms around her. But none of that came out of her mouth.

Instead she said, "What are you planning to do?"

"You and I are going for a little ride. If you try to pull any crap, I'll shoot you. Don't think I won't."

"Where are you taking me?"

"That's for me to know. Just move, slow and easy. Hands where I can see them."

It never occurred to Rose that he was bluffing. Clearly he was a dangerous man, and if not deranged, at the very least he was desperate. Desperate men hurt people.

Surely the vibrations from the shaking inside her would start a chain reaction that toppled glass, cast iron pots and books down on them. She hoped anyway, but it didn't happen.

With the pistol pressed into her back, Fowler forced her toward the rear door. She remembered Austin insisting on walking with her from ROOTS back to her town hall office at night. She'd teased him about his gallantry. This is Thunder Canyon. What could happen?

She'd give anything not to know the answer to that question. More than that, with all her heart she wished Austin was here now.

Rose wasn't sure when she'd learned to trust him so completely, but she knew in her heart that if Austin were here, he would know what to do. He would get her out of this.

But he didn't even know where she was.

Austin looked at his watch again. Rose was late.

Glancing around at the family-style picnic tables and the customers filling them, he noted that the Rib Shack was surprisingly crowded tonight. Maybe last-minute shoppers didn't want to go home and cook. Enough of that coming on Christmas Eve and the day after. Could be out-of-town-ers were spending the holidays at the resort and eating here. Whatever the reason, it was good to see DJ's place hopping again after all the weird stuff that had happened to put a dent in business.

From Austin's perspective in a booth against the wall, the place was busy and there were a lot of people in here, just like the last time he'd been stood up.

How many times could a smart guy pull a boneheaded move and still be considered smart? The call to Rose wasn't a reasoned-out engineering problem; it had come from the gut. He couldn't stand another second of not seeing her. Talking with Angie had simply brought those feelings to the surface. He didn't blame his sister for the problems with Rose. Her part in it had just put everything out there so they could deal with it. Now he was finished letting Rose push him away.

When she'd answered her phone, Austin swore she was happy to hear from him. He'd been sure that her sassy retort about not telling him no meant she was as eager to see him as he was to see her.

But it was possible she'd changed her mind. It had happened after he'd made love to her. She'd been all fire and passion in his arms one minute and the next she'd gone all skittish on him. Maybe she was thinking too much. He should have picked her up at work.

He was turning his water glass and studying the rings it left on the wooden table when someone stopped next to him.

"Austin?"

He looked up and saw Zane Gunther and his fiancée, Jeannette Williams. "Hi, you two."

"It's good to see you. I haven't had a chance to stop by ROOTS for a while," Zane said.

"He's been rehearsing like a maniac for the Christmas Day concert," Jeannette explained.

The singer shrugged. "This is by far the most important thing I've ever done professionally. It's not just about me."

"The foundation is a good cause." Austin had just been thinking about his conversation with Angie at the teen hangout. "Actually ROOTS hasn't been very busy. Hopefully that means the kids are with family and friends doing fun stuff."

"That's important," Jeannette agreed. "Tonight I got a babysitter for my little guy and convinced my big guy to take the night off so we could have a dinner date."

"Don't let me stand in the way of romance." Austin did his best to sound sincere and hide the anger and bitterness coursing through him. He'd fully expected to be doing his own romantic thing by now. "You two go enjoy yourselves."

"Are you waiting for someone?" Jeannette asked.

"I think what I'm doing is giving history a chance to repeat itself." He noticed the blank expressions on the couple's faces and realized neither of them had lived in Thunder Canyon when he got so publicly dumped.

Jeannette looked at Zane and by some silent form of couple communication they sat down across from him. "We'll keep you company."

Zane slid him a look, sympathy from one man to another. "Sorry, Austin. You opened the door to this. No way she's not getting the whole story out of you."

At that moment a waitress stopped by and took their drink orders, then dropped menus on the table. Austin wished he already had his beer because he knew Zane was right.

As it turned out, telling the details of the public proposal that had happened in this very place was like relating an anecdote without any power over him. He told them about asking Rachel to marry him, how she took the ring and then skipped town without a word. He knew if Rose were sitting beside him the story would make him laugh now.

"So that's my sad little tale. Except that after my heart got stomped to smithereens, both my sisters and pretty much all my friends told me that they never liked her."

"Nice," Zane said drily.

The waitress returned with beers for the men and a glass of white wine for Jeannette.

When they were alone Austin said, "It would have been helpful if they'd shared that with me before the whole town knew I'd asked her to marry me."

"You wouldn't have listened to anyone," Zane said. He gazed at Jeannette, love shining in his eyes. "Guys can be stubborn that way sometimes."

"Hard to believe, right?" Jeannette grinned.

"I hate to break this to you, but that trait isn't exclusive to men." Austin took a sip of his beer.

"You're talking about Rose." It wasn't a question and at his look Jeannette shrugged. "We work together. We talk. It just happens."

"Like a law of physics," Austin guessed. He shrugged and said, "I have two sisters."

"For what it's worth, Rose told us—"

"Us?" Austin stared at her.

"Calista and me. We had to keep ourselves entertained during a tedious and boring job." Jeannette toyed with her wineglass. "Anyway, she mentioned why she'd been holding back with you. The whole age thing. But I think she's starting to come around."

Austin had thought so too when she'd agreed to meet him, but now she was really late and it was clear that she wasn't coming. Definitely déjà vu all over again, but this time was different because he was different. Humiliation didn't even register and last time that had been the worst. Not now. He felt something he'd never felt before. Rose's rejection took the pain clear down to his soul because this time he was in love.

He loved Rose and knew he'd fallen hard the very first time he saw her. The foolish part had been trying to tell himself all he wanted was fun.

"I think you're wrong, Jeannette." He looked at his watch. "Not only is Rose not coming around, she's not coming tonight."

"Is she the one you're waiting for?" Zane asked.

All his life, Austin realized. And that was the hell of it. She was everything he wanted, all he'd been looking for. Beautiful. Smart. Funny. And that body... He'd been so damn sure that the excitement of wanting someone, finding someone had been the same for her, but now he knew he'd made another boneheaded mistake. This time, so far, only these two knew and with luck he would keep it that way.

"Yeah," he finally answered. "Rose said she'd meet me here."

Jeannette frowned and her blue eyes grew troubled. "When did you talk to her?"

"As she was leaving work. She said she had an errand to do first."

"Oh, no—" The woman suddenly looked really worried. "It shouldn't have taken her this long."

"What?" Zane asked.

"She was going to stop by The Tattered Saddle."

Austin stared at her. "The junk store?"

"Antiques," she clarified. "Rose volunteered to ask Jasper Fowler about something I found when I was cleaning out file cabinets in the mayor's office."

"What was it?" He was starting to get a really bad feeling about this.

"We found bank drafts that Arthur Swinton signed over to Jasper Fowler. Bo cautioned not to make assumptions, that there could be a legitimate reason for the transactions. Calista works part-time at the store and volunteered to ask him, but Rose didn't want her to put the job in jeopardy. She said she'd go, ask discreet questions, then we could put the matter to rest. We'd know whether to give it to the sheriff or the shredder."

"So she went alone?" For once, Austin wished she'd suppressed that spunky streak.

When Jeannette nodded, his insides knotted with fear. And speaking of jumping to conclusions... He should have known better. Rose might think too much, but she never kept the thoughts to herself. She was straightforward and honest. It was one of the things that had made him love her more. If she'd changed her mind about meeting him, she'd have done one of two things: called or come in person to tell him she wasn't staying. She would never have stood him up without a word.

"Something's wrong," he said. "I think Rose might be in trouble."

"Oh, God—" Jeannette squeezed Zane's hand. "What should we do?"

"I'm going to look for her car at The Tattered Saddle," he said, standing.

Just then his cell phone vibrated and he grabbed it off his belt. Looking at the caller ID he said, "Rose."

He hit the talk button, but before he could say anything, he heard her voice on the other end.

"Just let me go," she said, fear lacing the words. "Please don't hurt me."

Fear flashed through him, but some part of him realized she wasn't talking to him, that he should listen.

"Jasper, kidnapping me will just make things worse." There was a pause and her breathing was rapid and harsh, as if she'd been running. There was true terror in her voice. "Why are you taking me out of town? Just let me go." There was a voice in the background, then she said, "There's nothing out here on Thunder Canyon Road. I know because this is where Austin brought me to get my Christmas tree."

She was giving him a clue. Austin looked at the other couple and put his hand over the phone so he couldn't be overheard. "Fowler's got her. I know where they're headed. Call the sheriff first and then her brother Jackson. The rest of her brothers, too."

Austin asked Zane and Jeannette to pass on the information because he was going to get Rose. He could still hear her pleading as he ran out of the restaurant.

He had to help her. Failure wasn't an option. Fate couldn't be so cruel as to bring him the perfect woman only to take her from him forever.

Chapter Fourteen

Rose had never been so scared in her life.

She couldn't believe what was happening. This man was clearly unhinged. When he first shoved her into the truck, she hadn't tried to get away, too shocked by what was happening and petrified of getting shot. Then he started driving and jumping out of the passenger side door crossed her mind, but at this speed, hitting the road would cause serious damage, or death if she hit her head.

Then she'd felt the cell phone in her pocket.

Fowler was mumbling to himself and pointing the gun at her. There were no dashboard lights in the old truck, but she couldn't very well pull the phone out and expect he'd let her dial 9-1-1. Picturing her phone's keypad, she pushed the redial button, ringing the number of the last call she'd received.

Austin.

Not sure if road noise would camouflage the sound of dialing and someone on the other end answering, she started talking as loud and fast as she could. As terrified as she was, talking fast came surprisingly easy. She saw a road sign and mentioned this was where Austin brought her to get a Christmas tree. After that she kept up an endless stream of senseless chatter and peppered him with appeals to let her go.

"I can't hear myself think," Fowler said. "Just shut your mouth."

"I can't. I'm nervous. I can't stop talking when I'm nervous. Just let me go. Stop the truck, I'll get out and walk back to Thunder Canyon. You'll have a really good head start. Really good because I don't walk fast on these short little legs. And these heels? Forget about it. It will take me forever—"

"Shut the hell up."

"I told you, I can't. Why are you doing this?"

"Damn interferin' outsiders," he muttered. "Can't leave nothin' good alone. DJ's Rib Shack is still in business. Shoulda gone down what with everything I did. And those pushy Traubs are pumping buckets of money into Grant Clifton's hoity-toity resort."

She was a Traub. And what *about* DJ's? Was he behind all the recent funny business? "What is going on?"

"It's damn frustratin' is what it is. Couldn't just leave well enough alone."

"What do you have against all of us?" she asked.

"You don't belong here. None of you. You're not from Thunder Canyon, born and raised."

"Neither are you. You said you drove across the country with a coffin in your truck." If she got out of this alive, she was going to mention that little fact to the sheriff and suggest he check it out.

Fowler glanced at her and raised the gun just a fraction. "It's different."

"How?"

"Just is," he snapped.

Way to go, Rose. Antagonize him. Surely that would help a situation that until now had gone so well.

"So you hate us because we brought economic growth to Thunder Canyon?"

"New isn't always better. And this ain't personal. It's business. All about the money. You're a Traub. You oughtta know that. Now shut the hell up. Why couldn't you just keep your nose out of my business? Now you know too much. I have to think."

Probably about how he was going to get rid of her. Permanently. Rose was getting desperate now. This lunatic wasn't going to let her go and she couldn't be sure that Austin got her call. She couldn't just do nothing and let him hurt her.

She wanted Austin so much. She wanted a life with him. This was a really bad time to realize what a fool she'd been. The words Ben Walters had said kept echoing through her mind.

Foolishness is a waste of time, but you don't know that until the one you were foolish over is gone too soon.

She could very well be that one and would never get the chance to tell Austin that he made her happy and nothing else mattered a tinker's damn.

If Fowler stopped the truck, he'd have the gun and all his attention focused on her, making it all but impossible to make a run for it without taking a bullet in the back. Her only chance was to try something while he was driving, but he had that gun between her and the steering wheel. But as strategies went, grabbing the wheel was dangerous, too. The truck could go over the side of a cliff or just roll. There were no seat belts in this old thing.

Jumping seemed her only choice and she had no illusions about his intentions which meant she really had nothing to lose. She'd get ready. When he slowed a little going around a curve, she'd go for it. With her fingers on the passenger side door handle, Rose looked at Fowler, waiting to make her move.

"Son of a bitch," the man snarled, just before stomping on the brake.

Suddenly thrown backward and off balance, Rose tried to brace herself. She looked through the front window and saw an old truck blocking the road. A familiar truck. It was Austin's truck.

"Thank God," she breathed and started to grab the door handle.

"Not so fast." Fowler lifted the gun to stop her, then threw the truck in Reverse, hit the gas pedal and glanced over his shoulder. He braked again. "Damn it."

Rose looked behind her and saw another vehicle blocking the road behind them. It looked like Jackson's car and there were more behind it. Ethan. Corey. Dillon. Her brothers.

"You're boxed in," she said. "It's over."

"Not till I say so." He leveled the gun at her and slid across the bench seat before gripping her upper arm. "Get out. I've got *you*. That'll get me a pass outta here."

She had no choice but to do what he said. When the truck door opened, she heard the sound of sirens in the distance. Help was on the way.

But Austin was here now. He'd made Jasper stop and was standing in the road. At least she got to see him but she pushed away the thought that it could be for the last time. Her heart was pounding in her chest and she was shaking all over. Fowler had a gun in her back and was gripping her arm so hard that it threatened to cut off blood flow to her fingers.

Austin's angry expression was clearly visible in the glow of headlights. His hands were clenched into fists and there was a dangerous gleam in his eyes. He looked like a man ready to spring into action, barely held in check. Holding on to his cool with both hands.

"Let her go, Fowler." He took a step.

"Don't come any closer," the old man warned. "I've got nothing to lose and won't hesitate to use this gun. Push me and I'll shoot her."

Rose's legs were shaking and started to buckle. He yanked her up and she cried out.

Austin surged forward. "I'll break you in half, you son of a bitch—"

Fowler pressed the gun muzzle to her neck. "Stop right there."

"You're not going anywhere. Give it up," Austin ordered.

"I've got the gun. I'm calling the shots. Get it?" The old man laughed at his pun. "You all just let me go on my way. Get the hell out and I won't hurt the girl."

"You know we can't do that." A muscle jerked in Austin's jaw. "Let her go and *you* won't get hurt."

"Like I'd fall for that. Without her I've got no leverage at all—" He gestured with the gun, pulling it away from her.

Rose heard rock crunching beside her just before a body came hurtling out of the dark. As Fowler was tackled to the ground, she was knocked loose and stumbled forward. And then Austin was there, catching her. He pulled her against him. Strong, safe arms held her close. She never wanted to leave those strong, safe arms ever again.

"Oh, Austin—" She wasn't all alone in this anymore.

She didn't need to hold herself together. For some reason she started trembling even more. "I was so scared."

"I know, baby. I'm here." He held her at arm's length, checking her over. "Did he hurt you? Are you okay?"

"I will be. Now that you're here." She threw herself against him as several law enforcement cruisers came to a screeching halt around them.

Rose, from the safe haven of Austin's arms, watched two sheriff deputies pull her brother Jackson off Fowler and ease her other brothers back.

"I think the sheriff just kept the Texas Traubs from doing frontier justice to Jasper Fowler," Rose said shakily.

"They're not the only ones who want a piece of him." There was a dark, menacing look in Austin's eyes and his tone was low, threatening.

Before tonight, Rose might have been frightened by it, but not now. This was a man you could count on. He would be there to protect the ones he cared about and keep them safe. She loved that about him.

The cops had Fowler's hands cuffed behind his back. Apparently *he* was nervous now because he was suddenly talking up a storm, most of it not making much sense.

"This isn't my fault," he finally said.

Before he could go any further with that thought, one of the deputies informed him of his right to remain silent. If he gave up that right, anything he said could and would be used against him in a court of law.

"It's not my fault," he repeated.

Jackson moved beside him, breathing hard from the struggle. "You held my sister against her will. That's definitely on you, Fowler."

"I'm not going down for this alone." The old man stood there between two burly deputies, his shoulders slumped, his expression defiant. "It's all Arthur Swinton. He's the brains behind everything."

"That would explain the bank drafts we found," Rose said.

"But there's a whole lot more it doesn't explain." Austin stared at the cuffed man. "Like the fact that Arthur Swinton is dead."

"Austin's right," Jackson said. "He died of a heart attack in jail."

"Maybe he did. Maybe he didn't." The old man smiled a crazy, mysterious smile. "You'll never find him, or the money he stole."

"Get him out of here. We'll interrogate him down at the station." The deputy in charge of the crime scene looked to his partner who nodded.

Fowler was immediately hustled into the back of a cruiser and driven away. The red-and-blue strobe lights on the two remaining cars cut through the dark, cold night.

Jackson leaned over and hugged her. "You okay, Rosie? I nearly had a heart attack when I heard what happened."

"I'm fine. Thanks to you and Austin." She looked at her other three brothers and smiled, too choked up to say more.

Jackson held out his hand to the man who had his arms around her. "Thanks, Austin. I owe you."

"No, you don't. I'd never let anything happen to her."

"She's pretty shaken up." Jackson studied his sister. "You can come home with me. Laila and I will take care of you. Or Ethan—"

Rose shook her head. "I'm not leaving Austin."

She looked up and he nodded, then sent her brother a look. A current of understanding passed between all the men.

Jackson finally nodded approval. "Keep her safe."

"Count on it," Austin said.

She rested her cheek against his chest and savored the sound of his strong heartbeat. "In that case, would you take me home? I just want to go home. With you. Please."

"I would do anything for you."

Austin had never been so scared in his life.

It was quiet in the truck as he drove to Rose's apartment. The "what ifs" were torturing him. He could have lost Rose tonight and life without her was no life at all. If he hadn't been able to keep Fowler talking while Jackson moved into position to jump the guy, things could have turned out differently in a lot of ways. All of them bad.

He kept looking over at her in the passenger seat and hated how terrified she still looked, how white her face was.

"Are you doing okay?" he asked.

"As well as can be expected after surviving a kidnapping by a crazy old man who put a gun to my head." Her voice trembled, but the attempt at spunk reassured him.

He reached over and squeezed her hand, resting on the seat between them. "We're almost home."

Thirty seconds later he pulled into the lot and parked near the stairway to her second-floor apartment. Before he could get out of the truck, Rose gripped his hand. Parking lot lights showed the pleading in her eyes as well as the lingering fear and emotional bruising.

"Austin?"

"What?" he asked.

"Please come in with me."

"Just try and get rid of me."

"Thank you," she said.

"No need. I'm doing it for me. Letting you out of my sight would just about kill me."

He went to her side of the truck and helped her out, then

put his arm around her, holding her close against him. He needed to feel that she was there, reassure himself this was real because the other part of this night felt like a really bad dream.

After letting them into her place, Rose locked the deadbolt. As if she'd just let her guard down, she started to shake all over again.

Austin took her hand and led her into the bedroom, realizing it was the first time he'd seen it. He'd made love to Rose in front of the fire and it had been the best night of his life. Until it turned into the worst. Even that paled compared to almost losing her earlier.

He flipped the wall switch and the matching bedside lamps came on. The bases were delicate cream-colored ceramic with three-dimensional white roses. The shades were scalloped at the bottom. A floral comforter in shades of pink, purple and green covered the bed.

Still holding her hand, he could feel her trembling—part reaction, part cold. "You're freezing."

She nodded. "And I feel dirty. That store—Jasper's place—was all dusty and cluttered. Dark and awful. And he had his hands on me—"

"Don't think about it." Still keeping her fingers in his, Austin took her into the connecting bathroom and filled the tub with hot water. "This will warm you up."

"Please don't leave me," she said when he started to walk out of the room.

He cupped her cheek in his palm and gently touched his lips to hers. "I'll be right outside. I'm going to get you a towel, some tea and a nightgown—"

Her mouth curved up a little in the ghost of a smile. "What makes you think I don't wear pajamas?"

"Because I can't picture a girly girl like you in anything else. Am I wrong?"

"No."

Austin made sure she had everything she needed, then left her to make some tea in her kitchen. He wished there was brandy, but had to make do. It took him about five minutes to find what he needed and get the hot drink ready. He was about to check on her when she appeared barefoot in the kitchen. Her white satin nightgown with pink roses on the bodice was both innocent and erotic. The look made him want her and he knew beyond a shadow of a doubt that he always would. But right now taking care of her was priority.

"You had orders to soak and relax in the tub."

"I didn't want to be alone. It all kept replaying in my head. The gun. That mad, glittering, evil look in his eyes—" The words stopped when her teeth started chattering.

"That does it." He was beside her in a heartbeat and scooped her into his arms, carrying her into the bedroom. He'd already turned down the bed and set her on the sheets before pulling the comforter over her. After propping pillows behind her back, he said, "Stay put. I'm just going to get your tea. I'll be back before you miss me."

"Not possible. I'll miss you the second you're gone."

The words and serious expression on her pale face gave him hope that he hadn't allowed himself before. As promised, he was back in seconds and handed her the steaming mug, handle first. She slid over, making room for him on the bed and he slipped off his shoes before joining her.

She leaned her head on his shoulder and dragged in a shuddering breath. "Oh, what a night…"

"There's an understatement." He laughed. "I've aged ten years. So that makes me older than you."

"Oh, Austin…" Her words caught and tears filled her eyes.

"What is it, Red?"

"I've been so stupid about this age difference thing. The foolish ideas that were stuck in my head seem so trivial compared to—everything. I'm so sorry."

"Don't be." He rested his cheek on her hair.

"I can't help it." She brushed a tear from her cheek. "When I left work, I was so excited about having dinner with you. I just had to do that one errand. Then it all got crazy and Jasper kidnapped me—"

"Don't think about it, sweetheart."

"Can't help it."

When she shuddered, he took the mug and set it on the nightstand, then slipped his arm around her and pulled her close. "Maybe you need to talk it out."

"Yeah." She put her hand on his chest. "At first, when he forced me into his truck, I didn't know what to think."

"You were smart to call me and give me clues about where he was taking you. If you hadn't…"

"Thank goodness you didn't talk and just listened. He might have heard your voice and then who knows what he'd have done."

"I knew right away something was wrong."

She shuddered. "It was clear pretty quickly that he had no intention of letting me go."

"God, Rose—"

"The thing is, I thought I was going to die and that was terrifying enough. But it wasn't the worst thing."

"It was to me—" Emotion choked off his words.

She smiled at him. "I only had one regret."

"What?"

"That I never told you I love you." She snuggled closer. "I decided that I had to do something to help myself or he would win. I was getting ready to jump out of the truck."

"Geez, Rose. You could have been killed."

"Thanks to you I didn't have to."

"Thank God I got there in time." He kissed her hair. "So can we talk about the fact that you love me?"

"I do. With all my heart. I feel so safe with you. And that's not all—" She couldn't hold back a yawn, a big body-shaking yawn, proof that she was finally relaxing.

"You're not the only one with hang-ups," he said. "After what we've been through tonight it sure puts everything into perspective. Helps straighten out priorities. And if there's any silver lining in what happened, it's that we got to the same place emotionally and did it a lot faster than we might have otherwise if—"

Austin stopped and heard Rose's deep, even breathing. She was asleep and he was glad. They'd been through hell tonight but came out of it more together than before. Now there was all the time in the world to say what needed to be said. But he wanted her big, beautiful, blue eyes open when he said it.

"Sweet dreams, Red." He snuggled them down into the bed and held her as he went to sleep.

A difference of years had stood between them, but not anymore. Now they had all the time in the world.

Rose's eyes drifted open, putting an end to her lovely dream. But two lovelier realizations penetrated her sleepy consciousness. It was just starting to get light outside and there was a man in the bed with her.

Austin.

She smiled, then everything flashed back to her. Desperately wanting to get to him while a deranged and increasingly desperate man took her hostage. The fear started to crawl inside her, but in the safety of Austin's arms, she was able to push it away. She curled closer to him and put her hand on his chest.

"Good morning." His voice was raspy from sleep.

"I didn't mean to wake you," she said.

"You didn't."

She sat up and smiled. In the half light she could see his dark hair rumpled from sleep, the shadow of beard on his jaw. She wanted to feel the scrape of it, to reassure herself he was real and they were truly together.

"I was having the most wonderful dream," she said. It was her wedding and they were standing in front of the minister. "Then I opened my eyes and the reality was even better."

He propped the pillows behind their backs and took her hand, threading his fingers through hers. "I've been dreaming, too, and strangely enough there was no sleeping involved."

"Tell me," she urged.

"We were standing in front of our family and friends and promising to love and cherish each other for as long as we live."

"That sounds a lot like a wedding." She stared into his eyes, hoping he was serious. "And for most guys, that would be their worst nightmare."

"Not for me. Marrying you is my dream. I knew you were the one for me pretty much from the first moment I saw you. But two things stopped me."

"Only two?"

"You and me." He grinned. "My head kind of got in the way of my heart. Then I had to wait for you to grow up."

"A near-death experience will certainly speed that process along," she said ruefully.

"I have a feeling you're not a woman who meekly does what she's told and it's one of my favorite things about you. But just for me, please, no more near-death experiences ever again."

"It's not on my list," she agreed.

Intensity darkened his eyes. "What I'm trying to say is that I love you, Rose. So much that it scares me."

"I love you, Austin." She lifted their joined hands and kissed the back of his. "You're everything I've been looking for my whole life."

"Does that mean you'll marry me?"

"Yes."

He lifted up on an elbow and looked into her eyes. "I thought the best news of my life was when your brother gave me more responsibility in the company and a promotion at work. But that was nothing compared to hearing you say you'll be my wife."

"I should warn you that I want children," she said.

He grinned. "Works for me."

"Maybe more than two. In fact, it's pretty likely that four or five could be in our future."

"The more the merrier."

"So we have a deal? For better, for worse. In sickness and in health. Until death do us part."

He nodded. "I promise to honor you above everything. I'll be the best husband I know how to be and take care of you and our children for the rest of my life."

She smiled. "I now pronounce you the husband of my heart, the mate of my soul. You have permission to kiss your bride. And you'll do it now if you know what's good for you—"

He touched his lips to hers, but the touching didn't stop there because the promises they'd just made were sacred. If that wasn't commitment, she didn't know what was. In their hearts they were as married as married could be. Austin made her feel alive in a way she never had before. It was their first Christmas Eve together and started in a way more promising than she'd ever imagined.

The legal part would come later.

Chapter Fifteen

Holding tightly to Austin's hand, Rose walked into DJ's Rib Shack with Claudia and Pete Wexler, her mother and stepfather. The two had arrived earlier that day to spend the holidays in Thunder Canyon. They'd come to surprise her, but got one back when she introduced her fiancé. And there were more surprises to come. She grinned at Austin and he returned her conspiratorial look.

Rose slid her arm through her mother's. "All day a group of volunteers has been taking shifts to cook and deliver holiday meals to people in Thunder Canyon who need assistance. We're going to do our part now."

Claudia frowned. "Are you sure you're up to it, sweetie? After that horrible ordeal you went through?"

"I'm fine." She studied her mother. Claudia was in her early sixties but looked younger. Not a strand of her light brown hair was out of place, but weariness was there on her face. "But if you're tired…"

"No." She looked at her husband. "How about you, Pete?"

"I'm ready to pitch in."

And that was the soul of Pete Wexler. Several inches under six feet, he was an average-looking man with receding gray hair that was getting a little thin on top. He had married her mom when Rose was four and "pitched in" right from the start to be her dad. And he was a good one.

The interior of the restaurant looked like it had on Thanksgiving and the Presents for Patriots project. There was a decorated Christmas tree in the corner of the room, shiny and bright with ornaments, ribbons and white lights. Tables were pushed together and filled with food, to-go containers and insulated carriers to keep things warm or cool as needed.

As always, a large volunteer group had turned out. Rose saw the Cates family and lots of Cliftons milling around. Jeannette Williams and Zane Gunther were there with their little guy. Angie Anderson was around somewhere and Rose would find her soon. From grandparents down to newborns in infant seats, the people of Thunder Canyon took care of their own.

And speaking of hers, they hadn't moved from just inside the door when they were surrounded by Traubs—Ethan, Corey, Dillon and Jackson, along with their significant others gathered around to welcome Claudia and Pete.

"Hey, Mom." Jackson was the last of her sons to get a hug. "Why didn't you tell us you were coming?"

"Because I didn't plan to until I heard what happened to Rose." She clutched her son's arm, an anxious expression on her face. "If you hadn't been there for her…"

"If it hadn't been for Austin, I couldn't have done anything."

"All I did was talk." Austin shrugged.

"You couldn't have done that if you hadn't blocked the road and then distracted him." Rose slid her arm through his. "You're an engineer, so talking isn't part of your skill set. That's what makes it even more heroic."

"I don't know." His eyes twinkled. "When necessary, my skill set can be pretty convincing."

"Yes, you can."

"Hey? Where's Jason?" Jackson asked his mother.

"Your brother," Claudia said, frowning a little, "is holding down the fort for the company in Midland."

Rose translated for Austin. "That's code for my brother is having a fling with a really hot bathing suit model who is more interesting to him than family right now."

"Rose," her mother scolded.

"Am I wrong, Mom?"

Claudia sighed. "Sadly, no."

Rose spotted her boss across the room. Bo Clifton met her gaze, then threaded his way through the crowd to join the Traubs. He greeted the newcomers, then moved a little off to the side with Austin, Rose and Jackson.

"I have some news about Arthur Swinton," he said quietly.

"What?" Rose instinctively leaned into Austin. With him by her side, she could face anything that came their way.

"Jasper caved pretty quickly under questioning. He figured Swinton was double-crossing him and told us where he could be found."

"So Fowler wasn't lying. Swinton's not dead," Jackson said.

Bo shook his head. "The investigation is ongoing, but right now it looks like someone in the clinic at the jail helped him fake a heart attack to cover his escape. He's been hiding out in the next town over."

"And calling shots behind the scene with Jasper Fowler doing his dirty work," Austin guessed.

"That's right." Bo looked grim. "He's been paying off Fowler to ruin DJ and God knows what else. Swinton's back in custody and pretty much spilling his guts, too. Apparently years ago he fell in love with Dax and DJ's mother—"

"There's a big eww." Rose shuddered. "We could all have been related to him."

"Don't go there," Bo warned. "Anyway, she had the good sense to not get involved with him, but over the years he watched the family be successful. Bitterness drove him a little crazy."

"A little?" Jackson's voice dripped sarcasm. "I'd say he's more than a little whacked out. This whole scheme is right up there in lunatic land."

"Yeah," Bo said. "But I thought you should know that the two of them are in custody and singing like a couple of canaries. There's nothing to worry about."

"What a relief." Rose smiled at Austin, then her boss. "In that case, it's time for our surprise."

"Okay." Bo whistled, a high-pitched sound that carried through the room and stopped conversation. "Can I have your attention, please? Who's up for a wedding?"

"Not another one." Evelyn Cates was standing nearby with her husband, Zeke. The fiftyish, blue-eyed blonde faked a frown at the mayor. "Two of my nephews just got married and two of my daughters are engaged. I think I've had just about all the romantic stress I can stand. Please, I beg you, tell me it's not one of my kids."

"You can't afford to be a wedding scrooge, Evelyn," someone whooped. "Heck, you've still got four single kids left."

Rose couldn't see who said it, but someone who sounded

a lot like Ben Walters called out, "And there's a whole bunch of Cliftons still looking for love."

Claudia moved beside her daughter. "Who's getting married?"

"Me, Mom."

Austin looked at his soon-to-be mother-in-law. "More than anything I want your daughter to be my wife, Mrs. Wexler. I love her very much."

She looked confused. "Rose? You're getting married right now?"

"We called the mayor earlier today and he used his considerable influence to expedite our marriage license so we could have the ceremony on Christmas Eve."

"But, sweetheart—" Claudia's light brown eyes filled with concern. "You always wanted a big wedding."

Rose held out her hand to indicate all her family, friends and acquaintances from Thunder Canyon. "This is big."

"I mean all the bells and whistles. From the time you were a little flower girl, you wanted the veil, the long train, white lace and promises. Flowers." Her mother studied her. "You're wearing a red dress."

One that Austin had picked out. It was long-sleeved and high-necked. The skirt swirled around her legs and her black patent, peep-toed pumps made her feel feminine and sexy. What she kept to herself was that Austin chose this outfit because it was festive and later, he could get her out of it fast.

She squeezed his hand. "I guess I finally grew up because decorations and what I wear aren't important. What really matters is being Mrs. Austin Anderson. I learned something, Mom. Foolishness is a waste of time. And you don't know that until the one you've been foolish over might be taken away too soon."

Claudia's eyes filled with a bittersweet understanding.

Pete had made her happy, but she understood that sentiment the same way Ben Walters did. Still, she looked at the two of them.

"You're sure about this?" she asked.

Rose met Austin's gaze and at the same time they said, "Very sure."

"I thought the two of you were a little overdressed for a volunteer gathering."

"So we didn't fool you?" Rose glanced at her groom and thought he looked pretty spectacular in his dark suit and the red tie that matched her dress.

"Only a little," her mother admitted. "I guess we're going to have a wedding. And Austin?"

"Yes, ma'am?"

"Don't ma'am me. It's Claudia. Or better yet, Mom." Claudia's eyes misted. "I think I'm going to cry."

Rose put her to work and everyone together made it happen. A short time later her maid of honor, Angie Anderson, led things off. Then Pete Wexler walked Rose down the "aisle" that was created because her family and friends parted to create it. Once upon a time she'd expected to be sad that Charles Traub wouldn't see her get married, but she wasn't sad at all. She believed with all her heart that her father was there, her guardian angel, watching over her.

Austin waited beside the Christmas tree with the mayor, who was going to marry them. Ben Walters, his best man, stood next to them.

To Rose, the setting was just as perfect as the double wedding she'd gone to with Austin. She had her poinsettias and white lights glittered through the branches of the pine tree. When it's right, everything is right, she thought happily.

She could hardly wait to get to Austin and all she could

see was the love in his eyes. On her stepfather's arm, she stopped in front of the mayor.

"Who gives this woman to this man?" Bo asked.

"Her mother and I do," Pete answered.

Rose stood on tiptoe and kissed his cheek. "I love you, Dad." Then she kissed her mother. "I love you, Mom."

Claudia's brown eyes filled with tears. "Be happy, baby girl."

"I'll see that she is." Austin took Rose's hand and placed it in the crook of his elbow.

Holding tight to his arm, Rose faced the mayor for the ceremony.

"Austin Anderson, do you take this woman to be your lawfully wedded wife?"

"I do." His voice was clear, strong and sure.

"Rose Traub, do you take this man—"

"I do," she answered before he could finish.

Bo grinned, then continued the ceremony and reading of the traditional vows, which they each repeated after him. The ceremony was short and incredibly sweet. It made them one in the legal sense, with all the rights and privileges allowed by law. But in Rose's heart she'd become Austin's bride that morning when she'd promised to love him forever.

The mayor cleared his throat. "With the powers vested in me by the great state of Montana, I now pronounce you husband and wife. You may—"

This time Austin didn't wait. He pulled Rose into his arms and kissed the living daylights out of her while everyone whistled, clapped and cheered.

Then he lifted his head and whispered in her ear, "I can't wait to get you out of that dress. You can keep the heels on."

"Oh, my." Her breath caught at the look in his eyes.

Then they grinned happily at each other.

Jackson shook Austin's hand, then gave his sister a hug. He held her at arm's length and said, "So this means you lost the dating bet."

"No, I didn't."

Her brother shook his head. "You're telling me you just married a man you've never dated?"

"That's right. Because I never fell in love with anyone I dated." She leaned against her husband. "We never even set a date for the wedding."

"I think you're pulling a fast one, sis."

"No, she's not," Austin defended. "Technically she's telling the absolute truth. I asked her out repeatedly, but she never accepted."

"Like I'd believe *you*," Jackson scoffed. "She'd lie and you'd swear to it."

"Think what you want." She only had eyes for her groom. "I would happily lose the bet because I just won my happily ever after."

The next day, Christmas Day, Rose and Austin spent the morning in bed. He decided to give his sister Angie the house they grew up in and make Rose's apartment home until buying or building one of their own. But on this most sacred of gift-giving mornings, their presents to each other didn't come in packages tied with ribbon. They were personal, full of passion and pleasure. As perfect as alone with him was, as much as she'd loved it, she knew it couldn't last because they had family to see and a benefit concert to attend. So propped up against pillows, Rose snuggled against her husband, making the time count.

Austin picked up her left hand and kissed the fourth finger. "I'm sorry you don't have a ring."

"It all happened so fast. And I don't mind." She

shrugged. "Rings don't make us any less married and that's all I care about."

"Me, too. But first chance I get, I'm taking you to the jewelry store."

She kissed his neck. "I'd be lying if I said I wasn't looking forward to that. It's like saying I've got no estrogen."

He laughed. "Not only do I want to buy you the biggest diamond in the place, I want a ring on your finger to show God and everyone that you're all mine."

She looked at his handsome face, studying his eyes for any lingering pain about the girl he'd lost along with the ring he'd given her. All Rose saw was happiness and a sparkle that was for her alone.

She smiled up at him. "Back at you, bud. I'm putting a ring on your finger, too, so the ladies won't have any doubt that you're spoken for."

"Amen. I worked awfully hard to convince you we were exactly the right fit for each other."

"I'm told you appreciate things more when they don't come easily."

"Then I appreciate the hell out of you," he said sincerely.

She tapped her lip thoughtfully. "It did take a while for me to realize you have all the attributes on my man-must-have list."

"And what would those attributes be?" he asked, one dark eyebrow lifting.

"There are only six."

"Wow," he said. "No pressure."

She ignored him. "Every last one is a deal breaker and sense of humor is right there at the top. Followed by handsome."

"So you don't think I'd have to wear a bag over my head walking up Main Street?"

"Not a chance," she said, running a finger over his strong, rugged jaw. "Number three is a good kisser."

"Oh?"

"Yeah. I checked that one off the list that night in my office when we were working on the mayor's Christmas cards."

"I confess to putting a lot of effort into that one. It might have been my only shot," he admitted.

"Mission accomplished. It worked better than you could possibly know." She thought for a minute. "Next is sexual chemistry. Since we're both here naked after a pretty spectacular night, I think it's safe to assume that that one is crossed off the list."

"I aim to please." His grin was wicked. "What else?"

"My man had to be smart," she said. "Little did I know he'd be scary-smart."

"Thank you, I think."

"And last but not least, he had to be just the right age."

"Since we *are* both here naked and everyone in Thunder Canyon saw us get married last night, I made the cut on that one?"

"Oh, yeah." She leaned over and gently bit his earlobe. "You're perfect."

He sucked in a breath, then said, "I'm liking being married to you, Red. Life is going to be really fun and full of surprises."

When he put his arms around her and pulled her down, Rose sighed. "We'll be late for Christmas dinner at Ethan's."

"Do you really care?"

"No." She laughed when he kissed her neck and slid under the covers.

Later that evening Rose and Austin sat in the front row, a few feet from the stage, at the fairgrounds arena. They were waiting for Zane Gunther's concert to start and she watched a scattering of stragglers hurrying in. A hum of murmuring voices echoed and buzzed in the tiered seats behind them. The place was sold out; it was going to be a capacity crowd.

The high ceiling was dark, shadows hiding the equipment that would light the stage when the show started. It was being broadcast on the local TV and radio stations.

Rose felt Austin's warm hand wrap around her smaller one as his thumb rubbed her left ring finger. A smile curved her lips as she remembered their earlier pillow talk. She felt as if their relationship had gone from forget it to forever. Tonight Zane's journey was coming full circle.

After a horrible, unimaginable accident that resulted in a young girl's death at one of his concerts, Zane had been changed, withdrawing from his life which only seemed to get worse. The girl's family had brought a lawsuit against him which was eventually settled out of court. With Jeannette by his side, he was finally able to move on with his life and career, but he was using that platform of fame to do good.

A few moments later the overhead stage lights clicked on. An unseen announcer welcomed everyone to the charity concert. Rose recognized Drew Casey's voice, the radio personality she'd seen at Presents for Patriots. And then he was introducing the singer.

Zane Gunther walked out onto the stage with his guitar draped across his chest. He stopped in front of the microphone stand and looked into the audience. His green eyes glittered in the bright stage lights.

"Thank you all for coming tonight to share a part of your Christmas for a cause that is close to my heart."

When he self-consciously dragged his fingers through

his hair, Rose realized it was probably the first time she'd seen him bare-headed.

"I'm here to pay tribute to a life cut short and it would be disrespectful to wear my hat."

"That explains that," Rose whispered to Austin.

Zane continued, "There's been a whole lot of publicity about what happened to Ashley Tuller and I'll carry the sadness of her loss with me as long as I live. If I could bring that little girl back, I'd do it in a heartbeat, but I can't. All I can do is reach out to kids in a positive way, help their growing up go a little better, a little easier. So I'm here to announce that I'm starting the Ashley Tuller Foundation to fund high school music programs and support for families with teens who have sustained a traumatic brain injury. With your help we can reach out to young people—"

From where she and Austin sat, Rose could see people off stage, in the wings. Someone was beckoning to the singer, getting his attention. There was shock and emotion in Zane's eyes just before he made an announcement.

"Ladies and gentlemen, it's just been brought to my attention that Ashley's family is here tonight. I'm humbled and very grateful for that." He looked offstage at them. "Would you like to come out here and join me in honoring your daughter?"

As the spectators applauded encouragement, a middle-aged man and woman walked out on stage with an older teenaged girl protectively between them. Father, mother and daughter held hands.

"Please welcome Ashley's family," Zane said, "Mr. and Mrs. Tuller and their daughter, Tania."

The audience erupted into applause again and everyone was on their feet. The pounding noise seemed to go on forever, as if somehow it could bring them a measure of comfort. Finally Ashley's father walked to the microphone and the arena grew quiet enough to hear a pin drop.

"Thank you all for being here tonight. Ashley would have loved this," he said, smiling as he looked around. "When she died, her mother, sister and I wanted someone to blame. She was only thirteen and went to her favorite singer's concert. She loved music and it was going to be the best night of her young life. But she never came home again and someone *had* to be responsible for that. However unfair it was, the target of our anger was Zane Gunther. Our daughter, Tania, made us realize it wasn't his fault. It was simply a horrible accident and revenge wouldn't bring her back." He pulled his wife and daughter close. "We'll always miss our Ashley and never forget her." His voice was husky with emotion. "Now with a foundation named after her, the rest of the world won't forget either. When we learned about Zane Gunther's tribute, we had to be here. We're grateful to him for helping us to keep her memory alive. With his permission, her mom, Tania and I would like to be involved in the Ashley Tuller Memorial Foundation."

Zane walked over and held out his hand to the other man, but Mr. Tuller brushed it away. Rose felt more than heard the audience gasp, then hold a collective breath, before the whole Tuller family embraced the singer. Zane's shoulders were shaking with emotion and the three people who had suffered such an unimaginable loss circled around and comforted him.

Rose's eyes filled with tears and she was pretty sure there wasn't a dry eye in the arena because she heard sniffling all around her. She fumbled in her purse for a tissue, then felt Austin's arm around her.

"I think we just saw a Christmas miracle," he said.

After all the anger, accusations, recriminations and sadness, what she'd just seen here tonight was truly miraculous. The power of forgiveness filled the arena and no one who'd witnessed it could ever forget.

Rose looked up and through her tears she saw Austin smile. "A perfect ending to a perfect day. The spirit and season of forgiveness and the magic of love that brought so many of us together tonight is the best beginning to the rest of our lives."

A heart wants what a heart wants, she thought, and wouldn't settle for anything less. She'd found her prince and he was the last man she expected when she'd least expected him.

"This is the best Christmas ever," she said.

Austin kissed her. "That goes double for me."

"I never even opened a present, but I got everything I ever wanted. I got you."

* * * * *

A sneaky peek at next month…

Cherish™

ROMANCE TO MELT THE HEART EVERY TIME

My wish list for next month's titles…

In stores from 18th October 2013:

❏ Marry Me under the Mistletoe – Rebecca Winters

& Proposal at the Lazy S Ranch – Patricia Thayer

❏ A Little Bit of Holiday Magic – Melissa McClone

& Stranded with the Tycoon – Sophie Pembroke

In stores from 1st November 2013:

❏ Marrying Dr Maverick – Karen Rose Smith

& A Maverick under the Mistletoe – Brenda Harlen

❏ A Cadence Creek Christmas – Donna Alward

& How to Marry a Princess – Christine Rimmer

Available at WHSmith, Tesco, Asda, Eason, Amazon and Apple

Just can't wait?

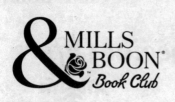

Join the Mills & Boon Book Club

Want to read more **Cherish**™ books?
We're offering you **2 more** absolutely **FREE!**

We'll also treat you to these fabulous extras:

- Exclusive offers and much more!
- FREE home delivery
- FREE books and gifts with our special rewards scheme

Get your free books now!

visit www.millsandboon.co.uk/bookclub
or call Customer Relations on 020 8288 2888

Wrap up warm this winter with Sarah Morgan…

Sleigh Bells in the Snow

Kayla Green loves business and hates Christmas.

So when Jackson O'Neil invites her to Snow Crystal Resort to discuss their business proposal… the last thing she's expecting is to stay for Christmas dinner. As the snowflakes continue to fall, will the woman who doesn't believe in the magic of Christmas finally fall under its spell…?

4th October

www.millsandboon.co.uk/sarahmorgan

Come home this Christmas to Fiona Harper

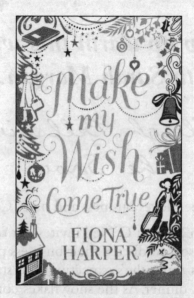

From the author of *Kiss Me Under the Mistletoe* comes a Christmas tale of family and fun. Two sisters are ready to swap their Christmases—the busy super-mum, Juliet, getting the chance to escape it all on an exotic Christmas getaway, whilst her glamorous work-obsessed sister, Gemma, is plunged headfirst into the family Christmas she always thought she'd hate.

www.millsandboon.co.uk

1113/MB442

She's loved and lost — will she ever learn to open her heart again?

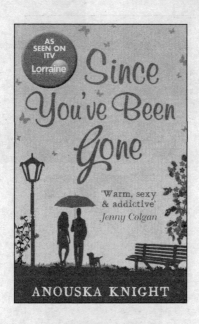

From the winner of ITV Lorraine's Racy Reads, Anouska Knight, comes a heart-warming tale of love, loss and confectionery.

'The perfect summer read — warm, sexy and addictive!'
—Jenny Colgan

For exclusive content visit:
www.millsandboon.co.uk/anouskaknight

Meet The Sullivans...